Unfolding Nights

A NOVEL

Jim Foreman

CLAIREMONT BOOKWORKS

San Diego, California

CLAIREMONT BOOKWORKS
P.O. Box 179191
San Diego, CA 92177
www.clairemontbookworks.com

Publisher's Note: This is a work of fiction. Names, characters, places, and incidents are a
product of the author's imagination. Locales and public names are sometimes used for
atmospheric purposes. Any resemblance to actual people, living or dead, or to businesses, companies, events, institutions, or locales is completely coincidental.

Book Layout ©2013 BookDesignTemplates.com

Ordering Information:
Quantity sales—Special discounts are available on quantity purchases by corporations,
associations, and others. For details, contact the "Special Sales Department" at the address above.

Unfolding Nights / Jim Foreman — 1st Edition
Printed in the United States of America

20 19 18 17 16 15 14   1 2 3 4 5 6

ISBN 978-0-9912265-2-8

This book is dedicated to Debbie, who has walked with me through all the unfolding nights, through all the unfolding days, through all the unfolding years of being wedded in the living Word.

Table of Contents

Dear Doc

Grace and peace abounding to you in Christ Jesus! Doc! It happened! Jesus answered your prayer for me—he gave me a dream to follow, gave me his calling on my life! And he gave me this calling by coming to me in my dreams while I was sleeping! I wrote down each of the dreams, given to me in successive nights, arranged them in order, and then had them bound into a book. I packed the book into a box and placed this letter on top of the book—so you'd have to read this letter before you even looked at the book!

My dreams chronicle the unfolding journey that led me to discover the true calling on my life! I've given a title to each dream, so that you'll have a sense of how Jesus revealed himself to me in each dream, what he taught me, and how he guided me through them.

I can't close this letter without letting you know that another of your long-standing prayers for me has been answered definitively: I'm dating a woman! I can't wait for you to meet her. She's a peach! By the way—knowing this will spark your curiosity—she shows up in my dreams! I'm overflowing with gratitude as I think of your fierce commitment to our friendship. Jesus has set free so much in my life—much that has your fingerprints on it. You, Janice, and your precious children are in my prayers daily—that the Holy Spirit will continue to bathe and soak you in waterfalls of mercy and rivers of joy.

So, for now, Doc, I leave in your hands my book of dreams, and I pray that your dreams are energizing, animating, and full of the Jesus who comes to us in dreams—to heal our pain, to call us into new life!

Much love, in Christ, from the Hug Zone,

Travis

Welcoming Sleep

Every night for over two years, this is the prayer I've been offering to God: "Father, should I become a counselor?" I'm still waiting for his answer.

In the beginning, when I started offering my prayer to the Father, my words felt light and swift, reaching upward and outward, unfolding in inviting openness, words fueled with a flexing power and set on a course so certain that no earthly thing, no demonic force, and no person could block or alter their direction, words that seemed to pierce the night sky, reaching beyond the stars, words whose only destination was the ears of the Father in heaven, seeking his welcoming throne, there to find, to hear, and then to embrace his will for my life: "Yes, you should become a counselor," or "No, you should not."

For two years I was eagerly expectant, unwaveringly hopeful. Every night, as I walked to my bedroom to pray, I thought: *Thank you, Father, for I believe that this is the night that you're going to answer my prayer.* But every night the result was the same—I heard silence.

I thought that perhaps there was something lacking in my obedience in the way I prayed. So, at least once a week I reviewed my routine. My routine was precise and punctual. I always started my prayers fifteen minutes before midnight and continued praying until fifteen minutes after midnight, reasoning that my prayers would span two days, the day passing away at midnight and the day just beginning after midnight. In praying that way, I knew that by the time I'd fallen asleep it would already be the next day, and even though I was asleep, I'd been obedient, even wise, in praying—covering two days during one prayer time. I followed this routine to the letter, not once altering, forgetting, or failing to do it, regardless of whether I was sick or healthy, or whether it was a work week, or a weekend, or whether I was on vacation. I had to be certain that I was being obedient. I was convinced beyond any doubt that my precise, punctual, and obedient praying to the Father was the only way that he would grant me an answer.

At one point, to be sure I'd considered all possible avenues of intercession, I met and prayed with my pastor, and then I met and prayed with the elders in my church. I sent my request for prayer to over twenty churches, asking their prayer teams to intercede for me. I phoned ten of the top evangelists on television, requesting of them and their intercessors to pray for me. I asked my friends to make a commitment to pray with greater frequency and for longer periods of time. The result of their prayers was the same as mine—they heard silence from the Father. And I, too, continued to hear nothing but silence.

But a week ago, no matter how strictly I followed my routine, no matter how long I prayed, no matter how intensely I prayed, I heard a silence I'd never heard before—It was a dead silence—as if my prayer in some way, even as it left my lips, had died, that the words themselves, each one of them, were now dead, void of sound and emptied of sense, a dead silence, so dead and so silent that it took from me all of my strength to lift off my lips the single sentence: "Father, should I become a counselor?"

Two nights ago, as I said the words of the prayer, my lips felt heavy, and then felt heavier and heavier as I spoke each successive word of the prayer, until, when I reached "counselor?" the last word of the prayer, my lips became so cold, so rigid, and so fixed, that I couldn't say "counselor?" I lay in bed, in the dead silence, and couldn't finish speaking my prayer, but I was able to finish my prayer by thinking the word *counselor?* And as I thought *counselor?* I knew that my prayer was completed.

I believed that I'd been painstakingly obedient in my prayers to the Father, and that because I'd been so painstakingly obedient for so long, I deserved—even had the right to!—the reward of his answer to my prayer.

But no answer has been given to me, and yet I've continued to offer my prayer. And I've continued to hear nothing but dead silence, a dead silence with no sense of the Holy Spirit's presence, with no hint of the Father's direction. I've cried out for Jesus to make his presence real in my bedroom, real in the dead silence, begging him to be nothing more than a witness in the dead silence, to be someone who is near me while I am praying in the dead silence, a witness who doesn't have to speak but who is a witness to my long struggle to hear an answer to my prayer, a Jesus who is a sustaining witness to my prayer, a prayer that itself has become as dead and as silent as the dead silence.

I'd hoped that Jesus would be someone who'd sympathize with me, the Jesus who for three days was dead inside the silence of the rock-encased tomb. But Jesus has shown no sympathy for me, no compassion for my soul-tearing struggle as I've prayed obediently again ... again ... again ... abandoned ... invisible ... irrelevant ... desolate ... in the dead silence ... and still I've prayed obediently ... again ... again ... again ... ashamed ... enraged ... afraid ... in the dead silence ... and still I've prayed obediently ... again ... again ... again ...

But it was last night, while I was in the dead silence, beginning to pray, but able to speak only the word "Father," that the dead silence wrapped itself around me, seeming to envelop my body. The dead silence felt like a large fist gripping me, its fingers of stone a cold and heavy clench tightening around me, making it difficult to breathe. I tried to call out *Father!* but now my tongue felt like a stone fist clenched on the word *Father!* squeezing the sound out of the word. I was mute. Panic seized me.

I had to find inside me the will to marshal the energy to break the clenching fist of the dead silence. A thought flashed into my mind: Cry out only one word— *Father!* —that word will break the tightening clench of the dead silence.

I lay flat on my bed, lifted my arms high, my palms and fingers stretched wide and open. Suddenly my hands clenched—my hands had become fists! They felt like large and heavy stones! I couldn't hold the weight of them. They thudded onto the bed. Still clenched, I couldn't move the stones.

The dead silence tightened its clench.

Now my eyes felt like clenched fists of stone. I couldn't see anything in my room. Suddenly I realized that I couldn't hear any sounds. The inside of my ears felt sealed by fists of stone.

The dead silence tightened its clench.

Now my body itself—all of it—felt like a stone fist tightening its clench—more and more—squeezing me, my lungs being constricted, narrowing with each breath. The dead silence was suffocating me. *I'm dying!* filled my head, my silent words desperately searching for a way to scream. No sounds came from my lips.

Father! arose from somewhere inside me. As soon as I thought the word *Father!* the very feel and force of the word released an arterial throb coursing through me, its pulse a rhythmic language resonant with its own life-giving sounds.

A gathering hope laced with a warming joy filled me. I let the word *Father!* speak in me, let *Father!* move in and through me, the very sound of *Father!* creating space inside me, my chest rising, my lungs opening so I could take one last breath, one last breath that could carry with all my strength the word *Father!* the one and only word that could free me from the stone fist of the dead silence and release me into the life-renewing words flowing from the Father's presence.

I took a deep breath, and instead of hearing my own voice speak "Father," I heard the sound of myself sighing, a joy-filling yet slowly-releasing sighing that was filling me with widening and deepening peace, and on my sighing a voice arose, the gentlest, safest, and yet most power-filled of whispers I'd ever heard, the whisper itself dissolving each and every fist of stone clenched on my body and piercing the dead silence with the words: "In a dream, a vision of the night, I will open your ears and seal your instruction, that you may turn aside from your conduct, and keep you from pride." Stunned yet smiling, bewildered yet filled with awe, I said out loud, "Father, that's no answer to my prayer!"

My sigh became a relaxing breath. Then the voice whispered, "He walks upon the wings of the wind, and makes the winds his messengers." The words "wings of the wind" seemed to stroke my brow, making me drowsy, and then I felt lifted by those wings, my body so free and so light that I began to float, letting those wings be my protection and guide, now so safe inside those wings that I let myself glide into the smooth flow of welcoming sleep.

Grave Measures

I heard a voice say, "You're sleeping, but your heart is awake." The words "your heart is awake" seemed to create a scene with me in it—I was dreaming!

It was night, and a full moon was casting its light through a cloudy sky, covering everything with a dull silvery haze. I was standing in the center of a tract of hard ground, and I appeared to be surrounded by very high walls, but the silvery haze made the walls look blurry, making it difficult to judge accurately how far I was from them.

I walked to one of the walls, and I began to jog, my fingertips moving lightly across the surface of the walls, feeling what I now could see was smooth rock. I picked up my pace, my jog becoming a run, my fingertips searching for any crack in one of the walls, for any sign of a door, for any way out.

When I completed making a round of the walls confining me, I knew that the walls formed a rectangle of thick rocks, the rectangle enclosing a space around fifty yards by one hundred yards. What appeared to be lookout towers were built upon the four corners of these formidable walls. The towers seemed empty. I shouted, "Is anyone up there?"

No answer.

Then it struck me—the lookout towers were the kind used to monitor the actions of inmates—I was in prison!

I didn't see any guards anywhere on the grounds or notice any other prisoners. But I was certain: I was being held prisoner, and I was being punished for something! "Father, what did I do to deserve this?" I shouted, looking into the blurry night sky, desperate for a response.

Silence was all I heard.

"You have no right to keep me here!" I shouted, this time aiming my words at the wall nearest me. I heard only the sound of my own voice. Anger surged through me. I shouted louder, repeating, "You have no right to keep me here!" hurling my words at the wall, hoping my words would have the force of a battering ram that would break through the rocks and open a doorway for my escape. But the rocks seemed indifferent and unmoved by the sound of my words, denying me even a single echo, refusing to let my words affect, in any way, the walls of my prison!

I screamed, "I'm in solitary confinement!" Suddenly I felt dizzy, caught in a swirling funnel of images spinning at a speed too fast to identify. My body felt shot through with a burning liquid, turning my insides, even my bones, into a mush, the funnel spinning faster, the images now splotches of color, the mush giving way, the dizziness now a churning wind whipping me around—my body weaving—my hands clutching for something solid to hold me up—my legs sagging, too weak to stand—my breath gasping—my legs buckling, folding in on themselves—mush turning into slimy mud, its thick ooze saturating me—my insides out of control—falling to my hands and knees—shuddering—sobbing— "Help me!" I cried ... "God! ... Please! ... Come! ... Help me!"

I collapsed, my chest and legs flat on the ground, my head heavy, my face pressing hard on the ground, my fingers clawing at unyielding dirt, struggling to pull myself up. Only my hands and fingers felt strong—I kept clawing. Pain stabbed my fingers, and I saw my fingertips, bloody from clawing. No matter. Desperate, I kept clawing but couldn't right myself.

Nausea flooded through me, its waves of stench frenzied, insistent, and furious, drenching everything inside with a sickening odor of decay. I was rotting, decomposing. I tried not to smell my body, but the stink, so putrefying and so penetrating, kept forcing its way into my nostrils. I was disgusting! My insides—the slimy mud—the thick ooze saturating me—the waves of stench—the rotting—the decomposing—the putrefying and penetrating stink—all of this was disgusting me—and it was me! I was disgust—disgusting to the core—I was made of disgust!

I began to heave, trying to vomit, to throw up who I was. I heaved and heaved, but I couldn't throw up, couldn't get rid of myself.

The memories of my past sins and my refusal to confess them to the Father and to those I'd wounded—that disgusted me!

The self-centered goals I'd set for myself—that disgusted me!

The fantasies of how I'd serve God and how popular and famous I'd become—that disgusted me!

The secret envies I had of others and my intentionally withholding encouragement from them—that disgusted me!

The smoldering resentments of others and my refusals to forgive others who'd hurt me—that disgusted me!

The pleasures I derived from seeing others fail, blaming them for the tragic events that assailed them—that disgusted me!

The ignoring of the suffering of those who'd directly asked me for prayer or for money—that disgusted me!

My twisting the truth in conversations about the Bible—that disgusted me!

My turning my back on Jesus, making the approval of others more important than his acceptance of me—that disgusted me!

Drawing on my own strength, and blocking the Holy Spirit's attempts to fuel me with his power and renewing life—that disgusted me!

My hypocritical praying to the Father, saying out loud that I want the Father's will for my life, but inwardly telling myself that I'll only accept an answer to prayer that's in accordance with my will—that disgusted me!

A kaleidoscope of images of me sinning kept assaulting me, each one disgusting. I was guilty, guilty of being disgusting, guilty of being a disgusting sinner. "I am so disgusting," I said, my words coming in groans. "I'm not worth God's love. I am nothing, nothing but a sinner who deserves death!"

Sorrow welled up in me, and suddenly I began to grieve, my grieving moving in me like a spiral of expanding pain: As my grief was deepening, my grief was widening.

I became aware of tears pouring from my eyes, coming in gushes, flowing down my nose and onto the ground, the ground growing dark where my tears were falling, the hard ground absorbing them, the circle of wet darkness increasing.

As more tears formed a widening pool on the ground, the ground started to open before my eyes, the fissure in the ground growing wider and deeper, beginning to take the shape of a grave. My tears! They were digging a grave—my grave! My head—too heavy to lift—my body—too weak to move—my fingertips—too painful for me to keep clawing. I could only watch as my tears continued to dig my grave.

Suddenly I realized that my tears were being released in a way that was making me feel clean. It was as though my grieving was cleansing me of my disgust, that my tears were washing away my guilt and my sins. My tears kept flowing, the ground kept widening and deepening, I felt cleaner and cleaner. *I'm ready to die,* I thought. *My death—that's what Jesus wants!* My tears stopped. The digging of my grave stopped.

I felt light, free, and completely clean, inside and out, my body inches from the mouth of my grave. *The grave is wide enough,* I thought, *and deep enough. I'll roll myself into it.* I closed my eyes, planted my bloody fingers in the ground, and with one motion raised my body and then started rolling toward the grave, shouting, "Jesus, my life is yours! ... My death is yours! ... Forgive me, sinner that I am!"

But—I did not drop into the grave! I rolled and rolled, feeling only solid ground underneath me. I opened my eyes. The grave was gone. I rose to my knees, looking at my bloody fingers, scanning the ground for any sign of the grave. There was none. I looked up. The sky was clear, the moon bright, and the air a cool refreshing breeze.

A man's voice behind me said, "Travis, if you lose your life for my sake, you will find it," his voice resonant with power and suffused with peace.

He spoke my name! I spun around, my eyes wide. A man was standing there, his smile welcoming, his eyes radiating warmth, his arms extended toward me, his palms open and upturned, his fingers stretched in a way that invited me to touch his fingertips with my fingertips. I placed my bloody fingertips on his alabaster fingertips, and instantly my fingertips were healed. "Oh! —My! — God!" I cried, "Jesus! It's you!"

I threw myself on the ground, and began kissing Christ's feet, then shouting, "Praise you, God!—Thank you, Lord!—Praise you, God!—Thank you, Lord!" He reached down, took my hands and lifted me to my feet. "Lord, why are you here, in this place, with me?"

Jesus smiled, and said, "I'm here because you made space for me."

"Made space for you?"

"Yes, when you asked me for forgiveness."

"How did my asking for your forgiveness make space for you?"

Jesus put one hand on my shoulder, and with the other hand pointed to the ground. "There," he said, "that is where your repenting tears made a grave for you as you were confessing your life as a disgusting sinner. You believed that the space opening in the ground was a grave to swallow you in death, and when you rolled toward your grave, with all your heart believing yourself to be a dead man, pleading for forgiveness—then—at that very moment—your plea for forgiveness opened a space for me."

I asked, "A space for you to be with me, to be in my life?"

"Yes, Travis, and more."

"More?"

Jesus leaned close to me, his lips next to my ear, and said, "Forgiveness opens the space that my love fills."

The words "my love fills" flowed into me as a song, its full-bodied melody seemed to sing in me "just for you." I felt grateful just to be standing there, feeling the music of Christ's love reverberating through me. "Lord," I said, "thank you for loving me so much. But"—I hesitated, thinking that what I was about to say might sound like ingratitude. Then I said, "I must admit that I'm confused."

"Confused about what?" Jesus said, his voice reassuring.

"Well ... Lord ... We are in a prison!"

"Travis, wherever I am, there is no prison." He laid his arm gently across my shoulder and guided me toward one of the walls of the prison, saying as we walked, "I am the door."

The Door Between
Should and Should-Not

I was with Jesus—both of us—again—inside the rectangular prison made of thick rocks. He and I were standing shoulder-to-shoulder, a few yards from one of the walls. What appeared to be two doors were fixed in the wall, each door around ten-feet high and four-feet wide. A span of rock five-feet wide separated the doors.

"I'm puzzled," I said.

"About what?" Jesus asked, his voice engaging.

"The doors, I can't figure it out: Earlier I checked every inch of all the walls, and I didn't see or feel any door."

"You can discover only what you are ready to find."

"You mean these doors were here the whole time?"

"Yes," Jesus said, "and now that you see them, tell me what you see."

"They look like they're made of steel," I said, "and, at least from where I'm standing, they appear to be very heavy and impossible to break down or to break through. Each one has a doorknob, but I can't tell from here whether the doors are locked." I believed that I saw something else on each door, but I thought that my eyes were deceiving me. I squinted, focusing my gaze, trying to confirm what I thought I saw.

"Is that all you see?" Jesus asked, his tone inviting.

"For a moment … I wasn't sure, but now I am certain. I do see something else."

"What is it?"

"There are letters written on each door," I said, "all capital letters that spell out words. On that door," I said, gesturing to the door on my left, "is written one word—SHOULD. And on the other door are written two words—SHOULD-NOT."

I began to recall my prayer to the Father, the prayer I'd hoped he would've answered by now. "Lord," I said, turning to face Jesus, "are these two doors the Father's way of providing me with his answer to my prayer? If I open SHOULD and could walk through that door, maybe that would mean that the Father is saying Yes: that I should become a counselor. But if I open SHOULD-NOT and could walk through that door, perhaps that would mean that the Father is saying No: that I should not become a counselor. But how can I know which door to open? I don't even know whether I'll be able to open either one of the doors. The doors are wide apart, but I think I have just enough reach to open them both at the same time. If I could do that, I have no idea of what would happen. But one thing is certain: If I could open both of them simultaneously, I wouldn't be able to walk through both of them at the same time. Would that mean I'd be trapped between two—"

"Travis!" Jesus said, interrupting me, "all your questions will be answered soon. Go to one of the doors and open it."

"I'm afraid," I said, my voice tight, my body tense. "Lord, what if I walk through the wrong door?"

"Opening a door does not obligate you to walk through it."

"Does that mean that I can't be wrong—no matter which door I open?"

"That's right, Travis, you can't be wrong."

Feeling relieved, I went to SHOULD, and when I drew within an arm's length of the door, I heard a muffled sound coming from behind the door. I slowly opened the door.

The muffled sound became a voice, clear and commanding: "I am SHOULD. Walk through me and you'll always know what is your goal in every situation, always know what is morally good, always know what rule to follow, always know how to perform your duty, always know what is true perfection, always be able to explain the purpose of your life, always be able to justify all of your actions, always be able to define in finest detail every concept you use to analyze whoever or whatever confronts you in life, always be able to dominate others with arguments composed of irrefutable logic, and always be filled with the self-admiration of knowing that you are superior to others because you worship your god."

I was stunned, my head felt invaded by SHOULD's words, words with such force that they were drowning out my own thoughts. I struggled to hear my own thoughts, trying to gather my own words into a coherent response. I managed to shape some words into a question, speaking haltingly: "And ... who ... is ... my ... god ... Jesus?"

"I am your god!" SHOULD proclaimed. "You should worship me, and you should have all that you deserve. And I will bestow on you every second of every day the greatest gift I can give—Pride!"

I turned to Jesus, to ask him for help—but he wasn't there!

"Come on, Travis," SHOULD cajoled. "Walk through my door. It's easy: just one step across the threshold and you'll be in the best of all worlds—your perfect world!"

SHOULD's words were like a strong magnet, drawing me toward the threshold of the open door. Angry and frightened at SHOULD for his commanding me what to do, I resisted the pull, shouting, "I need time—to think!" I slammed shut the door, and with both hands pushed myself away from the door so that I wouldn't be able to hear the muffled voice behind it.

I wondered what happened to Jesus, and yet I felt an urgency to approach the other door. My eyes riveting on SHOULD-NOT, I crept toward the door. I stopped, listening for a muffled voice, but I couldn't hear any sound coming from behind the door. I drew closer, near enough to place my ear on the door, straining to hear even a whisper. I heard nothing.

With caution I opened the door, and saw a metallic object inside the door, flush with the edge of the threshold. I recognized the object as a CD player. I heard the click of a button being pushed, and I knew that someone or something had starting playing a CD.

"I am SHOULD-NOT," the voice on the CD said, "and I knew that I should not speak directly with you until I was adequately prepared for a give-and-take between us. And because I was not adequately prepared, I recorded my message to you, so that I could give you one uninterrupted expression of my inadequacy, my one-sided defense of why I am not worthy of being defended, why I am not worthy of being seen and heard live, because that would mean that it would be possible to be affirmed by someone in the flesh—and that should not happen. I am the perfect master of inducing guilt in my mind, of generating shame in my being. I am the always-sharp scalpel of a relentless conscience, always making a new incision—without anesthesia—into my body, into my soul, and into my spirit, laying bare whatever in me is trying to become whole, for I should not become whole until I am wholly nothing. I am the perfect master of self-reflection, critically examining without end why I should not be free until I know every aspect of my helplessness, know every nuance of thought, every subtlety of image, and every shade of memory that makes me too vulnerable to pain, too subject to disease, and, hence, too unworthy to be free. I mistrust the word 'trust,' and then mistrust my mistrust, and then mistrust my mistrust of my mistrust, and so on, always able to find another layer to dissect, and then another layer, and so on. I should not see myself of worth until I examine microscopically every dimension of what is negative in me, dismembering every part of my imagination, of my feelings, and of my proposed actions, employing reason to show why I am so unreasonable in my use of reason, judging as defective every quality of my personality, and detailing, down to every iota, why I am a failure as a human being. Travis, if you worship me as your god, I guarantee that you will become perfect in what you should not be and not do. For until you know with perfect negativity what you should not be and not do, you should not be and not do anything. And, Travis, to be able to know at the core of all you are, know what you should not be or not do, and to know it all the time, will this not produce in you the greatest godly quality of all—Humility? So, Travis, if you pick up the CD player, put it under your arm, and carry it across the threshold of my door, that very act will be the sign that I am your god and that you will worship me." Then I heard a click—the CD player was shut off.

I closed the door, my palms pressing hard against the cold steel. I backed away from the door. Standing a few yards from the doors, I looked at SHOULD, and said, "You offer me perfect pride if I worship you as my god." Then, directing my gaze at SHOULD-NOT, I said, "You offer me perfect humility if I worship you as my god." I stood there, my eyes moving back-and-forth from SHOULD to SHOULD-NOT. "Two choices," I said, "Perfect pride or perfect humility. Somehow, there must be a way to bring the two of them together, to make them one."

"No!" said Jesus, his voice emphatic, "there is no way to make two idols into one god! But there is a third choice."

I turned around.

Jesus was standing there, smiling.

"Where were you when I needed your help?" I asked, my voice demanding, so demanding that the force of it frightened me. *What if I've offended him?* I thought. *What if he abandons me to the crushing loneliness of this prison?* Too ashamed to look at him, I took a few deep breaths, and then I asked, "What is the third choice?"

Jesus walked to the wall that separated the two doors. He showed me his right index finger, and then, using the tip of his finger, he drew on the rock wall the outline of a door, the outline was bright red and the bright red substance appeared to be coming from the tip of his finger.

"My God!" I cried, "Is that your blood?! Are you drawing the picture of a door with your own blood?!"

"Yes," Jesus said. "It is my blood. But you seem surprised."

"Well, Lord," I said, "I don't mean any disrespect, but that wall is made of solid granite."

"Nothing can stand against my blood!" Jesus said, his voice bold and electric.

My mouth agape, I could only stare in wonder at what I saw unfolding. The bloody outline was bleeding, all of his blood seeping into the rock wall, moving toward the center of the door, until the entire rectangle that made up the picture of the door was saturated with his blood.

"But Lord," I said, "that rock … it is granite, the toughest kind of rock, the kind of rock used for tombstones—made to last for the ages!"

Immediately the door made of blood was split in two, the granite shattered, and then his blood, its sound like a rushing stream, dissolved the shattered granite, washing it away, leaving in its place a perfectly-shaped rectangular passageway for us to walk through.

As we stepped across the threshold of the passageway, I shouted, "My God! You are the door!"

"Yes, I am!" Jesus declared joyfully, "and I am always open!"

Armor of Light—
Wonderful Counselor

I studied the high walls surrounding me—I was back—in the same prison—with Jesus! We were both looking into the passageway he created in the rock wall with his blood. The passageway was filled with light, the light warm, sunny, embracing, and clear. As I was walking with Jesus, I recalled the psalmist who cried out, *Send out your light and your truth, let them lead me.* And they were sent—to me! I was being led out of my prison by the very one who is the light of the world, who is the way, and the truth, and the life! Waves of joy washed through me, each wave making me feel more alive.

I'm almost free, I thought, when suddenly I started to sense a pressure on both sides of me, hardly noticeable, yet somehow, threatening and unrelenting, seeming to come from behind the walls, as though something behind each wall was trying to break through the barrier between me and it, something whose only aim was to block my way to freedom.

"Lord!" I said, my heart racing, my feet moving faster, "I'm afraid that these walls will collapse before we can get out of this prison!"

"It's not the pressing weight of the rocks you feel," Jesus said, his voice calm. "What you feel is the heavy pressure of SHOULD and of SHOULD-NOT still vying to be the god of your life. They are on the other side of the walls, but as long as you stay with me, stay in the space between SHOULD and SHOULD-NOT, they cannot in any way touch you, or hurt you, or draw you into sin."

Feeling comforted by the calm in Christ's voice, I asked, "Why can't they?"

"When I became your door, and you stepped into the passage-way, you put on the armor of light. I am that armor! I am that light! And you are now inside the light, completely surrounded by me—safe inside this floor, these walls, and this ceiling, and as long as you remain inside the armor, you are covered and protected by the light."

Christ's words seemed to embrace me. I felt reassured. "Yes," I said, "I can feel it: the armor of light is a barrier against SHOULD and SHOULD-NOT, holding them at bay. I never knew light could have so much power."

"It can," said Jesus, "but only when light is shining forth from love."

"I see what you mean, Lord." I paused, mulling over whether to ask Jesus a question. Then I asked, "Have SHOULD and SHOULD-NOT ever pressured you to worship one of them as your god?"

"Yes, they have, but I've never felt threatened by them."

"How come?"

"Because I live in the space between all shoulds and all should-nots."

Baffled by Christ's answer, I asked, "What space is that?"

"That space is called the heart of my Father," Jesus said, "and it is from his heart that his will is flowing. So, to be in that space is to be in union with the Father, a union so intimate that to feel the beating of your heart is to feel the pace and rhythm of his heart beating. To be in that space is to experience from the depths of your heart the Father's power, his purpose, his plan, and his living presence—all of them joining together as one holy and majestic force, surging in your heart, surging upward and outward, a surging that is overflowing with love that is nourishing and affirming every action you are doing, and it is in your releasing into this life-directing overflow of love that you discover—moment-by-moment—the will of the Father—my Father and your Father."

The words "your Father" took my breath away. I felt a bit dizzy, my legs wobbly. I stopped, bent over, grasping my knees, struggling to catch my breath. *Can anyone except Jesus really be that close to the Father?* I asked myself. I breathed deeply and slowly. I stood up, took a few steps, my legs felt steadier. I continued walking, noticing that we were about halfway through the passageway. "Lord," I said, "I want"—but suddenly my tongue seemed thick and frozen.

"Yes, Travis," Jesus said, "What's on your mind?"

"Well, Lord, I ... it's difficult to ask but ... hard to believe ... I know it's true ... I want with all my heart ... with all my heart ... to be in that space, living out the will of the Father, to experience the union ... intimacy ... overflowing love of the Father ... my Father."

Jesus was filled with delight, his smile wide, his eyes accepting, his arms outstretched toward me, inviting me to come to him. I took one step toward him, and fell into his welcoming arms. Jesus held me close, held me tight. My chest secure on Christ's chest, my head safe on his shoulder, and his arms a protective embrace wholly around me, he said in the most tender voice: "Travis, you already are in that space: when you are with me, you are with the Father, for I and the Father are one."

I don't know how long I stood there, my arms tight around Jesus, feeling our hearts beat as one, feeling his heart creating a peace-resonating humming that was like a lullaby being sung to my heart. I felt like a child at peace with his loving Father. From somewhere inside me I heard faint sounds of the words *Father, should I become a counselor?* The sound quickly faded, as though blown away by the lullaby being sung to my heart, leaving in place of the words only the lullaby, the peace alive in its music, now gentler and deeper.

"My peace I give you," Jesus said, his voice the rhythm and tone of the lullaby.

I was being bathed and soaked in the peace of Christ. "Thank you, Lord," I said, tears streaming from my eyes, "thank you."

We both let go of our embrace, turned, and started walking, able to see clearly the end of the passageway.

"Lord," I said, "I don't know what the Father's will is for me in this season of my life, but I just realized something."

"What's that, Travis?"

"That my being with you—my knowing you—my letting you love me—the way we met—how you saved me—our ongoing relationship—what I've been through and how you've been with me in it—all this must be part of his will for me."

Jesus smiled, and said, "Yes, Travis, you and I, our being together, is part of his will. And there is so much more to know. Where do you want to start?"

"I want to know more about you," I said, feeling expectant and adventurous. "The prophet Isaiah said that you are Wonderful Counselor. I believe that you are the greatest, the wisest, the most loving, and the most merciful counselor who will ever live. And yet the Holy Spirit inspired Isaiah to name you 'Wonderful' rather than call you by any other name. I'd like to know more about what it means for you to be that Wonderful Counselor."

"All right," Jesus said, "let me begin with the word 'Wonderful.' All counseling that glorifies the Father begins with wonder. If a person can't wonder, he will never be of any service to the people of God." Jesus stopped talking. He seemed to know by the expression on my face that I was shocked and confused. "Is there something that you want to say, Travis?"

I stopped, went to one of the walls and leaned the length of my back against it. I felt dull tension ripple down my back muscles, and sensed what seemed like a pin trying to prick the skin at the center of my spine. Ignoring the feeling and the sensation, I said, "I can't see how a person's being able to wonder could ever help anyone who is suffering. People need a counselor to do something, need someone to take action to relieve their pain. When you're wondering, you're not doing anything." I let my head rest against the wall, and then felt a muscle twitch at the base of my skull, but I kept my eyes and ears focused on Jesus.

Jesus stopped walking, and standing in the middle of the passageway, said, "Has anyone in pain ever come to you for help?"

"Yes," I said, feeling twinges of anger, "mostly friends. I know that I'm not a trained professional counselor, and I don't have a license to practice. But everyone who knows me says that I'm a good listener, that I'm insightful, and that I give good advice. And I've read more books on Christian counseling than anyone I know. Friends have told me I have a gift for counseling. But no one has asked me whether I know how to wonder."

"And what is the first thing you do when you're in the presence of someone in pain?"

"I diagnose that person," I said, feeling angrier and sensing the need to defend myself, "because I have to categorize that person's pain. If I've determined that she's depressed—Depression is her category. If I've assessed that he's anxious—Anxiety is his category. If I've concluded that she's an addict—Addiction is her category. If I've interpreted his behavior as hostile—Hostility is his category. Every person must be diagnosed, be put into a category that defines his or her mental disorder, because only then can a plan of interventions and goals be formulated to treat that person's problem. All the books, whether written by lay counselors or by professionals, state emphatically that what I said is the only way to do effective counseling. Not one book ever mentioned wonder."

"The breadth and depth of your reading in psychological theory is impressive," Jesus said, "and your detailed examination of clinical texts complete with successful treatment plans, along with your long hours of pouring over hundreds of case studies in which the counselor failed to help the person in pain, not to mention your ability to analyze every person in pain and to slot him or her into the appropriate mental disorder category—all of these diligent efforts and many works, works you've been doing for years, can be matched by very few trained professionals, and by even fewer lay counselors."

"Thank you, Lord," I said, taken aback by his compliments, the flow of his words cleansing me of anger and defensiveness, the force and feel of his words magnetic, drawing me toward him. As I moved away from the wall, to join Jesus where he was standing, the thought flashed through my mind: *Did Jesus really mean as a compliment what he just said?*

"Travis," Jesus said, "did you know that I was struck with wonder?"

"You were!" I said, stunned by his question. "That's hard to believe. You? ... Really? ... When did that happen?"

"When I was in Capernaum, a centurion, a Gentile of high authority, came to me, calling me Lord and begging me to heal his servant who was lying paralyzed at home. His servant was being fearfully tormented, with no relief in sight. I said that I would come and heal his servant. But the centurion said that he was not worthy for me to come under his roof, and that if I just said the word, his servant would be healed. When the centurion said this, I was struck with wonder, and I proclaimed to all those following me that I had not found such great faith with anyone in Israel. You see, Travis, I had a category into which I had slotted the people of

Israel: I believed that the greatest expressions of faith in me would come first from my own people—from Israelites. But when that depth of humility and faith in me came from a commander in the Roman army, a Gentile of very high rank who was actually part of the oppressing forces occupying the land God had promised to the Israelites—wonder took me by surprise!"

"Lord," I said, "help me understand: What's it like to wonder?"

"When the categories you relied on to label types of people, or the categories you relied on to assign meaning to events occurring around you, or the categories you relied on to enable you to fit together the pieces of your life into a framework that makes sense—when those categories fall way, then you are experiencing wonder," said Jesus.

Still stunned, I said, "Categories? ... falling away?"

"Yes," Jesus said, "I believed my framework of categories to be an established reality that I assumed would be verified as true. One of those categories was that an Israelite would become the first one to profess great faith in me. So, when a Gentile was the first person to show such great faith in me, that category I'd relied on, that such great faith would come first from an Israelite, dissolved and fell away, leaving me in a state of wonder."

"Wondering sounds chaotic to me," I said, "and it sounds as though there's no structure to hold your life together, that there's no social order that's predictable, that human reason can't find a definable purpose in what's happening to you, and that wonder is even beyond the reach of articulate speech. And wonder seems to happen to you—and against your will!"

"Travis, I can understand why you might think of wonder in those ways. But experiencing wonder is much more than what you think. Wonder can't be commanded! Love, kindness, for-giveness, compassion, humility—all these can be commanded. But you're right about one aspect of wonder: Wonder can't be willed into happening, and it arises seemingly from out of nowhere, overwhelming a person without warning. But in truth, Travis, wonder is a gift from the Father to a person with an open spirit."

"Lord," I said, my voice quavering, "I must ask you for your forgiveness."

"What do you think you did that needs my forgiveness?"

"Well, a few minutes ago, when you were talking about wonder and how foundational it is to being a godly counselor, I became angry at you, and felt this strange urgency to criticize you and to defend my own view of counseling. I couldn't seem to stop myself, and even more—I didn't want to stop myself! I wanted to prove you wrong and then, somehow, convince you to agree with my view. Lord, please forgive me."

"I forgive you, Travis," Jesus said, his voice tender and affirming. "Do you know why you acted and felt the way you did?"

Feeling on the verge of crying, I managed to force out, "Because I'm a sinner."

"Yes," Jesus said, "but there's a more specific explanation, and hearing the explanation will equip you to make choices that flow from the will of your Father in heaven."

"I'm at a loss, Lord," I said. "I thought that the explanation was simple: I was acting from my flesh."

"Do you recall walking away from me, leaning your back against the wall, and then laying your head against the wall?"

"Yes, and it was then that strange feelings and odd sensations pricked my back, spine, and skull."

"Those weren't strange feelings and sensations," Jesus said. "That was SHOULD."

"SHOULD!" I said, my voice close to a shout. "I thought SHOULD was out of my life. Are you saying that SHOULD was directly involved in my sin?"

"Yes," Jesus said. "When you chose to follow your own will by walking away from me and leaning against the wall, SHOULD realized that you were just on the other side of the wall, that you had moved away from me and had drawn close to SHOULD. And because of that shift in distance, SHOULD knew that you were vulnerable to having your actions shaped and controlled by SHOULD. Through those feelings and sensations you were experiencing, SHOULD was letting you know that SHOULD was backing you up as you were taking a stand against me, that you could lean on SHOULD anytime you wanted to choose your will over your Father's will, and that SHOULD is always there for you, ready for you to switch your faith from me as your God to SHOULD as your god."

"But Lord," I replied, "you were only a few yards away from me! I had no idea that even when I know that you're in my presence, and that even when I know that I've put on the armor of light—even then, when I choose to follow my own will, I can still be powerfully affected and controlled by SHOULD. Now I can see that I need to stay in that space between SHOULD and SHOULD-NOT, to live with you in that space where you live. But, Lord, I feel uneasy, because in my mind I see this picture of a highway with a single yellow line in the center, the yellow line dividing the highway into two lanes of equal width. That's how I picture the space between SHOULD and SHOULD-NOT. You are sinless and are continuously in the Father's will, so I understand how you are able to walk with unwavering faith on the yellow line, living perfectly in the space between SHOULD and SHOULD-NOT. But someone like me, a sinner, well, we've both seen how easily I can walk away from the yellow line. I feel discouraged, believing that I'll spend more time off the yellow line than on it."

Jesus smiled, his eyes warm and embracing, and said, "Travis, let's recast your highway analogy. Let's see the highway as a one-way, single lane road with no yellow line. And the entire length and breadth of the highway is the Father's will—with one direction and one destination. When you choose your own will—whether you turn left or turn right—and step off the road, you are walking away from his will, making into your god SHOULD or SHOULD-NOT. But my love always knows where your love is lacking, and I will always invite you to come back with me, back onto the highway, back into the flow of the Father's will. And you are living in that space between SHOULD and SHOULD-NOT this very moment, Travis—you are with me, walking on the highway of the Father's will!"

"Thank you, Lord!" I said as joy rippled through me. "Thank you for your grace! Thank you for your mercy! Thank you for not giving up on me!"

Jesus' smile widened, his face had the look of someone about to shower a person with a gift beyond anything that person could imagine. "Travis," Jesus said, "that space you are living in right now, I have a special name for it: I call it my Hug Zone. Anyone who joins himself to me is one spirit with me, and that person is, there and then, in my Hug Zone, near enough to me that I can encircle him with my arms. When you stay inside my Hug Zone, no matter how you are moving forward in your faith, you are bringing with you both me and the Father's will, keeping me in intimate union with you, and wherever I am loving you, I am bringing with me both you and the Father's will, keeping you in intimate union with me. Right now, we are in the Hug Zone, together, one in the Father's will. If you would have leaned against the wall while you were in the Hug Zone, SHOULD could've tempted you to sin, enticed you to step off the highway, but SHOULD, by himself alone, couldn't have caused you to sin. Recall what the Spirit led my apostle James to write: 'But each one is tempted when he is carried away and enticed by his own lust.

Then when lust has conceived, it gives birth to sin; and when sin is accomplished, it brings forth death.' As long as you remain with me in my Hug Zone, SHOULD and SHOULD-NOT can lure you toward the shoulder of the highway, can tempt you to step off the highway of the Father's will, but whatever lust is enticing you, it can't conceive and give birth to sin, it can't force you off the highway. When you walk in the will of the Father, it is not of utmost importance that you stay in the center of the highway. You may move across the entire breadth of the highway, move back-and-forth, move in zigs and zags, or even move to the very edges of the sides of the road where SHOULD and SHOULD-NOT are lurking to tempt you into choosing one of them as your god. What is of ultimate importance is that you remain in my Hug Zone, for only in my Hug Zone are you free to realize the hope of your calling in the unfolding of your Father's will. Come on, let's keep walking."

As we started moving forward, the words Jesus speaks in *John's Gospel* moved through my mind: *As the Father continues to love me, I also continue to love you—continue to stay in my love!* I threw my arms around Jesus, and shouted, "I love being in your Hug Zone!" He encircled me with his protecting arms, and responded, "So do I, Travis, so do I!"

We continued walking on, nearing the end of the passageway.

"Lord," I said, feeling confused and frightened, "I question whether the Father will ever see me as a person with a spirit open enough to receive the gift of wonder."

"Travis," Jesus replied, "do you remember when we had our arms around one another and you were feeling our hearts beating as one?"

"Yes, Lord."

"But you couldn't put into a category your experience of our hearts beating as one."

"No, I couldn't. As a matter of fact, I didn't think of trying to find a category for what I was experiencing."

"That's because all of your categories regarding our relationship fell away. Travis—you were wondering!"

"I was?!"

"Yes, Travis, you were. And do you remember how you heard music playing through your heart, music that created through its melody resonating through you a gentler and deeper peace than you'd ever known, and you had no category for that experience?"

"Yes, Lord, I do remember: I did experience peace I'd never known before."

"And, again, you didn't try to define your experience, or try to force it into a formula that you believed you could repeat at will anytime or at any place, or try to make it into a category that would be a part of a larger system of theological categories."

"No, I didn't. I was in your presence, and I was experiencing what was arising and unfolding from my being in your presence—nothing more, nothing less!"

"Yes, Travis!—You were wondering! Experiencing wonder is beyond all knowledge grounded in measurable behavior and in fixed criteria for the attainment of goals, beyond all definitions and categories, beyond all pronouncements of logical analysis of phenomena, beyond all persuasive arguments and theological debates, beyond all claims of specialized knowledge no matter what the field of study, and beyond all claims to wisdom based on privileged position and social status. Wonder is always surprising, new, immediate, spontaneous, and embracing. It's always engaging the whole person, saturating him with a presence that he experiences as a mystery. Wonder keeps a counselor open to someone in pain, so open that the counselor believes that both suffering and healing are mysteries, mysteries whose purpose and meaning only the Father understands."

"Then what can a counselor really do to help anyone, Lord?"

"A counselor remains fully awake in the space my presence creates between suffering and healing."

"How will that help anyone in pain?"

"It's not meant to help anyone in pain—it's meant to help the counselor."

"What?! ... help the counselor?! ... how, Lord, please tell me. I want to know."

"When a counselor remains fully awake in that space, he can't slot a person into a category of suffering or into a category of healing. That makes the counselor so open that I can pour into him how precious he is, that the Holy Spirit can lead and empower him, and that the Father can reveal to him the Father's unfolding plan. A counselor needs the Father, the Son, and the Holy Spirit if he is to be a counselor who glorifies God."

"Yes, Lord," I said. "I see what you mean, and I can see that your Word says that there is a love beyond comprehension, that there is a peace that surpasses understanding, that there is a power working in me beyond all I can think or ask, that there is a surpassing grace, and that there is joy inexpressible and full of glory—all of these experiences arising and unfolding when categories fall away. I thank you, Lord, for your patience with me. And I thank the Father for the Spirit of revelation that enabled me to see why you are the Wonderful Counselor. And I thank God that he has called me out of darkness into God's wonder-filling light. Lord, I've been asking the Father whether I should be a counselor. Maybe I need to know whether the Father is calling me to be a counselor. Lord, I want to do whatever it takes for me to know whether that calling is on my life."

"Take a moment, Travis," Jesus said, "and gather yourself, and then let me know whether you still want to do whatever it takes. The path that you'll follow in your attempt to answer that question will be full of unexpected challenges and life-threatening dangers, and you might not discover what you hope to find."

I stopped at the edge of the passageway, one step from freedom. I closed my eyes. Then I fell to my knees, and allowed to wash through me the apostle Paul's declaration: that God calls into being that which does not exist. I kept concentrating on Paul's words until I believed that the Father would one day call into my being that which did not yet exist in me: the calling to be a counselor. I rose, faced Jesus, and said, "I'm ready to do whatever it takes."

"All right, Travis," Jesus said. "In the world you have tribulation, but take courage; I have overcome the world."

We stepped out of the passageway. I smiled as I felt the soft, green grass under my feet, and then joy surged through me, and I shouted, "I'm out—out of my prison—I'm free!"

Killing Time

A cool breeze played across my face as I sat on the crest of a hill. I felt refreshed and at ease.

"It's nice here," Jesus said.

I took a slow, deep breath, and remarked, "Yeah, it's very relaxing."

Jesus was sitting with his ankles crossed and his knees slightly raised, his forearms resting on his knees. His eyes were closed, his head was bowed, and his hands were folded.

"Lord," I asked, "are you praying?"

"No, Travis, I'm not."

"Well, then, what are you doing with your eyes closed?"

His eyes still closed, Jesus replied, "Travis, as I said before: It's nice here and I'm enjoying it."

"But the flowers, the trees, the grass—the entire landscape is so delightful! How can you enjoy all of this with your eyes closed?"

Jesus smiled, and said, "Travis, perhaps I can assure you of one thing about my eyes."

"What's that, Lord?"

"My eyes are closed now, but my eyes were wide open and wild with joy-filling delight when I created this landscape according to my Father's plan and through the power of the Holy Spirit."

I closed my eyes, clamping them shut. *He's God, you idiot!* I thought. *Why do you keep forgetting that?* My head felt hot, throbbing with shame, my face slick with sweat. *I know he's looking at me!* I thought. *I wish I could disappear—vanish from his sight!* Suddenly I couldn't think—my mind blank—my tongue too heavy to move.

"You seem unusually quiet, Travis," Jesus said, his tone caring, his words gently probing. "Are you all right?"

As Jesus was speaking, my eyelids began to feel light, as though the sound of his voice was an invitation to release the clamps on my eyes. My eyes opened—wide. I looked at Jesus. His eyes were still closed! Tension drained from me, and I relaxed. I knew I could speak.

"Lord," I said, "I'm sorry for the way I questioned you. With my questions … well … I was just passing time."

A voice responded to me, saying, "Did I hear you say that you are passing time?" That was not the voice of Jesus. A man was walking toward us, his voice sounding scratchy as he said, "Passing time! I know a great deal about that!" Pointing both index fingers toward his body, he shouted, "See what I mean!" His body, except for his head and his hands, was covered with pocket watches, the watches themselves functioning as his clothing, the chain of each watch appearing to be sewn into his skin. "My name is Emitt," he announced, "spelled with two 't's."

Taken aback by the sight and the ticking of so many watches, I replied, "My name is Travis," raising my voice just high enough to override the sound of the ticking.

"When you were passing time," Emitt said, "were you thinking of becoming a counselor?"

"How do you know about my interest in counseling?" I asked cautiously. "I don't recall ever meeting you."

"My name is Emitt, and Emitt is time spelled backwards, except for the extra 't', and time knows everything."

Jesus opened his eyes, and fixing his gaze on Emitt's eyes, declared, "No, you don't!"

The authority booming in that "No, you don't!" seemed to sub-due the sound of Emitt's watches, their ticking barely audible. Emitt looked frightened and angry. "Yes, yes," Emitt agreed reluctantly, "he's right. I don't know everything, but I do know—"

"Know what?" Jesus asked sharply.

"Oh, I know that time marches on," Emitt fired back. "But I was talking to you, Travis. And I want you to know that time is on your side." Emitt glanced at Jesus, scanning Jesus for signs of response. Jesus looked at me, nodded his head, which I interpreted as affirmation to continue speaking with Emitt.

"What do you mean by time being on my side?" I asked.

"Time is a counselor's greatest friend and ally, and if I'm not your greatest and best friend, you'll never be an effective counselor."

"The way you talk about time, you make it sound like time is as real as a person, as real as someone you can see and hear."

"What do you think you're looking at?! You see all these watches covering my body, don't you?"

"Yes, of course."

"Don't you hear all the watches, hear all of them ticking as one?"

"Yes, I do."

"I am real, and although he won't admit it to you!" Emitt boomed triumphantly, pointing at Jesus, "I have more power in the world than he does!"

I was shocked at Emitt's words. I looked at Jesus, and asked, "Are you going to let Emitt say that without a fight?"

Jesus smiled, and gestured to me to continue speaking with Emitt.

Moving toward Emitt, I shouted, "That's outrageous! What power? Who do you think you are—God?!"

"I wouldn't say that I am God," Emitt remarked, "but I do say I have more power in the world than Jesus does. I'm sure that you've heard the statement 'Time is of the essence,' haven't you?"

"Of course," I said. "It's a cliché, and everyone has heard it."

"A cliché is a truth that people take for granted," Emitt said, "but that doesn't change the fact that it is a truth. The fact that people take it for granted only proves how pervasive that truth is in their lives. The essence—the one indispensable quality, the one absolutely necessary thing—of the lives of people all over the world is determined by time: birth, aging, death. All of them are controlled by time—by me! The minute people wake up, the hour that they go to work, when they celebrate holidays, when they pay their bills, when planes take off and land, the seasons of the year, how your week and weekend are scheduled, when and for how long you take vacations—all this, and much more, is determined by time. So, time is the one and only essential for how lives are constructed and coordinated for everyone on the planet. And because time is essential, time and time alone determines how human life will exist on earth. The lives of all the people on earth are determined by time—by me!—not by Jesus! That's what I mean when I say that time has more power in the world than Jesus does."

I looked at Jesus. "I need your help," I said pleadingly. "I don't know what to say. What Emitt says makes a lot of sense."

"It makes a lot of sense," Jesus replied, "but is it true?"

"I don't know ... Emitt says it's true, but I guess—"

"No need for any guesses, Travis," Emitt insisted. "Let me show you how time is of the essence for a counselor. Someone with a problem comes to you for help. First thing you're going to ask is: 'When did the problem start?'—that's a point in time. Then you'll ask: 'How long has the problem been going on?'—that involves a segment of time. You'll meet with the person for an hour—that's sixty minutes of time. You'll meet once a week—that's a particular day in time. You'll meet with the person until the problem is solved—that's over a course of time. When the person has completed counseling—that closure involves an ending in time. And the person will pay you for your services because, as you know, time is money."

As Emitt was speaking, the ticking of the watches grew louder, the sound seeming to push out of my mind any way to argue with him. I felt a bit dizzy, my eyes blurry. My chest felt tight. I put my hands over my heart, and took a labored breath, trying to block out his relentless ticking.

"Travis, I see you've got your hands on your heart," Emitt noted. "You don't have a bad ticker, do you?" Emitt laughed, and said, "'Bad ticker'—get it?! … time … even a heart beats—ticks—to time. You're not laughing, Travis."

I shook my head, angry at his mocking me but still unable to speak.

"Travis, I see by your face that you are almost—but not quite—convinced," Emitt said. "So I'll go on. My name Emitt is time spelled backwards for a reason: without me, no one could recall anything. I enable a person to go back in time. It's what people call History or the Past or Memory. But my name Emitt is also the verb 'emit': I emit time, producing a forward succession of intervals, these intervals people call the Future. Without me, no one could imagine any goals or envision any picture of a changed life. I enable a person to go forward in time. Only I alone can give a counselor the ability to remember and to talk about the past of someone with a problem. And only I alone can give a counselor the ability to talk about the future of someone with a problem and to imagine a future without that problem. Without me, you'll never be an effective counselor. That's why you need me to be your greatest, best, and closest friend."

I felt paralyzed, the ticking of the watches feeling like hundreds of ice picks stabbing my skull, eyes, ears, and tongue. My head throbbed. I was on the verge of fainting.

"Excuse me, Emitt," Jesus said, his voice strong and incisive. "I'd like to ask you a question. All right?"

"Go ahead," Emitt responded, "I'm sure I've got the answer, because, as you must have heard: time reveals all things."

"Yes, I've heard that," Jesus said. "And you must have heard someone say: 'There is no time like the present.' My question is: What do you think of that—the present?"

Emitt tensed. The sound of the ticking grew quiet, almost inaudible. "There is only the past and there is only the future," Emitt insisted. "Time is either looking backward or time is moving forward. Time can never stand still and can never stop. Therefore, time can never have a present."

"Yes," Jesus said, "that is true for time, but it is not true for eternity! Emitt, you know so painfully well that when I was hanging on my Cross, the nails, the spear, and the thorns that were piercing my body, wounding me—those same nails, spear, and thorns were also piercing time, creating wounds in time so large and so wide that I was able to bring eternity and the eternal God with me, through the doorway created by my wounds. That's why I am called Emmanuel—God is with us, for when I am with a person who receives me as Savior, my presence makes the eternal God present, and anyone who lives with me, lives in the eternal present. I am the dawn who is always breaking. And that is what a counselor needs more than anything: to stay rooted and grounded in my presence, embracing those in pain from the perspective of eternity, believing that I am the dawn who is always breaking. To be a counselor of God, a counselor doesn't need to understand time, he needs to live in the presence of eternity."

"That's a lie!" Emitt boomed, his voice angry, the ticking of the watches erratic, "Your words are smoke and mirrors—nothing more!"

"Travis," Jesus said, "Emitt wants to deceive you by concealing something from you, something that needs to come into the light of truth."

"What is that, Lord?" I asked, the pain of the ice picks gone, my eyes clear and focused.

"The second 't' in Emitt's name. Emitt, would you like to tell Travis the truth—the story behind how you got that second 't' in your name?"

"No," Emitt blustered, "if Travis is stupid enough to believe that story, then he'll see that time flies, and time will have flown without him!"

"All right," Jesus said, "I'll tell the story. The second 't' Emitt refers to, the 't' that he, in fact, has such contempt for, is not really a second 't'."

"What is it, Lord?" I asked.

"That 't' is the sign of my Cross. And as I just said, when I was crucified, my wounds on my Cross created wounds in Emitt, and that 't' in Emitt's name is my permanent reminder to Emitt that he has been wounded, that his wounds have been created by my wounds, that my wounds in him have made a doorway in time, and that eternity has come through that doorway, triumphing over the limits of time—sickness, aging, and death—my resurrection being the proof of eternity's triumph. Emitt can never get rid of my permanent reminder, the sign of my Cross, because no matter how he twists and distorts what he calls himself, that 't', that sign of my Cross is nailed to his name, permanently wounding him, permanently altering his identity, permanently making him unable to stop eternity from coming through the doorway created above and beyond time. That 't', that sign of my Cross, that permanent reminder of the wounds in Emitt that he is powerless to close—that's why Emitt is so full of rage and envy toward me, and that's why he hates me."

"I do hate you!" Emitt screamed, "and I'll never stop hating you! But you are wrong! Yes, your Cross may have opened a doorway in me, and you may have made eternity triumph over me, creating something new, the eternity above and beyond me—something I could never be! But I invented the phrase 'killing time,' and I alone—not you!—can kill time! I'll prove it to you!"

Emitt begin ripping from his body the chains that held the watches to his skin, and as he did, he threw the watches on the ground and with his heel smashed the face of each watch. Every time he ripped a watch from his skin, he left a gaping wound that gushed blood. He was in a frenzy, ripping and smashing watch after watch, pausing, wildly and momentarily, to show the smashed watches to Jesus and to me. Then he continued on, ripping and smashing watches until only a few watches remained chained to him. Blood was gushing from his wounds, the blood covering his body and the few remaining watches. With only a few watches chained to his body to armor him, and being able to draw little strength from their feeble ticking, Emitt seemed helpless, unprotected, and was becoming more and more weak.

"Emitt, you're bleeding!" I shouted. "The bleeding—it can't be stopped! And your wounds—they're too deep to heal!"

"You're wrong!" Emitt replied, his voice weak but defiant. "I've still got a few watches left. I'm not out of time yet! And in case you haven't heard, let me inform you—time heals all wounds!"

"No!" Jesus said, his voice commanding. "That is a lie! The truth is—time causes all wounds! Only the eternal God and my Cross heal all wounds!"

When Jesus said "time causes all wounds"—at that moment— Emitt collapsed to the ground, face down. Emitt tried to speak, but instead of a voice, only the sound of an uneven, rasping ticking came from deep within his throat, and then there seemed to be no sound—only silence.

"Lord, isn't there anything we can do to help Emitt?" I asked.

"No," Jesus resplied. "He can't be helped, because there is a truth that he can never learn."

"What truth?" I asked.

"That time will always run out, but eternity is everlasting." Jesus looked at me, smiled, and said, "Let's go from this place."

"But Emitt's hurt really bad," I pleaded. "I can't leave him ... maybe I can do something."

"You can't do anything that will make a difference," Jesus remarked as he started walking away.

I walked to Emitt, scanning his body for the smallest sign of life. "I think Emitt is dead," I said. "He doesn't look as though he's breathing."

"He's not dead," Jesus remarked, his voice confident. "But Emitt knows for certain that he is winding down, that he is mortally wounded."

"So Emitt really is going to die?" I asked.

"Yes," Jesus replied.

"When?" I asked, expecting a definitive answer.

"Only the Father knows when he will make that come to pass," Jesus said, his voice serious and certain.

Emitt rolled over, onto his back, the watches ticking, the ticking slow and faint. "No, Jesus," Emitt rasped, managing a grin. "You're wrong: Only time will tell."

Jesus stopped walking, turned, looked at Emitt, and proclaimed, "No, time will not tell—time will be told!"

Love is Patient:
First Delivery

Jesus and I were walking down a low-sloping hill of rolling green grass, and I saw the figure of a woman coming up the hill, approaching us. She was wearing a uniform, and as she drew closer, I could see that her neatly-pressed jacket and slacks were the standard issue of the United States Postal Service.

"I have a letter for Travis," she announced, her eyes focused on me. "Is that you?"

"Yes," I replied cautiously. Impressed that she knew where to find me, that she knew my name, and that she was delivering a letter to me, I asked, "How did you know I'd be here?"

She tilted her head slightly, raised her eyebrows, and said confidently, "The U.S. Postal Service will not rest until a piece of mail reaches its proper location and is delivered to the person whose name appears on the envelope." She handed me the letter, and said, "I hope that it's good news. My supervisor told me that he noticed the letter lying on his desk when he came to work. A Post-it was pasted on the front of the envelope and 'Very Important Delivery' was written on it. My supervisor handed me the envelope, and his instructions were clear and pointed: 'Make this delivery top priority on your route today, and don't rest until you find Travis and put this letter into his hands.' I've made good on my promise to my supervisor: you have the letter. So, I'll be on my way. Take care, and God bless you." She turned and walked away.

I sat down, let my fingers and palms feel the texture of the verdant green envelope, then turned it over and saw that it was sealed with what looked like red wax. I opened the envelope and removed the letter, unfolding it to its full length. The so-called letter was nothing but a blank piece of paper—its color verdant green! Inside the paper was a 3-inch by 5-inch note card. The note card was blank—its color verdant green! The verdant green of the envelope, the blank piece of paper, the note card, and the feel of their leafy texture in my hands, energized me, imbuing me with a feeling of hope. I looked at Jesus, searching for cues for what I might do next with the note card, with the feeling of hope growing in me.

Jesus scanned my face, and from what I saw in his look, my face must have appeared as blank as the note card, and then he said, "I'll catch up with you later ... try looking at the other side of the note card ... maybe there's something written on it. By the way," he said as he turned and walked away, "it's good for an aspiring male counselor to embrace a feminine presence in his life."

I felt confused, and for a moment wobbled, dizzy, barely able to keep my balance. "Are you telling me that all of this—stuff!—was sent by a woman? ... feminine presence? ... embrace? ... what do you mean? ... a woman? ... the letter carrier? ... which feminine presence? ... in my life? ... is this for real? ... is this a joke? ... or what?" I asked with my voice loud enough to bridge the widening distance between Jesus and me. Jesus lifted his hand above his head, waved good-bye a few times, and without uttering a sound, kept walking, his pace brisk and deliberate.

I turned the note card over, laid it on the grass and read the words lettered on it:

LOVE IS PATIENT

I sat there, staring at the words, the inside of my head crowded with question marks, each question mark like a fishhook trolling my brain, the stinging barb of each fishhook desperate to catch and haul up a question, a question with a reasonable answer, an answer to make sense of what was happening to me.

More question marks ...

More fishhooks ...

More trolling ...

More stinging barbs ...

No answers ...

With my index fingers and thumbs I stretched my eyelids wider apart, thinking that I could open enough space to let in the full meaning of *Love is patient*—no help!

I picked up the note card and drew it close to my eyes, studying each letter of each word closely and slowly for any clues that might unlock an answer hidden from normal viewing distance—no help!

I shouted repeatedly—*Love is patient!*—my shouts loud enough to produce rolling echoes, my hope that the reverberating words would shake loose a meaning from somewhere—anywhere!—that would dispel the muddle in my mind and replace it with purpose to my plight—no help!

I thrust my tongue hard into one side of my mouth and then hard into the other side, believing that the thrusting might open space inside my mouth, a space for more words to take shape and form an answer to my troubling situation—no help!

I crumpled the note card, and then opened and smoothed it out, trusting that the new texture of the note card would point to an answer to my quandary—no help!

The sight of the note card caused my fists to tighten. My eyes burned. My ears buzzed. I hated the note card! I loathed its very presence! I had to rid myself of its being there, right in front of me—I had to!

With my fingernails I clawed feverishly at the grass and ground, digging a 4-inch by 6-inch grave. I tossed the note card into the grave, and with all the strength I could muster combined with the full weight of my body concentrated in my right thumb, I pressed the note card deep into the grave. Then I covered the note card with dirt. I rolled a large rock over the grave, and then stood there for a moment, studying the rock, making certain that the rock obliterated any visible trace of the note card.

"What does a note card with *Love is patient* written on it have to do with me?!" I cried. "I—am—a—patient—man!"

I felt something hot oozing from the soft part of the thumb I used to press the note card into the grave—it was blood! A paper cut! The note card made me bleed! I kicked the rock, and cupping my hands into a makeshift megaphone over my mouth, I yelled, "Jesus! I can't see you, but I know you can hear me! Yes, you let the paper cut me! But the note card is in the grave—not me!"

Stunned by the grating sound and crazed sense of my words, I paused, took a deep breath, gathered my thoughts and feelings, and with upturned palms dropped to my knees, cleared my throat, and spoke, my voice imploring and solemn, offering an appeal, "Jesus, I'm sorry! I may have sounded like a mad man just now but you and I know I'm not crazy, and I pray that you saw and accepted my patience in the many inventive ways I searched for an answer to my painfully confusing situation, and I pray that what I did to the note card is proof for you that I will not show love to just any anonymous source. Your Word says that Satan disguises himself as an angel of light, and for all I know that note card came from Satan, using *Love is patient* to deceive me into believing that the note card was a message from you, that it was a learning experience you created for me, to help me grow as a Christian, when, in fact, it was Satan tempting me—somehow—to come under his influence."

My eyes searched for any sign of Jesus. "Well, Lord, as far as the letter carrier is concerned, she seemed like a loving and committed person, and a believer in God—not an agent of Satan. Is she the feminine presence you want me to embrace? She was polite, humble, persevering, and she called me by my first name. Who wouldn't want to know her better? But better yet, right now, Jesus, I'll prove beyond doubt my ability to love. I'll dig up the note card and keep it with me, even though I don't know why it was given to me."

I walked over to the rock, bent down to roll it away and retrieve the note card and—suddenly—I froze, my eyes riveted on the words carved into the face of the rock:

LOVE HOPES ALL THINGS
LOVE ENDURES ALL THINGS

The Stranger

My windshield wipers were no match for the rainstorm, so I pulled my car into an open parking space on the street, near an intersection. I put the gearshift into neutral, let the car idle, and watched the wipers laboring to skim off sheets of rain pummeling the windshield, making everything I saw through the glass murky and a blur of colliding colors.

Deciding to wait out the downpour, I shut off the engine. The driving rain banged louder on the roof of my car, and fell harder and heavier on my windshield as the storm grew fiercer, blinding me to whatever was happening outside my car.

Then—suddenly—the rain turned into a steady drizzle. I started the car and turned on the wipers, the swishing of the wipers warding off enough water to keep the windshield clear. I looked through the glass and spotted a figure standing on the corner. It was a woman, her gaunt body a few feet from me. Her oily and blotchy skin, her tongue-less and lace-less shoes, and her torn and threadbare clothes were the desperate signs of someone who is homeless.

The woman's left hand was wrapped in a blood-stained rag, the rain making the blood run, further staining the rag and slowly dripping blood from the palm of her hand. Her face was festooned with sores, and her nose appeared broken in two places. The woman's hair was wound into a tight cylindrical bun nearly a foot in length, sticking straight up from the middle of her head. The location and length of her gray-and-silver bun combined with an unusually small head, made her hair and head, taken together, look like an exclamation mark set precariously on her spindly neck and slumping shoulders.

Feeling compassion for her, I rolled down my window a crack and pressed her urgently, "C'mon in, out of the rain!" As a show of good faith, I opened the car door on the passenger's side, and said in a calm voice, "Please, dear lady, I won't hurt you … I want to help … you're drenched to the bone … and you could get sick … you need to be in a dry place."

The woman was studying my every movement while I was scanning hers. Bare, leathery skin stood in place of her eyebrows, and her yellowish eyeballs suggested a diseased liver. Her fingernails were chipped and broken, and the little finger of her left hand seemed dislocated. Plastic bags from a supermarket were stuffed into the front pockets of the men's trousers she was wearing, and a rip in the trousers, from her knee to her ankle, exposed her bruised leg to rain and cold.

"Dear lady, I fear for your health—for your life!" I pushed open the door as wide as it could swivel, and pleaded, "Please, come in! … come in!"

Her eyes furtive, the woman cautiously edged her way into the seat next to me. I kept a roll of paper towels in the backseat, and I grabbed it and offered it to her, "For now, you can dry off with these."

The woman took the towels and laid them in her lap. "Do you read the Bible?" she asked, her tone inquisitive.

Taken aback by her question, I paused, my eyes focused on the severely chapped lips of her wide smile. "Of course—yes!—I do." I pointed to her cracked lips, and asked, "Doesn't it hurt when you smile?"

"No, it only hurts when I don't smile! The Bible! We were talking about the Bible—"

"Yes! I told you that I read it, but you're so wet and your hand is bleeding, and—"

"Hold off on that! The Bible! Do you ever let the Bible read you?!" she asked, her voice curious, eager to hear an answer.

I felt sad, thinking that her question may be a sign of a mental disorder, and then I was struck by the fact that in the midst of all of her physical and mental pain—she was still alive! "I'm not sure what you mean by the Bible reading me."

"Listen and feel—feel and listen! Do you know the prophet Hosea?"

Wary about her mental stability, I said, "Are you asking whether I know him as a person ... and ... actually met him? ... talked with him?"

"Absolutely! What else could I mean?"

"I'm really concerned about you! I think we should go to the ER!"

"Absolutely not! Listen and feel—feel and listen! If you don't feel and hear the voice of God through Hosea's words, then how can God be real for you? Do you see how drenched I am?"

"Yes," I said, my words soft and confirming. I moved my hand toward the key in the ignition—

"Absolutely not!" she shouted, the palm of her bloody hand covering the key and blocking my access. "What's your name?"

"Travis. What's yours?"

"Travis, I'm drenched."

"Yes, I can see that you are."

"That's because of Hosea."

Believing that I could easily dislodge her grip from my key and start my car, I reached for her hand and—suddenly—felt repelled by the sight of her blood oozing from her palm onto my steering column, her blood like a force field repelling me and protecting her hand. I turned so that my back rested against the side of my door. Agitated, I thought of escaping from the car. Feeling pity, I echoed her words, "Because of Hosea? … Because of Hosea? … "

Seeing me give up on trying to start my car, the woman removed her hand, laid it on the roll of paper towels, and proclaimed, "Absolutely! Hosea! He's why I'm wet! I was standing on the street corner—hearing—feeling—his words—you know, where he proclaims—well God does—every believer—has a part—that's dry—parched—hard—cold—dead—absolutely!—a part … it needs plowing up—made ready—for new growth—then wait—wait—wait—until the Lord rains righteousness—upon you—absolutely!—then let God grow you up—absolutely!—when I felt the rain pour over me—it was cleansing—was soothing—I was feeling—God's in the rain!—speaking—to me—through Hosea's words—God's raining his righteousness—on me!—absolutely!—waiting's over—new season—growing—now!—then you drove up in your car. Listen and feel—feel and listen! That's how the Bible reads you!"

The woman's words were rivulets rippling through me, feeling their way through me, seeming to be searching for some place in me that needed watering. My mouth felt dry. I was thirsty. The woman let out a sigh and sagged sideways, her shoulder pressed against the door, her mouth ajar, exposing wide gaps between her broken teeth.

"Are you all right?!" I asked. "Even in this dim light I can see that your color isn't good. I don't care what you say or do, I'm taking you to the ER!"

"Ab—so—lute—ly not!" she shouted, her tone resolute. "There's something I must do … absolutely more important than taking me to the ER."

"But you're hurting so bad! Your hand hasn't stopped bleeding! —and your yellow-stained eyes!—I fear your liver is diseased!—and the sores festering on your face!—the sickly look of your skin!— your rawboned body!—your decaying teeth!—your ragged clothes!—no protection from the elements!—and you're soaked through with cold rainwater! Let's go! I mean it!"

"Not until I do this one thing. It's a matter of life or death!"

"Refusing to go to the ER—that is a matter of your life or your death! I'm starting the car—we're leaving—now!"

"No! Not before I pray for you!"

"Pray ... for me?!"

"Absolutely! My prayer for you is a matter of your life or your death!"

Confused and feeling my back and shoulders pinned to my door, I fumbled for words—my heart pounding—then—suddenly—words surged from my mouth, "You'd delay going to the ER!—even if it means sacrificing your life for me!—just so you could say a prayer for me! Do you know how crazy that sounds?! Why on earth would you do that—for me?!"

"Because I was a stranger, and you invited me in!"

Heaven's Dental Plan

I was enjoying a walk in the cool tingles of a March morning when the sight of a figure kneeling on the sidewalk brought me to a halt. I drew closer and saw that it was an old woman, hunched over, her head wilted into a bow. She was shuddering, her fists pressing hard against the tops of her thighs as she strained to keep herself from pitching forward.

Cautious, I stood motionless, confused about what was unfolding before my eyes. People passed by her, no one stopping to ask her whether she needed help, no one calling out for someone to call the police. *Is it safe for me to approach her?* I wondered. *Will she be violent? ... Is she mentally deranged? ... Is she in the final throes of a deadly and contagious illness?*

Slowly the old woman raised her right fist until it was pointed upward, toward the sky. Her fist seemed fastened securely in the air, the clenched knot of flesh insistent and unyielding.

I stiffened, and started to back away.

She began to sob.

I stopped.

She lifted her face, her sobs growing louder.

I rushed to her. "Are you all right?" I asked, offering her my handkerchief to dry her eyes and to soothe her wrinkled cheeks.

"Yes, I am," she said, waving off my offer. "Thank you, but I'm fine."

"Are you sure? ... You're alone ... crying ... Did you fall down? ... Are you hurt? ... Should I call for help?"

"You're very kind, but I'm fine, really. I didn't fall down, and I'm not hurt." The old woman stood up, turned in circles, and walked back-and-forth. "See," she said, "there's nothing wrong with me."

I watched her every movement carefully. Still undecided about her mental competence and still confused about what I just saw her do, I asked, "Will you sit down for a moment and talk with me?" Pointing to a nearby bench, I asked, "Is over there all right with you?"

"Okay," said the old woman. "You're a nice man, and you have a sweet smile."

"Thank you," I said, smiling wider.

"And your teeth are beautiful—so even and white! Are they all yours?"

"Yes, they're all mine," I said, laughing, "but too many have fillings and a few have crowns. I can see that you're fascinated by teeth. Well, I'm fascinated by names. May I know your name?"

"Hilary Green, and I am seventy-five years old. And your name, may I know it?"

"Of course, Hilary. My name is Travis."

"Hello, Travis," she said politely, "I'm pleased to meet you."

"And I'm pleased to meet you, Hilary," I said, my voice mildly apologetic. "I trust that you won't think I'm trying to intrude into your life, but may I ask you what you were doing kneeling in the middle of the pavement? I think you can see how strange and crazy that might seem to some people."

"I was praying to the Lord Jesus!" she shouted, her face radiant with gratitude.

"Hilary," I said, "why … ?" I paused, caught by the magnetic draw of what I was seeing in her face—it was her smile! Wide and long, her smile transformed her wrinkled, ashen face into a soft pink glow that was an invitation to come inside the circle of warmth generated by the safe expanse of her full lips. Two tooth-less gums stood on display along the length of her smile. Her soft pink face, her gums without any teeth, the invitation, warmth, and safety in her smile—all of this made her face appear like that of a baby's. "Why pray there," I asked, "on the pavement?"

"I couldn't keep it in any longer," said Hilary. "I was too happy. And when I'm that happy, it doesn't matter to me where I am or what I'm doing, I drop to my knees and pray to Jesus. And today I just had to pray to Jesus, thanking him for the gift he sent me, thanking him for how happy his gift has made me."

"Happy?" I asked, weighing what she was saying now against what I'd watched her doing only minutes ago. "You were sobbing loudly when I saw you, and you didn't seem happy to me."

"Travis, those were tears of joy!"

"And that fist you were shaking in God's face, what was that about?"

"You mean this?" said Hilary, holding out her fist. "Open it and see for yourself what's inside."

I cradled her fist in my hands and tenderly unfolded her fingers. "Teeth!" I shouted, surprised at the two smooth, sparkling white shapes that seemed so out of place in the palm of her hand. "You're carrying around your teeth?!"

"Why not? After all, they are mine! For years they were the on-ly two teeth left in my mouth. My dentist pulled them out yester-day. Just now, I was on my way to his office, to tell him my good news and to let him know that I won't be needing his dental plan, when I fell on my knees and began thanking Jesus for the gift he sent me!"

"Dental plan?" I asked. "If you don't have any teeth left, why would he think that you still need more dental work?"

"My dentist is very thorough," said Hilary. "He has a step-by-step plan for preparing and fitting a mouth for dentures. I reached the stage where all my teeth had been pulled out except these two teeth. And because the two teeth I had left were eyeteeth, my dentist made a joke about it: 'These eyeteeth have seen a lot of food come and go into your mouth. They have been there for you, they were the eyes of your mouth, the first line of defense for what you decided is or is not safe to let into your mouth and let your teeth bite into. Remember that mugger you bit on the arm, bit him so hard that he screamed in pain and ran away? Maybe that was your eyeteeth protecting you, commanding you to attack! I know that you'll miss your own eyeteeth, but they have seen the last of your mouth!' My dentist is always trying to do something to relax me before he begins to work on my mouth. But this time he didn't realize the depth of what he was saying. Neither did I. But Jesus realized it, and he showed me that depth—through his gift!"

"Gift?" I asked. "What gift, Hilary? I don't understand."

"Yes, Travis, Jesus' gift," said Hilary. "I was holding up the gift while I was praising Jesus' name. That's when you came along."

"Do you mean to say that the gift is what you had in your fist?!"
Hilary nodded.

"Then the gift must be your two eyeteeth—right?"
Hilary nodded again, a smile wide on her face.

"I still don't understand," I said. "The dentist pulled out those teeth, probably because they were too decayed or too abscessed to repair. The dentist wanted to get rid of those teeth, teeth that were a threat to your health. So, how can those teeth be Jesus' gift to you?"

"I can answer that for you, Travis," said Hilary, her voice eager. "Let me explain. As far back as I can remember, I've had bad teeth. Every time my parents brought me to the dentist, the dentist would always end the checkup by reporting: 'Hilary's teeth need work.' Then my parents would scold me, and say with absolute certainty, 'Little girls with bad teeth can't go to heaven.' I did everything I was told to make sure I'd have good teeth, but nothing helped. The cavities came. The fillings came. The root canals came. The crowns came. The bridges for my teeth and mouth came. The procedures on my diseased gums came. And the pulling of my teeth, that came too—"

"That must have been hard to take, I—"

"It was ... yes ... it was. But every time one of my teeth was pulled, I carefully placed it under my pillow. I would beg the Tooth Fairy to please take my tooth, give it to Jesus, tell him I'm sorry my tooth is bad, and ask him to make the tooth good, so I can go to heaven. But the next day, I'd find the tooth exactly where I'd placed it, and it would look just as decayed as it was the night before."

Twinges of sadness tugged at my throat. "That must have made you feel like you did something wrong," I said. "I mean, you—"

"That's not the worst of it, Travis. Later my mother would come into my room, take the tooth from me, drag me by the arm to the trash can outside our house, throw my tooth into the trash, and shout with angry disapproval, 'See! That's where God thinks a bad tooth from a bad little girl belongs—in the trash! Never in heaven!'"

"Hilary, your mother was cruel, I don't know how you—"

"But last night was beyond anything I could've imagined. I hadn't done it for over sixty years, but I felt the strongest urge to place my eyeteeth under my pillow. At that time, I didn't know why I felt such a powerful urge, since I don't believe in the Tooth Fairy. I held my eyeteeth in the upturned palm of my hand, my eyes riveted on how yellow, dull, decayed, and blood-stained they looked. A wave of nausea crashed through me, and I hesitated to lift my pillow and to follow wherever the urge would take me, but then a voice seemed to arise in me, saying, *Your eyeteeth are now blind and dead to your old life. They can no longer see anything that would cause you shame*—the words saturating me with their confident sound and washing away the nausea. I lifted my pillow, let both eyeteeth roll from my palm into their resting place, gently covered them with my pillow, and then I went to sleep."

"Your faith, Hilary ... your faith ... amazing, even knowing what happened in the past, you—"

"Today, when I woke up, I felt under my pillow ... felt my eyeteeth ... held them in my hand ... looked at them ... to see what their eyes had seen ..." Hilary's words dissolved in heavy sobs and gushing tears.

"Don't cry, Hilary," I said. "It's not your fault that Jesus didn't take your teeth. He must have his reasons for what he did. What matters is that you tried: You showed Jesus that you wanted to go to heaven. You showed Jesus your faith, the faith of a little girl. That's all you can do."

"Yes," said Hilary. She took a slow, deep breath. "That's all I could do. But that's not all that Jesus could do." She smiled, her gums in full view. "You see, Travis, when I felt those teeth—my two eyeteeth—I knew that Jesus had come and taken them to heaven. He let my eyeteeth see heaven! Then he returned them to me. And the instant I felt them in my hand, I saw heaven, saw heaven as clearly as I am seeing you right now. I saw heaven, and I knew that I'd be going there tomorrow. I've been holding my eyeteeth tight in my hand, all the time seeing heaven, and I haven't opened my hand until just now, when I let you see Jesus' gift to me. I gave my eyeteeth to Jesus, and in return he gave me the eyes to see heaven. We have quite a God, don't we, Travis?"

"Yes, Hilary, we have an amazing God," I said, my tone affirming. "And he continues to work in ways that are truly beyond comprehension." As I heard the sound of my words, they seemed hollow, trite, and scripted.

"Well, I better be on my way to cancel my appointment with my dentist and to tell him that tonight I am stepping into heaven. I can't wait to see his face when I tell him what my eyeteeth saw! He was right: My eyeteeth have seen my mouth for the last time!" Hilary tossed back her head and laughed, her gums glistening in the sunlight. "He'll be happy for me! And he'll be smiling. I know it!"

Hilary rose from her seat. I stood up. Feeling vigilant and invigorated, I ran my tongue across my own eyeteeth.

"God bless you, Travis!" said Hilary, her voice full and free. She hugged me, looked into my eyes, and asked, "Will you celebrate my stepping into heaven tonight by lifting up a smile toward heaven tomorrow?"

"Tomorrow?" I asked, surprised and confused. Needing time to gather my thoughts, I repeated the question, "Tomorrow?" my voice louder to express greater surprise. Then I added a question that I knew would call for a detailed explanation from her, an explanation that would give me time to piece together how I would respond to her belief that she was going to heaven tonight: "Why so soon?"

"Yes, tomorrow, Travis! And why so soon? I told you that Jesus showed me heaven and that tonight I'm going to step into heaven. Tomorrow there will be a graveside service for me, and I've invited some Christian friends to come. I've requested one thing of all those I've invited to come: that each person lift up a smile toward heaven. Will you come?" She smiled, her face soft and pink.

"I believe that you're sincere in what you believe, Hilary. But I can't understand how you can be so sure that you are going to heaven tonight!"

She reached into her sizable handbag and drew out a thin but large object. "Maybe this will deepen your faith in what I say and believe, Travis," said Hilary, as she displayed the object before my eyes. "This is a photograph of my grave. As the colors and details clearly show, the grave has already been dug. The photograph has been taken from the perspective of someone standing alongside the open grave. Notice that there is nothing covering the opening of the grave. I've left written instructions to the funeral director and to the personnel at the cemetery, that my casket is not to cover the opening of the grave during the graveside service, that no artificial grass is to be used as a border to my grave—everything during the celebration is to be open, real, and natural. And when everyone arrives at my grave, my grave must and will appear as this photograph appears, and people will be allowed to stand only at the side of my grave. No one may stand at the head or at the foot of my grave. Now, Travis, do you see why I know that I'm going to step into heaven tonight?"

"No," I said, "I don't." I felt pressured to find an answer to a question I was convinced I could never answer. Cold sweat oozed onto my forehead. I kept focused on the photograph of the grave, thinking the answer was in that picture—but where?

"I see that you're looking at the grave!" said Hilary, excitement ringing in her voice. "Look closer! What do you see?"

"A photograph of a grave."

"No!" said Hilary, her voice edgy but expectant. "It's a photograph of my freshly-dug grave! Look closer! Imagine yourself standing there. What do you see?"

"Your open grave."

"Yes, Travis. And what is it about my open grave that makes me so certain that tonight I'll be stepping into heaven?"

"I think I see something taking shape, but I'm not sure."

"What does my open grave look like, what does it remind you of?"

"I think ... maybe ... I see ..." My unfolding words seemed to be taking me to an answer, but I could not stay focused on them, the words breaking apart and fading away. Pausing, I shut my eyes. Then I slowly opened my eyes and looked at Hilary. She was smiling her widest of smiles, her face even softer and pinker.

Then I looked at the photograph—then at her smile—then at the photograph—then at her smile. And then I shouted with joy, "Yes, I see the truth of what's there! Yes, I know that Jesus really let you see heaven! Yes, I know that you're going to heaven tonight! Yes, I know why your faith is unshakable in Jesus! And yes, tomorrow I'll be at the cemetery, standing alongside your grave, lifting my smile toward heaven! I shout yes!—yes to it all, because now I see that an open grave is like a smiling mouth without any teeth, a smiling mouth lifting its smile all the way up—straight into heaven!"

Charming Snakes

I was sitting on a long wooden bench inside a large circus tent crowded with people when I heard the clack of switches turning on spotlights—that was the signal: the show was beginning. Harsh red beams poured from spotlights, breaking the darkness inside the tent and drawing a narrow circle of crimson light around two closed coffins lying on the stage, making their metallic skins appear bathed in blood.

A chant rose within one coffin, its single word becoming loud and heavy, straining to be heard through the closed steel lid, a lid now slowly opening and raising higher with the quickening drone of the chant: "I—I—I—I—I—I—I—I," the last "I" seeming to raise the lid to maximum height, the "I" expanding to "I—am—Mongo!"

Mongo leaped from the coffin, the bloody light faded, then vanished, the glistening presence of Mongo's white robe and white turban seeming to absorb the bloody light, filtering it until the light was purified of the blood, leaving Mongo, the two coffins, and the round stage a scene of crisp and polished clarity—ready for drama.

Mongo pointed to the open coffin and began to speak: "The Lord said to Moses, 'Make a snake and put it up on a pole; anyone who is bitten can look at it and live.'" Mongo paused, looked at the audience, and said: "Behold, Ladies and Gentlemen, how I have obeyed the Lord."

He reached in the coffin and removed a white wooden pole. A bronze cobra adorned the tip of the pole, the cobra's hood fanned, its fangs bared, its body coiled and ready to strike. Mongo set the pole in a holder located inside the coffin, fastened his eyes on the bronze snake, bowed, then turned to the audience and said: "This is an exact replica of King, my cobra. I had it made to protect me when I'm working with him, in case the day ever comes when my skill fails to keep me safe from King's vicious bite, for, as you know, the venom of a king cobra is fatal. So I must have God's promise to save me from death, or else I wouldn't risk what you're about to see. So, Ladies and Gentlemen, pray that I don't need God today."

With one hand Mongo drew a white soprano recorder from his robe, displayed it, and walked to the coffin that held King. The fingers of his other hand slid behind the coffin and pressed a hidden button that released a catch, popping open the lid with a bang as loud as a gunshot. Mongo began to play the recorder, the notes undulating and insistent, calling King to show himself.

King refused to appear.

Mongo switched tunes, now waving the recorder as he played, side to side, up and down, his face looking strained and confused, as if he was asking himself why the movement of the recorder wasn't drawing King out.

King continued to hide himself.

Mongo played louder, his gestures with the recorder becoming more forceful, changing from smooth waves to jerky starts and stops.

King did not show himself.

Mongo stopped playing. He faced the audience, his mouth a hollow silence, his eyes a daze, his white turban dotted with sweat. He offered the recorder to the audience, in self-mockery, as if to say: "Will someone do what I can't do—charm King out of his coffin?"

"Fake!" shouted a voice from the audience.

"Rip-off!" boomed a man. "Snakes are deaf!"

"Yeah!" jeered a voice in response. "Mongo's deaf, too, or he'd hear that he's being laughed off the stage!"

"Not only that," yelled a man from the back of the tent, "I'll bet there's no snake in that coffin!"

Thunderous booing rocked the tent. Clusters of grumbling people stood, some hurried away, some hurled empty cans of cola at Mongo, and some demanded refunds.

Mongo tossed aside the recorder, rushed to the coffin, aimed his hands at a target only he could see, and thrust them into the coffin, and, with one heave, drew into view the thick, squirming tail of a snake.

"Here he is!" screamed Mongo. "Here is King! My cobra!" His fingers clamped on King's tail, Mongo pulled, exposing the dark sheen of half the body, pulled again, harder, dragging a seething knot of coils onto the rim of the coffin, pulled again, the force of his effort increased by whipping his arms and twisting his shoulders, wrenching away the coils and hauling up the hissing head, the head still fighting to keep hidden in the coffin as the snake's twenty-foot body thudded onto the stage.

King rose up, fanned his head as if to strike, then quickly dropped to his belly, and with rapid turns slithered to the coffin and started to wriggle up one of its metal sides. Mongo seized King, dragged him clear of the coffin, and, putting both hands on the lid, slammed it shut!

"There!" Mongo shouted at King. "It's closed! I closed it! And what do you think you're going to do about it?"

King slid behind the coffin. Mongo grabbed King and pulled him into view. "You'll perform!" commanded Mongo, "one way or another, even if I have to beat you into obeying me!"

Mongo picked up the white soprano recorder and put it to his lips, but before he sounded a note, King darted toward the other coffin. Mongo shrieked, and using the recorder as a club, he swung wildly at King, and, missing him, thrust his white-robed body in front of King, blocking King's path to the coffin.

King drew himself up, fanned his hood, then he froze, motionless but for his forked tongue tasting the frenzied air.

Mongo stripped off his white robe, sneered at King, and then draped the robe over the length of the open coffin, keeping firmly in place the pole with the bronze cobra on it. "Ha!" shouted Mongo. "Now you've had it! Nowhere to go! I control the coffins around here! They're both mine! I own you! This is my show! I make the show! And I made you! You're my bread and butter! And you're ruining me! This is my final warning: either you perform, or—"

King's fangs, taut with venom, struck, sinking into Mongo's eyes, the two deadly needles injecting both eyes at once, the venom filling his eyes with scalding emptiness.

"My God!" cried Mongo, holding open his eyelids, "I'm blind! No! It can't be! I've got to see my bronze snake! Where's my pole? I claim God's promise: if I look at the bronze snake, I can be saved. But I can't see the bronze cobra! God, save me! Let me see the bronze snake! I don't want to die! But I can't see the snake! God! Help! Let me see again!"

Mongo groaned, sobbed. He began to flail his arms, looking desperate to find the pole with the bronze cobra on it. Suddenly his body twisted and jerked as if the pain was biting him, gnawing at his face and mouth, chewing its way into his flesh. He pitched forward, caught himself, then lurched, the wrist of his right arm hitting the pole, snapping it at the spot where it stood in its holder, the pole and the bronze cobra crashing to the floor, and Mongo, his fists buried in the sockets of his eyes, convulsed as venom appeared to flood more layers of his flesh, one spasm doubling him over, causing him to fall into the coffin, his dying body jarring the lid, shaking loose its supports and closing it on him. "I—I—I," muffled and fading, was heard from within the closed coffin, the last "I" contracting into a gasp. Mongo was dead.

Most of the audience bolted from the tent, except for me and one other man.

Stunned by this scene of agony and death, and with my eyes tracking King's movements, I asked the man, "What are we going to do now?"

The man didn't answer me. He was sitting in the front row, leaning forward, his eyes seemed clogged with questions. As King was sliding across the stage, the man stood, took a few steps toward the snake, and asked, "Why?" his plea either unheard or ignored by King, who with every looping move seemed to wrap himself deeper and deeper into silence.

King edged himself up the side of Mongo's coffin, not stopping until he had pulled himself to the top.

Something caught the man's eye while King was pulling himself up. "Look!" he shouted, pointing at King, "There! Do you see it? On King's back! There's a break in King's skin: long, jagged, and yet thin, as if a surgeon had made an incision in his back!"

"Yes," I said, "I see it—King's broken skin, along the entire length of his body. Do you believe the break in King's skin is somehow related to his killing Mongo?"

The man didn't answer me. "Why?" he asked again, his question aimed at King, "why are you trying to hide yourself?"

"I don't think that you're going to find the answer to that question," I said. "Some questions must remain unanswered."

"That's nonsense," said the man. "Every question has one true answer. I am Doctor Lesner Files, Full Professor of Philosophy, and a philosopher's task is to love wisdom so much that he will expand the boundaries of his mind until the answer is found—

even if the price he pays for wisdom is his own mental break-down!"

"That's a huge claim," I said, "especially when you're dealing with a creature who doesn't know how to speak—I mean the snake, of course."

"There are ways of speaking that do not involve words," said Files. Frustrated with me, Files sighed, pointed at King, and said, "Inside the snake's coils of silence, those shrouded places where King was hiding from us his broken skin—there the answer to my question is waiting to be spoken to me!"

I opened my mouth to respond, but was interrupted by a sudden and loud—Pop! the sound of canvas on canvas as a security guard threw open a side flap of the tent. Startled and speechless, my body tensed, and for a moment I was unable to move. "Get back!" yelled the security guard. "That snake's a real killer! No time to wait for people from the zoo! For your own safety—get out of here!"

King rose, his coils flexed, his forked tongue searching the air.

The security guard drew his pistol, aimed, and fired, the guard cursing the snake as the bullets missed King's swaying head. The guard rushed to Files, and demanded, "Give me your coat!"

"My coat!" said Files, his voice loud, his tone angry. "Not a chance! This coat is made of snakes' skins, the skins of pythons to be exact. It was a gift from one of my students, who always used to say that I was like a python, and like that constrictor, I could wrap my mind around any belief and then squeeze it until my logic crushed it to death."

In slow, deliberate, and sinuous ripples, King began moving toward us, a heavy defiant hiss spewing from his mouth.

Seeing King's movements, the security guard shouted, "Shut up! Now's not the time for your head trip! Give me your coat!"

"No!" insisted Files. "You might soil the lining. The lining is made of the whitest silk, and it's never been stained, and there's nothing to mar the purity of the silk: the lining has no label on it, and it doesn't even have my name on it, to identify me as its owner."

The guard seized Files' shoulders, spun him around, and wrestled him to the floor, face down, his arms and legs splayed, squirming to free himself. With speed and force the guard pressed his knee on Files' neck. Files moaned, and then his body went limp. In one surprisingly swift and fluid motion, the security guard peeled off the snakeskin coat, jumped onto the stage, and flung the coat at King, the coat landing on the snake, covering King's head and blanketing his swaying body.

The security guard paused, watched King writhe in the folds of the coat, looked around, spotted the pole with the bronze snake on it, grabbed it, and, as if using a spear, drove the bronze snake into the snakeskin coat. The writhing stopped. A pool of blood began to spread throughout the coat. The security guard used the pole to pry off the snakeskin coat, casting it a few feet from King.

King quivered. He was still alive, but his mangled head could not move: it remained fixed in place while his body twitched.

"You want more?" shouted the security guard, his voice vindictive and victorious. "Okay! Take this—Die!" he roared as he raised the pole and drove its splintered end into King's head, halting only when he saw the white slivers of wood going into King's head turn into bloody splinters coming out of his head. "I've pierced him!" shouted the security guard, pierced him clean through!"

King didn't move. King was dead.

The security guard dropped the pole, glanced at me, looked at King, sneered, and then locked his eyes on Files. "It's over," he said to Files. "Thanks for your snakeskin coat. I couldn't have killed the snake without it. Hey," said the guard, chuckling, "I guess it takes a snake to kill a snake—you follow my drift?! I've got to report what happened. Stay here and wait. The authorities might need a statement from both of you later. Okay?"

I nodded, and said, "That's fine with me."

Files muttered something, dulled and choppy sounds I couldn't understand. Then he yelled to the security guard, "You idiot! My snakeskin coat is soaked with blood. You've ruined my coat—forever! I'll never wear it again!"

"Maybe so," said the guard, his voice smug yet calm, "but I saved your life, and I did it without being a professor of philosophy!" Laughing, the security guard ran from the stage.

Files quickly got to his feet, and climbed onto the stage. "I must know why King was trying to hide himself," he said. "It's a philosophical question, and I must find the one philosophical answer—no matter what it takes!"

I joined Files on the stage, curious to see how he would try to find an answer that would satisfy him.

Files knelt beside King, Files' eyes eager for answers as they followed the course his fingers were marking across the long, jagged, but no longer thin break in King's skin: the break was now uneven and much wider. "No scalpel cut this skin," said Files, "or any other kind of blade. So the break was not an incision."

Files leaned closer, his eyes inches from the broken skin, his fingers deftly probing it, drawing it apart, wider and wider, and then he saw what was just under the broken skin, hardly visible between his cradling hands—"New skin!" he shouted, his words carrying the force and feel of certainty. "King had begun to slough off his old skin, and new skin was breaking through."

Files paused, seeming to be taken off guard by his own words, and then he went on: "Oh, my word!" he exclaimed, "I think I'm close to an answer … somehow … the answer … it must be in

King's new skin breaking through the old skin … but why would he want to hide that?"

Drawing a large pocket knife from his trousers, Files said, "The answer is in King's new skin—I know it: I've got to see more of the new skin!" With purpose and precision, Files began to flay the old skin from the length of King's body, his one hand cutting while his other hand was stretching and pulling away skin.

"There—it's gone!" he declared. "All the old skin is stripped off!" He laid down his knife, and slowly moved his eyes across the length of King's body. Then his eyes froze—into a long stare. "I can't find the answer—not yet," said Files, his voice taut and pressing. "Philosophy has never failed to give me answers! I just need more time. But that idiot security guard and a crowd of thrill seekers will be here any minute, and this place soon will be swarming with police, zoo officials, and the press. I've got to find my answer—and fast!—before those intellectual riffraff arrive and ruin my thinking process with their stupid questions. Stupid people who are too stupid to think philosophically—those mindless zombies really get under my skin!"

"Doctor Files," I said, "when I heard you say that stupid people get under your skin, I remembered your snakeskin coat, and what your student told you when he gave it to you: that your mind was like a python, and that you, like that constricting snake, could wrap your mind around any idea, no matter how false or stupid, and then squeeze it until your logic crushed it to death."

"Your memory is not bad," remarked Files. "That's not far from what he said to me. But get to the point—the mob will be here soon!"

"Put on your snakeskin coat, Doctor Files," I said, increasing the speed of my speech, "your coat made of pythons' skins, then you'll be able to crush with your logic the question of why King was trying to hide himself, and you'll know with finality the one true answer."

I walked the few steps to where the coat was lying, picked it up, and, holding it open, open in the way someone offers to help someone slip into a coat, I started walking toward Files.

Files' eyes focused on the inside of the coat where the pure silk was stained with King's blood. "No!" screamed Files, his eyes glazed and gawking. "That can't be true!" He rubbed his eyes, looked at me as I moved closer, then he shrank back. "Take the coat away!" shrieked Files, his eyes locked on the inside of the coat. "What's inside the coat—it's a lie! That's not the answer! What's inside the coat—it makes my skin crawl!"

"What are you talking about, Doctor Files?" I asked, confused by his strange and unexpected words. "There's nothing inside your coat, well, yes, okay, I can see by looking at the back of the coat, there's some blood that's seeped through the skin. But this is your snakeskin coat, the one that you wear so that your philosophical mind can enable you to find true answers to philosophical questions. Hurry up, Doctor, put on the coat—quickly, I think I hear some shouting in the distance ... the shouts are getting louder ... they're getting closer."

Files started sobbing, his eyes thick with terror, as if he was staring at someone who was telling him that he was losing his mind, his voice raving, "Take the coat away!—I can't bear to look at what's inside!—It's making my skin crawl!—Crawling with snakes!—Pythons!—They're on my feet!—On my legs!—Don't you see them?!—They're around my waist and chest!—On my arms—Around my neck!—Don't you see them?!—They're crawling on my face!—Wrapping themselves around me!—Squeezing me!—I can't bear to look at what's written inside the coat!—The words inside the coat!—They're squeezing me!—Breaking me apart!—The words!—Inside the coat!—Squeezing me out of my skin!—I'm coming out of my skin!—I'm coming out of my skin!—I'm coming out of my skin!" Files rushed off the stage, his mouth foaming, his arms flailing, and as he fled from the tent and disappeared from my view, I heard him shriek, "Help me!—I'm coming out of my skin!"

I stood on the stage, still holding the snakeskin coat, stunned by Files' psychotic ravings, his words swirling through my mind: "I can't bear to look at what's written inside the coat!"

I decided to look inside the snakeskin coat, to prove to myself that no words were written inside, and to confirm that what Files claimed that he saw was only the hallucination of a mind gone insane.

I turned the snakeskin coat around, to face me, and opened it wide, then, suddenly breathless, I dropped to my knees when I looked inside and saw what was written in King's blood:

CHRIST IS KING!

Holes Through The Night

In the dimming glow of dusk I was watching a little girl creep toward the back of a man sitting at one of the picnic tables that dotted a spacious park. A newspaper lay open and flat on the wooden table top, and the man pressed his forearms and palms on the paper, securing it against a gust of wind. The man glanced at me, flashed a smile, and then drew his eyes into squints, looking determined to finish reading the newspaper before the fading light dissolved into darkness.

The little girl crouched, hunched her shoulders, and shaped her fingers into sharp curves of claws. She was a jungle cat stalking her prey, inching closer and closer, until she was within pouncing distance. Slowly she rose up behind the man, her claws extended and ready to strike his head, and then, with one awkward leap, she flung herself onto his back, her arms around his neck, and shouted insistently—"Guess who?!"

The man did not flinch. His narrowed eyes stayed focused on the newspaper, as he used an index finger to track the sequence of words he was pouring over, finishing what he was reading just as night absorbed the last glimmer of day.

"Guess who?!" shouted the little girl, clapping her palms over his eyes.

"I don't know who you are!" exclaimed the man. "Give me a hint."

"C'mon, Daddy!" she cried. "Who am I? Guess!"

The man smiled. "I don't know who you are ... maybe a tiger? ... maybe a bear? ... maybe a gorilla? ... but you're very scary, and it's already dark outside. And now you've got your hands over my eyes, making it darker ... I can't see anything ... caught in your grip ... please let me go," gasped the man, pretending to be weary from his make-believe struggle to free himself, "I want to go home."

She pressed her palms harder on his eyes. "Guess first!" she commanded. "Then you can go home!"

"All right, Mystery Girl. I'll try. Are you Teresa the tiger?"

"No."

"Are you Betsy the bear?"

"No."

"Are you Gail the gorilla?"

"No! C'mon, Daddy! You know!"

"Hmmm. Are you ... are you—Carly?!"

"Yes!" she squealed gleefully, the sound of her name the signal to pull away her hands. "Daddy! You guessed me! You can go home now."

"Thanks," he said, a chuckle following his words. "I will go home. I'm sure glad I can see again, because I see that it's really dark outside. Hey, I've got an idea."

"What is it, Daddy?"

"Let's go home together."

She giggled. "Okay," said Carly. "But can we play the game to-morrow? Can we? Can we, Daddy?"

"Sure," he said, "but next time I get to put my hands over your eyes."

"Oh, Daddy," said Carly, "but that's not fair."

"How come?"

"Because I won't have to guess. I already know who you are!"

The man laughed, took his daughter by the hand, led her out of the park to their car. I noticed that the man had left behind his newspaper, for it lay there, still open on the picnic table. Thinking the man may have forgotten his paper, I rushed to the table, grabbed the paper, and turned to call to him, but he'd driven out of sight.

I began to walk toward my car, but a twinge of feeling arose in me, a feeling more like a tug at my heart, a desire to want to stay a while longer. I felt a smile play across my face as I recalled images of the man and his daughter—their playful yet unbreakable bond of love. I thought of the picnic table, how its weathered planks must have been for years a place of rest for the man, a place of reliable and solid quiet: the wooden table always there, in the same spot, an always steady, always secure place for him to lean on, a place to read his newspaper at leisure, while his daughter explored the wonders of the park and the freedom of having fun with her father.

As I took a deep breath I smelled the enlivening aroma of the ocean, its waves less than fifty yards from the edge of the park, and I imagined the aroma to be Carly's favorite scent, picturing her breathing deeply, letting sea breezes gently blow salty wet perfume across her face, making her feel fully awake to the fact that she was embraced by God's glorious creation, an embrace that affirmed her as a precious little girl sitting on her special bench with her father, her mind already dancing with new ways to play with him.

Smiling wider, I leaned against a tree, my eyes caught by the look of the waves in the night, their liquid velvet swelling into curling peaks, peaks turning inward while arching forward, and then unfolding their spraying white foam as they rolled toward and onto the beach. A gust of sea-filled air wafted across my face, and I took a deep breath. I felt relaxed, open. Peace washed through me and over me. I felt safe, receptive, even welcoming. I let my head rest gently against the tree, my head tilted up, toward the sky. My eyes moved across the sky, its dark gray expanse making the sky appear moonless and starless.

Suddenly I sensed someone nearby. I stepped away from the tree, but before I could turn my head, the heavy force of a lunging body fell on my back and seized my neck, driving me sideways, threatening to buckle my legs. "What?!" I shouted, trying to keep my balance. "What's going on?!"

No answer.

My fingers tore at the arms locked around my neck. The arms tightened. I spun left—lurched right, struggling to shake off the burden weighing me down. "Hey!" I screamed. "What do you want?"

No answer.

The body clamped its legs around my waist. "Get off me! Are you crazy?!"

The body clapped its palms over my eyes.

"If you want money—take mine! Take it all!"

The body clung to me, squeezing me, its draining load becoming heavier, more unwieldy. "Let me go!" I cried. "Please!"

The heft of the body grew heavier, its legs constricting, its palms tightening their seal over my eyes. "Help!" I pleaded. "Someone! Help me!"

"Guess who?" asked the body, its voice a piercing and commanding whisper.

I felt paralyzed—my mind a cold blank—I staggered forward—my legs gave way—my arms outstretched in front of me—clawing at the empty air—trying to brace my fall—I shrieked in pain when my splayed hands skidded across the top of the wooden picnic table, splinters stabbing into my palms. "Guess ... who?! ... Is this ... a game?! ... This isn't funny!" ... I'm hurt! ... I can feel my palms—they're bleeding! ... Do you know me? ... Tell me who you are—please!"

"Guess who?" said the body, its voice the same piercing and commanding whisper. Its palms still tight over my eyes, the body lifted me from the picnic table.

"Your voice—I don't know it! ... don't know you!" I cried. "This is insane! If you let me go, I won't press charges!"

No answer. I just felt those hands—strong, fixed in place, and unbreakable in their grip over my eyes. Suddenly I felt waves of warmth flow from the palms covering my eyes, flow in circles around my eyes, then the warmth radiated from my eyes across my face, filling my face with warmth, and then my head and body became bathed in this same flowing warmth.

Then I heard a voice, a man's voice, deep, full-throated, and emphatic, command, "Tell me what you see!"

"I can't see anything," I said. "Your hands are covering my eyes. But I can feel warmth flowing from your hands into me."

"Look again," replied the man. "Open your eyes. See the truth!"

In an instant I realized that all this time I'd been keeping my eyes shut tight. Slowly I opened my eyes. The palms over my eyes still fixed in place. But I could see! The man had holes in his palms, and I was looking through these holes!

The man kept his hands over my eyes, and asked, "What do you see?"

"I see through the holes in your palms."

"And what else?"

"What do you mean?"

"See the truth!"

"I see stars. Before you covered my eyes, the sky seemed starless."

"Keep your eyes on the stars. What are they? See the truth!"

"The stars are points of light—eternal parts of God's creation."

"No, my precious one," the man said softly and firmly. "You're looking at the stars. Whenever you look through the holes in my palms, you see through whatever you are looking at—then you see the truth! Look again. Look at the stars and see through the night—see the truth!"

The warmth of the man's hands bathed and soaked my eyes with waves of pulsing light. My eyes were like doors flung open, to let in more light, light that was brighter than sunlight, cleansing light that was streaming into my eyes through the holes in the man's palms.

"Yes!" I shouted. "I see the truth! The stars are holes through the night, and I see through and beyond the night! I see heaven! Everything is light! There is only the face of my Father in heaven. He is smiling at me! And his smile—it is heaven!"

"Oh, yes, precious one!" exclaimed the man, "and he is my Father too!"

"You are the crucified Christ!" I shouted with joy. "And you are the resurrected Jesus!"

"Yes, I am, Travis. Now lean back against my chest, and feel me backing you up."

I leaned back, and thoughts arose from somewhere inside me: *Jesus is the only begotten God who's in the bosom of the Father. The bosom of the Father! My back is leaning against the chest of the Son of God who was and is himself in the chest—the very heart—of the Father!* I felt safe, trusting my whole body to Jesus.

"Raise your hands, waist-high," Jesus said, "and place them, palms open, close to your hips."

As I did as Jesus directed, I felt trickles of blood running from my splinter-pierced palms.

He took his hands from my eyes and placed his open palms on my open palms. "Yes, Travis, I am the crucified Christ. And I am the resurrected Jesus." Then he drew his palms across my bloody palms, declaring, "You are being healed, because I am also your new skin—your only skin, skin newer than the skin of a baby just born into the world. I am your born-again skin, your eternal covering. Every time you look through the night, look through the holes in my palms, your born-again skin will always be new, you will always be new, and everything you see will always be the truth that is new, for I am making all things new."

A warm sea breeze floated across my face. As I breathed in the refreshing fragrance of the ocean air, I gazed at my healed palms, struck by how fluid and light my hands felt. Suddenly I realized that the hands of Jesus—were gone! I turned around—he was gone!

The sea breeze was steady, and as the air gently drifted past my ears, I heard words rising on the wind: "Look through my holes—see the truth—live!"

Research Scientist

I was waiting in the windowless room of a laboratory, my wristwatch the only proof that I'd been sitting in the metal folding chair for an hour, the chair the only piece of furniture in the blank-walled, bare-floored room.

I heard a firm knock on the door, and a voice asked, "Is your name Travis? And are you alone?"

"Yes," I said, "I'm Travis, and I'm alone."

The door opened. A man walked into the room. "I am Doctor Shearson," he announced, "and I am Director of The World Academy of Research Scientists. We are an elite group of committed researchers, and we refer to this facility and our group of scientists as 'The World.' Or, if you wish, you may refer to us by our acronym: W.A.R.S.—W.A.R.S. because we make war on every form of intellectual pretense, every expression of hypocrisy, every moronic superstition such as organized religion, astrology, palmistry, and magical thinking in all its posturing guises. In other words, we make war on everything that is not based on research science. Travis, you are in one of the small labs at The World, and, as a matter of fact, I am director of the project you may be about to undertake. And this, Travis, is our creed and war-cry at The World: Life is a laboratory for the advancement of Science."

Shearson moved toward me, his demeanor one of consummate precision: the efficiency of his swinging arms, the mannered pace of each step, the manicured glitter of his calculating white hands, their porcelain burnish heightened by the fluorescent glare pervading the room, the polished lines and planes of his hairless face and head, their angles looking honed and sharp enough to cut anyone who touched them—all this combined to produce a monolithic figure whose cold and hard presence dominated the room.

Casting a diagnostic glance at me, Shearson said, "Travis, I told you The World's war-cry and creed, and I want you to burn into your memory this one more thing: Science is God! Every laboratory is one of Its temples, every research scientist is one of Its priests, and I am Its chief priest! Don't you ever forget that—Never!"

I locked my eyes on Shearson's face, struck by the clenched force of the doctor's words, words that hit me with the heft of final authority, final in the way that a ruling from the Supreme Court is final—it's the Law beyond which there is no appeal.

"How long have you been waiting?" asked Shearson.

"For an hour," I said. "Exactly one hour."

"Excellent! You are punctilious, a quality that the research scientist must have if he is to succeed." Shearson inspected my eyes, looking for hints of pretense. "And yet you remained in the room. Why didn't you leave after fifteen or twenty minutes?"

"I made an appointment," I replied, crossing my legs at the ankles. "I kept my word."

"Superb! Commitment! A scientist must remain committed to the course dictated by his research design—no matter what results that course may bring!" Shearson paused, folded his arms over his chest, his clinical eyes appearing to calculate some meaning he detected in my shifting posture. Then he asked: "What hypothesis would you advance to account for my lateness?"

I drew my lips between my teeth, as if to halt the words poised on them. I needed more time to consider an answer to Shearson's question. I let a few moments pass in silence.

"I deem reflective thought necessary for a scientist to do his work," Shearson asserted, "but you had an hour to ruminate on my question, a question I am sure that you anticipated while you were waiting for me. So, if you have an answer, let me hear it now. Or, perhaps, you are not the next person to become a research scientist whose life is committed to The World."

"I have a number of hypotheses," I said, surprised by the calm yet challenging sound of my voice. "One: Your lateness was intentional, designed to test whether I'm prepared to do my own research. Two: You forgot the appointment. Three: A personal emergency prevented you from arriving on time. Four: You—"

"Outstanding!" exclaimed Shearson, almost shouting. "Say no more. You manifest a mind that is flexible enough to imagine new scientific possibilities and yet resolute enough to formulate analytical distinctions and use them to guide scientific practice! Those who trained you before you came to The World knew what they were doing. You are well-trained because your trainers knew what you are about to discover: that no one can become a counselor, an economist, a sociologist, an anthropologist, a psychologist, a physician, or engage in any other professional endeavor that claims to be a science unless that person worships Science as his God. Your training and this interview are now complete. Representing The World, I have designed a project for you so that you can do your own scientific research. Are you ready to go to the site?"

"Yes, I am." I rose from the chair and walked to the door.

"One more point to remember," inserted Shearson. "Research means to search again and again and again until the truth emerges from the jumbled mass of disconnected observations. This will be your initial attempt at research. So, you will not be asked to know the previous research done on this topic. And you will not be asked to create a research design before you begin your project. So, you will not be required in advance to have any imaginative grasp or analytical understanding of what you are going to observe."

"I'm confused, Doctor Shearson," I said. "All the qualities that you insisted a qualified research scientist must have, qualities you said I have, are now the very qualities you tell me I won't need to complete the research project you've designed for me."

"Logic!" said Shearson, his voice emphatic. "Once more you display a quality of utmost importance for the research scientist. But that is beside the point, at least for now."

"What is the point?" I asked, my tone probing.

"Commitment!" said Shearson, his voice commanding and confident. "I mentioned it earlier: commitment is the quality that kept you in your chair for an hour. I have to examine further your sense and depth of commitment before I can sanction you as a research scientist worthy of being in The World."

"Excuse my presumption, Doctor Shearson, but you were not the doctor originally assigned to be my director. I think that his name is Doctor Waverly. I received his name in the mail, informing me that he would be my project director, but I never met him or heard from him again. What happened to him?"

"That is classified material. What I can tell you is that some personnel adjustments had to be made at The World, adjustments that involved Doctor Waverly." Shearson paused, slowly stroked his chin, and then said, "Furthermore, The World regards me as the only research scientist who has the credentials that are necessary to guide someone like you. You are a special case, a rare specimen, indeed." Shearson walked to the door, opened it, and asserted, "The project site is waiting for us. We do not want to get a late start, do we?"

"No, we don't. Let's go."

I matched my stride to Shearson's measured pace as we walked down the long, empty corridor that connected the main building to the underground parking lot. We didn't look at one another, and the only sound we shared was the rhythmic click of our heels on the recently waxed and polished floor.

Shearson led me to a car, the doctor sliding behind the wheel, and I taking the bucket seat next to him. Shearson drove for over an hour, repeating zigs and zags until he came to a block of my hometown unfamiliar to me.

"We are here," said Shearson. "This is the research project site. Notice that there are no street signs. I planned it that way. I want you to rely on your own well-trained inner resources to locate and develop who you are as a scientist and what you are doing as a researcher." The doctor stopped the car. "Get out!" he said, the push of command in his voice.

"All right," I said as I opened the door. I got out of the car and stood on the corner. "What's next?"

Shearson leaned sideways and reached for the handle of the door I'd left open. "No matter what happens," he said as he pulled shut the door, "search again and again and again, until the truth emerges."

"What am I to look for?" I asked, my question both a plea for the doctor to stay and a request for information and direction.

"Commitment!" shouted Shearson. "Look for commitment!" He drove away and vanished in the distance.

I looked right—then left, my eyes confirming what my ears were hearing: Many cars, many trucks, many noises. This much was certain: I was standing on a busy street corner. The frenetic swell of traffic rose, threatening to flood me with its relentless din and sweep me off the sidewalk. I wanted to hold on to something fixed and solid, something that would anchor me in the rolling buzz rushing about my ears.

I looked over my shoulder and spotted the tall office building that occupied both sides of the street corner, its heavy stone façade a promise of support. I ran to the building, spun around, and carefully let my back rest against the façade. I felt safe there: No one could approach me from behind, and no one could do anything without his actions being detected by me. I made the building my observation post, from there surveying the street corner and the intersection, searching for a sign—any sign—that would lead me forward in my research.

A bench with "35 Bus" lettered on its back caught my eye. A bus stop. Yes. A fact. A man appeared from the other side of the corner, walked to the bench, and sat down. A man. Walking. Sitting. Yes. More facts. Then the man stood up, moved to behind the bench, pacing back and forth. He cast a glance in my direction, a glance that turned into a grating stare. Standing. Moving. Pacing. Staring at me. More facts.

I gazed into the man's stare, to determine whether it would be the central fact that I could use to construct a picture of commitment, but the grip of the man's stare became too weak to keep me in it, and his eyes let go their hold of me. *A weak will!* I thought. *That's a sign of cowardice. And no coward has ever had the will to stay committed to anything.*

The man yawned.

A yawn! I noted to myself. *A sure sign of boredom. And when a man is bored he can never be committed to anything.*

The man coughed.

"A cough," I whispered, my words aimed at the ears of the man but not loud enough to reach them. "That's a definite sign of sickness. And commitment can never be based on anything that's sick."

The man drew in a deep breath, paused, and then let out a long groan edged with anger.

All right, I thought, *I see it. The fact is clear: Impatience is the enemy of commitment. But I—*

The man shook his head, the sharp movements seeming to cut off the words I was about to say to myself. The man studied his wristwatch, glanced down the street, and asked, "Why is the bus always so late?" He began to shuffle his feet, his step agitated and uneven. Mumbles and half-audible phrases were squeezed through his pinched lips.

The man halted, looked skyward, and, with his hands raised high, proclaimed, "Love your neighbor as yourself!" The man doubled his hands into fists and began to shake them at the sky. "It's your commandment, God! Why don't you follow it yourself?! If you can create the universe and never be late for your work, why won't you create a bus that can get me to work on time?! Hey, God, I'm your neighbor, right?! So, why don't you love me as you love yourself—and make that bus come on time?!"

A stream of mumbles poured from the man as he resumed shuffling his feet. He stopped. Looked for the bus. Shook his head. He put his hand into one of his trouser pockets, his fingers fumbling to locate something. Suddenly, in a wide sweeping motion, he drew out a straight-razor, lifted it skyward, and shouted, "If I'm late again, I'll lose my job!" He brandished the straight-razor, slicing the air with its stainless steel blade. "Take that, God!" he screamed. "In your throat!" He paused, scanning the silent sky. "Hey!" he boomed, his angry blast meant to prompt a response from God. "Hey!" he repeated, his voice louder, "are you there?!" He walked to the curb, craned his neck so that he could see for blocks, looking for any sign of the bus. "It doesn't matter, God. It's too late. There is no bus. I don't care anymore. I give up—you win!"

The man looked at me, grinned, and said, "Love your neighbor as yourself!" Then he slashed his left wrist with the straight-razor, using the entire length of blade to open a long and deep gash.

"No!" I shouted. "Stop!" Shocked, I pressed my back hard against the heavy stone facade, my eyes darting.

Appearing more confused than in physical pain, the man, his lips quivering, stared at his sliced open flesh. He uttered no sound as he held out his slashed wrist and walked toward me, his tread shaky but undaunted.

My eyes glimpsing the deep wound, I cried, "My God! That looks really bad? ... Is ... it? ... Is ... "—I began to heave at the horror inches from my eyes, the burn of vomit spraying the back of my throat. "You ... you're ... slashed!" I said, my words forced out in coughs and gasps. I turned away my head, and in that moment, while my eyes were shut tight, I realized that something that should be in that gash was not there.

I returned my gaze to the slashed wrist, my eyes widening, searching for what I knew should be there—it wasn't! "No blood!" I shouted. "Slashed to the bone! But no blood!" I looked into the man's eyes. "My God!" I said, my voice tight, barely a whisper. "You ... look ... dead!"

"No," said the man. "I'm not dead. But I want to die. My slashed wrist proves that. But I need blood. No one can die unless he sheds blood. Will you give me some of your blood?"

"What?" I asked, my eyes moving along the white empty space in the man's wrist. "My blood?!"

"I have a right to die whenever and wherever I choose," insisted the man. "Not even God can take away that right!"

"I'm not sure ... about a right ... to die ... but ... my—"

"Killing myself!" interrupted the man. "That's the only thing I can make happen on time. Death never comes late when you commit suicide, and suicide is the greatest commitment anyone can ever make. But I need your blood to help me realize that commitment, to help me to die! Commit some of your blood to me! Please!"

"Commit? ... my blood? ... I ... would ... if —"

"I think I hear the bus coming," said the man, keeping his eyes fixed on me. "I'd know that sound anywhere. I must have your answer before the bus gets here. Please! My death is in your hands! Yes or no! Your blood! May I have it?!"

I felt dizzy, my legs weak. "I need more time," I uttered, "I—"

"Time?!" shouted the man. "More time?!" He cocked his ear. "The bus! It's coming!" The man stepped back, raised the straight-razor, his arm poised to strike. "I've run out of time!" he boomed, his voice thick and tense. "And so have you! Your blood—Now!"

"No!" I cried, flinching, covering my eyes with my palms, trying to shield myself from seeing where the blade would rip into me. My body tensed, I waited for the feel of slicing pain. Time dripped by. The blade didn't cut me. Cramps in my arms forced me to drop my hands. My eyes scoured the street corner for the man, but I saw only a bus pulling alongside the curb.

I stood there alone, sweat oozing onto my forehead and trickling down my cheeks and nose. I reached into a back trouser pocket for my handkerchief, to wipe away the sweat, but found that the handkerchief was gone and in its place was another object—the straight-razor!

I drew the straight-razor from its gold-plated case, its stainless steel blade sharper than I'd imagined. I examined the blade, turning it over as my eyes searched its surface, and then, seeing an odd array of lines take shape on one of its highly-polished sides, I stopped turning the blade and looked closely at the lines. The lines formed words, words etched on the side of the blade, their clean, broad letters engraved with the precision of a master craftsman. For a moment the sun glinted on the stainless steel, filling my eyes with a brilliance that blinded me, making it impossible to read what was etched on the blade. Slowly I experimented with the angle of the blade, adjusting it until, in an instant, I saw what the words engraved into its side commanded:

LOVE YOUR NEIGHBOR AS YOURSELF

"God," I moaned, my pleading voice directed at the command on the blade. "I meant to help. My blood ... I would have given ... committed some blood ... needed more time ... please believe me ... I—"

The sound of the bus door springing open jarred me, interrupting my response to the command on the blade. I peered into the bus, looking at the man sitting behind the wheel. It was Shearson!

Shearson removed his coat, and then rolled up one sleeve of his shirt. He held out his exposed wrist, the white empty space in his flesh the same size and shape as the space the man on the street corner had slashed into his wrist. Then Shearson said: "Hello, neighbor!" Shearson grinned, and then went on: "Do you love your neighbor as yourself?"

"Doctor!" I cried. "You?!—That wrist?!—The blade?!—Me?!" I paused, my eyes fastening on the command on the blade—then on Shearson's wrist—then on the blade—then on the wrist—then the blade—then the wrist—back and forth, until the only thing I saw and heard was "LOVE YOUR NEIGHBOR AS YOURSELF."

Unblinking, my eyes locked on Shearson's wrist, I shouted, "Yes! I love my neighbor as myself!" I placed the blade of the straight-razor on my wrist. "And here's what you want! My blood! Take it!" One swift, hard, and deep stroke of the stainless steel blade severed arteries and veins, the gash in my wrist erupting blood, splattering the sidewalk and my clothes. I staggered into the bus. "See," I said weakly, showing Shearson my bleeding wrist, "I am committed ... I love my neighbor ... my blood for him ... my blood is his blood ... " My legs buckled. "But ... I'm bleeding ... losing blood ... no one's taking my blood ... to give to my neighbor ...

where is my neighbor? ... who is my neighbor? ... " My voice fading, I collapsed onto the floor.

"Quick!" shouted Shearson to the only other person in the bus. "Give me a hand! We can't let him bleed to death!"

The man rushed to the front of the bus. Carrying a white towel, he took hold of my hand, and using the towel as a tourniquet, he applied it to the spurting gash in my wrist. "There," he said. "That will stop the flow." He scooped up the straight-razor, guided the blade into its case, and placed the razor in his shirt pocket. Then Shearson and the man picked me up, placed me on a seat of the bus, and secured me with a seat belt, my head facing the front of the bus and leaning against a window.

Suddenly I recognized the man—it was the same man from the street corner, the one who had slashed his wrist!

"Now what?" the man asked Shearson.

"Let's take him to the hospital, Doctor Waverly," said Shearson, his voice calm and insistent. "We can talk on the way."

"Which hospital?" asked Waverly. "County General?"

"No," countered Shearson, his voice decisive. "I have a different hospital in mind. And do not give a second thought to his physical safety. I guarantee you that he will not die before we arrive at the hospital."

"Well, you are the Director of The World, and I know that you have a plan designed for what's best for the advancement of Science."

They moved to the front of the bus, the seat facing the steering wheel wide enough to accommodate two people. Shearson sat down and took hold of the wheel, and Waverly sat next to him. The bus surged forward onto the street as Shearson said calmly, "I guaranteed you a result, and I am committed to achieving that result. So I will not delay, even if I have to exceed the speed limit!"

"Excuse me, Director," Waverly probed, "but have you decided whether you're conferring on me the title 'Research Scientist,' a title that would mean that I'm accepted as a member of The World?"

"I do not at this moment see any problem with you being a member of The World. You operated at the highest scientific levels in this project, carrying out your assigned duties without a hitch. Yours was a first-rate professional performance—you played your role with dramatic force and believability. And the special effects expert that you hired to show you and me how to make our wrists appear as if they had been slashed—that was an ingenious move on your part! You convinced Travis that you actually had slashed your wrist, and he was equally convinced that I had slashed my wrist—all of this your doing, and all necessary additions to the experiment, additions that reinforced the illusion of our being hurt and the illusion that we needed Travis' blood. I do not think that he would have slashed his own wrist had it not been for your research brilliance and unmatched acting ability. So, all of your analytical foresight, combined with my legitimate authority as Director of The World and with my insisting that Travis must believe and live out how unwavering commitment to a course of action is the foundation of research science—all of this made the experiment a success of the highest importance. You are a research scientist, Doctor Waverly. There is no doubt about that. When we return to my office at The World, I will announce to everyone that you are one of us, that you are a member of The World."

"Thank you, Director Shearson. I am honored to be a member of The World. I am committed to Science. Research is my life. I don't know what I'd do without it. Speaking of research, may I inquire what your research design has prepared next for Travis? I mean, to which hospital are you taking him?"

"New Horizons Mental Hospital," announced Shearson.

"A mental hospital?!" asked Waverly, his voice tight, his words probing. "We never discussed that as a part of the experiment."

"Look," said Shearson, "my research design is flawless: After the doctors treat Travis for his wrist wound, I'll observe him at the hospital for a while."

"What if the psychiatrists don't agree with you, don't believe that Travis should be kept there for observation?"

"I am way ahead of you, Doctor Waverly. I have already determined that Travis is mentally ill, and that his mental illness warrants his being institutionalized. I merely need to demonstrate that I have amassed the psychiatric evidence, record it on official documents, and present it to the court. Then the court will commit him to be confined in the hospital for life. It is all part of correct legal procedure, and correct legal procedure always serves the advancement of Science. Remember the motto of The World: Life is a laboratory for the advancement of Science. And Travis' life is no exception. His life must serve the advancement of Science, and that means he must be kept in a mental hospital for the rest of his life."

"That sounds as if you're defining him as mentally ill before all the facts are in, before he's assessed by any qualified mental health professional," said Waverly, his voice growing louder with each word. "That course of action not only sounds like a roadblock to the advancement of Science—it is Bad Science! You don't have the facts to prove that Travis is mentally ill, and you're not qualified to make evaluations of someone's mental health status. Besides, even if you do get as far as a court, how do you know that the court will agree with you?"

"You are beginning to disappoint me, Doctor Waverly," said Shearson, his tone clinical but victorious. "I am certain that the court will agree with me that Travis is mentally ill, because I have for years known the judge who decides these court cases, and I can state as a fact that he wants for Travis exactly what I want for him—a life of commitment!"

"A life of commitment!" shouted Waverly. "Travis' actions proved that his life is committed to the advancement of Science! He was willing to give his life's blood for research science, willing to die for Science! I would think that you would see his slashing his own wrist for Science as the height of mental health! And I don't know why you didn't embrace him on the spot as a member of The World!"

"No, Doctor Waverly!" shouted Shearson, his voice insistent. "A scientist never uses words such as 'embrace.' I must tell you that my disappointment in you is quickly becoming frustration. I am starting to question my decision to make you part of The World. Travis failed the experiment, failed in a way that is a threat to the advancement of Science. And the fact that you cannot see why he failed—that fact alone exposes blind spots in your scientific thinking."

"Then tell me why Travis failed the experiment!" demanded Waverly.

"I will tell you," said Shearson, his voice angry and incisive, "and your response to what I say will determine whether you have a future in The World. Travis failed because he did not see that the life of a research scientist is a bloodless life. When you showed your slashed but bloodless wrist, he became a bit disoriented, but I thought that he was going to deduce that the experiment was set up to show that Science and Its scientists must be bloodless to do their work. It was right there, at that point, that he should have stopped the experiment and declared to me that Science and Its scientists must be bloodless, and that there is no such thing as a soul or any god other than Science, and—"

"You're headed down a dangerous path!" declared Waverly, "and you—"

"And then, when I displayed my slashed but bloodless wrist—he cracked up, slashing his own wrist. There and then he proved that he was a failure as a research scientist, demonstrating beyond any doubt that he slashed his wrist because he loved his neighbor. Anyone who loves his neighbor can never be a research scientist. A scientist must be coldly objective and be willing to use anyone, to deceive everyone, and even to lie to people in order to obtain whatever data the scientist needs to complete his experiment. When Travis slashed his wrist, he was not demonstrating his commitment to Science. No! No! No! He was demonstrating that loving a neighbor is more important than doing research for Science. Love clouds judgment, distorts logic, and prevents an experimenter from seeing the truth. I do not understand why you are protesting, Waverly, since until now you were a willing participant in the experiment."

"Doctor Shearson, you promised me that the State Ethics Committee, the committee that oversees the work done at W.A.R.S., had approved in writing this experiment on a human subject. And you know that it is by law an unethical and punishable offense to experiment on a human subject without the approval of that committee. I want to see that official document, notarized, and signed by all members of the committee—now! And if you don't show it to me, I'll—"

"You will do what?!" taunted Shearson. "In the final analysis, when it really counts for the advancement of Science, you are like every member of that ethics committee—a fool who is more concerned about following rules of right and wrong, rules made by bureaucratic ignoramuses who do not have a clue about what it costs to be committed to the advancement of Science. I do not have the approval of the State Ethics Committee. As a matter of fact, I never submitted a request for them to review the experiment. Science is a higher authority than any committee, and I obey whatever Science commands me to do. This is your last chance, Waverly. I am only going to ask this one more time: When we arrive at New Horizons, are you going to—"

"I'm going to call the police and the State Ethics Committee," boomed Waverly, "and I'll expose you as a fraud and as an imminent danger, and I'll prove that you are the greatest threat to the advancement of Science!"

"No, you will not! At the hospital, I will present Travis as someone who tried to commit suicide, someone who became suicidal because he was not qualified to become a member of The World. And I will prove that you were the one who goaded him to keep trying to apply for membership to The World, and that you pushed him until he became so depressed that he tried to take his own life. Because I have always been suspicious of you and skeptical of your abilities as a research scientist, I have kept a secret file on you, a file that contains classified material that could be used as evidence against you. And I will tell the police and the psychiatrists at New Horizons that you threatened my life because I would not admit you into The World."

"Well, Shearson, you haven't thought through your research design on your latest scheme," shouted Waverly, his voice caustic. Waverly reached into his pocket and drew out the gold-plated case housing the straight-razor, and, waving it in front of Shearson's face, he said defiantly, "Do you see this?! This case has your fingerprints on it, has my fingerprints on it, and has Travis' fingerprints on it. And DNA tests will confirm that the blood on the blade is Travis'. I'll tell the police, the psychiatrists, and the State Ethics Committee that you went berserk when Travis and I would not perform an unethical and illegal experiment, and in a state of psychotic and murderous rage, you claimed that Science is God and that you are Its chief priest, and that your God commanded you to kill Travis and me, but I managed to stop you only after you seriously wounded Travis, and that I regretted that I had to use force to restrain you so that I could pry the razor out of your hand."

Suddenly Shearson grabbed the case housing the razor—Waverly grabbed Shearson's hand—They struggled for control of the razor—The bus veered left—veered right—veered left—right—left, both men shouting threats and insults—Waverly broke free of Shearson's grip—For a moment Shearson's hands flailed about, his fingers moving in spasmodic jerks clawing at the air, and then his fingers seized Waverly's neck—"Put your hands on the wheel!" screamed Waverly—"The bus is out of control! We're going to crash!"—Shearson began choking Waverly—"No!" shouted Shearson—"You are wrong! I am in control—of you! Give me the razor—or I will kill you!"—Waverly struggled to breathe, arching his body while prying at Shearson's fingers—"You're ... a threat ... must ... be stopped!" gasped Waverly, as he in one flick of his wrist snapped the strait-razor from its case. He held the blade inches from Shearson's eyes, and said in a rasping voice, "Look ... at ... what's ... on the blade, Mr. Scientist ... I'm going ... to teach you ... what it means ... to love ... your neighbor ... as yourself ... feel the blade ... cut into you ... feel ... the love!" Waverley pulled back his hand, aimed the blade at Shearson's neck—but before Waverly could strike, the bus shot through an intersection with a four-way Stop, narrowly missed what seemed to be a hitchhiker displaying his outstretched arm and upraised thumb, and slammed into a tree, throwing both men forward—hard!—their heads hitting the windshield, then the force of the blow throwing them backwards. The straight razor flew into the air, making an odd whirring sound as it moved in twists and turns until it fell, landing in a seat across from mine. Slowly the men sagged against one another, appearing unconscious as each slumping body held up the other one, keeping both of them from falling to the floor.

My seat belt had held me firmly and safely in place. I felt alert but shaky.

I looked at the damage to the bus. Shattered windshield. Front door smashed, hanging open.

The hitchhiker approached the bus, peered inside, and said, "Hi, is anyone in here going my way?"

"Jesus!" I shouted, joy surging through me. "What are you doing here?"

Jesus entered the bus, walked up to me, unfastened my seat belt, and sat next to me. "I'm checking to see if anyone in here is going my way," said Jesus. "But first I want to heal you." He removed the towel from my wrist, and then drew his index finger along the gash in my wrist, his finger closing my wound as if he was a surgeon suturing an incision—except, unlike a surgeon, there was no scar! "There," said Jesus, smiling. "Now you're as good as new!"

"Lord, what about Shearson and Waverly?" I asked. "Are you going to tend to them?"

"Shearson and Waverly are dead. But paramedics from New Horizons Mental Hospital will soon be here to transport both of them to the hospital, and then from the hospital to a funeral home."

"Lord, may I ask why you were standing out there, hitching a ride?"

"I wasn't hitching a ride, Travis. One of my greatest joys is to stand at a crossroads and hold up my thumb. That is one of my ways of inviting those who are driving and being driven to stop their vehicle, get out of it, come over to me, and hitch a ride with me—walking with a new direction and with a new destination."

"So that's what you were doing when the bus almost hit you— you were inviting us to hitch a ride with you. But Shearson and Waverly never saw you. They were fighting with each other, focused on the straight-razor and who was going to control it."

"But you saw me, Travis, and I know that you are a hitchhiker who is going my way." Standing up, Jesus said, "I hear a siren. The paramedics are coming. Let's leave before they arrive. Come on, Travis, let's continue on. I know the way."

Jesus rolled up the towel and placed it under his arm. As we started to walk toward the door, I paused to pick up the straight-razor. "No!" said Jesus, his voice firm. "The razor stays here, stays with the dead research scientists."

As I reached the front of the bus, I stopped, and looked at the faces of Shearson and Waverly—No cuts. No swelling. No bleeding from anywhere. Their eyes open but hollow globes, seeming to be staring both from and into a bottomless loneliness.

"Lord, wouldn't it be right to throw a cover over their faces, to be respectful of them even in their death?"

"Yes, Travis it would be respectful to them, even though they believed in idolatries: that Science is God that is a thing, a loveless It, that feelings are frauds people use to justify their cowardice to give their all to what Science requires, that there is no soul in a person, that scientists are bloodless priests who worship their loveless It, that people are things to be used, deceived, and lied to—all for the advancement of Science, that my Father's creation is nothing but a laboratory for the advancement of Science, that Science is not to be held to any standards of right and wrong, that Science is The World, that Science is the truth that judges and wars against my Father's truth as moronic superstition, hypocrisy, and intellectual pretense, that scientists, with their immutable logic and punctilious research methods, are superior in every way to all other professions and occupations—and that all of these elements that make up a research scientist are undergirded and pro-pelled forward by one thing and one thing only—A commanding and demanding commitment!"

"Lord," I said, "your kindness ... it's so touching ... yet you speak the truth with so much power, I—"

"Travis, even though Shearson and Waverly believed all of this, they deserve to have their faces covered. And I believe that it is only fitting that I cover their faces with the towel that is soaked with your blood, because on that towel is spelled out the truth of commitment, the truth that all scientists, all those who work at New Horizons, and you, Travis, as an aspiring counselor, need to see emblazoned in blood."

Jesus took the towel from under his arm, and holding it by two of its corners, he let it unfurl, and with one motion draped it over the faces of Shearson and Waverly. And then I saw words on the towel, emblazoned in my blood:

AND YOU SHALL LOVE
THE LORD YOUR GOD
WITH ALL YOUR HEART,
AND WITH ALL YOUR SOUL,
AND WITH ALL YOUR MIND,
AND WITH ALL YOUR STRENGTH

Beauty—
Minding the Blood

I was sitting on the back porch of a house, gulping a large cup of coffee while studying my list of tasks set for the day. The thirty-eight tasks were neatly written with permanent ink on lined three-inch by five-inch note cards, one task per note card. The note cards were compiled in one stack, and I began to read through the stack, rating the importance of each task, and then assigning each task to one of three piles: To-Do. Must-Do. Absolutely-Have-To-Do.

After I organized the tasks into three piles of note cards, I examined the Absolutely-Have-To-Do pile, prioritizing the tasks according to their bearing on the efficiency and effectiveness of my day, calculating the geographical distance needed to travel to accomplish the task, anticipating the volume of traffic between me and the destination, and scheduling blocks of time for achieving each task.

I repeated the same procedure for the Must-Do and the To-Do lists, and then numbered them from one to thirty-eight, starting with the Absolutely-Have-To-Do list, then the Must-Do list, and finally the To-Do list.

I then revisited what I'd just done, analyzing in detail the logic, the scope, and the feasibility of my plan and how it was embedded in the routines for my day.

I felt satisfied, even proud. I patted myself on the shoulder, and thought, *The best mind is a mind that can make and carry out a comprehensive plan, because planning is the key to having an ordered life. A mind that can't plan—that's the mind of a numbskull!*

I gathered together the note cards, finished my coffee, and—suddenly a white dove descended from the sky and perched on the stump of a tree about ten feet from me. The bird, at least seven-feet tall, full-feathered, muscular, and sleek, stood there in silence, his golden eyes gazing at me.

Startled by the massive size of the bird, I froze in my chair. My thoughts were swirling, my mind searching for an explanation for what I was seeing: *Some kids from the block must be playing ... a huge balloon they inflated into the shape of a dove ... the balloon got away from them ... drifted into my back yard ... This is a kite ... looks like a giant dove ... kids were flying the kite ... the string broke ... the kite landed here ... There's something wrong with my brain ... I had a stroke ... this is an hallucination ... This isn't real ... It can't be! ... There are no birds this tall ... this big ... This is not real!*

The white dove spread his wings, their length casting a shadow over the back yard. Then his wings began to move, their easy power lifting him off the stump. He hovered near my face, the whir of his wings the music of an ecstatic hymn, a holy melody being sounded with fierce eloquence created from an alphabet of sounds in harmony with—and yet beyond—the lyrics of human speech.

Like a diamond giving off glints of glory, the dove turned smooth and wide circles in the sunlight, each exquisite facet of his beauty set free by the sunlight into a kaleidoscope of silver, ivory, and brilliant white, his majestic body creating a display of delicate yet power-filled splendor alert with decisive energy dancing in the freedom of weightless air.

Then the dove glided to within a foot from my face, hovering there, the sonorous rush of his insistent wings claiming my full attention. He then darted to a few feet away from me, then back to inches away, repeating this back-and-forth gesture until I realized that he was beckoning me to follow him. His eyes flashed their dazzling gold in the sunlight, and I heard myself say out loud, "All right, Beauty, all right, I'll follow you!"

The instant I called him Beauty, his wings whirred with delight, and he took flight, dancing in play-filling circles, his body painting spirals of luminous white on the blue canvas of morning sky. In one fluid motion the dove swooped down, drawing close to me, and for a moment he hovered before my eyes, and then he began to fly slowly and with unwavering purpose. The direction of his deliberate flight was clear, but his destination, certainly known to him, was unforeseeable to me.

Drawn on by him, I followed.

The white dove led me into the alley behind my apartment. I heard noises in the distance but couldn't see where they were coming from or who was making them. The noises were more like a din, growing louder and louder with each step I took, a din that broke through my ears to my skull, where the din felt like a heavy stone wheel grinding on bone itself, uncovered and unprotected bone, the stone wheel breaking through to bone to pierce inside my skull, exposing my brain to the relentless grinding inside my skull. I struggled to hold a thought, a memory, an imagined future, strained to speak even a single word, or utter a wordless cry—anything to stop the relentless grinding on the bone inside my skull.

Nothing helped.

My skull seemed like a prison for my brain, my brain, once the safe place and source of all my self-reflections, and my skull, once my cloistering armor of bone where no one could stain my truth with their polluting lies, where no one could block my thinking up plans for my life, my skull, now a sound-proof prison cell of bone where I felt condemned to a life-sentence with the grinding din my only cell mate.

I wanted answers, explanations.

None were given to me.

Everything seemed a question mark. The heavy stone wheel kept grinding, the inside of my skull seething with raw, excruciating pain. I halted, afraid to go on, the grinding din threatening to crush my skull.

Beauty drew closer, his eyes level with my eyes, the soothing and energizing music arising from the whir of his wings blunting the sound of the grinding din, and the bright sheen of his feathers like splashes of reviving water flowing over my head and ears as he whirled across the space between us, his whirling inviting and exhorting.

Beauty flew on.

I followed, quickening my pace as I kept walking down the alley, its long path one of potholes and broken slabs of concrete. Each step I took intensified the grinding inside my skull, a grinding met immediately with the blunting force arising from the pain-relieving anthem resounding from Beauty's wings, until, with the end of the alley in sight, the grinding din—all of a sudden—turned into shouts, as clear as they were condemning, "Crucify him! Crucify him!"

My Savior! My Jesus! I thought. *I can defend him! I can speak the truth of who he is!*

I ran ahead of Beauty, to the end of the alley, my steps rapid but unsure as I zigzagged my way through the torn up alley, and then I turned the corner, stunned by what I saw.

One man. One cross. And then I knew—the man was Jesus! He was dead, still hanging on the Cross. I was too late. In the short time it had taken me to reach the end of the alley, Christ had been nailed to the Cross—already crucified, already dead!

It was no longer morning.

It was late afternoon.

And there was no one there but me, and Beauty who'd caught up to me and was hovering nearby, his wings the sound and feel of a steady and gentle breeze.

I was surprised: Inside the bone of my skull—the din! It was gone, but it was replaced by my own thoughts shouting *Crucify him!* I was alone, and yet *Crucify him!* hammered at the inside of my head, shooting pain throughout my skull, pain as sharp as nail points, splitting open bone, as though the hundreds of "Crucify him!" I'd heard outside my head had been driven into the walls of bone inside my skull, as though the words "Crucify him!" were nailed to my mind, as though *Crucify him!* were now my own words shouting inside my skull—that I, exactly like all the other haters of Jesus, wanted to crucify him too!

Shuddering, then staggering on rubbery legs, and wailing, "No ... please! ... help me! ... I want the words ... go away! ... crucify him ... no ... a killer ... me?! ..." I collapsed, falling to my knees, then flat on my chest, my arms and legs splayed, my chin on the ground, my eyes inches away from the base of the Cross, where the Cross had been sunk into the ground—No! Not sunk into the ground. I was at Golgotha—the Place of the Skull. The Cross was sunk into a skull—The Skull!

I struggled to my feet, rubbed my eyes, and surveyed the landscape. I was standing in the parking lot of a Home Depot. The parking lot was deserted except for a massive skull that appeared to have erupted through the concrete. Only the vacant eye sockets, the empty ear holes, and the top of the skull were visible, the skull standing around forty feet high, and the slightly-curved width of the skull spanning at least ninety feet from ear hole to ear hole.

Somehow I'd been brought here, been transported here, been led here, by Beauty. And the Cross! Its vertical beam had been driven into Golgotha, been driven into the Skull, been driven, somehow, by the invisible but real hands of God, as though the Cross itself was—now—a nail driven into the skulls of all people for all time and in all places, a nail driven into my skull!

Beauty hovered before my face, his dance as expansive and free as open sky, his wing beats the sound of soft music creating waves of peace-filling melodies washing through my skull.

My eyes stayed focused on the Place of the Skull, at the base of the Cross, where I was watching a drop of Christ's blood fall on, splatter, and pierce the place of the Skull, the drop of blood a seed piercing dead bone, the blood-seed causing to sprout and bloom in an instant a sunflower, its face round and full of life, its head bowed, then slowly beginning to rise, facing upward.

Just then Beauty flew to the place where Christ's blood had pierced the Skull and created the sunflower, seeming to mark that spot by hovering there. In an instant Beauty turned his body in a way that invited me to climb onto his gleaming white back. I dived headlong onto his welcoming expanse of feathers, my arms around his neck.

Beauty began to elevate, lifting me up, past the wounds in Christ's feet—higher—past the wound in his side—higher—past the wounds in his hands—higher—to the place where the crown of thorns had been driven into Christ's scalp, driven into the bone of his skull. There, a single drop of Christ's blood was hanging on a jagged tip of one of the thorns, the crimson drop ready to fall from Christ's disfigured head, his head pitched forward and slumping in such a way that the crown of thorns extended outward, angled away from his face and body, so that when the drop of blood fell it would fall unfettered from the thorn to the Skull.

As the size and shape of Christ's blood swelled to the size and weight that would release it like a limb of a tree releases a fully-ripened fruit, Beauty hovered at that spot, letting me gaze upon the blood-dripping thorn, and I was struck with wonder at seeing the vast universe on display within that single drop of Christ's blood.

Then the drop of Christ's blood fell, free from the crown of thorns, free and moving, and Beauty moving with the blood, descending at the same pace as the drop of blood, my eyes fixed on that glorious drop of blood, the drop expanding to the size of my head, my eyes fixed on that drop of blood, falling together, free and moving, the blood and my eyes on the same plane, moving parallel through the same space at the same time, then—in a moment—my eyes beheld words arising inside that drop of crimson blood, words formed in scarlet letters:

The blood of Christ,
who through the eternal Spirit
offered himself without blemish,
will cleanse your conscience
from dead works to serve the living God

Then Beauty began to fall faster than the drop of blood, quickly dipping to a place inches below the falling blood-soaked words, a place directly over my head, and then Beauty stopped—hovering there, until I felt the drop of blood-soaked words strike the center of my head, the drop becoming a crimson wave of blood pouring over my entire head, the crimson wave expansive and electric with joy, now jolting and piercing my skull, now bathing the inside of my skull, cleansing my conscience, filling my mind, the blood-drenching words making my head feel light as a bird gliding on the smooth freedom of exalting air, my ease-filling flight a holy witness to my joy-fluttering victory over the relentless and boney grip of grave necessity.

The blood-saturating words washing through my skull seemed to ignite Beauty into flight—with a whoosh!—he soared, aloft on holy air laced with sunlight, his golden eyes wide circles drinking in the sun's nourishing rays, fueling him—and, somehow, fueling me—with shining streams of radiant and radiating power, the illuminating sunbursts charting his course, Beauty's direction and destination clear, straight, and true—the Son inside—and yet beyond—the sun!

Then whoosh!—Beauty leaned right, his flight a wide, smooth curve, his body feeling lighter and freer than the softest white cloud, his majestic eyes looking fearless, safe in allowing the sanctifying updrafts to guide him and hold him aloft. The open trust of Beauty's outstretched wings were suspended on a rarefied breeze, a lilting and inviting breeze, which, like a felt but unseen dance partner, led him—and me—fluidly and fluently in a slow motion ... slow motioning ... slow dance across a slowly-unfolding dance floor covered by the high-arching canopy of heaven.

Then Beauty flew in circles, the circles turned into a spiral that was returning me to my back yard, and as we neared the tree stump, Beauty fanned his wings, the rush of air created by the force of his fanning blew the thirty-eight note cards into the wind and out of sight.

Beauty landed on the tree stump, and bent slightly forward, making it easy for me to slide from his back. I stood next to him. We were both looking at the coffee table, swept clean of my list of tasks.

"From now on, and without my note cards, how am I supposed to think about my day?" I asked out loud, expecting some response from Beauty.

Beauty kept his golden eyes fixed on the empty table.

All of a sudden I felt blood flooding the inside of my entire skull, as though a dam had broken from somewhere inside my head, a dam no longer able to contain the power and presence of what it was holding back, and in the sound of that rushing blood I heard words forming and then arising, words as cleansing and gentle as they were urgent and commanding—*You have the mind of Christ!*

Defacing Shame

It was summer—but I didn't want to know the exact date. It was after midnight—but I didn't want to know the exact time. I was in the U.S.—but I didn't want to know my exact location.

I knew that the humid air of the hot night was clinging to my skin ... knew that the car I was driving had no air conditioner ... knew that my throat was parched ... knew I was looking for a place to quench my thirst—and that's all that I wanted to know.

I noticed a large neon sign atop the flat roof of a one-story building, the garish red light bulbs dotting the sign spelled the words *Railroad Bar*. Even a glance at the harsh red lights made me feel hotter, heightening my thirst. I pulled into a parking space just behind a car with a license plate that read *RHINO*, and then I moved toward the bar, the image of a refreshing cool drink quickening my steps.

The air-conditioned room was crowded with men and women sitting at tables and at the bar. I scanned the room and spotted the only open seat—a stool at the bar. The pasty dryness coating my mouth and throat drove me toward the barstool. I eased myself onto the stool while raising and waving my hand, trying to catch the bartender's eye. He seemed to ignore me, turning to serve someone who called him by name.

A large man was sitting to my right, the heat from his massive bulk coming in waves across my body, making me even thirstier. He was breathing through his mouth, his short, rumbling breaths the agitated sound of a complaint looking for a target. The entire back of his thick left hand displayed a tattoo of a Jesus hanging on the Cross. Just below the base of the Cross were the words *God Is Dead*. The man lifted to his mouth a long-necked bottle of dark beer, his protruding lips clamping around the rim of the bottle and guzzling the entire contents.

I don't think I've ever seen a bottle that big, I thought. *It's less than a quart ... more than a pint ... maybe it's one of those beers that contain twenty-two ounces ... and he gulped it down—in seconds!*

"Hey, you!" the man shouted at the bartender. "Another beer over here! No! You better make it two—and I mean now! Can't you see I'm hot and thirsty?! What kinda' joint are you runnin' here?"

"No problem," said the bartender. "Be right there." Carrying two opened bottles of beer, the bartender rushed to the man. "I'm sorry," the bartender said to the man. "We're really busy tonight. Take these two beers on the house ... as my apology to you for the delay."

"Hey, your service should be more personal: You should know the faces of customers on sight, and you should call 'em by name."

"You're right. That's a great suggestion," said the bartender, his voice brittle with fear. "And I do know most of my customers by name. But I haven't seen you in here before. So ... what's your name?"

"Rhino—that's my name! And, hey, I've never been in this bar or city before. I'm just passin' through ... don't like the Midwest ... never have . . . never will ... don't like cities with railroad tracks cuttin' through 'em ... I'm stoppin' only long enough to suck back a few cold beers—then I'm gone."

"Rhino is an unusual name. Is that a nickname? ... or your real name? ... or what?"

"Rhino! That's my name! That's all you need to know, Slick. Hey, you're not makin' fun of me, are you, sayin' that a real man can't have the name Rhino?"

"No, Rhino, I didn't mean anything by it ... just asking ... nothing more ... haven't seen your face before, so I—"

"Seen my face before!" shouted Rhino. "Are you mockin' the way I look?! Are you tellin' me there's somethin' wrong with my face?!"

"No, Rhino, I was just trying—"

"Because if you're makin' fun of me, we can step outside and I'll show you what this Rhino can do to the face of a nameless chump like you!" He made a fist with his left hand and showed the bartender the tattoo, bellowing, "Hey! Look! If you don't want to end up like this guy on the cross—dead meat!—you'll watch your mouth! You're runnin' a business here, and you need to show more respect to us folk who keep you in business!" Rhino snatched up the two bottles of beer, pressed them to his lips and quickly drained both bottles, a few drops of beer dribbling onto his sleeveless camouflage T-shirt.

Some voices, angry and yelling, broke through the din of the crowd: "Shut up, gorilla breath!"—"We can't hear ourselves talk over here!"—"Yeah, and I can't hear the jukebox!"—"Stop talking trash or get out!"—"This is a bar, you moron, not your own private soap box!"

Rhino stood up, scanned the crowd, and yelled, "I don't know who you are or where you are, but show yourselves, you punks!—or shut up!"

Silence fell over the room. No one stood up or spoke out. Someone played a song on the jukebox, and within seconds the din of the crowd rose to full pitch.

"Gutless cowards! Spinelsss punks!" Rhino snorted as he pounded the bar with both fists. "Step up! Take a beatin' like a man!" He paused for a few seconds more, and then he sat down. "Two more beers!" he shouted, his voice demanding and threatening.

"Right away," twittered the bartender as he tried to scurry away on wobbly legs.

"And I'll have a Coke—in a glass with lots of ice!" I called out. "It's a hot night. I guess we're all thirsty."

"You got it!" spurted the bartender, his quavering voice straining to sound like a man in charge. "A bottle of Coke—coming right up!"

"I see that you like the imports," I remarked to Rhino, hoping to shift his attention from his savaging words.

"What?" he asked, his glaring eyes still on the bartender. "What're you talkin' about? Imports? What imports? Are you callin' me a foreigner? Are you sayin' I'm not an American?!"

"No," I said calmly, "that's not what I meant at all. I was referring to the dark beer in the bottles with the elegant long necks." Smiling and pointing at the bottles, I noted, "You don't find any beer brewed or bottled like that in this country. The bottles themselves are beautiful works of art. You must be a connoisseur of fine beers."

Rhino glanced at me, and proclaimed, "I like what I like—period!"

Craning my neck to see whether the bartender had gotten my Coke, I said to Rhino, "Well, that's all that matters, I suppose."

"You suppose right!" spouted Rhino, his tone sarcastic. "And you ordered a Coke. Where I come from, that's a little girl's drink. So, I guess you're more of a con—o—sewer of drinks rather than a con … con … or whatever, but, hey, you're an average American, and, oh yeah, a little girl!" He turned to look into my eyes, his neck bulging beyond the back of his skull, the pock-marked flaps of skin layered on his scarred face appearing rougher than the coarsest sandpaper, the bridge of his nose flattened as though broken and crushed, making the tip of his nose look like a small horn jutting straight out from his face, the horn appearing defiant and deadly, poised to gore anyone or anything that set off the rage seething in Rhino's hulking mass of flesh. "Little Girl! I bet that's your name!"

"No!" I blurted, feeling my hands turn into fists, "that's not my name!" I kept my eyes locked on his glare. "My name is Travis." Sweat oozed onto my forehead. I looked away, suddenly feeling ashamed—then feeling angry at myself for feeling ashamed—then feeling more ashamed—then feeling more angry—then deeper shame—then anger flared into rage shooting through me. I wanted to unleash my rage on Rhino, but my shame held me back. Caught between rage and shame, I felt paralyzed, too helpless to speak or to move. I sat there, my face now a hot and throbbing mask of sweat stinging my eyes and dripping from my chin.

"Hey, I said your name is Little Girl, and that's what you're to me."

The bartender brought Rhino's two beers and my Coke, and he set the drinks in front of us.

Rhino looked at my drink, and nodded his head. "Hey, there's your Coke," said Rhino, his voice smug and victorious. "See what I mean, a Coke for a Little Girl? A Coke for a joke—you're a joke as a man!" He bellowed with laughter. "Hey, I'm a poet: A Coke for a joke! It rhymes! Get it? A Coke for a joke!" He nudged the Coke toward me, and said, "Here, Little Girl. Hey, remember to sip it. Too much sugar and you won't be able to sleep tonight."

"Little Girl!"—the words made me feel defective, flawed in some way that was beyond repair.

"Hey, Little Girl! Ain't you gonna drink your Coke?"

Rhino's words—"Little Girl!"—tore at me, seeming to strip me of my clothes—*I'm naked!* I thought. *Everyone can see me!* Shudders of panic rocked me—"Little Girl!"—the contracting grip of those words squeezed my body. I felt diminished, and seemed to be shrinking while at the same time struggling to breathe, but sensing that I was incompetent to free myself from Rhino's words, and yet thinking that I should, somehow, know what to do to stop the degrading force of Rhino's words—"Little Girl!"—words now tearing off chunks of my flesh, exposing my ribs, and then the force of the words hacking at my ribs until they cracked and fell away under the assaultive weight of "Little Girl!" My heart felt exposed, as if the secret mystery of what makes me special and keeps me alive was now being exposed for all to see and know without my permission. I was defenseless, unable to guard my heart, unable to keep my secret hidden and protected by the walls of flesh and bars of ribs that once denied entrance to all intruders. I moved my hands across my chest, trying to convince myself that my hands could shield my heart from the judging eyes of others and from Rhino's relentless shouting of "Little Girl!" but my hands couldn't protect my heart, my entire body now feeling like a huge heart, that I was nothing but an exposed heart beating as I was being beaten, that all of me was a heart being wounded from every angle by "Little Girl!" and everyone in the bar could see the blood pouring from my wounds, and no one helped me, no one stopped the onslaught—"Little Girl!"—the words piercing me as though being driven by Rhino's horn-like nose, the words like the horn on his nose covered with filth, making my heart feel dirty, my heart quickly swelling with polluting disgust, disgust shot through with heaves of nausea. *You don't deserve help!* flashed through me. I felt abandoned. I felt worthless, the feeling carrying the thought *You are unlovable, and grotesque.* My heart felt like tissue paper so fragile and so clogged with shame that the goring sound of one more "Little Girl!" would be the final blow, breaking my heart and killing me!

Rhino reached into his left pocket, apparently searching for something, but when he withdrew his hand nothing was in it. As Rhino's left hand moved upward, the back of his hand moving across my line of sight, I saw the tattoo, my eyes fixed on Jesus hanging on the Cross, and as the arc of Rhino's hand continued upward, my eyes and then my head lifted, still focused on the crucified Jesus, as if my seeing an image of the crucified Jesus was enough to lift up my head and eyes.

As I kept my eyes riveted on the crucified Christ, his naked exposure on the Cross seemed to drain off my shame and draw it onto himself. I could feel the full weight of my body again, and I felt covered with flesh, ribs, and felt three-dimensional. As more of my shame was being drained away, my rage began to fill the spaces vacated by my shame. Rage fueled my flesh, bone, and mind.

Rhino's hand reached out, grabbed a bottle of beer, and then he turned to face me. He took a long gulp of beer as if he was rewarding himself for the next "Little Girl!" he was about to spew out on me. Glaring at me, he used his left palm to wipe dribbles of beer from his chin, and again I saw Jesus hanging on the Cross, and my rage erupted from me.

"Before you say one more word," I commanded, "I want you to look at that woman over there!"

Rhino seemed taken aback by my sudden forcefulness. "Which woman?"

I pointed in the direction of the crowd. "Over there. Don't you see her?"

He followed my extended finger. "No."

"Well, you better look again."

"Why? What's so important about a woman in this rat hole?

"Well, you were really angry at the people who were telling you to shut up."

"Yeah, but, hey, you saw it. They're all cowards and punks—all too chicken to say anything to my face."

"Yes, but this woman didn't say a word, but she did give you the ugliest look I've even seen! I mean the ugliest look!"

"Hey, show me where she's sittin', and I'll go over to her table and teach her how messed up her face is."

"I can't point her out to you, but I can tell you who she is."

"Hey, that'll be enough for me. You tell me who she is, and I'll call her out right here and right now."

"Okay. Her name is Mother Nature, and when she made you she gave you the ugliest face I've ever seen! I mean, you're so ugly that the word 'ugly' can't even capture how ugly you are! Not even 'ghoulish' or 'grotesque' can describe how ugly you are! Or when someone says that a person is uglier than sin—not even that can put into words how ugly you are! But I wouldn't use the name Rhino to describe you, the same name on the vanity license plate of your car parked outside. A rhinoceros is a beast too noble for your namesake. You should change the license plate to FAT PIG. You look and smell like a fat pig, and your nose is more like the snout of a slobbering oinker, you know, one of those garbage-eating, mud-wallowing swine whose only real purpose in life is to be slaughtered and made into ham for civilized people to eat, and to be reduced to ham bones for dogs to chew on. You know, as far as porkers go, you're the first one I've seen who can oink sounds which occasionally sound like English words. I read somewhere that in France pigs are trained to sniff out truffles so that they can be taken from the ground and served as delicacies for cultured men and women. Ever plowed the dirt in France with that snot-caked honker you have? I'll bet with that horn-like growth on the end of your nose you could make some serious money digging in the dirt for truffles. And I'll bet that you are considered by all who see your snout plowing through dirt, mud, and slime to be the porker among porkers, the garbage-faced oinker who makes a living digging through garbage!"

The barroom was silent, and I felt the stare of eyes fixed on me and Rhino. I scanned the room, and shouted, "This porker who calls himself Rhino told the bartender that this barroom needs to be more friendly, that everyone should be called by his or her first name. Well, I'd like to introduce you to Fat Pig, and please greet him with the respect due to his specie, and so when I say 'Now!' I want all of you to shout his special greeting: 'Oink, oink, Fat Pig!'" I paused, glared at Rhino, looked around the room, and then shouted, "Now!" And everyone bellowed in unison, "Oink, oink, Fat Pig!"

"I'll kill you!" screamed Rhino. As he drew back his left hand and made a fist, the fingers of my right hand grabbed one of Rhino's empty bottles, and I barely glimpsed Jesus hanging on the Cross as Rhino's massive fist clubbed my jaw, my body lurching backwards and falling off the bar stool, Jesus hanging on the Cross seeming to recede from my eyes as I fell hard onto the floor. I stood up, still holding the bottle. The bottle was intact except for the bottom which had been broken off when I fell. The bottom of the bottle looked like a row of uneven shark's teeth, the row a perfect circle of jagged and sharply-pointed glass. I held the neck of the bottle in my hand, felt the heft of what was now my deadly weapon, and then aimed the broken end of the bottle at Rhino, and shouted: "C'mon! I'll take my shark's teeth over your rhino's puny horn! C'mon, Fat Pig!"

Rhino lunged at me, grabbing me by the shirt, his left hand tight on my chest, and I saw up-close Jesus hanging on the Cross. Suddenly I thought, *What am I doing?! I don't want to fight this man!*

We scuffled for a moment, and I tried to break free, to end the fight. But hands and arms from the crowd lunged at us from every direction, instantly restraining us. The bartender yelled, "Take it outside!" Another voice shouted, "Somebody call the cops!"

We were pushed outside, and the door closed behind us. I started to run. "You're just another gutless coward, Little Girl!" bellowed Rhino. "You're dead meat!"

I looked at my car, and I knew that I wouldn't have time to get in and escape Rhino's fury. So I ran, quickly increasing the distance between me and Rhino. I spotted an alley, ducked into it, and started to run faster, thinking to evade Rhino for good, but—it was a blind alley! I turned around, and then began to run toward the street, hoping that Rhino had given up the chase or hadn't reached the entrance to the alley, but Rhino was standing there, blocking my way out.

I moved to the farthest end of the alley, my back against the wall facing the street. Extending from the wall, and a few feet above my head, was a dull yellow light bulb with a tin lampshade. The light bulb was making a crackling sound as its light flickered on and off, as though the bulb was about to burn out.

Rhino crept toward me, his bearing menacing, his movements those of an animal stalking its prey. "Now we'll see who lives and who dies—Little Girl!"

"I don't know what got into me back at the bar," I said, "and I want to apologize for the way I spoke to you."

"Hey, it's too late for that," shouted Rhino, his voice decisive, the veins standing out from his huge neck a sign of the depth of his rage. "I said I was goin' to kill you, and I'm goin' to kill you!"

Rhino edged closer to me.

"I can see that you're really angry," I said, "but, you know, you shouldn't have made fun of me back there ... that wasn't right . . . maybe we were both wrong ... maybe we can work out a compromise here ... maybe both of us can offer an apology and call it even."

"Even!" Rhino yelled. "Call what even?! You think the trash talk that came from your mouth was no worse than mine—right?!"

"Right," I said, my voice hopeful, "I couldn't agree with you more."

"And you think we can apologize, shake hands, and go on our way— right?!"

"Right," I said. I extended my open hand as I slowly walked toward Rhino. "Maybe we could find a way ... somehow ... to leave as friends."

"Friends!" bellowed Rhino, his voice cutting, his hands clenched fists. "I don't make friends with phonies with big mouths, weaklings who can't walk the talk. You can't walk your talk, and that's why your name will always be Little Girl. And Rhino's goin' to give you the spankin' not of your life, Little Girl, but a spankin' that'll snuff out your life!" He looked at the jagged bottom of the bottle in my hand, and declared, "A little girl shark's baby teeth are no match for the full-grown horn of a real man—me!—Rhino!"

"Little Girl!" —Rhino's words exploded somewhere inside me, exploding at that place where my rage was being held in check by a dam hidden somewhere inside me, a dam I'd believed was too strong to collapse again, a dam now blown apart and pouring rage throughout my body and mind.

"No, Fat Pig!" I yelled. "I'm going to kill you! You have a face that no mother could love, let alone stand to look at! You deserve to die because you're too ugly to live! C'mon, Swine Face! My shark is hungry for a fat ham sandwich!"

Rhino's eyes drilled into my eyes. He slightly lowered his head, and then let out a snorting bellow as he charged me, his horn catching me under my ribs, lifting me off my feet and driving me against the wall. I felt pinned to the cold brick wall, my breathing strained under his massive weight pressing on my chest, and for a moment the light bulb on the wall flashed on, its yellow light bright and steady, and I caught a glimpse of the veins in Rhino's neck, standing out, tensed and throbbing, the pipelines sustaining his strength, rage, and resolve, and I quickly mustered all the strength within me, and then plunged the jagged glass into that bulging cluster of veins—twisting the sharply-pointed teeth as I drove in the jagged glass—feeling and hearing flesh being torn apart, the glass teeth biting and chewing their way through veins and arteries—Rhino's blood erupting from his neck, blood pouring and spurting from his neck seeming to carry with it the energy fueling his strength—I felt him—all of him—rapidly become emptied of strength, drained of resolve, and devoid of rage.

Rhino slumped to his knees, his hands on his neck, trying to stanch the gushing blood. The light bulb crackled, then flickered on and off—then stayed off. I grabbed Rhino by the straps of his T-shirt and spun him around, pushing his back against the wall. Slowly he slid down the wall, his body flat on the damp concrete.

Suddenly the light bulb flashed on, crackling and flickering, and as I looked at Rhino's face—the light flickered off—Rhino's face shrouded in thick shadow—the light came on, burning brightly—I saw not Rhino's face—but the face of my second grade teacher, who in front of the entire class had slapped me across my face because my mother had given me coffee for breakfast. Rage seethed through me, and I drove the shark's teeth into Rhino's face, shouting—"Guilty of shaming me! Face it and die!"

Then the light bulb flickered—went off—flickered—came back on, the light bright and clear, and I saw the face of my junior high school principal who'd slammed my face into a wall as punishment for beating up a kid from my class—"Guilty of shaming me! Face it and die!" I screamed as I drove the shark's teeth into Rhino's face, feeling his tissue, skin, and muscle being chewed to scarlet pulp as I ground and twisted the jagged shark's teeth deeper into his face.

Rage kept pumping vengeance through me as the light flickered—went off—flickered—came back on again, the light steady and shining, and I saw the face of the policeman who'd hit me in the face, dragged me to his car, and forced my face into the floor of the car, ridiculing me for being a punk kid stupid enough to be caught by him. The beer bottle felt like a judge's gavel as I pounded the jagged glass into Rhino's face—"Guilty of shaming me! Face it and die!"

The light bulb crackled, dimmed—went off—then came on again, and I saw the sadistic eyes of the man who'd kidnapped and tortured me, the memories of his cruel and humiliating voice and fists for an instant freezing me with fear, then quickly burned away by the fire of hate blazing in me—"Guilty of shaming me! Face it and die!" I screamed as I gripped the neck of the bottle with both hands and plunged and twisted the jagged glass teeth into Rhino's face.

The light bulb continued to crackle and flicker off and on, each time the light came on, bright and clear, a face appeared in place of Rhino's face, and I gouged and marred each face with the shark's teeth at the end of my judge's gavel, the gavel plunging, biting, and chewing deeper and deeper into Rhino's face.

The faces of the two men who assaulted and robbed me.

The purple face and swollen and jutting tongue of my dead grandfather hanging by a rope in the basement.

The face of my drunken father, home from the local bars for another of the many nights of teaching me to fight by hitting me in the face.

Each and every face met with—"Guilty of shaming me! Face it and die!" until I felt Rhino's nose collapse, horn and all, his face now a mass of red goo.

The shining light bulb flickered and then went off. Darkness covered Rhino's face, but I felt his fingers grab my shirt, fingers clutching and edging their way up, taking hold of my collar. "No more," said Rhino, a pleading whisper barely audible through his shredded lips. "No more ... please ... help me," his voice begging from somewhere in the darkness, the sound of his words desolate yet urgent, as if his words were desperately struggling to overcome his terrifying loneliness trapped in that enshrouding darkness, words hoping to be heard, a final, convincing appeal for mercy.

The light bulb suddenly flashed on, brighter than before, and I saw what was clinging to my collar. It was his left hand, the one with the tattoo, Jesus hanging on the Cross and *God Is Dead* inches away from my face.

"No!" I yelled as I lifted high the jagged teeth of my judge's gavel, "God is not dead!—you are!" Hate, rage, and revenge burst into fires within me, each blazing with a white heat so intense that it felt as though three fires were burning as one inferno, creating a surge of power fueling an unstoppable force within me as I plunged and twisted the shark's teeth deeper and deeper into Rhino's face. His fingers went limp on my collar, and his arm began to slide down, making a dragging sound as it flopped its way to the ground. I pressed my ear to his chest. No heartbeat. I searched for a pulse at his wrist. There was none. I placed my palm on his chest. No movement. Rhino was dead.

I heard a siren in the distance. "The cops!" I said out loud. "I've got to get out of here! No! Wait! Evidence! I've got to get rid of evidence!"

I stripped off all of Rhino's clothes, looking for anything that police could use to identify him. I removed his wallet, his watch, his two rings. I probed his mouth. He had dentures, upper and lower. They were broken at places from my blows, but I took the plates and every other piece of denture I could find. He had only one tattoo. I placed his hand flat on the concrete and using the jagged shark's teeth I cut into the skin of his hand and with one fluid motion I sheared off the tattoo. The skin rolled up into one intact piece.

I turned the beer bottle upside down, and used it as a container to collect and contain Rhino's personal effects. I put in the rolled up tattoo first, and then the rest of his items. *He complained that he didn't like the Midwest,* I thought, *that he was passing through. Well, I'm passing through. Nobody in that bar knew either one of us.*

Then I thought of our cars. *They're evidence ... easily traceable ... how can I get rid of them?* The siren grew louder. Then I heard a staccato of tiny hissing sounds. They were coming from the tin lampshade covering the light bulb. *Drops of water! It's starting to rain!*

Suddenly there was a cloudburst, pouring rain. The light bulb flickered and crackled as the rain increased, then a loud popping sound came from the light bulb as it exploded, short-circuited by the rain. The alley was dark. The rain increased, falling harder.

I snatched the beer bottle with Rhino's effects and began to run toward the street. When I reached the mouth of the alley, I noticed that a gang of car thieves were in the last stages of stealing both of our cars. They sped away before anyone could try to stop them. *Good,* I thought, *the cops will never be able to find the cars— they're untraceable now!*

The gutters were swollen with rain, the water flooding into open sewers at the corner of each street. I rushed over to one of the sewers, thinking, *The sewer will take Rhino's stuff to where no one will ever be able to find it.*

I took all his money from his wallet, ripped into small pieces all his photos and all his other cards, and then I flung them into the torrents of water pouring into the sewer. I threw his dentures on the ground, stomped on them, grinding them into dust, and then kicked them into the sewer.

Rhino's rings had no inscriptions, so I stomped on them and then hurled them into the open sewer.

I smashed the beer bottle, kicking the shards into the sewer, but I was still holding the neck of the bottle, and as I drew back to throw the neck into the sewer, I noticed something protruding from the lip of the bottle—it was the skin bearing Rhino's tattoo. I removed the skin from the neck of the bottle, smashed the neck, and kicked the broken glass into the sewer.

I wanted to tear up the tattoo and throw the skin into the sewer, but the tattoo was stuck to the tips of the four fingers of my right hand, the skin unfurled and with the crucified Jesus facing me and in full view. I pulled hard on the tattoo, but it was as if the tattoo was fastened to my fingertips, and Rhino's skin was thick and tough. I couldn't tear off any part of his skin. I tried a few more times to remove his skin, but the tattoo remained in full view while excruciating pains kept piercing through my fingertips and into my hand.

The siren grew louder, the police just seconds away. The rain was falling faster and harder. I heard the sound of a train approaching the city, and I ran toward the railroad tracks, and there it was—a freight train, and I caught sight of a boxcar with a half-open gate, the gate appeared made of heavy planks that looked weathered and arrayed with thick and long spike-like splinters.

So I ran for the train and managed to hurl myself onto the edge of the boxcar and pull myself up and in, avoiding the danger posed by the splintered planks.

As the train moved out of the city, I saw the police arrive and people starting to come out of the *Railroad Bar*. I felt cautiously safe, relieved to be leaving town.

Then I looked at the tattoo stuck to my fingertips, with Jesus hanging on the Cross. The words *God Is Dead* were gone. As I looked at Jesus on the Cross, I started to feel shame—"I killed a man!" I cried, "No! I murdered a man! Rhino begged for mercy but I judged him guilty and sentenced him to death. I was his judge! I was his jury! I was his executioner! And Rhino was wrong. God is not dead—I am god! Or I believed I was god—Rhino's god!"

As I spoke the words "I am god!" I felt Rhino's skin on my fingertips, and I looked at the crucified Christ on the Cross, his slumped naked body made me feel naked, exposing me as weak, exhausted, and helpless. I pulled and twisted at Rhino's skin, skin which now felt grafted to my skin, as if Rhino's skin and my skin were one! I hated his skin, hated my skin, hated having to feel and see the dead Jesus hanging on his Cross, the picture of his dead body somehow felt as heavy as a real life-size body—too heavy for me to bear, and I strained to keep my body from collapsing under the weight I felt just by my looking at Christ's dead body.

My fingertips were racked with searing pain. Torrents of burning shame shot through me, scalding my insides, my heart felt as if it was being boiled in my shame, the scalding humiliation like teeth of fire biting and shattering the idol I'd made of my heart, made of myself. I had no right to take Rhino's life. I was the one now who was guilty as charged—a murderer!—and I deserved death!

Kill yourself! I thought. Then I declared with resolve, "Kill yourself! Yes! I'm guilty! I deserve to die!" I drew myself to my feet and stood on the edge of the boxcar, the fingers of my right hand wrapped around one of the weathered planks, the plank my only support. The rain fell harder and began to blow toward me, whipping into my face and body. The train picked up speed. I knew that if I leaped from the train, my arms outstretched, my face aimed at the stony ground roaring by me, I knew my body would be shattered, and my face crushed. In one motion I leaped from the train, but pain jarred my shoulder and arm as I dangled from the plank, my body hanging outside the boxcar, veering left and right as I was suspended between the floor of the box car and the stony ground. Something was holding onto me, preventing me from committing suicide, and as I was dangling by one arm, I looked up and saw that Rhino's skin had become impaled on one of the large spike-like splinters, Rhino's skin, fused to my fingertips, was holding me up, his skin was the only link between me and death, his skin still displaying Jesus hanging on his Cross.

I swung back and forth until I had the momentum to hurl myself back onto the boxcar. I stood up. I saw that one of the splinters had pierced the face of Jesus. I removed Rhino's skin from the large spike-like splinter, and I looked at the crucified Christ. The splinter had pierced Christ's head, making him appear faceless. My legs turned into jelly, and I heard a groan come from somewhere inside me as I collapsed to my knees, unable to utter a word.

A voice spoke to me from somewhere in the darkness pervading the boxcar, "Travis."

"Yes. That voice … I've heard it before … Is that you … Jesus?"

"Yes."

"I can hear you, but I can't see you. Come here, please. I need to see your face!"

"Tonight you've already seen my face—and more than once!"

"No … Lord … please forgive me … but that can't be! I didn't see your face. Tonight I've seen many faces … and I saw the face of one man … the man I murdered … I destroyed his face … and not once did I even think of your face."

"Yes, you murdered Rhino and while you were destroying Rhino's face—that's when you were looking at my face but you didn't know that it was my face."

"Rhino was an atheist, and he wore a tattoo for all to see, to shout to the world that God is dead, to ridicule your love and mock your saving death on the Cross as a sham that only idiots and fools believe. How could I see your face in the face of an evil man who is slated for hell?"

"Do you remember what Isaiah prophesied about my face?"

"Yes, Lord, I think so ... but ... no ... not now ... I can't recall any of his words ... but what I did to Rhino's face ... what are you going to—"

"My face was marred to the point that I was unrecognizable as a human being. That is the truth—the truth you need to know—that Isaiah prophesied."

"I believe you, Lord," I said, feeling shaky and a bit dizzy, "but what does that have to do with me? ... with my murdering an evil and ugly-faced man like Rhino, who didn't believe in you? ... and what about the violence done to my face by all those cruel hypocrites from my past—all those religious phonies who shamed me while they professed to believe in you?"

"My face was unrecognizable as a human face, so that you could see me in every human's face," the voice of Jesus now a breeze that caressed my face and then floated into the rain-soaked night, the rain immediately stopping, and a bright moon now lighting the inside of the boxcar.

I scanned the boxcar. Jesus was gone. But the breeze that had caressed my face lingered there, still alive on my skin, and suddenly I felt an urge to feel the wind on my face. A metal ladder was riveted to the side of the boxcar, a ladder allowing access to the roof. I climbed the ladder, walked to the center of the roof, and sat down. The train slowed as it continued traveling due east, and the wind at once became a breeze—brisk, tingling, and steady as it lightly stroked my face.

I looked at the tattoo grafted to my fingertips, my eyes locked on the dead Jesus hanging on the Cross. Suddenly I was drawn to the hole where the face of Jesus used to be. I closed my eyes, and then pressed the tattoo to my cheek, letting the crucified Jesus rest tenderly against my face, feeling the empty space made by the spike-like splinter, and through that empty space that was once Christ's face was now wafting that caressing breeze, the breeze becoming a liquid warmth filling that hole, the warmth like a consoling salve gently being applied to an infected wound, the warmth becoming a cauterizing heat, trying to penetrate me and reach that life-condemning infection still lodged deep in my heart, the cauterizing heat longing to heal that hole still hollowed out in me, clogging me with impenetrable and bottomless darkness. I felt the cauterizing heat touching my face through the hole that was once Christ's face, but the healing was halted, unable to move any further than the surface of my skin.

A light, growing brighter, stronger, and warmer played across my face. I opened my eyes. Dawn was giving birth to a new day. I set my eyes on the rising sun. Suddenly from somewhere inside me, I saw, vivid and real, the bloody mass of pulpy flesh that was once Rhino's face, a face unrecognizable as a human being, a face I destroyed ... I was his murderer ... a murderer ... still alive ... a murderer ... facing the radiant glory of a new day breaking through my darkest night ... I sensed Rhino's skin on my fingertips ... I turned my face toward the faceless Christ hanging on his Cross ... the dead Jesus ... Rhino's dead skin ... felt nailed to my fingertips ... hope stirring ... facing a new day. . . hoping ... it was enough.

Love Is Patient:
Second Delivery

I was walking, nearing my home, when I glimpsed the back of someone wearing a drab blue uniform and carrying a shoulder bag—it was the letter carrier! Standing in front of my mailbox, she began sorting envelopes and packages.

"Hey!" I called out. She turned around. "Do you have any mail for me?" I asked as I drew closer to her. Displaying a large bundle of envelopes in her extended hands, she asked, "Do you mean these?"

Incredulous at her serious tone and struck by the thickness of the bundle, I replied, "You can't mean all of those are for me … can you?!"

She laughed, and said, "No, I was just kidding … I hope that's okay with you."

"Sure," I said, "and you really had me fooled! Maybe next time I'll be the one fooling you!"

"That sounds like fun! But—of course—now that you've warned me, I'll be on the lookout for you playing a trick on me. Today … though … I really do have some mail for you." Still grinning, she began to sift through the mail, picking out the envelopes sent to me, her fingers moving with fluid tenderness over the letters. I let my eyes focus on her fingers, following their every supple move, and began to picture their fluid tenderness stroking my face.

"Travis," she said, her voice interrupting my reverie, "here's your mail." Looking into my face, she offered me the letters.

As I gazed at her—suddenly—the magnetic pull of her presence captivated me: the exquisite strength of her head, adorned with ribbons of sunlight braided through cascading strawberry blond hair, the gracious simplicity of her face, its beaming elegance nearly able to conceal a faint scar on her right jawbone—her majestic forehead, the expanse of its curving space an alluring call to glide on the glory of its mysterious radiance—her eyes, their intricate perseverance, delicate order, grounded vulnerability, and tranquil freedom interlaced with emerald green irises nestled in soft coronas of warm golden yellow—the size and shape of her nose—balanced, compact, straight, and petite—reminded me of the dainty bill of a songbird, and I sensed that at any moment she might burst into delightful music, a love song composed and sung only for me!

"You are the most beautiful woman I've ever seen!" I blurted, each word a fragile bubble I was blowing to her, each bubble bursting the instant I blew it into the air, the bubble's see-through skin unable to contain the wild passion that formed it. The tip of one of the envelopes stood out from the rest of the mail, the sight of its two verdant green corners felt like two splinters of wood being thrust into my eyes. *Oh, no!* I screamed inside my head, *not another "Love is patient" note card—please, Lord, not that!* I buried my eyes in the crook of my left arm, and bit my lower lip. "The pain!" I cried, "In my eyes! Oh!—God!—make it stop!"

"What's wrong, Travis?" she asked, gently pulling back my arm. "Your eyes are bloodshot, tears are pouring from them, and your lip is bleeding! You're deathly-pale! You're soaked with sweat! I'm going to call 911!"

"No! ... no ... I'm fine ... my eyes are clearing ... the pain is gone ... just give me my mail ... I'll go inside ... sit down for a while ... I've been in direct sunlight too long—that's all."

Her hands on my shoulders, she studied my face, and said, "Are you certain that you're okay?"

I nodded my head.

"Your color looks good, and you've stopped sweating and bleeding."

"Don't call 911."

"All right ... I guess."

"Promise me?"

"All right: I promise."

"Thanks for caring ... please ... I should go inside."

"Travis, what you said to me ... how you see me as the most beautiful—"

"I'm not sure what I said ... I really have to go ... sorry ... maybe we can talk tomorrow ... or ... I don't know ... soon." I snatched the envelopes out of her hand, opened my door, stumbled into my living room, closed and locked the door, and sank into my couch, tossing the letters onto the cushion next to me.

"God bless you, Travis," she said, her encouraging words loud enough to hear through my door, "and take care."

I stared at the verdant green envelope—reached for it— hesitated, pulled back—stared at it—reached for it—hesitated, pulled back—then quickly seized the envelope—tore it open— grabbed the verdant green sheet inside—clawed it apart—glanced at it—unmarked—spied the verdant green note card—turned it over and saw written on it:

LOVE IS PATIENT

I grasped the ends of the note card, bending them toward one another, making the note card bow-shaped, relishing how I was controlling the look of the words—the deeper the bow, the more the words appeared to slide into one another, and at its deepest bow, without creasing the note card, the words vanished from view.

I returned the note card to full length, held it between the thumb and finger of my right hand while I tapped it on the fist of my left hand, thinking, *What shall I do with this albatross that Jesus keeps hanging around my neck?*

I recalled the chair in my dining area, the chair with one uneven leg. *I'd been meaning to fix that leg for months,* I thought. I walked over to the chair, tested the leg, to see how much it was out of balance. Estimating the thickness I needed to restore balance to the chair, I folded the note card, wedged it under the leg and tested the balance with my hands—it was solid. Then I sat on the chair, tried rocking it back and forth—it was solid.

I stood up, turned to the chair, and said, "Well, you've been patient all these months, waiting for me to repair your leg, and you've never complained once, always showing me your love by letting me sit on you whenever I felt like it. And so, as a way of apologizing and of acknowledging your patient love for me, I fixed your leg with a note card that says 'Love is patient,' a small gesture of how much I appreciate you. Hey, Jesus, how's that for a confession and an expression of how my love can be patient?! I know you're here somewhere! Say something! Show up!"

I waited for Jesus to answer me or to make his presence obvious. A silence unfolded, the arc of the silence long, empty, and heavy, the heaviness a growing burden I needed to shake off. "All right, Jesus, I give up. I get it: I'm not worth your time today!"

I returned to my couch, looked through my window, squinted as I glimpsed the fiery-red force of the setting sun, took a slow deep breath, and then let my eyes rest on the envelopes lying next to me, the same envelopes her fingers had touched with such fluid tenderness. I let my fingertips move lightly and gently across the skin of the envelopes, and I felt a fluid tenderness flow across the skin of my fingertips, her fluid tenderness still lingering on the skin of the envelopes, waiting patiently to offer love to anyone whose skin needed to be touched by tenderness.

Suddenly I was awash with vivid contours of her face and hair, picturing her vibrant lips flowing with "My love is patient," her words feeling like refreshing water streaming through me, cleansing me, quieting me, and then a singular feeling arose in me, a feeling I could not name, a feeling for a woman who was not there, and whose name I did not know.

Love Is Patient: Third Delivery

I was sitting on my couch, about to read the Bible, when I heard footsteps outside my apartment. I looked through my living room window and saw a woman dressed in the uniform of the U S. Postal Service—it was the letter carrier! I opened the door.

"Hello, Travis," she said, her tone welcoming.

"I've been thinking about you," I replied, my eyes scanning her face for a reaction.

"Really?"

"Yeah, really."

"And you've been on my mind."

"Really?"

"Yes ... your words celebrating my beauty were so—"

"Any of those special deliveries for me today?" I interrupted, feeling too panicky to hear where her words were leading.

"As a matter of fact, I do have another special envelope for you, and my supervisor was just as insistent this time as he was last time—'Find Travis and make certain that you put this letter into his hands personally!' Those were his exact words. But when he said the word 'personally,' it made me realize that my relationship with you has become personal."

Taken aback by her candor and inviting tone, my tongue locked in place. I looked away, tugged at my ear, willed my eyes to focus on her, and then asked, "What do you mean?"

"Let me give you an example," she said. "I've been calling you Travis, and I've never asked you if that was okay with you. I feel like I know you, feel at ease around you. So I didn't give it a second thought the first time I called you Travis. Should I have asked your permission?"

"There's no need for that kind of formality. Of course! Please! Call me Travis."

"And then when you told me how beautiful I looked to you, I sensed a connection between us that—"

I feigned a cough, its harsh sound cutting off her flow of words. Feeling my body tense and my face flush, I asked, "What's your name?"

"You may call me L.C., the initials for Letter Carrier." Handing me a verdant green envelope, she announced, "Here's your important letter."

"Thank you, L.C.," I said as I took the letter and hurriedly slid it into my back pocket. "Is it against the rules of the Postal Service to give anyone on your route your given name?"

"L.C. is my given name. My parents told me that when they prayed to God the Father for what to name me, they both received a clear leading that L.C. was to be my name, because I had a calling on my life to be a Letter Carrier for God. People may see me as working for the government, but they're off the mark: I have a calling to fulfill what the Father has in his plan for me. I don't merely drop-off mail at correct addresses, Travis. I deliver letters from God. I am a messenger sent from Father God."

"I knew it!" I said joyfully. "You're a Christian! So am I!"

"That's wonderful! Travis, I'm so blessed to know that you're a believer!"

"Speaking of being blessed! What about you? To be told from your earliest age what you are called to do for God, then to be given a name that's a constant affirmation of that calling, then to believe in that calling, and then to live out that calling day after day and year after year—what a blessing from God, a blessing all Christians hope for!"

"Amen to that, Travis! I'm filled with gratitude when I think of how God has used letters and those who delivered them as agents to carry out his plan. Hezekiah's letters of invitation to all of Israel, Judah, Ephraim, and Manasseh, that they should come to the house of the Lord at Jerusalem to celebrate the Passover; King Artaxerxes' letters of safe passage for Nehemiah to return to Jerusalem to repair the holy city's walls; Esther and Mordecai's letters to all the Jews in the entire kingdom of Ahasuerus, words of peace and truth; Paul's letters, Peter's letters, John's letters, James' letter, and Jude's letter, to name a few, letters to equip believers so that they're encouraged and filled with hope as they persevere in their faith."

"That's glorious, L.C.—just glorious! I've longed for years for my heart's desire—to be a counselor for Jesus—to be confirmed as my calling. I've waited alone, I've wandered with Jesus, I've prayed with believers, heard that saints I don't know and never met are praying for me, and I've struggled with the Father's silence—but I've received no clear confirmation that I'm to be a counselor for Jesus. But I have hope! I'm not ready to give up!"

L.C. smiled at me, adjusted the mailbag on her shoulder, and said, "May you be blessed with an answer today," and started to walk away.

"Thank you, but do you have to go so soon? I think a good talk with you might help me clarify things even more."

Pointing to a bandage on her left forearm, L.C. said, "This has slowed me down today, so I'm a bit behind on my route … I've got to keep moving."

"That looks like a nasty gash," I remarked. "How'd it happen?"

"Yes, it was bad. It runs the length of my forearm. I cut it on the rusty edge of a mailbox."

"Your forearm looks like it's still bleeding."

"That's mostly dried blood." L.C. grinned, her eyes widened. "Travis, I've come to believe that every calling has blood in it, or it's not a calling at all. Don't you agree?"

"Well ... I never thought of it ... not in that way—that's why I need to talk to you."

"Travis, Scripture says, 'How beautiful are the feet of those who bring good news of good things!' And I want to honor Father God's proclaiming that even my feet are beautiful as I deliver his good news of good things." L.C. turned and walked away, her pace brisk, her voice trailing off as I distinctly heard her say, "Okay ... let's talk again ... I'd enjoy that ... maybe get together ... meet somewhere."

Traffic noise swelled as I watched L.C. quickly disappear around a crowded street corner, the traffic noise drowning out my shouting "How can I reach you?"

I went into my living room, switched on a table lamp, slid from my pocket the verdant green envelope and held it against the bulb in the lamp. I could see through the envelope and the sheet of paper inside, the verdant green note card clearly visible but the words were blurry. I opened the envelope and took out the note card and saw the words:

LOVE IS PATIENT

I carried the note card to my refrigerator, took a magnet from the door of the fridge, the magnet fashioned in the shape of a small cross, and used the cross to fasten the note card on the door, next to the handle, so that every time I reached for the handle, I would see the cross holding in place and displaying in full view:

LOVE IS PATIENT

Mothering Courage

With the silvery disc of a full moon the only light in a starless night, I started walking. I was late for an appointment, but I didn't know the purpose of the appointment, didn't know who made the appointment, and didn't know the address for the appointment, and yet I was walking at my top speed, turning left down this street, right down that street, and yet sensing with each turn that I was farther and farther away from my appointed destination.

I spotted an alley, and asserted, "Shortcut!" even though the moment I heard the sound of my own voice, I thought, *Shortcut to where? You have no idea of where you're going!* Pressing on, I wheeled into the alley and started to jog, thinking that quickening my pace would get me to my appointment faster, and then I became aware of an approaching danger, the feel of a thickening presence, ominous yet invisible. I pushed my legs onward, into the thickening presence, its dense resistance heavier, harder to move through. *There's an emergency somewhere* raced through me, the words jolting me to double my effort to move forward, *I've got to get there before it's too late!* I rushed down and through the end of the stony passageway, my feet coming to a halt on the sidewalk adjoining the alley. I stood there, bent over, breathing hard, and then I noticed something near my feet.

A long shadow appeared on the cement pavement before me, the head of the shadow like the point of a large black spearhead, moving toward me, aimed at me. I stopped, planted my feet, fixed my eyes on the shadow and scanned it from its head to its source, a figure standing on the curb of a cement sidewalk—it was Jesus!

"Why did you scare me like that?" I asked, my voice quavering. "I'm rattled to the bone!"

"What are you seeking?" Jesus replied.

Stunned by the question, I paused, then gathered my thoughts, and said, "There's an emergency … I have an appointment … don't know where I'm going, I—"

"You've made it to your appointment. Now, what are you seeking?"

"My appointment? … here? … in this deserted street?"

"Yes, here. Now, what are you seeking?"

"I don't know!" My hands clenched into fists. "Stop asking me that!" I blurted, my voice demanding, "I told you I don't know what I'm seeking!" I edged toward Jesus, shaking a fist at him, and shouting, "You're playing games with me! You know what I'm seeking—I don't know!—but you know and you won't tell me! You're always preaching to me about how I need to persevere in the ambiguities of life, and that when the time is right, answers to my questions will emerge! I'm sick of hearing that hogwash! Admit it: You like messing with me!"

"Travis, you haven't lost your passion to know the truth, even when you want to know the truth only on your own terms. But you're right about one thing: There is an emergency, you're deeply involved in it, and it's one you're seeking."

"Ridiculous! I'm not seeking an emergency and I'm not involved in it! More double-talk! More word games!"

Jesus stepped to the right, and I saw a woman lying on the ground. She looked injured. "I'm broken, dying," she moaned, her eyes focused on me, "I'm your emergency … help me … please!"

Jesus walked past me, and without looking back, left the alley.

I hastily grabbed my cell phone, and said confidently, "I'll dial 911! Help will be here soon!"

"No!" she said, her voice an appeal and a command, "it's too late for that! I need your help—now!" With an insistent, urgent, and bleeding arm the woman beckoned to me. I ran toward her, rubbing my eyes at what I thought I was seeing, and then I looked again—it was my mother! Her ripped slacks and blouse exposed her torn body, spasms jolting her limbs and head while she was pressing her folded hands against her belly, as though she was praying for relief from the agony assaulting her.

As I knelt beside her, her spasms stopped. She appeared calm and focused. The interlaced fingers of her praying hands rose from her belly, her fingers separating, opening outward and upward until her upturned palms framed my face. I let her wounded palms guide me, gently turning my head, drawing my right ear to her belly, to the place where she'd been offering her prayer.

"Listen and remember, my son," she said, her voice halting and quavering as she pressed my ear deeper into the welt-ridden hollow of her belly, both her palms tenderly covering my face, eyes, and left ear, sealing me in silence, the silence inside her hands, the silence of her prayer. "What do you hear?"

I waited ... listened ... in the silence ... praying. "Nothing ... Mother ... I'm sorry ... I don't hear anything."

"What do you remember?"

"I'm sorry ... again ... nothing comes to mind."

"It's time!" she cried, "time for you to hear ... time for you to remember! It's an emergency!" Her hands gently lifted my head so I could look into her face. As a faint trace of a smile played across her lips, she took my hands in hers, squeezed them reassuringly, then let them go. "Listen ... hear and remember what happened that terrible night nine years ago."

My folded hands cradled by my lap, I sat next to her. I was focused on her, ready to listen.

"It was your thirty-fifth birthday, and we capped off your celebration with an evening visit to your favorite bookstore. As usual, you were the last customer to leave the bookstore. You gave me the stack of books you wanted and I went to the cashier to pay for the books. You decided to go outside, catch a breath of cool night air, and wait on a swing just inside the park across the street."

The pressing feel of her words made me feel edgy, and a vague pain spread across the back of my head.

"As I was leaving the bookstore, I saw you swinging and laughing, and images of you as a little boy flooded my mind. I ran toward you, into the street, my arms full of books, my heart full of joy. Then it happened!"

"Mother, I don't think this is the best time to recall—"

"Yes, it is! I heard squealing tires, the squeal like a deafening sound coming at me. I spun around—too late!—a drunk driver smashed into me—running me over!"

Sorrow rippled through me as she told her story. "Mother, I—"

"Stop, my son! Not now!" Breathing deeply, she went on, "After being hit, I don't remember much, except being hurtled through space, books sent flying—my head whirling and hurting—dull snapping of bones—shattering of glass, the jagged glass like a hundred knives stabbing my belly and slicing off body parts—my skin being raked and shredded across the potholed macadam street—my head and shoulders flung into the curb and onto the cement sidewalk on the other side of the street. And then—for a moment—everything in me and around me seemed frozen in place. My face, half in the gutter, half on the sidewalk, felt numb and paralyzed, and I seemed to have only one eye, that eye able to see only the surface of the cement sidewalk, the other eye submerged and trapped in dark blur of gutter water."

"It was horrible, Mother, but—"

She laid a fingertip on my lips, stopping them. "Then you were there, wailing 'Oh!—My!—God! Mother! No!' You lifted my head out of the gutter and laid my head on something soft—maybe your new birthday sweatshirt, I don't know—and then you said the paramedics were on their way. You held my broken body, stroked my face, and you started to pray, choking back sobs. I told you that I was dying, that it was too late for the paramedics to help me, and that Jesus wasn't going to heal me. I told you that I loved you, thanked Jesus for you, and said that I wasn't ready to die—to leave you—but I knew I couldn't stop Jesus from letting me die."

"Mother, I can't take much more of—"

"You must, my son. It's an emergency! It's your time to hear, your time to remember. That night, I remember pleading, 'Lord, if you're going to take me—then take me! But don't make me suffer anymore, and don't make my dear Travis have to see me like this, see me so maimed ... so mutilated, see me in such horror ... such pain—spare my son from having to see how ugly death can be!'"

I stroked her face, and let my fingertips lightly brush across her lips.

"Yes, Travis, what you're doing now, that's what you did that night: You gently touched my lips, and spoke so softly, 'Shhh, Mother, say no more. You're still here ... stay with me.' Then I said, 'I'm sinking, Travis ... further ... further ... falling away ... can't stop it. I'll wait for you in heaven. Good-bye, my dear, dear son.' Do you hear, my son, do you remember?"

"I do hear and I do remember that night I said to you, 'Mother, please don't go! Jesus, don't take her from me!' And then an ambulance roared around the corner, pulled alongside us, and two paramedics rushed toward us. 'Get back!' shouted one of the paramedics, his words so jarring that I couldn't speak. He grabbed me by the shoulders and pushed me to the side, commanding, 'Let us help her!' I stood up, my eyes focused on yours, Mother, and I watched as they worked with skill and speed to keep you alive."

"Yes, my son, that's how I remember it. While the paramedics were trying to keep me alive, I was trying with all my fading strength to keep my eyes focused on yours, and then—quickly, surprisingly, and horrifyingly—you shrieked, jammed your fingers into your ears, jumped up, and ran away! I never knew what you shrieked, or why you ran away, or why you abandoned me while I was dying—your own mother ... dying ... constricting loneliness like a huge snake coiled around me ... squeezing the last gasp of life out of me ... dying ... needing to see your face one second more ... dying ... in the cruel silence of night—among strangers!"

"Seeing you, hearing you, on that ghastly and gory night, and wanting with all that was in me to come to you, to hold you, to comfort you—without warning the full force of a horrifying memory seized me: Dad's sudden death from a heart attack during Christmas dinner, less than a year before you were hit by the drunk driver! What I shrieked was 'Blot it out! Blot it out!' I was gripped with the—my!—irrevocable truth: for the rest of my life, remembering Christmas would always remind me of the birth of Jesus and the death of my father. And remembering the day I was born would always remind me of my birthday and the death of my mother. I couldn't bear to hear your last dying groans, couldn't bear to see your body bleeding and disfigured beyond repair, and I couldn't bear to remember Dad's startled, vacant eyes as he clutched at his chest, collapsing to the floor, his face turning blue. *Blot everything out!* roared through my mind. Rage at Jesus thundered through me! I couldn't face what he let happen to you ... couldn't face the grisly mess he arranged for me to suffer through year after year! I had to escape his ghoulish plot! I had control over one thing: I could blot out everything: the birth of Jesus—the death of Dad—my birth—your death! Blot it all out! Forever! So I ran and ran and ran, the words *Numb up!* loud in my head."

Mother lifted her hand, rested it on my knee, and said, "Yes, you are hearing ... you are remembering."

"I saw a barroom ahead, ran to it and stumbled inside, sucking at the air—*If Jesus is here, I'll kill him!* the words exploding in my skull. I ordered a whiskey, and said to the bartender, 'Are you Jesus disguised as a stranger, and do you want me to take you in? Well, I won't—and you know why!' Taken aback, the bartender poured me a shot, and said, 'I'll leave the bottle with you, Mack.' I drank shot after shot until I heard the bartender bark out, 'It's closing time, Mack. Time to leave! If you have car keys, give them to me? You're too drunk to drive.' I felt numb through and through, so numb that I couldn't form a sentence. The bartender told me that he couldn't understand any of the noises coming from my mouth, that he was going to step into another room, call the police, and that I should rest my head on the top of the bar until he came back."

"Did the police come for you?" Mother asked.

"No ... at least I don't think so. What I remember next is waking up in an alley ... the faint light of dawn ... the hard metal of the dumpster I was slumped against ... the pain of a headache hitting me like a trip hammer. I fumbled for my cell phone, drew it out of my pocket, and called the hospital I thought that the paramedics would've rushed you to. The official I spoke with was sad to inform me that you'd died in the ambulance."

"Thank you, my son," said Mother, "for hearing, for remembering, and for telling me the truth, and yet—"

"I know, Mother, there's still an emergency."

"Yes, and it's your time ... now ... I'm dying ... all things are possible with God ... it's your time to make things right."

"I'm not going anywhere this time. I'm staying with you until Jesus takes you home. And I confess that I sinned against you when I abandoned you to die alone. Mother, will you forgive me?"

Spasms returned, jolting her limbs and head. She struggled with her twitching fingers, managing to interlace them and press them against her belly, as though she was praying for strength to say something. Slowly the interlaced fingers of her praying hands rose from her belly, her fingers separating, opening outward and upward until her upturned palms framed my face. I let her wounded palms guide me, gently turning my head, drawing my right ear to her belly, to the place where she'd been offering her prayer. "Travis, I"—her voice halting and quavering as she pressed my ear deeper into the welt-ridden hollow of her belly, both her palms tenderly covering my face, eyes, and left ear, sealing me in silence, the silence inside her hands, the silence of her prayer.

My ear and the skin of her belly felt sealed, made one in the silence, and as I sensed her fingers losing their grip on my head and heard her enter a peace-filled stillness that followed her final breath, I pressed my ear deeper into her belly, listening deeper into the silence, and I heard words rising from the center of that fertile silence inside her where my life was first conceived, words freeing, warming, and hope-filling—"I forgive you!"

Dogged Faith

Jesus and I were sitting on plastic lawn chairs. Jesus was reading a newspaper. We were inside a large room, and standing out from the walls were stalls, all but one of them covered with thin wire mesh. Each stall stood by itself, a distance of roughly ten feet separating one stall from another. And the stalls were empty. I didn't notice anyone in this room but us.

"Where are we? … What're we doing here?" I asked.

"We're answering an ad," said Jesus.

"An ad for what?"

"I'll read it to you: 'Four dogs need a good home. Come to Animal Ark Shelter on 1 August. We open at 8:00 a.m. It is vital that the dogs be placed in a good home before we close at 5:00 p.m.'"

"There's no one else here," I remarked, "and I don't see any dogs. We must be early."

"Yes, we are," said Jesus. "I wanted to be here before anyone else arrived, to make sure that we have the best view, because I'm very concerned about what could happen to those dogs."

"The ad says that the doors open at eight," I noted. "How is it that we're already inside the shelter?"

"I know the director of the shelter," replied Jesus, "and he told me that he'd leave the door unlocked for us."

A man walked through a back door, and, approaching us with an outstretched hand, said, "Hello, I'm Clyde Fields, Director of Animal Ark Shelter, or, as I like to call it 'Clyde's Ark.'" Jesus shook hands with Clyde, and then Clyde firmly took my hand, gently shaking it. "I see that you had no trouble finding Clyde's Ark, and I trust that you made yourselves comfortable."

Clyde looked at Jesus, and asked, "Is the view to your liking?"

"Yes," said Jesus, "this view will do just fine. Thank you for your generous hospitality."

"I'll be right back," said Clyde. "I've got to bring in the dogs before this place becomes crammed with people." Clyde left the room, and within a few minutes he returned with four dogs, not one of them on a leash. He petted and talked to the dogs as he guided them into the stall without thin wire mesh, the stall spacious enough to house a large horse. "You're magnificent—all of you!" Clyde declared to the dogs, "and it will be difficult to see you go … but go … you must. It can't be any other way."

Clyde wiped tears from both eyes.

The dogs looked at one another, and then, all at once, sat down, side-by-side, in a straight row, facing Jesus and me.

"That sounds like someone's at the front door," said Clyde. "People are starting to come. Excuse me, I've got to go. Limited seating, you know … folks can get rowdy … even get rough physically when they're not happy with their seats … I have rules … there must be order to the process … like Noah had with his ark … my Ark is shelter for the dogs … the dogs need to be safe … they deserve a good home—animals have rights, you know!"

Clyde began welcoming people as they arrived, directing them to empty chairs. All the seats quickly filled. People with no place to sit began clamoring as they elbowed and edged their way toward the front of the room, men and woman loudly proclaiming "This is my spot!" as they staked out their places to stand in the aisles. The number of people swelled to a crowd of over one hundred.

Clyde closed the front door and locked it, waving off those who were still trying to gain entrance, saying, "I'm sorry, my Ark is full. There is no more room."

Clyde pushed his way through the crowd, forcing open enough space to be able to reach the stall where the dogs were sitting.

"Welcome to Animal Ark Shelter," said Clyde. "I'm pleased that you could come, and the fact that there are so many of you, only proves how much you all must care about the dogs being placed in a good home. I'd like to begin with a short history of my Ark, and how I believe that the Lord wants me to see myself as a modern day Noah. Just as God commanded Noah to build an ark, build it in a land where it would be absurd to believe that there could ever be enough water to float an ark that size, let alone enough water to keep the ark afloat while carrying all the animals—just like all of that, God commanded me to build Animal Ark Shelter, and to—"

"Yeah, yeah! Clyde!" shouted a man from the back of the room, his face barely visible, "we all care about the dogs! Now cut the speech about yourself, and let's get on with why we're here—to talk about the dogs!"

"This is not a show, sir!" said Clyde, his voice sharp. "And I can assure you that the life of each dog matters—matters enough for you to have to endure the length of any speech I choose to make on behalf of the dogs!"

A tall woman, wearing a well-tailored business suit and stylish hat, remarked loudly, "Your ad was expressive of such urgency regarding the dogs, Clyde, so I'm confused as to why you're delaying the start of the proceedings. I don't care about the history of 'your' Ark, and I'm beginning to doubt that you really care about the welfare of the dogs."

"I agree with her!" boomed an unseen woman.

Cupping his hands into the shape of a megaphone, a man bellowed, "Me, too!"

Grumbling that sounded like a collective groan rolled through the crowd.

"All right! All right!" shouted Clyde. "Let's get down to business! I only thought that some historical context would be instructive for anyone who may be here for the first time, for someone who has not been to one of these proceedings at my Ark."

Spontaneous applause and loud whistles erupted throughout the crowd.

"We love you, Clyde," a woman said, blowing a kiss to Clyde. "You know how we like to tease you. Now do what you do best: tell us about the dogs."

"Thank you for your support," Clyde replied, "but I do have some formal business to take care of that involves the former owner of the dogs. And I have to speak of that before we can talk about whether there is anyone here who could provide the dogs with a good home."

A gravel-voiced man with a goatee said, "Every time we've done this in the past, without exception, someone met the specific criteria for what a good home had to be for the dog under consideration."

"That is true, sir," said Clyde, "but this time is different for a number of reasons. Please give me a moment to clarify what I mean."

A shout—heard as one "Oh, no!"—burst forth from people in one section of the room, and then a woman, shaking her fist, shouted, "Clyde, come on, you—"

"Please!" Clyde shouted back, his voice stern. "Control yourselves! I am the Director of Clyde's Ark, and I am in charge of these proceedings. I have responsibilities to the dogs, you know, responsibilities that are mine and mine alone." He paused, surveying the crowd, poised to respond to any further disturbance.

"Do what you have to do, Clyde," said a man wearing a green blazer and neatly-pressed slacks. "When I say that I'm sorry, I'm confident that I'm speaking for all of us. We all know that you have a protocol to follow. It's just that we really want to hear about the dogs."

"Thank you," said Clyde. "Now I'll continue." Clyde held up a piece of paper, waving it while he was saying, "This document bears the seal of a public notary, and it is signed by a lawyer as a witness, the same lawyer who wrote the document. And it also bears the signature of the former owner of the dogs. The former owner is deceased, and he has no surviving family members that could be located, even though an extensive search was made by a private investigator. So, the former owner's wishes—and that means his non-negotiable conditions—must be followed to the letter, and if they are not, then no one gets the dogs."

"What happens to the dogs if the conditions aren't met?" a squat man asked as he fingered his lower lip.

"I don't want to address that now," said Clyde. "It makes me too sad to even think of that ... so ... let's not get ahead of ourselves. All right?"

"Okay," replied the man fingering his lower lip. "Let's hear the conditions of the former owner of the dogs."

"Yeah, let's hear the conditions!" ten to fifteen people shouted as one voice.

"Before I speak of the conditions, I must make one more point regarding procedure," said Clyde. He paused for a moment. Then he bowed his head as though he was offering a silent prayer, and then, fixing his eyes on the Lord's eyes, Clyde went on, his voice yielding, "Because I know how important it is that the dogs are placed in a good home, I have memorized the document. I'll refer to it as the procedure unfolds, and I'll show what's written in the document to anyone who doubts that what I'm saying is, in fact, in the document."

"Clyde, we know you are a man committed to attending to the finest details of life," said a woman wearing an electric blue sweatsuit and fire-engine red running shoes, "and although your manner is plodding, even at times tedious, we know that you're a man who is single-mindedly devoted to adhering to a course of action to which you've been charged to follow. For you, this is more than fulfilling responsibilities. For you, it is the highest expression of a moral life."

"Preach it, lady," a man shouted, applauding as he spoke.

"Right on!" boomed a man sweating profusely and wearing a straw hat. "You can't say it any better than that!"

Chuckles along with clapping of hands rippled throughout the crowd.

"You're too kind," said Clyde, "much too kind. But I appreciate the sentiment. And now, I'll return to the document. First, the former owner wanted me to say a few words about each dog."

Clyde pointed to the dog nearest him, saying, "This is a Bloodhound. He is four years old. Bloodhounds are famous for their ability to follow scents that are hours and even many days old. Their tenacious and tireless tracking ability is unrivaled, being able to follow and locate lost people, escaped criminals, and wounded animals. And they can do this over trails that cover great distances. Their noses can detect a scent on as few as one or two cells left by someone on a trail that one would assume would be cold and a dead end. Bloodhounds have a gentle disposition, they easily show affection, and they are even-tempered." Clyde patted the dog on the head, and declared, "This bloodhound has been credited with fifty finds. Any questions?"

"I've got one!" boasted a square-jawed man standing in the center aisle. "What's the dog's name?"

"His name is 'Fido,'" said Clyde.

"Fido!" the man roared, and then bent over with laughter. "No one has ever named a dog Fido! I don't believe you! Show me the document!"

Clyde motioned to the man to come forward, indicating on the document the place where the dog's name was written.

The man came forward, looked closely at the name, then turned and walked away, announcing to the crowd, "Yeah, it's there ... Fido ... I still can't believe it!"

"I don't know why you can't believe it," said Clyde. "Fido means 'Faithful.' When you think of the qualities of a dog, isn't 'faithful' the first word that pops into your mind?"

"Of course, you're right," said the square-jawed man, "you've got me nailed on that one."

Clyde pointed to the next dog in line, saying, "This is a Saint Bernard. She, too, is four years old. Saint Bernards were bred for rescuing people trapped in snow and ice in threatening mountainous regions. Their pulling strength is unmatched by any other dog, and they can cart and pull a weight of over two tons. The Saint Bernard sitting right here—she has been credited with fifty rescues. Saint Bernards are extremely loyal, very friendly, and quite affectionate. Any questions?"

"Yes," said a young woman with a wide smile. "What's her name?"

"Fido," said Clyde, "and I can show you where her name is on the document if you would like that."

"No," said the woman. "I'm sure it's there. But this former owner must've been weird—giving two dogs the same name!"

"This next dog is a Newfoundland. She, too, is four years old. Newfoundlands were bred as working dogs for fishermen. Newfoundlands have a dense, oily and waterproof coat, webbed feet, enormous lung capacity, massive size, and tremendous strength—qualities which make these dogs ideal for rescuing people in distress in icy seas and very cold rivers. The head and mouth of the Newfoundland is shaped in such a way that it can keep breathing even while its mouth is full of water and being bombarded with waves. Newfoundlands are universally acclaimed as exhibiting the sweetest and most dignified temperament, and they are the breed that shows the greatest benevolence, kindness, and gentleness. They are excellent guardians, and are especially good with children. Also, they are unshakeable in their loyalty. This Newfoundland is credited with preserving fifty lives. I—"

"And I'll bet you that her name is Fido!" shouted a broad-shouldered man, his mouth tensed into a sneer.

"And you'd win that bet, sir!" remarked Clyde, his words delivered with flare and force. "Fido is her name."

A teenager, leaning against a wall, yelled, "Please don't tell me—no, better yet, let me guess: the German Shepherd's name is Fido, he is four years old, and somehow, like the other dogs, the number fifty is part of his story! Right?"

"Right, you are!" said Clyde. "His name is Fido, he is four, and the number fifty—"

"This is too strange," uttered an elderly woman. "All four dogs named Fido. Was the former owner ever evaluated to see whether he was in his right mind when he wrote that document?"

"Please, ma'am," said Clyde, "let me return to the document. Remember? ... the former owner's final will and testament? ... I must inform you of all of his conditions. And the former owner insisted that you know specific qualities of the German Shepherd. German Shepherds were bred to herd sheep and to protect them from predators of all kinds—animals who would try to prey on them, as well as evil men who would try to steal them. The hallmarks of the breed are keen intelligence, willingness to learn, eagerness to pursue purposeful activity, quickly-accelerating speed, great agility, courageous strength, a discriminating sense of smell, and a powerful bite, the force of their bite second only to the Rottweiler. And last, but not least, they bond deeply with persons they know and remain unwaveringly faithful to those persons.

This male German Shepherd is credited with serving and protecting fifty sheep. Any questions?"

"Can you move through this document any faster?" asked a pregnant woman. "I want to take one of the dogs home before my baby is born!"

"That's funny!" said Clyde, his tone sarcastic, "very funny! But I have bad news for you. All four dogs must go to one and only one new owner."

Voices boomed throughout the crowd—"That's ridiculous!"—"Who could afford to feed all of them!"—"Who could house all of them!"—"I only want the bloodhound!"—"I want the German Shepherd!"—"The Newfoundland's mine!"—"My Saint Bernard just died, and I deserve to have another one!"—"The former owner's a nut case, and that document should be shredded!"—"Yeah, Clyde, toss the document!"—"Let's start over!"—"I think we should bid on each dog!"—"No! We should draw lots for each dog!"—"No! We should all remain quiet and still, and wait until each dog makes a move, and the first person each dog goes to, that person gets that dog!"—"No! That's stupid! I don't want the Newfoundland or a female dog, but what if she comes to me? Am I to be forced to take her?"—"Are you calling me stupid?"—"Your idea is stupid!"—"If my idea is stupid, then you think I am stupid!"—"When you put it that way, it sounds like you're saying that you are stupid!"—"I can't see you in this crowd, but if you show me where you are, I'll come over there and slap some manners into you, stupid!—"

Clyde shot up both hands, over his head, in the gesture that means "Stop!" and yelled at the top of his voice—"Quiet!"

The booming voices stopped, became a muttering din, then faded quickly into an uneasy silence.

Hearing their silence and seeing their attention fixed on him, Clyde said, "Thank you, animal lovers. Just be patient. We're almost finished. And let me be crystal clear: Anyone who is not interested in giving a home to all four dogs is, of course, free to leave."

People looked around the room, to see what others might do or say, and to note whether anyone was actually making a move to leave. No one left his or her place staked out in the room. No one spoke.

"From this point on," proclaimed Clyde, "according to the document, anyone who will provide a home for all four dogs must first, state your name, and then second, explain why you believe you should be the new owner. The person who gives the explanation that matches the former owner's explanation, the explanation he has written on this document as the true explanation—that person will be given the dogs."

A woman immediately spoke, "I am Regina Wilson. I am the C.E.O. of my own corporation, and I have a net worth of over five-hundred million dollars. No one else in this room could ever provide the indoor and outdoor space, the food, and the housing that I can give the dogs, let alone could anyone else, in here, pay the cost of the best medical care in the world. I could provide that for the dogs. Of course, I will give each dog a new name. What has made my corporation so successful is the combination of corporate vision and individual talent. A person needs to be part of an embracing purpose within which that person's talents can be developed to the fullest. And dogs are no different than people—dogs need that combination, too."

"I'm sorry, Regina," said Clyde, "that is not the true explanation. And I have to add: the former owner insists that all the dogs are called by the same name."

Regina fired back, "But if I wanted to change their names, neither you nor that screwball former owner could stop me!"

"In your case, Regina," said Clyde, his voice definitive, "that is a moot point, since you didn't give the true explanation—you don't qualify! Besides, the dogs will not answer to any name except Fido."

"Regina spoke of providing medical care, and speaking of medical care," a man said, "I am a Doctor of Veterinary Medicine. My name is Doctor Waggerson, and—"

"Excuse me, Doctor," interrupted Clyde. "Just for the record, what is your first name?"

"Oh … of course," the doctor said, "It's Oscar. And because I'm a vet, I know the anatomy, chemistry, and nutritional needs of each one of these breeds, as well as each one's average life-span. And I've done complicated—and I might add, successful—surgeries on each one of these breeds. And I know the kind of environment in which each one will optimally thrive. Who else but me should be the one to be given the dogs?"

"I'm sorry, Oscar," said Clyde, "that is not the true explanation."

A man in full military dress stood up, and said, "My name is Colonel Chester Irons, Retired. I was the Commanding Officer of the United States Army's Precision Drill Team. I, more than anyone else in this room, know how to teach obedience. Under my command, the dogs will execute behaviors that will integrate them into a team. Each dog will learn to sacrifice his or her own individuality for what's best for the team. In winter, when they are out of doors, each dog, although of a different size, will wear coats identical in design and identically tailored to the smallest detail, so that each dog knows that neither size, nor breed, nor any other characteristic that may have, in the past, distinguished him or her as a special breed—none of that matters and never will matter. The former owner's idea that the dogs do have and will continue to have the same name—that's a brilliant tactic, no doubt grounded in a strategy to guarantee the most efficient, precise, and unflinching obedience. When can I take the dogs home?"

"I'm sorry, Chester," said Clyde, "but that is not the true explanation."

"Who do you think you're talking to, Clyde?" replied Chester. "I am Colonel Irons to you! Where is your respect for authority? I commanded men in the United States Army, a position with greater respect and prestige than someone who is a lowly director of a trivial animal shelter."

"I am truly sorry, Colonel Irons," said Clyde, "but the fact remains: your explanation is not the true one."

"Clyde, I'm over here," a woman said waving her hand. "Last year, I hired a professional who specializes in researching family histories, a person who can trace your family tree as far back as he is able through his research. Then he gives you a report of what he found. Although it cost me a lot of money, what he found I think will convince you that I should have the dogs. Oh, I almost forgot: my name is Winifrid Menthon. The research into my family tree revealed that I am related to Bernard of Menthon, a monk from the eleventh century. This monk was named Saint Bernard, and he established a hospitality lodge on Saint Bernard's Pass, the Pass being given the monk's name. The Pass was a very dangerous place in the Alps, and the lodge was a place of safety and recovery for travelers going through, or having been trapped in, Saint Bernard's Pass. Saint Bernard was the name given to the dogs working on the Pass to rescue travelers in trouble, travelers who were then brought to the lodge to recuperate. Because I am related to Saint Bernard the monk, I believe that the Saint Bernard sitting near you, and who can see me, can, even now, sense that I have a very deep connection with her through my family and through her family—both of our bloodlines originating from one source, a spiritual man, nearly ten centuries ago, and, to top it off, we are both females. I am convinced that the other dogs would sense that I could connect with them in the same deep way, and we could become, in a uniquely spiritual way, a family. Clyde, you called your shelter 'Clyde's Ark,' so you know how important a spiritual connection is with animals. Surely, you must agree that the dogs must be given to me."

"I'm sorry, Winifrid," said Clyde, "but your explanation is not the true one."

"Look my way!" shouted a man in a three-piece suit. "I'm a German, born and raised in Germany, and now I'm a citizen of the U.S. My name is Wilhelm Steiner, and I'm a professional dog trainer. The Colonel may know how to train men, but he doesn't have a clue about how to train dogs. I do it for a living, and training German Shepherds is my specialty. Only a native German would really know how to train a German Shepherd, and I—"

"Please, Wilhelm," Clyde interrupted, "let me stop you there. I already know that you do not have the true explanation."

"What about me?" asked a small but strong voice rising from inside a group of people clumped in one of the side aisles. The voice, louder, determined, clear, and incisive, repeated, "What about me?" The people pressed around the voice seemed to be peeled away, leaving standing in an open space—a child!

"Regarding the dogs, there are no limits on age," said Clyde. "The former owner was resolute on that point. Come up here, little boy, please."

The child came forward, stopping within three to four feet of Clyde. The ears of all the dogs perked up, and they all sniffed the scent of the boy, but the dogs stayed in their places.

The boy looked at me and then at Jesus, lingering for a moment to smile at Jesus, the boy's face shining with delight. I was puzzled, but felt—somehow—expectant.

"Where are your parents?" asked Clyde.

The boy turned toward the front door, and pointing to two faces pressed against the plate glass door, said, "There they are.

When you closed and locked the door, you blocked them from coming in." Both parents were smiling as they waved at the boy.

"Will someone open that door and let them in?" asked Clyde.

"There's still no room for them," someone observed. "It's so tight in here that I couldn't open the door even if I wanted to."

"That's okay," said the boy. "As long as they can see me, they'll be fine. They brought me here so that I could give the dogs a good home."

"How old are you?" asked Clyde.

"Seven," replied the boy.

"And what is your name?"

"Fido!" said the boy, his voice magnetic and electric with passion, his eyes sparkling as their moving warmth touched the eyes of each dog, and then he turned and faced the door.

When the dogs heard "Fido!" their tails wagged with wide, gleeful sweeps, and then the dogs bounded to where the boy was standing, quickly encircling him: the Bloodhound in front of him, the Saint Bernard on his right, the Newfoundland on his left, and the German Shepherd directly behind him.

The boy started walking toward the door, the crowd parting as he and the dogs walked in unison.

"Hey, Clyde," someone shouted, "why does an elementary school boy get the dogs?"

"Why?—well, it's not because he's a boy or that he's in elementary school," said Clyde. "He gets the dogs because of what the former owner wrote." Clyde looked directly at the document, and read out loud, "'When a person who is named Fido calls for the dogs—that person's name—Fido—is the first part of the true explanation.' And now for the second part of the true explanation: Why do you want the dogs, Fido?" asked Clyde.

The boy and the dogs stopped walking. The boy looked at the Lord, the boy's face knowing, open, excited, and radiating hope.

Then the boy looked at Clyde and proclaimed, "I want the dogs because their faith and my faith is one faith in Jesus, and that makes Jesus the Saint in me, makes Jesus the New—Found—Land in me, makes Jesus the Shepherd in me, and makes the Blood of Jesus the Redeemer in me."

Clyde held up the document for all to see, and said in a commanding voice, "That is the right answer! That is what the document states is the reason for wanting the dogs. Fido, the dogs are yours."

"This has all been a set-up!" shouted a man as he kicked over his chair. "That boy's been coached by someone—his parents, I bet! He could've never come up with those answers on his own."

A voice arose from somewhere at the back of the room, the voice strong and insistent, crying out, "Jesus once said: 'I praise You, O Father, Lord of heaven and earth, that You have hidden these things from the wise and intelligent and have revealed them to infants.' It's in the Bible. The Lord of heaven and earth revealed the true explanation to the boy—he deserves what God has ordained!"

"That's bogus talk!" raged a man with a tattoo of a large skull on his forearm. "Bringing in the Bible is nothing but more mumbo-jumbo to throw us off track. The boy's a fake, a lackey for someone who wants to keep his or her identity secret while we are conned out of the dogs!"

Ignoring the malicious remarks, the boy and the dogs started walking toward the door, and as the boy drew near the door and reached to open it, a middle-aged woman, her face shocked that the boy was leaving with the dogs, said, "Hey, kid, you're too young to be responsible for all those dogs. Don't you think you should grow up before you try to take care of them?"

"Hey, kid," said a burly man with a gruff voice, his voice half-mocking, half-serious, "that lady makes a strong and valid point!

You owe it to us: Give us a picture of what it's going to look like in the future when you're an adult with a responsible job, a job that can make you enough money to take care of the dogs. At the very least, kid, tell us this: what're you going to be when you grow up?"

Fido opened the door, and, as he was briskly walking through it, he spoke out, his voice the sound of the crescendo of a joy-filled and victorious song—"A counselor for Jesus!"

Love Is Patient:
Fourth Delivery

I was coming home from work, feeling tired and irritable, feelings impossible to shake off, feelings further aggravated by the fact that every parking space near my apartment was taken. Two blocks from home I found a parking space. I nabbed it seconds before a man in a truck spotted it.

As I was walking toward my home, I mumbled, "What's with the company? ... Why the overtime? ... Why now?" The weight of my briefcase made my fingers cramp a bit, so I switched the bulging leather thing to my other hand. "And why on a Friday ... cutting into my weekend?"

I noticed the faint glow of dusk, and thought, *Oh, rats! I missed seeing L.C. today! She's made all her deliveries by now!*

I stopped in front of my mailbox, opened it and saw a single item waiting for me—a verdant green envelope. I plucked the envelope from its metal container, deftly stripped away an inch of the envelope, drew the open end to my mouth, blew a current of air into the envelope, my breath expanding its paper sides, then swiftly turned the envelope upside down, and with a quick snap of my wrist the verdant green note card was launched into my welcoming palm. I looked at the note card:

LOVE IS PATIENT

The words seemed fixed on me, trying to move me in some way. As night was absorbing the last glimmers of twilight, I held the note card high over my head, *Love is patient* facing the darkening sky, the sky, soon black, became dotted with twinkling stars.

"Yes, Lord!" I whooped, my feet dancing in place, "Love! Is! Patient! And you are that Love who is patient!" I reached into my back pocket, drew out my wallet, unfolded it to its full length, fingered the place where I keep my paper money, and gently placed the note card next to a twenty-dollar bill, the face of the note card snug against the back of the bill. Suddenly laughter seized my insides, then rolled through me, laughter touching off shockwaves of joy, buckling my legs, causing me to drop to all fours, and then turn, sag backwards, now in a sitting position, all of my weight being supported by the wall that housed my mailbox. I looked at the note card pressed seamlessly against the twenty-dollar bill, and barely able to constrain the laughter rocking every part of me, I cried out, "Lord, from now on"—laughter tickled my tongue, making me squeal—"even if I have only a single dollar bill"—titters tied up my tongue—"in my wallet, *Love is patient* will always be face-to-face with IN GOD WE TRUST!"

Blood Types:
Crossed and Matched

J esus and I were seated at a table in a coffeehouse. My eyes lingered on face after face, looking for signs to help me understand why every face was shining with delight. *Why is everybody so happy?* I thought. *It can't be caffeine. I've been wired on caffeine and I've never had a happy look in my eyes.* Suddenly I became self-conscious, aware that I was licking my lips, my tongue moving like a windshield wiper. A slight chill rolled along the length of my spine. I rubbed my palms, cupped my hands and blew into them. I leaned close to Jesus. "I'm chilly," I said. "Is it cold in here or is it just me?"

"It's just you," said Jesus. "Do you feel sick? Or is something else bothering you?"

"I feel out of place here. I noticed that there are many tables here, and most of the people seated at these tables are holding sheets of paper in their hands. When I look at these people, gaze into their eyes and sense their eyes catching mine, their eyes appear filled with delight—but not delight at seeing me. No! They're staring at me—judging me because I don't have any papers in my hands!"

I glanced at Jesus' face, his eyes flashed that same look of delight. A deep shiver racked me with shame. In the midst of all these delighted faces, I felt worthless, useless, unwanted, and condemned to unending loneliness. "I'm freezing! My blood's turning into ice water! I need something to warm me up. A hot mocha might be just what I need. Is there a waiter to take an order for drinks?"

Jesus laid his hand on my shoulder. "No," said Jesus. "We arrived too late for drinks but we got here just in time to hear the readers."

"What readers?" I slipped on a heavy jacket and zipped it from bottom to top. I began to feel warmer.

"This is Open Mike Night, and this evening is advertised as *Blood Types: Crossed and Matched—A Night of Poetry*. People who've written poetry on this topic go to the microphone and read to all of us what they've composed."

"Blood types! That sounds ghoulish! Don't tell me this is one of those New Age gatherings where bloodless intellectuals and anemic poets are going to drivel on about the cultural importance of vampires!"

"No, Travis, tonight is not about vampires."

"Well, then, is it about a bunch of atheistic quacks—bloodsuckers who'll try to con me into buying their ten magical tips for wellness, tips that can work their magic only if I know how to take proper care of my blood type? You've taught me to see through all these kinds of trickery for what they are—Idols! Death dressed-up to look like life! What would be your purpose in testing me further?"

"Travis, as you can see, this room is filled to capacity. And I know that every customer in here claims to be a Christian. If you listen to the readers, your concerns will be addressed and your questions will be answered." Jesus pointed to someone moving through the crowd. "Look, Travis, here comes the manager."

Light and steady applause greeted a man as he was walking to the microphone. "Thank you," he said, his face beaming. "As most of you know, my name is Tobias, and I welcome all our regulars—and each person here for the first time!—in the name of Jesus!"

Applause grew louder, laced with shouts of "We welcome you in the name of Jesus!"

His voice overriding the applause and shouts, Tobias cried out, "Thank you, Jesus! Thank you! Jesus said that wherever two or more come together in his name, that he'd be there among them! And by how excited you are when you shout out 'in the name of Jesus!' ... well, there is no doubt that Jesus is here among us, his presence stronger than ever!"

Tobias bowed his head and raised his upturned palms.

The room grew silent.

"Let us pray," said Tobias. "Father, I thank you that Jesus is here among us, and I thank you for this place where those who are led by the Holy Spirit can be released to build us up by reading the words that were given to them by the Spirit. Father, I pray that you richly bless those who come forward to share with us what has been placed on their hearts about the blood of Christ. In Jesus' name, I pray. Amen!" Tobias stroked his wisp of a goatee, his face the look of someone reviewing what he'd just said.

"I'm so excited!" cried someone from a far corner of the large room. "C'mon, Tobias, let's hear the first reading!"

Tobias laughed. "I know ... I know that I've gone on and on! But I want to make certain that everyone understands the process of how we share at these readings. As a matter of fact, I just remembered to let you all know that out of respect for those who are reading, we don't applaud them while they are reading. We wait until after they've finished sharing and then respond ... oh, also, we turn off all cell phones during the readings. And last but far from least: after the last reading, those who wish to leave, may go in peace. Those who wish to stay, we will have our monthly agape feast! Servers will come by your table and take orders you have for food and drink. Are there any questions?"

Tobias scanned the room, looking for raised hands and waiting to hear a question sounded out. "Since there are no questions," said Tobias, "is there anyone who'd like to start the sharing tonight?"

From the back of the room a couple stood up, and, holding hands, walked to the microphone. They hugged Tobias, and then he gestured to them that the microphone was theirs.

The man introduced himself, "I'm George."

"And I'm Enid. George and I are married. We're going to read as one voice a poem we wrote. We've entitled it *Marriage in Christ.*"

George and Enid held a sheet of paper between them, drew close to the microphone, and began to read out loud, the harmony of their voices musical:

Marriage is the commitment of wills in
A spirit-saved love, a garlanded light
Binding broken circles of sorrowed sin
In Easter beginnings, a lifetime plight
Of unfolding freedom in discipline
Born of Jesus' blood, stretched beyond the night
Where Mercy heals despair, and our embrace
Is enfolded in the Living Word—"Grace!"

Applause rippled throughout the room as voices shouted— "Glory be to God!"—"What a celebration of marriage!"—"A song of love!"—"Yeah! Like a *Song of Solomon* for today!"—"You're two lovebirds for Jesus!"

His hands clapping along with the applause, Tobias walked to the microphone, and said, "Thank you! Thank you! That was wonderful! Is there anyone else who'd like to share?"

A young woman stepped onto the stage and walked to the microphone. "Hi, I'm Brenda. And this is a poem I wrote about Mary giving birth to Jesus. I decided not to give it a title." She smiled, scanned the room, and then began to read out loud:

Heavenly lips ablaze with stars
Draw a breath and blow a kiss to Mary.
"I feel warm. Something is touching me!
Where is it? There's no one here."
Stars become suns.
"No, the heat on my face—it's a fever!"

A second kiss.
"I'm burning up! What's wrong with me?!"
Suns become the Seed.
"My ears! My belly!"

A third kiss.
"The fire! He wants me! He's in me!"
The Seed becomes the Son.
"I love you—my Lord and my God!"

The Son waits, visible in swelling promise.
Mary labors in blood and water
Under heavenly lips ablaze with stars.
She blows them a kiss—Christ is born!

A young woman began to weep. Applause burst forth, followed by steady clapping amidst shouts—"Praise you, Lord, for taking on flesh!"—"Thank you, Mary, for your faithfulness!"—"Thank you, Mary, for being like me—a sinner saved by grace!"—"Kisses from heaven, kisses from earth"—"Wow!"—"What simple words!"—"What passion!"—"What humility!"—"You've got love, Brenda, real love for Jesus!"

Tobias leaned close to the microphone, and said, "Thank you, Brenda! Your words have honored the Lord and his mother."

"I have five children," said Brenda, "so I know what it's like to be in labor and to give birth. But my words are only poor guesses at what Mary experienced in giving birth to our Savior."

"Well recited, Brenda, very well recited indeed! Does anyone else have a poem to read?"

A middle-aged man sprang to the stage. "My name is Tony, and I'm single. I don't have any children … and I've never given birth, but—"

Rolls of laughter interrupted Tony's train of thought.

"I'm embarrassed! My face must be bright red … I wasn't trying to be funny. But I do have a poem, and it, too, is about the birth of Jesus. I call it *Christmas Bread*." He paused, appeared to gather himself, and then began to read out loud:

Born into the dark hollow of a cave,
Jesus, His palms spread in pardoning grace,
Felt the black silence of a distant grave
Fall as shadows on His radiant face.
His ears, circles of hallowed innocence,
Listened for the song in His mother's voice,
That psalm of nurturing benevolence,
Praising His name, calling Him to rejoice.
Christ, sacred flesh bound in a plain cradle,
Heard her song, but no words could mute His pain,
For His pain is Living Wine and Ladle,
Thirst-slaking blood of the Lamb without stain,
Redeeming food for the godless stranger,
Crucified Bread rising from a manger.

Loud applause rose from pockets of the room, applause laced with voices varying in tone and volume—"Very deep theology, you've got me thinking!"—"His flesh is our true food!"—"From his manger to his Cross, Jesus is my Bread of Life!"—"I was a godless stranger, Jesus redeemed me!"—"If you ever have children, you'll be a loving father!"

"To write in truth," said Tobias, his tone convincing, "you don't need to have children, but you do need to understand and believe how the blood of Jesus makes you a child—a child of the Father! I see someone already stepping onto the stage."

"Yes, I'm Mandy, and I'm very nervous. I have a poem I wrote about my child, a child I had, born out of wedlock, a child whose father—his name is Chet—abandoned us. The title of my poem is the same as my daughter's name—*Bree.* Thank you for letting me share it with you." Mandy took a deep breath, held it for a few seconds, and then began to read out loud:

Bree was conceived in a drunken stupor,
By two strangers who slurred
Their way into convincing themselves
That lust was the truth of sexual pleasure,
And that love was a liar's game,
Each player manipulating the other.
The goal of the game: each player to keep
The other player enslaved
For a lifetime of pretended commitment,
While both, in secret, played the other for a fool.

When Mandy told Chet that she was pregnant,
Chet slapped her across the face,
And said, "Don't try that with me!
I can't be the father!

You're trying to make me part of the liar's game!
You always made fun of the suckers
Who swallowed that swill they peddled—
Romantic love, sex with one person for life,
One marriage for life, and having their own kids!"

Chet knocked Mandy out cold, her face bleeding,
And after she got out of the hospital,
She searched for Chet,
But never saw him again.

When Bree was born, it was like her first cries
Were loud pleas to her parents' destroyed lives,
Pleas calling them back together,
To find healing peace in the blood of Jesus,
Pleas to them to stop thirsting for hope in booze,
But find hope in Christ's words,
"He who believes in Me will never thirst."
But Mandy refused the pleas of her daughter,
And Chet never heard her cries.

But the Lord heard her pleas,
And His hands were on her life from birth.
With wide palms of courageous trust,
Bree reached for Jesus, and He reached back,
His embrace unbreakable.
Jesus implanted in Bree's heart
A tenacious search for honest answers
To real questions, and a freedom to receive
The Lord's truth and grace without relent.

So when Mandy sees Bree's ever-widening smile,

A sure sign that Bree's moving deeper
 Into knowing Jesus, filling her with wonder,
Then Mandy listens, hears Bree praying,
"Jesus, this is Bree.
I need a home … a real mom and a real dad.
My mom and dad need Jesus.
I want to know my dad,
But please don't let him hurt my mom anymore."
When Mandy hears Bree praying that prayer,
Mandy cries out, "Jesus, you are the God of love,
You're not part of a liar's game.
I don't deserve Bree.
I'm a sinner who deserves death.
I need your blood! Save me!"

A sadness, thick and heavy, pervaded the room. No one clapped. Tobias walked onto the stage, placed his hands on Mandy's head, and every person raised in prayer an open right hand and angled it toward Mandy. Power seemed to gather in those open hands and began to flow in spontaneous streams toward Mandy—"I love you!"—"Jesus loves you!"—"Your pain is real!"—"Your daughter is a blessing!"—"You're forgiven!"—"Praying for reconciliation between you and Bree's father!"—"There's an anointing on you, Mandy!"—"May the hand of the Lord's mercy guide you!"

The room fell silent, except for a few muffled sobs and the voice of Tobias saying, "Mandy, I pray that you accept Christ's acceptance of you where you are and as you are, and that you rest in the protecting comfort of the Holy Dove's wings. May Bree's father, Chet, be convicted of his parental responsibilities by the Spirit, and may Chet come to love Bree the way that the heavenly Father loves Chet. In Jesus' name, I pray. Amen!"

Tobias hugged Mandy, and everyone gave her a sustained round of applause. "Is there anyone else with anything on his or her heart to bless us? Whether in sorrow or in joy, you bless us with your heartfelt words."

A young man who looked to be in his late twenties came to the stage. "My father died recently, and I wrote a poem for him, entitling it *Forever Free*." He began to read out loud:

My father bled to death, now clenched by earth,
Alone in dust and silenced faith—until
Tongues of tombs are a Maranatha mirth
Where Love heals the suffering Tree and Hill,
And Truth wakes sleeping faith with—"Rebirth!"
O sleep well! For the Kingdom of His Will
Lives for that Hallelujah Day when we
Are risen—all children—forever free!

Waves of "Hallelujah!" rocked the room along with sounds of clapping so loud that I felt the top of my table vibrate. Jesus leaned close to my ear, and asked, "How are you feeling now?" I unzipped my jacket and took it off. "Things are heating up in here. The Spirit is really cooking … he's on the move! I feel excited! I can't wait to hear the next reader!"

A woman with fiery red hair jumped up and started cheering, "Forever free!" repeating "Forever free!" each "Forever free!" seeming to lift more people from their chairs until nearly everyone was standing and cheering "Forever free!"

His hands waving, Tobias shouted, "Everyone! Please sit down!" People murmured as they took their seats, and once seated, focused on Tobias as he continued, "Whether we are awake now or are sleeping in the grave—nothing can stop us from rising and soaring into heaven!" He folded his hands, took a deep breath, then opened his hands in an inviting gesture. "Does anyone else have a poem to share?"

A thin man, his sunken eyes appearing fixed on a space just beyond the tips of his shoes, slogged onto the stage. His body trembling, he fought to keep steady the paper he was holding tightly in both hands, and said, "My poem's called *Doubting Thomas*. His lips drawn between his teeth, he let a silence go by, and then began to read out loud:

I am resolved to be resolved to be
Resolved, or so I seem to myself when
I reflect on Christ's blood poured into me,
Into me, knowing who I am again,
And again, and again, until who I
Am turns round to question who I am and
Comes upon my Self asking my Self why
Asking the question why is the command
I follow day and night, day and night, day
And night, my Self commanding my Self to
Repeat the same question in the same way,
My Self returning me to the review
Of my reflections upon my reflections into me,
I resolving why, Christ in me, why, I revolving.

"You've captured Doubting Thomas!"—"That's what that disciple must have felt!"—"Endless reflection!"—"Yeah! And with no decision!"—"Right! And with no action!"—"He's frozen!"—"He's terrified to risk believing!"—"His heart is a cage!"—"And he's imprisoned in it!"—"Solitary confinement!"—"A life sentence!"—"I've questioned the Lord!"—"Me too!"—"Never like that, not with such wracking self-torture!"— "Is the Thomas in the poem saved or isn't he?" Suddenly—almost in unison—the voices became subdued, and many people folded their hands and bowed their heads.

Tobias stepped onto the stage, and asked the thin man, "I didn't catch your name."

"Thomas!" he shrieked, "and doubt is killing me!" Then he impaled his poem on the microphone—rushed to the door—flung it open—ran through it—quickly disappearing into the night.

Focused on Tobias' stunned eyes, I spoke to Jesus, asking, "When Thomas came to you and said he would believe in you only if he could touch you, was he saved?" Not hearing anything, I turned my head, to face Jesus—he was gone! I hadn't heard him leave. I stood up, my eyes swept the room—no sign of Jesus. The sound of Tobias' voice broke the sweep of my roaming glances. I sat down.

"Heavenly Father," prayed Tobias, his voice pleading, "I ask in Jesus' name that you make the presence of your Son real for Thomas tonight, so real that he experiences an assurance of his salvation like he's never known before." He looked upward, his gaze seemed focused on something beyond the ceiling.

"Amen!" shouted a young woman. "And amen and amen!" cried out a man with a handlebar mustache.

Tobias smiled, extended his arms, his palms upturned, and said, "Anyone else?"

"Yes," replied a gray-haired man. He lumbered toward the stage, clearing his way with a cane.

"Very cool cane," said a woman with flowing silver hair.

"I made it myself," he remarked, "carving it out of a limb of a tree I found on a walk." Waving off Tobias' offer to help him, the gray-haired man managed to drag both feet onto the stage. "I think there's been some of Satan's use of smoke and mirrors here tonight. Jesus told us that Satan is the father of lies, and so he is. Sometimes, though, as the apostle Paul warned us, Satan can appear as an angel of light. Is there anyone here who doesn't like the light? My name is Bart, and I wrote a poem on how Christ protects us from the lies and deceptions conjured up by Satan. I entitled it *I Atone!* Bart's eyes searched the room, his intense gaze lingering on a few faces, and then he read out loud:

"Your blood had a disease," I thought I heard
Satan whisper from behind me. "To save
Your life, I had to void all your blood. I gave
You all my blood. And I give you my word:
No disease I've fixed has ever recurred.
My blood is yours—even beyond the grave!
All I ask is that you promise to rave
About your new blood and call God absurd
Whenever I ask you to bow to me."
With a needle I pierced my bone clear through.
 "It's my blood!" I declared, "inside my bone!"
"Are you sure? Make a blood smear. Test it. See
Through this microscope the blood I gave you!"
I turned—saw Christ: "Satan lies! I atone!"

Sustained applause filled the room, loud from some tables, soft from others—"The blood of Jesus is the light!"—"You saw through Satan's cunning tricks!"—"Satan's the Prince of Darkness!"—"Yes! And he always will be!"—"The blood of Jesus makes Satan's tricks go up in smoke!"—"Oh, yeah! And the blood of Jesus shatters Satan's deceiving mirrors!"—"Glory! Glory! Glory! Jesus is our atonement!"—"I can see the Truth because of His blood!"—"His atonement is the only mirror I need!" The applause and the praises tapered off.

Tobias walked onto the stage. "Bart," said Tobias, "your cane looks like a constant reminder of how you're protected by the bloody wood Christ was crucified on."

"Thank you," Tobias. "That's how I see my cane."

"If you carved a cane like that for me, do you think I could write poetry as well as you?"

"If I could walk without this cane, I'd give it to you right now. But how about this: I'll search for a fallen limb, and when I find one, I'll carve you a cane and bring it to you."—"How about canes for all of us, Bart?!" someone cried out from the back of the room—"All right! All right!" said Tobias, his tone firm. "Let's leave it there! Let's give Bart a break, and let him go back to his table!" Tobias shook his fist in mock anger at the person who'd asked for canes, smiled, and asked, "Is there anyone else with a word for us?"

No one made a sound or made a move. I craned my neck, my eyes lingering on the cane as Bart was returning to his seat. I sat down, felt a presence next to me—Jesus was back! "I searched for you but couldn't find you anywhere. Did you need a men's room break?"

"No, I had to leave for a while."

"How come?"

"Thomas was in deep trouble, on the verge of falling apart, and he needed something from me."

"Needed what?"

"Acceptance."

"Yeah … doesn't everyone need acceptance from you?"

"Yes, Travis, but the real faith issue for a person is whether he can accept my acceptance of him. You know something about that, don't you?"

"Oh, yeah, I know something about that … know too much … know my many failures at that … know how hard it is for me to do that."

"Don't you mean that you know how hard it is to receive that from me?"

I shook my head—"No!"—shook my head again—"That's not what I mean!"—I nodded my head—"Yes"—nodded my head again—"Yes … yes … that is what I mean."

A teenager with short, green-dyed hair and piercings through her nose and eyebrows strode to the stage. Her black nail polish stood in stark contrast to the white sheet of paper she was holding. "My name is Phoebe, and I love Jesus with all my heart, but I've got to tell you that I'm tired of fake preachers, tired of them making Christ into Kool-Aid, tired of them treating me like a kid who can't understand Scripture, tired of these politically correct wimps who've made church into a numbers game, tired of their fear of offending people with the truth, tired of being tired, tired of them telling me that my time will come but my time isn't now—but now is my time, and now is the time for saints—no matter what your age!—to know the real Jesus! I've written three limericks, and I call them *Listen, Preacher!* I'm going to speak them out, one after the other, without stopping. These are for you, preacher!" exclaimed Phoebe, her voice ready for a fight. Then she read out loud:

There once was a preacher of piety
Who desired great notoriety.
He denied ever needing
The Jesus who is bleeding,
Now famed for his death-bed anxiety!

There once was an obedient sheep
Whose pastor always preached him to sleep.
When pastor asked, "Why are you snoring?"
The sheep cried, "Because you are boring,

And of Christ's blood there's never a peep!"

A preacher declared that Christ's blood is pure,
Then he slipped on a pod of dog manure.
He fell hard on his rear,
Was so jolted with fear,
He doubted his faith was ever secure!

Blasts of laughter shook the room along with spurts of thunderous clapping mixed with gasps of disbelief—"Ewwwww-ee!"—"Tellin' it like it is!"—"You're crossing the boundary separating satire from ridicule!"—"That's coarse speech, even St. Paul is against that!"—"Cut her some slack, dude, she's exposing stuff that needs to be exposed!"—"Write on, sister, write on!" Her eyes closed, Phoebe laid her right hand on her chest and began gently to tap it with her open palm while she lifted her left hand straight up, and prayed, "Jesus, I trust that you were glorified through my words and the gift you gave me to proclaim them!" Then she quickly stepped down from the stage as Tobias was stepping onto it, passing one another without saying a word.

Tobias folded his hands and placed them under his chin, as though his jaw was resting on a prayer, a prayer asking for what to say next. "Is there anyone here who has a poem about being a poet?"

"I do," said a man wearing baggy pants held up by frayed suspenders. As he walked to the stage, he kept adjusting the cuffs of his plaid shirt, moving them from single-rolled to double-rolled and back to single-rolled. "Hi, my brothers and sisters, I'm Mickey." Pointing to a man sitting two tables away from him, Mickey declared, "There—right there!—that man is a poet! He's a cousin of mine, and he's very shy. I've written this poem about him and his poetry. I call my poem *Poet of Arterial Faith*, and I hope you enjoy hearing it." His voice serious and enthusiastic, Mickey read out loud:

He is of Adam and Eve origin,
A fig-leaf poet, a flesh-clenched fist of blood
Called by the Holy Dove's freedom-releasing coo,
To live in a resplendent gyre of blood and bread
With dazzling white its vortex of mercy.
I name him Poet of Arterial Faith,
Who writes from the place of deepest red,
Where arterial blood gathers in the heart,
Its chambers like wombs giving birth
To blood-infused words,
Their crimson images pouring forth,
Slaking the soul's thirst for meaning,
Fueling every cell with renewing life.
His bloodshot pen is moved by Hope's possibility,
Making his poetry sing in longing gratitude.
He writes from raw knees,
Each poem a prayer offered in faith
By rhyming shadow and light with the awe
Of promise in the rainbow Noah saw.

A few people clapped lightly, then clapping grew louder, quickly reaching a crescendo, lasting for 10 or 20 seconds, then applause faded away—"Thank you, Jesus, for poets!"—"Praise you, Lord, for loving families!"—"The mercy of God!"—"The healing possibilities of God!"—"The poet for Jesus must be in the blood of Jesus!"—"The hope God has for us!"—"The rainbow Noah saw!"—"Awesome!"—"Let's hear a poem from Mickey's cousin!"—"Yeah!"—"Oh, that would be glorious!"

"Well, Brock," said Mickey, "you've heard them. How about sharing a poem?"—"C'mon, Brock! Bless us with your arterial faith!"—"Yeah!"—"Yeah!"—"Yeah!"—"Yeah!"—"Yeah!"—"Yeah!"— "Yeah!"—Brock raised his hands in feigned surrender. "Okay!" he said, "You've got me! ... I'll do it! I have something I've just written, and I have it with me. His gait wobbly, Brock walked onto the stage. "The doctors tell me that I've got terminal cancer, and here's the poem expressing my struggles with cancer, and my hope in Jesus. I call my poem *The Roar*. If while you're hearing my words, the Spirit nudges you to pray for me, in a private place in your spirit—please do. Here's the poem." Brock cleared his throat, swallowed hard, and then read out loud:

I've been bitten by Death's cold fangs,
Its venom infecting my blood with leukemia.
The doctors say that they're helpless,
That the Devil is like a prowling lion,
That he is Death seeking to devour me,
And that the Devil's growl
So threatened the doctors,
It forced them to give up on me,
Telling me that they were sorry,
But they needed to protect themselves
From being devoured by the Evil Lion.
But I believe in the Lion of Judah!
His healing paws are greater than a doctor's hands,
And He's bigger and stronger than the Evil Lion,
His roar can drown out the caterwauls of the Evil Lion,
His massive jaws can crush the Evil Lion's fangs,
His ferocious blood can devour
The Devil's venom infecting my blood.
Drive out the prowling Devil, O Lion of Judah!

Hold me in your healing paws, O Lion of Judah!
Heal me with your blood, O Lion of Judah!
And Roar! Roar! Roar! new life into me!

Spontaneous weeping broke out, the force of compassion flowing from every person in the room, flowing in waves, each wave building on the next wave until they embraced Brock, encircling him with empowering tenderness. Brock started to sway, stagger, grope at the air, trying to balance himself, but the increasing force of the empowering tenderness buckled his knees, causing him to sag to the floor. Their hands under Brock's arms, Tobias and Mickey supported his limp body.

Tobias cried out in a commanding voice, "I want all those who have the gift of healing to come forward—now!" A group of ten or more people rushed to the stage. "Help Brock to the prayer room in the back and pray for him!" Two men and two women lifted Brock and carried him away. "He'll be prayed for mightily, and we're all going to believe right now for his swift and complete healing! Amen!" We all shouted back at the top of our voices— "Amen!"

"This has been quite a night of poetry bathed in the blood of Jesus. We magnify you, Jesus! We give you praise, Jesus! And we give you all the glory for what you are still doing here tonight, for you are the Lord of glory. I'm sensing that there is one more person or persons who've been led by the Spirit to share with us tonight. And I don't want us to move into our time of agape feasting if what I'm sensing is accurate."

"We have something on our hearts to share," said a woman who appeared to be in her early thirties. She and a man who looked to be her age came to the stage. "I'm Rose," said the woman. His hand soft around Rose's shoulder, the man said, "And I'm Nate."

"We've known one another for around three months," said Rose, "and we're deeply in love, in love with Jesus and with one another. I've worked on this poem almost from our first date. The poem was written for Nate, but after I prayed about it, it was made clear to me that I was to read it here, to all of you. I call it *Redemption*, and I offer you my words as an expression of thanksgiving to our Savior who redeemed us." Her face beaming, Rose read out loud:

Our parents were made of heavy clay,
Their unvoiced freedom trapped
In the dumb weight of working-class bodies,
Bodies used up in the consuming labor
Of a consuming society,
Bodies worn out in the making
And raising of new child-flesh,
Bodies struggling together
In the silent heat of weary passion.

These men and women of sweaty hope,
In one all-out effort of gathered strength,
Pressed their urgent shoulders against
The relentless drag of their muted lives
And forced open a space
In the dumb weight of their heavy clay,
Creating in that seed-and-egg space
A place for us to grow,
Their creating leaving them exhausted,
Alone, lying in their consuming silence,
Their silence consuming
Every attempt to bring words to birth,
Their only sense of closeness

The nameless sighs they heard
Being breathed into their dark bedroom,
Sighs longing to give birth
To a never-known language of intimacy.

But ... our parents did not know
That the unnamed sighs they breathed
Inside the silent heat of their weary passion
Were breathed into our just-conceived
Flesh-and-blood,
Their sighs unintended prayers
Offered in sweat to their sweaty hopes for us,
Sighs that breathed open a space in our spirits,
A space where the generational trudge
Of exhausted flesh could find pauses,
And in the freedom of those pauses
Imagine new lives,
Different from our parents' lives,
And give voices to those lives
And give names to those lives.

In those pauses, you and I,
Unknown to one another,
Each found a refuge,
A shelter without bars of encasing flesh,
A protective embrace made of our thoughts
Generated by our minds,
Minds giving birth, moment-by-moment,
To marvelous words, words building on words,
Words becoming names, words and names
Constructing worlds of images and ideas,
Minds dizzied by the delight of thinking

And speaking, thinking and speaking that was ours
And ours alone,
Free of the dumb weight of heavy clay
Passed on to us from our parents
And from their unnamed and unvoiced ancestors.

And so we lived in the open mind-spaces
Made by the fertile sounds of our parents' sighs,
Their sighs their greatest gift to us,
Sighs that released into us the freedom
To be in-spired by our own adventurous spirits,
Creating new universes of meaning,
Each one generated by names
Bearing the stamp of our unique individuality.

We believed that we were happy, even though,
In our most creative moments, you and I,
Separated by time and space,
Were still unknown to one another,
Still incomplete,
Still unaware that we were going to be called by name.

One day—quite by surprise—the Father
Called us by name, sewed our spirits
Together with scarlet threads
Made of the blood of Jesus.
Then the Father blew—as His kiss—the Holy Spirit,
The kiss a tender breeze alighting on us,
Brushing our cheeks as touches of comfort,
Playing across our ears as sighs of love,
Until—in one puckering sigh—the Spirit's kiss
Blew into the wind the sighs of our parents,

Sighs now set free, purified
By the sanctifying breath of the Spirit,
And our own sighing now transformed
Into joy-filled words resounding
In melodies and lyrics
Arising in the singing kiss of the Spirit's song.

Clapping erupted! It was continuous, the unbroken and unbreakable sound melting away the weight of worries hanging on weary bodies, making the room feel light, open, free, and lifting into a wide smile the corners of every sad and depressed face—"Thank God that His Word says righteousness and peace have kissed!"—"Oh, Yes! And now they've kissed their lives!"—"Kissed your love!"—"Will be kissing your marriage!"—"As long as there's life, nobody's beyond redemption!"—"Redemption!" interjected Tobias. "What a glorious word, no word better fitted to conclude our night of *Blood Types: Crossed and Matched—A Night of Poetry!* We are all redeemed by the blood of Jesus! And let us keep our redemption in mind as we celebrate our fellowship in Christ with an agape feast. Servers will come to your table for your orders. Let our celebration continue as the Spirit leads us."

"Wow!" I said to Jesus. "I'd no idea of how important and impactful the art of writing poetry can be for your people. And the breadth and depth of gifts expressed here tonight ... Wow!" I chuckled. "I just said 'Wow!' didn't I?"

"Do you think that you have a gift for using words to serve the saints and to glorify me?"

"Well, I think I do ... I mean ... isn't that what a counselor does—use words to heal those in pain, and that healing glorifies you—right?"

"Yes, that's much of what a person does who counsels in my name. But I was speaking of writing poetry. Do you think you have the gift?"

"Excuse me, my brothers," said a voice interrupting me before I could answer, "I'm Gabe, your server. Would you like to see a menu and order some food and drink?"

"I won't need a menu," said Jesus. "I'll have a hot mocha."

The server started to write down Jesus' order—"Just a second ... and I'll have extra chocolate and extra whipped cream."

"Very yummy," said the server. "You're a man who knows his mocha and knows how to get into the spirit of an agape feast!"

The server handed me a menu. I opened it. Surprised by what I saw, I said, "The selections look very attractive, including the main dishes, and all of the items listed are written as poems!"

"You're very observant, and you're quite right. Every menu we put together reflects the theme of that particular Open Mike Night. Is there any item on the menu that appeals to you?"

"I'm hungry, so I'm looking at the main courses. They look tough to read as poems." I turned the menu toward him, angling it so that Jesus could not see what was written on the inside. "Rather than try to read each selection and invariably get the meter and rhyme wrong, if it's okay with you, I'll point to the selections I'm interested in, and if you're willing, you may answer any questions I have before I make my selection."

"That's fine, and I understand your nervousness. You're not the first person who found daunting a menu full of food items written as poetry. Is there any main course you'd like me to explain?"

I drew a pen out of my shirt pocket. "I'll point to a selection and then ask questions. Okay?"

"Sure. Point and fire away."

I placed the tip of my pen on a main dish. "If I order this, it must be cooked at 145 degrees, and it must be a scrumptious medium-rare."

"I can guarantee that, my brother. Our chef is the best Christian chef in the state."

"The meat must be warm and red in the center, and then the red spreading out, becoming pinkish in color. I must see the blood, and the meat must be soft, soft enough for me to see it ooze blood if I press on it with my fork. Can your chef do all of this?"

"I assure you, brother, yes he can." He took the pen from my hand, and pointed at other selections, explaining in detail how they could be cooked to any specifications I laid out.

"No, I want the main dish I pointed at and I want it prepared the way I detailed. And one more thing. I'm going to give you my order now, and it will be in the form of a poem I will create right now, on the spot, a poem that I sense will be the most beautiful poem ever written, the most serious poem ever written, the most joyful poem ever written, a poem that both encompasses and goes beyond every poem read here tonight and every poem ever written, a poem that satisfies hunger as no other poem ever written, and a poem that is the shortest poem ever written."

"I'm overwhelmed!—I can't wait any longer!—I must hear your poem! Brother, what do you want to eat?"

"The Lamb!"

Revealing Words

This looks like the campus of a large and prestigious university," I said, my eyes scanning the landscape for signs of certainty. "I think I once saw a picture of it in the newspapers. Am I right, Lord?"

"Yes, Travis," replied Jesus, "you're right. And we're in the middle of the campus during change of classes."

"Are we here because you want to show me why counselors need a university education?"

"I want you to meet some people."

"Some people!" I said, feeling the force and speed of my speech quicken. "Of course! You want me to meet the top professors in psychology and psychiatry, the top practitioners in their fields, the top minds with the newest ideas on healing souls who are suffering—all the key people who can teach me what real professional counseling is all about!"

"No, Travis," said Jesus, his voice firm. "Those are not the people you're going to meet."

"Then who are they?" I asked, pressing Jesus for an answer, my voice loud and prickly. "And where are they? And how long do I have to wait to meet them? And are you ever going to stop making me search for an answer to the question of whether the Father's plan includes me in it as a counselor?"

"Patience, Travis," said Jesus, his voice warmly insistent. "Patience, wise choice of revealing words, and knowing when and how to express them!—now these are qualities of those who do

counseling in my name! Whether you believe that real professional counseling is the same as doing counseling in my name, now
that is indeed a different issue, one that's critical for every person
to figure out if he wants to be a counselor—in my name!"

I felt disappointed and agitated. I wanted to argue with Jesus, to
prove to him that I have patience, that I'm wise, that I know how
to speak in the right way, but I deliberately held my tongue, calculating that Jesus would interpret my silence as proof that I am a
patient and wise man. But even as I was holding my tongue, I
knew that Jesus sensed hypocrisy in my posturing silence.

We turned a corner and I followed him into a building.

"This looks like a restaurant," I noted, my stiff and awkward
speech an attempt to distract me from thoughts of judging myself
a hypocrite.

"It is," replied Jesus, "and this is a place where you may seat
yourself." He pointed to a small table for two near a wall, and said,
"Let's sit over there."

We sat down.

His words firm and instructive, Jesus said, "Travis, whatever
you see and hear, do and say nothing. Stay in your seat, and watch,
listen, and learn."

"Watch, listen, and learn what?"

"How words matter."

Puzzled, I asked, "When you say 'how words matter,' what do
you mean by that?"

"Watch, listen, and learn, and say and—"

"I know, I know—and say and do nothing!"

Seeming to take no offense at my curt interruption, Jesus said,
"That's right."

I scanned the large room and observed that all of the seats were
taken, except one. Directly across from us, in the middle of the
room, not more than six feet from us, was a large circular table

with four equally-spaced chairs. On the table was a card that read:

RESERVED

A party of four walked to the table, paused in front of it, talking for a moment about who was going to sit where, when a tall, well-dressed man appeared and interrupted their conversation.

"Excuse me," said the man, "I'm the manager of the restaurant and I'm sorry to tell you that this table is reserved."

One of the four, a thin man whose young face clenched in anger, said in a loud and tight voice, "You're sorry! Yeah! Right! I'm sorry, too! Sorry to have to remind you that in this restaurant—your restaurant!—people may seat themselves!"

"I understand your frustration," remarked the manager, "but for over thirty years, long before I was made manager, this table has been reserved for a particular person, a very special person who eats lunch here every day starting at noon and ending whenever he decides that he has finished his lunch. If you come back later, not too early and not too late, you may enjoy your lunch at this table—if, that is, someone else has not gotten here ahead of you."

The thin man sighed, glanced at his wristwatch, and said, "It's three minutes to noon. I think my friends and I should all wait and see whether or not this prima donna arrives at noon, and if he doesn't, then you should let us have this table."

A man with a long bushy beard threw his arm around the thin man's shoulder, and said, "No, Harry. It's not worth the trouble. Let's get out of here and grab some pizza off campus."

"Yes, I agree with Mike," said one woman, her speech crisp and confident, "this kind of elitist attitude is disgusting! Let's get out of here!"

The two others, a woman and a man, hugged Harry, and shouted as one encouraging voice—"Pizza!"

Harry shrugged his shoulders, sneered at the manager, and then said to his friends, "You're right. No doubt. You're right. Let's go!"

They all left the restaurant, and then Harry stopped, turned, came back, and yelled to the manager, "One minute until noon ... I'm tempted to stay ... to see this great specimen of humanity who deserves such first-class treatment, but you're not worth it! As a manager you're a hypocrite, an elitist snob, and a lackey for the aristocrats that control this university and your restaurant! Haven't you heard the news! This is America! And we're a democracy! You know, I just thought of something: Maybe I'll see you sometime—but not too soon and not too late!" Harry forced out raucous laughter, and ran out of the restaurant, quickly catching up with his friends.

As the manager was walking away, he trained his eyes on his wristwatch, and said in a barely-audible whisper, "Hey, Harry, your watch is off a couple of minutes. Is your watch so cheap that it can't keep accurate time? ... or is it that cretins like you just don't know how to tell time?"

I looked at Jesus, and asked, "What was that all about? Those people are gone. The manager is gone. Surely they were not the people you want me to meet."

"Patience, Travis, patience and wisdom," Jesus replied gently, a smile slowly forming across his face. "It's now exactly noon."

A neatly-attired, clean-shaven man walked into the room, his strides purposeful and measured, his direction and destination certain: He was moving toward the table, pulling behind him a large, white leather suitcase sporting two wheels and a retractable handle. He lifted the suitcase off the floor, set it carefully on the seat facing me and Jesus, and turned the suitcase slightly, as if it were a person focused on the man and always available for conversation.

The man sat to the right of the suitcase, angling himself in such a way that I could see his face. His Adam's apple was so prominent that its size and shape gave the impression that he was constantly in a state of trying to swallow something that was stuck in his throat. The man began to twiddle his thumbs, his manicured fingernails catching light from the long fluorescent bulbs overhead. After a few seconds, he said in a commanding and stern voice, "Jonathan!"

The manager walked briskly to the man's table. "Yes, Most Reverend Tomes, I am here. Do you want your usual?"

"Of course, but you better make it for two."

"I'll have it brought immediately," said the manager as he scurried toward the kitchen.

I looked at Jesus. He motioned to menus lying on our table, and said, "Check out the food they serve here, and order whatever you want."

I reached for a menu and then drew back. "I'm not hungry."

"Something to drink?"

"I don't know ... maybe ... a lemonade."

A waiter approached us. "Hello," said the waiter, "my name is Sam, and I'll be your server today. Are you ready to order?"

"Two lemonades," said Jesus.

"Anything to eat?"

"Not now," replied Jesus, "but maybe later."

"Two lemonades," said the waiter, "coming right up."

As he was walking away, I added, "I like mine with extra ice!"

"Extra ice," the waiter confirmed, "Got it!"

A man entered the restaurant and advanced toward Tomes. The man was wearing black shoes, white slacks, a black belt, and a long-sleeved shirt printed with white and black squares. "Are you the Most Reverend Tomes?" asked the man while he gingerly fingered his jet-black pompadour.

"Yes," replied Tomes, "I am he."

"We have an appointment for lunch. I'm Cosmo Pitcher, the owner of Cards For All Occasions. May I sit down?"

"Of course."

Pitcher pulled out the chair facing Tomes and sat down, Pitcher's face clearly visible from where I was sitting.

"Are you in the business of selling greeting cards?"

"Zingo! You're right on target, Most Reverend! I am in business and I do sell greeting cards, but greeting cards are a subdivision of my company. My cards meet needs of people no matter what their circumstances. Cards for grievers, cards for weddings, cards for newborns and their parents, cards for Christians and their holy days, cards for Jews and their holy days, cards for Muslims and their holy days, cards for every religion and its holy days, cards for atheists, cards for agnostics, cards for humanists, cards for, well, you name it and I have a card for it, or, if I don't have a card for it, I'll make a card for it—cards for all occasions, that's me!"

"You are very enthusiastic about what you do," observed Tomes. "But when we spoke on the phone, you sounded desperate, panic-stricken, almost, at times, suicidal. I thought that you wanted to meet with me because you were in the midst of a serious spiritual crisis and you needed the kind of advice that can come only from the most renowned systematic theologian who is also the most famous ordainer of clergymen, which, if national polls among systematic theologians are accurate, that would be your humble servant, me—the Most Reverend Tomes!"

"Zingo!" said Pitcher, his voice excited. "You're right on target but you missed the bull's eye. I was in deep trouble. You see, my business lives or dies by the jingles that're in the cards, and my two top jingle writers fell in love, married, left my company, and started their own card company. Their business has taken off, and unless I can turn things around in my company, I'm going to go bankrupt. I've interviewed hundreds of jingle writers—they don't have the gift. And my attempts to write a jingle always result in ear-splitting noise! I can't help myself out of this mess—but I do need help! Actually, Most Reverend Tomes, we can help one another!"

Tomes placed the tips of his index fingers in his ears and appeared to be lightly tapping inside of his ear canals.

"Anything wrong, Most Reverend?" asked Pitcher.

"Something you said … 'ear-splitting noise' … I heard a buzz … reminded me to do a quick check."

"A quick check of what?"

"Of how my hearing aids are functioning. I have been slowly losing hearing in both my ears. So, to amplify sounds, I wear hearing aids. Now and then, I hear a low buzzing sound, and sometimes, without warning, a shrill, piercing sound drills into my ears, a sound so painful that it can make me scream, even faint. This is my sixth pair of hearing aids. The company that invented them has examined each pair and their technicians can find nothing defective in the hearing aids. I keep using them because I believe their product to be the best on the market. Besides, just the phrase 'hearing aid' reminds me that in Scripture Jesus performed a miracle when he put his fingers into a deaf man's ears and healed him."

"Zingo!" declared Pitcher. "Bull's eye this time! Oh … before I go on … can you hear me, Most Reverend?"

"Yes," said Tomes, his voice thin, his eyes furtive.

"Bull's eye! Yes, Most Reverend! Bull's eye! If we both keep our ears open, we can help one another out of the trouble we're in."

"Trouble?" queried Tomes, his voice guttural and flexed, his body rigid. He reached for his suitcase, drew it closer, and asserted, "What presumption! You telling me that I am in trouble. What arrogance!"

"There's no need for you to pretend, Most Reverend. I've done my homework on you! You're in trouble. I'm in trouble. And I have a way out for both of us."

Tomes opened his mouth to speak, just as a waiter arrived with their food. The waiter stood just behind the suitcase. Tomes looked at the waiter, Tomes' mouth forced into a smile that was straining, appearing to conceal a sneer meant for Pitcher. As the waiter was placing their food on the table, he was saying, "Your lunch, gentlemen: The Most Reverend Tomes Special—for two." The waiter turned to Pitcher, and said, "The Most Reverend Tomes prefers no beverage with his meal. May I bring you something to drink, sir?"

"I don't see a menu," noted Pitcher, "so I don't know what my options are."

"I'll bring you a menu, sir."

"No need for that," insisted Tomes. "Mr. Pitcher, I—"

"Please, Most Reverend," said Pitcher, cutting off Tomes, "call me Cosmo."

Tomes sighed, his nostrils flaring. "I do not like to be interrupted in mid-sentence, Mis ... ter ... all right—Cosmo. I was saying that you do not need a beverage. My meal consists of meticulously prepared fruits. You see, I am a fruitarian, one who believes that every Christian should eat only what Adam and Eve ate before the fall—and that is fruit from trees. The fruit I ordered contains all the liquid you need to digest your food, to lubricate your body, and to release the nutrients into your body for optimal health."

Pitcher scanned the plate full of fruit, then looked at the waiter and exclaimed, "Zingo! The Most Reverend really seems to know what he's talking about. So, okay, no beverage for me. But ... just a second ... before you go. I have a few questions."

"Yes, sir, I'm here to serve."

"Have you ever written any poetry? ... ever played around with rhyming words? ... or written a jingle or two, you know, to celebrate a friend's birthday or to console someone who's lost a dear one to death? ... anything like that?"

The waiter appeared surprised and confused, frozen for a few seconds, and then he said, "No, sir ... never ... sorry I can't be of help." The waiter turned and walked away.

Snickering, Pitcher pointed toward the waiter, and said to Tomes, "What a loser! He can't see himself as doing anything but waiting on people, but me—I'm a winner! I'll try any tactic and stop and talk to anyone if what I do enables me to hire a new jingle writer!"

"You sound desperate again, just the way you sounded on the phone message you left me," declared Tomes.

"Don't give me that self-righteous tone, Most Reverend! You're as desperate as I am and you know it! For years enrollments for your classes and for your religious programs have been declining, a downturn which has now become irreversible—unless you do something radically different to attract students."

"I am not a 'radical,' so do not associate that term with me!"

"If you don't become radical, you won't only lose more and more students—you'll be out of a job!"

"The university would never terminate me! I am the Most Reverend Tomes! My national reputation alone is enough to guarantee job security in my position."

"Zingo! You missed the entire target this time! The university runs on money. If your department doesn't generate enough revenue from student fees and tuition, your department will be eliminated, which eliminates your position, which eliminates you. Let's face it: You use words to help people, and I use words to help people—we can combine forces, this time using our talent for crafting words for our mutual benefit, to help one another."

Tomes quickly fingered his hearing aids, then folded his arms, and said, "You are irritating, Cosmo, and yet there is something absurdly amusing, even entertaining, about you. I mean, consider the name 'Cosmo,' a name suggesting that you somehow represent a kind of cosmic truth, when, in fact, what you and your jingles represent is nothing but a collection of the shallowest clichés that masquerade as truth. The way you use words as pancake makeup to cover over what is real and true, I wonder why your parents did not name you 'Cosmetic.' And the way you dress! All your clothes are black and white, and that shirt with its black and white squares, it makes you look like you are wearing a checkerboard, a board the sign of—"

"Zingo!" shouted Pitcher. "You're on target, but you missed the bull's eye once again! My shirt represents a chessboard, and it's my way of showing to the public and to my employees that life is a business played like a game of chess, that the business world is black or white—never gray!—that each piece must know and play its part, and that the goal is to checkmate any and all people and obstacles that block you from making a profit. Even my pompadour has a purpose. I comb it into the shape of a wave about to break. It's my way of saying that, although you may feel stuck in your black-and-white world, good things are about to happen, that you're about to catch a break and move forward on a new wave of success!" Pitcher scanned his plate, picked up a piece of fruit and popped it into his mouth. "By the way, Most Reverend, unless your parents named you 'Most Reverend,' I assume that they gave you a Christian name, the name on your birth certificate."

"Ow!" squealed Tomes, cupping his hands over both ears. "My ears! The pain!"

The manager bolted from the kitchen and ran toward Tomes.

Pitcher stood, stretching his arms toward Tomes.

Tomes cautiously lowered his hands, then waved off the manager's and Pitcher's attempts to help. "No … thank you … the …

pain ... it came as one sharp stab—then it was gone." Tomes took a deep breath as he eased back against his chair. My Christian name is Casper."

"Zingo!" blurted Pitcher. "Casper! The same name as that animated cartoon character from years ago—Casper the Friendly Ghost! Not long ago I saw a few cartoons of Casper. He does look friendly. Surely you're old enough to remember him!"

Tomes sighed, and said, "Yes, I remember him, remember seeing his cartoons at movie theaters. But what is your point, other than the fact that he and I have the same first name?"

"My point! You really don't get it! *Retro* is in! If you work with me at *Cards For All Occasions*, we could market you as friendly in the same way Casper is friendly ... but, of course, I must be honest: you'd have a lot of work to do on your smile, which is non-existent, unlike Casper's smile, which is so cute, inviting, and playful."

"I still do not see your point! Do you ever say anything that is clear and without trying to sell something?"

"Zingo! You've missed the target—but just barely! Hear me out! Christians call the Holy Spirit the Holy Ghost—am I right?"

"Yes, some Christians still do, depending on their denomination and translation of the Bible they use."

"Zingo! Can you see where I'm going with this? This is the bull's eye! Now we can make a cash cow out of the bull's eye! Here's the marketing strategy. We'd tell people that your name is Casper, and that you love Casper the Friendly Ghost, and then we would show how the Holy Ghost is a friendly Holy Ghost, that, therefore, God must be a friendly God, and then we would use the fact that *Retro* is in fashion, and that would make it easy for us to sell you to the public and to sell your theology on my—I mean 'our'—greeting cards. Yes, we'd start with greeting cards. *Greeting Card Theology*—Zingo! Don't you just love the sound of that?! Is this a brilliant idea for a new product—or what!? This is the way out of the financial trouble we're both in! Am I brilliant or am I brilliant?!"

"Let me see whether I understand you, Cosmo. You want to take the nobility and semantic genius of my systematic theology and distort it to the point that it can be written as jingles on greeting cards?"

"Not distort, Most Reverend—never that! I have too much respect for you and for the many years that you've spent studying the Bible, and then designing and creating the volumes of written work that have made you so famous. No, not distort, but, rather, 'distill'—that is the key word here. You'd be taking the essence—and I emphasize the word 'essence'—of your systematic theology and distilling it so that it could be read, understood, and then seen and quoted by billions of Christians around the world."

"Billions of Christians?" queried Tomes, his eyes widening with possibility.

"Zingo! Yes, billions! The *Internet! Facebook! Twitter! Pinterest! Google!*—just to name a few sites. These are what I call 'short-burst' businesses and sites—and more are coming! They are the future—the future that's already here! And they're nothing more than businesses advertising and marketing themselves through a greeting card format—although they'd never admit to that. People want only short sentences, and they can no longer concentrate their minds beyond one to eight lines anyway, and many of those lines are even sentence fragments. Imagine billions of people reading your ideas. Imagine how your fame would become global. Imagine how many people you'd be helping to understand and to live the highest moral life, the kind of life Jesus lived—and all in the seconds it takes to read lines in a greeting card! We could go one better than *Facebook* by calling our enterprise *Gracebook Greeting Cards,* using the Christian word 'grace' as another way to tap into this virtually unlimited market. I envision profits soaring as high as what you'd call heaven! I can see us being hailed on the *Internet* and in all media as 'Geniuses for Jesus,' as visionary entrepreneurs who've wedded Capitalism and Christ, synthesizing evangelism and consumerism in ways never before conceived! ... of course ... there's still the problem ... of us ... not having a jingle writer ... but I believe now more than ever ... we'll find a master jingle writer. What do you think ... so far ... about my vision for us, Most Reverend? Or should I call you Casper, the man of God who personally knows the friendly Holy Ghost?"

Pitcher, his eyes fixed on Tomes, chuckled, and then picked up a piece of fruit, tossed it into his mouth, chewed it with vigor, and gulped it down, and said, "Zingo! This is scrumptious! You know, I've been an atheist all my life, but if Adam and Eve ate fruit that was this good, then I guess, no, not guess—I can see clearly how a person could be convinced that there is a God."

Tomes sighed, his eyes closed, his head tilted slightly backward, the palm of his right hand slowly moving up and down on his Adam's apple, as though he was massaging his throat, trying to ease the passage of something from inside his throat to his stomach. Suddenly he grabbed his napkin, covered his mouth with it and started to cough, the hacking bursts making it hard to breathe, his gasps for air causing his face to flush a reddish purple, his hands shaking violently, and then, seemingly with all the strength he could muster, he made one desperate lunge with his left hand, his hand grasping the suitcase next to him, and his coughing—instantly—stopped!

Tomes began to breathe slowly and deeply. His arm around the suitcase, he kept his eyes locked on it while he said to Pitcher, "What is in this suitcase, Cosmo, it is my 'zingo,' and there is nothing else on earth that can give me the peace and satisfaction I need. Just touching what is inside the suitcase brings me into a state of deepest calm and unshakable assurance. I do not need the *Internet*, greeting cards, or anything else to get me out of any and all trouble. I will show you what I mean."

Tomes lifted the suitcase, turned it on its side, and slid it onto the table. A large zipper held the suitcase together, and as Tomes reverentially unzipped the suitcase, he proclaimed to Pitcher, "Casper is a name that means 'Keeper of the Treasure,' and the treasure I am to keep is inside this suitcase." Tomes spread open the suitcase and one by one removed the contents and placed them on the table. "Behold, the books comprising my systematic theology, each one a tome. My surname, 'Tomes,' is descended from generations of Tomeses spanning centuries, each Tomes a writer of at least one or more tomes, the very word 'tome' etymologically meaning a large, weighty, scholarly book. The books you behold here are my tomes, each and every one of them a treasure, and I am the keeper of this treasure, so intellectually and theologically pure, that I keep it in this pure white leather suitcase. And I guard this treasure with my life."

Tomes paused, displayed the front and back of his hands to Pitcher, and commanded, "Look closely! There is not a single hair on my hands. I shave my hands and fingers daily, to make certain that my hands are sanctified when I write, to guarantee that there is no hair harboring any impurity that would contaminate the words being transmitted from the pure mind of God to my pure hands and fingers as I am writing down his words."

"Zingo!" shouted Pitcher, "what a salesman! You've got a flair for theater! People will swallow your act hook, line, and sinker! No doubt about it: We can use your shtick as part of our advertising campaign!"

Apparently oblivious to Pitcher's words, Tomes went on: "Notice, too, how each book stands there, a silent and immovable sentry, helping me guard against all assaults against the truth in the book. And notice how the covers of the book can be opened, exposing what is inside, vulnerable and transparent, never resisting the familiar touch of purified hands that love the truth, always allowing the truth-seeking eyes of a faithful reader to linger as long as he wants on any page, sentence, phrase, or word. It is the book, Cosmo, specifically the tome and the tradition that gave birth to it and also sustains it, the three-dimensional, embodied presence of truth in the book—that is the answer to any and all troubles—not the plastic, mechanical fraud of an e-book on a *Kindle!* Tomes and only tomes can save the people from themselves! God has ordained it in his plan."

Pitcher glanced at the books, moving quickly from one spine of a book to another until he'd glimpsed the spines of all six volumes set before him, and then he looked at Tomes, and remarked, "I told you that I was an atheist, and I am. But when I started my business, years ago, I took some time to read the Bible, not because I wanted to believe in God, but because I wanted to see if there was any book in the Bible I could use to increase my business. I mean, if billions of people are convinced that there is a God, then maybe I could somehow use the Bible to convince people to buy my products, products that they didn't know they needed until I sold them on the idea, just the way the Bible sells people on believing in God. And I found that one book for me in the Bible—*Ecclesiastes!* I studied that book inside and out, and you'll notice, Casper, that it is not a tome—it's short and to the point. I've used more information from that book to increase my business than tips from any other source. Solomon really knew what a hopeless mess people are when he pronounced 'Vanity of vanities! All is vanity!' He knew what gullible dupes people really are! He knew how empty and hollow their lives are, how they rush to consume whatever garbage they're fed as long as it feeds the image of themselves that makes them feel good about themselves and approved by others. Solomon knew how someone like me could use that hopelessness to create customers who, although they have no hope and remain a mess, can at least for a while be distracted from their hopelessness by my manufactured pleasures and comforts."

Tomes ate a piece of fruit, and retorted, "There is absolutely no end to your pursuit of rank commercialism and your exploiting of people! In the name of helping them in their pain, you convince them that they need the cheap and phony comfort you offer in the jingles in your greeting cards!"

Pitcher gestured toward Tomes' books, and shouted, "I suppose that you call that pile of abstract goobledygook comfort for people in pain!" Pitcher reached for one of the books.

Tomes grabbed Pitcher's wrist, and growled, "Do not soil the truth with your ungodly hands! God values highly the writing of books! He never values using people to make money off their pain!"

Surprised at the strength of Tomes' grip, Pitcher struggled to break loose, and growled back, "You claim that your books are full of truth, but Solomon says that increasing a man's knowledge results in increasing his pain and sorrow! People who read your tomes increase their pain and sorrow! How can words that increase a person's pain and sorrow be of help to him or to anyone else on the planet?!"

Tomes grabbed Pitcher's other wrist, snarling, "Solomon called himself the 'Preacher,' and I am the Preacher of today who seeks 'to find delightful words and to write words of truth correctly'— just like what Solomon said and wrote!"

Pitcher wrestled free his right hand, clawed at Tomes' hands, digging his fingernails into the back of Tomes' left hand, tearing skin, drawing blood, and snarling back, "Solomon issued a warning to fuddy-duddies like you when he said that 'the writing of

many books is endless, and excessive devotion to books is weary-
ing to the body,' and your body proves Solomon's point: Your
hearing is almost shot, your throat is screwed up, your coughing is
about to suffocate you, and with all that fruit you eat, you're, no
doubt, a diabetic—and who knows what other ailments you have
from worshiping your own books all your life!"

"I am bleeding!" shouted Tomes, "My sanctified hands are
bleeding! and you are the one who defiled the very hands that
writes books ordained by God!" Tomes reached across the table,
drawing the back of his bloody hand down Pitcher's shirt, smear-
ing with blotches of blood the black and white squares. "That is
checkmate, Cosmo! And with it goes your black-and-white
world!"

Pitcher slapped away Tomes' hand, and bellowed, "You've ruined my shirt! The material is the most expensive silk money can
buy! And you—you've spoiled my image of perfection! Here's what
I think of your precious tomes!" With one backhanded sweep of
his hand, Pitcher sent flying Tomes' six books, two of the books
falling between the feet of a woman, catching her between strides,
the books causing her to trip and fall.

Gasps filled the restaurant, followed by a moment of frozen silence.

The manager appeared, rushing toward the woman.

Pitcher stood up, and then bent down and helped the woman
to her feet.

Tomes snatched a large cloth napkin from the table and
wrapped it around his bleeding hand, then grabbed the suitcase,
gathered his books into a stack on the floor, and then carefully
placed the books into the suitcase.

Pitcher offered the woman a seat in the chair formerly occupied by the suitcase.

She sat down.

Tomes took his seat, bringing the suitcase to lean against his chair.

"Are you all right, ma'am?" asked the manager.

She nodded.

"Do you need anything?"

She shook her head.

"Most Reverend Tomes," said the manager, his voice commanding, "in all my years serving you, I've never seen an outburst like this! If it were anyone else but you, I'd ask the person to leave."

"I am sorry, Jonathan," said Tomes. "I can assure you that this will never happen again." He slipped his hand into the suitcase and drew out a small first aid kit, slid the napkin from his hand, removed a piece of gauze and dabbed the bloody scratches.

"And who is this man, Most Reverend?"

His eyes riveted on the back of his hand, Tomes muttered, "I thank God that I got a tetanus shot last year." Meticulous in applying to his wounds what appeared to be an antibacterial ointment, Tomes replied, "His name is Cosmo Pitcher. He is my guest. We had a misunderstanding that degenerated into behavior that is unacceptable and immoral." Tomes bandaged his wounds, and then took from his suitcase a white glove and with delicate precision inserted his hand into the glove. "There," Tomes said out loud to himself, his voice reassuring as he inspected the shape and fit of the glove, "that will keep my hand from any further exposure to infection."

"Zingo!" Pitcher said, his tone forcibly subdued. "The Most Reverend is right on target. I offer you, Jonathan, my sincerest apology, and, although I deserve to be thrown out and to be banned forever from this restaurant, I'd like very much to stay. I believe that Most Reverend and I haven't quite finished our conversation—this time, I promise and guarantee, we'll be talking in the most civil manner. And this sweet lady, whoever she is, Most Reverend and I need to see what we can do to seek forgiveness from her and to make amends."

"All right," said the manager. He held out his hand. First Tomes, and then Pitcher shook the manager's hand. The manager walked away, returning to the kitchen.

The woman stood up.

"You're not leaving, are you?" asked Pitcher

The woman pointed toward the end of the restaurant.

Pitcher focused on her finger, following it to where she seemed to be pointing.

"The ladies' room," said Pitcher, "is that where you're going?"

She nodded, and then she held up an index finger, her finger pointing toward the ceiling.

"One finger ... straight up ... meaning you'll be back in a minute—right?" asked Pitcher.

She nodded, and then walked away.

"Zingo!" Pitcher said with glee. "Can I read people or can I read people?!" When he saw the woman enter the ladies' room, he picked up the cloth napkin next to him and rolled it under his shirt collar, trying to angle it so that it covered the bloodstains on his shirt. He leaned forward in his chair, and asked Tomes, "Can you see any of the blood?"

"Yes," said Tomes, "when you lean forward like that and talk, the napkin flaps away from your shirt and I catch glimpses of blood. Sit back in your chair, let the napkin rest flat against your shirt."

Pitcher slowly pressed his back against the chair. "How about now ... can you see any blood?"

"No, and the way you have lengthened and narrowed the napkin, the napkin looks more like a rumpled white necktie than a napkin."

"Zingo! That's great! You're a real good sport, I mean, after all that's happened. That woman hasn't said a word. Do you think she's a mute?"

" I do not know. Her behavior has been odd to say the least."

"Maybe she has a serious disease, one that destroyed her ability to speak."

"A serious disease," said Tomes, his voice shaky as he pulled tighter his white glove, making certain that the glove was snug all the way around his wrist, "I hope not ... but ... if ... she is sick and contagious or was sick and is now a carrier of the sickness—I am leaving the table immediately. Perhaps she is thinking of suing us for damages ... damages for tripping her and making her fall ... claiming that we have injured her permanently."

"Zingo! You're not even in the ballpark, let alone near the target! The books that made her fall are yours!"

"You are the one that knocked the books into her feet, making her trip and fall! If you had not in an angry childish outburst sent the books hurtling onto her path, causing her to fall, she would not have a case against you!"

"Against me!" said Pitcher, his voice grating, "I'll—Shh! Casper! Quiet! She's coming out of the ladies' room."

The woman came to the table, smiled, took a seat, and said,

I was on my way to the ladies' room,
My thoughts on Jesus and His empty tomb,
When loud voices broke my concentration,
Each raging word filled with accusation,
But before I could turn my head to see,
To put faces to such ferocity,
Books crashed against my ankles and feet,
Making me stumble, my legs in defeat,

I fell—hard—on the rough carpeted floor,
The fall causing pain too sharp to ignore;
And that's when the nice manager arrived,
Who quickly discerned that I had survived,
That no dire injuries had occurred,
That I was all right, though I spoke no word,
My nod being enough to reassure him.
But when he chastised you, his face was grim.
Then you helped me to stand, the pain was gone,
And I checked my legs, ready to go on.

"Zingo!" blurted Pitcher. "She speaks in rhymes! She's our new jingle writer, Casper! Now, at last, it's all come together: Your national reputation for systematic theology, my highly-profitable and brilliant system of how to create consumers, and, now, her, with her limitless talent to crank out jingles on the spur of the moment and for any occasion, even jingles for tripping and falling in a restaurant! She's perfect for *Cards For All Occasions!* After hearing her speak in jingles, you may be right, Casper—maybe there's a God so big that He helps people who don't believe in Him!"

"I must confess that I am struck by the way you speak," said Tomes to the woman. "But why did you just nod or shake your head when we first spoke to you? Why did you not answer back?"

The woman's eyes and smile widened, and then she said,

I speak without disrupting halts or gaps,
Words streaming forth, unfolding without maps,
Without aims, logic, or self-reflection,
The words form a song of resurrection.
And so I let nothing cut short my song,
For the rhymes of my songs make me belong,
Belong to the Christ who makes me feel whole,

Who gives His transforming life to my soul.
When I sing my songs to their conclusions,
I trust God's truth, not my own delusions.

A grimace flashed across Tomes' lips, and he quickly fingered his hearing aids, and queried, "Are you professing that you are a Christian?"

"Zingo!" Pitcher shouted gleefully. "A master jingle writer and a Christian! What luck! But hold on a second, Casper. We don't know her name. Will you tell us your name, please?"

Her wide eyes a pale blue, the woman glanced at Tomes, and then chuckled, turned toward Pitcher, and said,

When Jesus saved my life, He changed my name,
And what Christ said to me, set me aflame:
'I give you this new name—Augusta Chimes,
 From this moment on, you'll speak only rhymes,
And your rhymes will be songs, worshiping me,
And celebrating the God who set you free,
Free to soar with the Spirit to new heights,
But you'll be one who sings but never writes!'
Christ spoke to me, words that set me on fire,
Words that empower, and words that inspire.

"No—Oh!—No!" shrieked Pitcher. "That will ruin all my plans! You must write down jingles!—You must!" Pointing at Tomes, Pitcher, his voice insistent, pleaded, "He writes tomes, the biggest, heaviest books in the world. I write greeting cards, the smallest, lightest books in the world! You are the answer to his and my troubles, and, at the same time, you'd be serving all mankind … er … I mean … of course … all humankind!" Agitated and near hyperventilating, Pitcher paused for a moment to catch his breath, and then went on, "Now ... before you answer, Augusta, please, you've got to hear me out. Your jingles would combine the knowledge from his big books and condense them into the compact spaces of my little books—spreading the word of Jesus Christ to billions of people throughout the entire globe!"

The Lord made it clear to me: 'Do not write!'
So I obey His command; it's a slight,
To me, to reduce my songs to jingles,
For my songs, while I sing, give me tingles,
The sign that Christ is present in my song,
Whether I sing to one or to a throng.

"I want to be certain I understand what you are claiming," said Tomes, his eyes narrowing. "Are you claiming that books are of no use to God?"

What your question implies, I don't believe,
But I can see the question makes you grieve,
And then panic at the thought, that your tomes,
Whether they're in libraries or in homes,
Are covered with dust, unread forever,
Your tomes a wasted, worthless endeavor.
As for books, God's word is in the Bible,
And to claim His book useless—that's libel!
God uses books, that's a fact I embrace,
But to write books—that's a matter of grace!

"Ow!" bawled Tomes, his fingers shooting to his ears. "Ow! The pain! My ears!" He bent forward, his shoulders slumped, his palms cupping and then massaging his ears. His neck limp, his head swaying from side to side, his mouth open, coughing, his

Adam's apple quivering, he seemed about to collapse onto the table, but suddenly sat up. "There," he said, "the pain has passed. I still think that there is a mechanical defect in these hearing aids."

Tomes smirked, as though he through his own will had conquered the pain, stiffened his back against his chair, and went on, "The Bible itself shows how important it is for those who believe in God to read books other people have written, books other than the Bible," said Tomes, his tone incisive and confident. "When the apostle Paul requests in *Second Timothy* that Timothy, and I quote, 'bring the books, especially the parchments,' Paul is providing irrefutable evidence that Paul himself needed books other than the *Old Testament*—for you will remember that there was no so-called *New Testament* at that time—to bolster his faith and to enhance his understanding of who God was in his life. The parchments were notes and memoranda from preaching and teaching and other writings that Paul must have needed to deepen his faith. And Paul also tells the Philippians that their, and I quote, 'names are in the book of life.' God makes it very clear in the Bible itself: All Christians need books other than the Bible; hence, my six-volume systematic theology, a set of tomes that is an absolute must for anyone who professes a belief in Jesus Christ."

"Yeah, here we go again," said Pitcher to Chimes, his face clenched like a fist, "this is right where we were when you tripped and fell—now we're right here again!—arguing about books, his tomes and my greeting cards, and how we could combine them, using our words and our verbal skills, to help confused, ill-informed, and hurting people, to get the most bang for our buck so that we both can stay on the chessboard of life, win the game, and not have to go bankrupt!"

He plucked the napkin from his chest, raised it high above his head, and, waving it about, blurted, "Zingo! You've got me, Augusta! I raise the white flag! I give up! There's no way either one of us is going to persuade you to write for us, even though you know that your refusal to help us will probably leave us penniless and begging on the streets. You'd let that happen to us, all because you believe Jesus commanded you never to write anything. Your Jesus sounds like a cold-hearted God who has no problem letting good people suffer. Are you and your God going to destroy my dream and look on from afar, watching me die a miserable death?"

Jesus is not a destroyer of dreams,
But He is a crucifier of schemes,
Killing what's false to bring life to what's real,
His loving mercy the balm that can heal.
So to those who follow dreams without fear
Of Spite's curse or Humiliation's jeer,
From credos and dogmas not yet spoken,
To end-of-time oaths which will be broken—
Situation Ethics shouts from the wings
That History mocks such one-sided things
As Standards, unchanging and ultimate,
For Art, Science, Religion, and the State.
But while Hate seeks to deepen the abyss
That blinds all beliefs from Hope's synthesis,
Christ is calling us, setting us free,
To love one another in unity:
The Communion of Faiths lived without strife,
Where Christ is the Resurrection and Life!

Tomes pointed at Pitcher's chest and said mockingly, "You have exposed the blood on your shirt, you idiot! There goes your image!"

Pitcher's face reddened, the look of a man embarrassed and angry. His mouth open but speechless, he stared blankly at Chimes, and then slowly uttered, "It's just pomegranate juice. It must've dripped on me when I ate a piece of the fruit."

"It's blood!" insisted Tomes. "My blood!"

"It's pomegranate juice!" Pitcher fired back.

"My blood!"

"Pomegranate juice!" barked Pitcher, throwing his napkin at Tomes, the rumpled cloth hitting him on the head, then inching its way down, draping his forehead and eyes.

Tomes grabbed the napkin from his head, checked to make sure that no blood from the napkin had stained his skin, and hurled it at Pitcher, Pitcher ducking, causing the napkin to miss its mark. Then Pitcher pushed back his chair, flashed to his feet, jumped onto the chair, and, aiming his finger at Tomes, declared, "This man is a sleazoid! He's a flannelmouth who claims to be a reverend, but who's a washed-up fake who reveres only himself! He's nothing but a shill for the carnival he calls the church!" Pitcher whirled around, and, with both hands on the top of his chair, he leapfrogged over it, landing awkwardly on the floor, his legs almost buckling. Staggering, he regained his balance, turned to Tomes, and retorted, "Zingo! You can't top that sales presentation! I've sold everybody here—you're a counterfeit Christian trying to sell us a counterfeit Jesus! I've exposed your pretense, and your game is over—that's check and mate!" Pitcher turned toward the door—stopped—his face blank.

"Your pompadour has fallen down!" shouted Tomes, his voice mocking and triumphant, "and that means that your wave of success has turned into a tidal wave, crashing down on the bigwig con man of capitalism. Now that I think about it, I would not be surprised if your coiffure is really a cleverly designed and custom-made toupee!"

Pitcher felt his pompadour, now collapsed and in disarray on his head, the matted strands oozing slender threads of grease onto his forehead. With a sequence of quick but jerky motions, Pitcher reached into his back pocket, pulled out a mirror and a comb, and then teased his hair back into a flawless pompadour. He glowered at Tomes, and then said with loud but hollow confidence, "Zingo! You pathetic geezer! You don't have a ghost of a chance of being right! I'm riding out of here on a new wave of success, a wave about to break my way!" Pitcher snorted, darted to the door, and as he was running out of the restaurant, he kept bellowing—"My hair is real! My hair is real! My hair is real!"

Tomes wheeled in his chair, trained his eyes on Chimes, and announced, "He is gone! What a relief! And you, my so-called convert to Jesus, you are not a singer of songs that celebrate Jesus. You are a bad poet, and your rhymes are tuneless noise that blasphemes the very Lord you claim to worship. Your words can help no one. Only my systematic theology can save the day for Jesus, these times where so many are lost, depraved, and who bow down to idols—idols, by the way, that are in your tuneless rhymes, for you speak in pathetically bad poetic images, but images nonetheless, and those images are the idols you worship every time you claim to be singing your annoying rhymes. I doubt that you have any understanding of church doctrine, and I am convinced that you are ignorant of the canon of Scripture, that your grasp of apologetics to defend the faith is nonexistent, that you could not give a proof for the existence of God if your life depended on it, that you cannot name the mental and moral attributes of God, that your knowledge of the Trinity would barely fill a thimble, that you cannot read a single word of Biblical Hebrew or of Biblical Greek, that you have never heard of exegesis let alone would be able to spell it so you could look it up in the dictionary, that you have no intelligible position on baptism, on the meaning of original sin, that you—" Tomes interrupted himself, paused, and then asked, "Should I continue enumerating the infinite list of your theological faults, to detail why I—not you—I am the only person who has the breadth, the depth, and the height of sophistication of theological wisdom to be of any help to Jesus and his ailing and confused church?"

Chimes, her eyes sad but her mouth flexed, ready for action, said,

Whether your rant continues is your choice,
But your blustering can't silence my voice.
You call me a poet, one that is bad,
And, for some reason, my songs make you mad.
May I refer you to the *Book of Acts*,
To Paul's Mars Hill sermon—its crucial facts:
'As even some of your poets have said,'
I quote Paul, straight from Scripture in my head,
And I highlight the word 'poet' for you,
To prove that poets are God's children too,
At least that's what Paul said was true for them,
For Paul preached to include, not to condemn.
I am a poet who makes songs from rhymes,
They may be tuneless, even sound like chimes,
But it's better to sing a tuneless song,
For my noise gives Christ joy—making me strong!
I'm a poet, my soul turned inside out,
Living at that place beyond faith and doubt,
Where the doors of life are riddled with locks,
That yield to one key—that of paradox:
That renewed promise that pain is ending,
That the soul, at its center, is mending,
That Christ nailed between life's opposite poles,
Creates, through pain, wider, embracing wholes,
That pain then transformed into healing song,

Its music drowning out the voice of Wrong,
Consuming Wrong's every sin-glutted sound,
Then music becomes a silence, unbound,
The deadest silence, one Christ consumes too,
Like a poem does when its song is through.
Alas, your eyes tell me your ears are clogged,
Your frowns say your brains are verbiage-logged,
So I'll change the course of my song for you,
And sing you the message that's just and true:
Christ's blood cleanses sin from the foulest heart,
And fills it with love no book can impart,
The love of Jesus, transforming and real,
His loving an embrace, one you can feel,
An embrace, unbreakable and divine,
The Living Presence no words can define!
So come to Christ—Act!—Your life's on the brink,
Confess your sins! Now! There's no time to think!

"Ahhhhhh!" screamed Tomes, his hands cupping his ears. "Ahhhhhh! The pain!" He slapped at his head, then dug his finger-tips into his ears, then, in a snapping motion, he jerked his head from side to side, aiming one ear then the other at the floor, like a swimmer fiercely determined to expel water trapped in both ears. "I have nothing ... to confess! I am ... the greatest ... man ... of ... God ... in Amer ... Amer ... —Ahhhhhh!—The ... hearing ... aids— Pain!—Can!—Not!—Get!—Them!—Out!—God has his book ... nothing to confess ... my books ... my words ... my pages." His voice a moan, Tomes lifted the suitcase onto his lap, squeezed it to his chest, and then pressed his lips to the pure white leather shell containing and protecting the books. "You are ... more real ... than any God ... I cannot see," muttered Tomes, appearing to talk directly to his books. "I am ... your father ... you are ... my ... sons ...

my … creations … always … there—always—unchanging—always—loyal—always!—always!—always!—Ahhhhhh!—The pain!"

Tomes shook in his chair, shockwaves of spasms wracking his body, his hands flailing, then his flat palms pounding the table, his teeth biting into his lower lip, blood oozing down his chin, blood dribbling from his ear canals and earlobes, then spurting from his ears, now a steady stream, staining the back of his white glove and dripping onto his suitcase, its white leather streaked with blood. "Everything pure is bleeding!" he wailed, "I … can … not … swallow … th"—suddenly his body went limp, and he began to slide off his chair.

Rushing to Tomes, the manager caught him under both arms before he fell to the floor. "Most Reverend, we've got to get you to the clinic—just around the corner."

"What did … you … say? … I … see … lips moving … can … not … hear—I—hear—" Tomes collapsed, appearing to be unconscious.

"Hey, you!" shouted the manager, his voice commanding, "Come over here!"

Turning his head, a waiter looked at the manager, and asked, "Me?"

"Yes, you! Help me carry this man to the clinic!"

They lifted Tomes off the chair and hurried him away.

Jesus turned to me, and said, "They left behind Casper's suitcase of tomes."

More curious than concerned, I asked, "What if someone steals his tomes?"

"No one will. But from this moment on, at the clinic, Casper is already learning a key truth."

"And what's that, Lord?"

"He who has ears, let him hear."

Chimes looked at Jesus, shrugged her shoulders, and stayed sitting at her table.

Jesus asked me, "Travis, what did you learn today?"

I struggled to speak, still reeling from what I'd just witnessed.

"Travis, did you hear my question?"

"Yes, Lord."

Jesus sipped some lemonade, and then asked, "Do you have anything to say? Or do you need some time to collect your thoughts?"

"No, Lord," I said, "I don't need time." I drank some lemonade, and gave what I thought was the right answer, "Words matter."

"In what way do words matter?"

"Well ... today, I'd have to say that words were a matter of life or death ... I mean . . .well ... the Bible says that life and death are in the power of the tongue. Today I saw firsthand how that Scripture was lived out."

"Very good, Travis. Would it be important for a counselor to know that life and death are in the power of the tongue?"

"I think so, because today ... the two men and the woman ... I noticed that when they spoke—"

Chimes interrupted me, saying,

Jesus, may I speak with you for a while?
I want to make sure I've sung without guile.

"Yes, Augusta," said Jesus, his tone welcoming, "come over and pull up chair."

Her movements fluid and free, Chimes eased into a chair.

"Augusta, meet Travis."

I said, "Hi," and shook her extended hand.

She smiled at Jesus, and her pale blue eyes widened as she spoke to him,

You have sown into my reborn spirit

Psalm forty-five, verse one, and I hear it,
The words alive and singing in my mind,
Words you, Jesus, through David have designed:
'My tongue's the pen of a ready writer.'
These words, singing though me, make me lighter,
But sometimes, like today, Lord I wonder,
Were those your truths, or my prideful thunder?

Jesus drank some lemonade, and said, "Augusta, today you served Casper and Cosmo, and you glorified me, but there is a truth you, now and then, forget."

What is this truth, Lord, please let me know it,
So that I can be a better poet,
One to glorify you, and not my pride,
Truth making me a much worthier bride.

Jesus offered Chimes his glass. She took the glass, swallowed a mouthful of lemonade, smacked her lips, and then gave back the glass.

"I'll remind you of the truth you need to keep alive as the Holy Spirit is giving you the rhymes flowing from your singing lips," said Jesus. "But before I do, I know that you have a prophetic word for Travis. You see, he cares deeply about people who are suffering, and so he wants to be a counselor, a counselor who knows how to make his words matter to people in pain."

Chimes folded her hands, and bowed her head, as though she was listening, the kind of listening that's awaiting an answer to prayer, and then, seconds later, she opened her eyes and looked into my expectant gaze. As I let her eyes rest on mine, I felt drawn into circles of pale blue, pale blue that now seemed more like sky blue, spacious yet embracing, as though the words she started to speak were coming from a heavenly place, that place where prayers are answered,

> He who judges a person's truthful place,
> Is imprisoned in Self and blind to grace,
> But he who is placed in Christ is set free,
> Grace and truth in unfolding mystery!

Chimes' words moved through me like waves of music, gathering in my throat, resonating as sounds—more like melodic notes—that seemed to be searching for lyrics, lyrics for a song—my song!—a song that I could sing, a poem of healing praise streaming from the heart of Jesus into the hearts of people in the night of their pain, but I couldn't find the lyrics for my song—I had only the music.

"Lord," I said, my voice pleading, "I can't find the words for my song. Scripture says that you are God my Maker, who gives songs in the night, and that I can remember my song in the night, meditate on my song, and in my spirit ponder my song—my night song, the words of counsel to those trapped in the agonies of their night pain, the darkest pain where the dawn of hope can't even be imagined ... Lord, I don't have my words, but I have only the words of the Psalmist, and I offer them as my prayer: 'O sing to the Lord a new song, for he has done wonderful things, his right hand and his holy arm have gained victory for him.' Lord, please give me a new song, a song for a counselor who sings into the nighttime of pain."

Jesus slipped his left arm around my shoulder, holding me close, his embrace safe, gentle, and reassuring. Then he turned to Chimes, his right hand moving toward her face, and then, with a caress of his fingertips that seemed to glide across the length her mouth, words, like the music and lyrics of a song, flowed from his lips, words spoken to her, but words I sensed that were also meant for me:

> Your counseling room is the gracing wind.
> Your thoughts are picture frames etched on the wind.
> Your words are blown kisses pressed on the wind.
> Your passions are wing beats warming the wind.
> And I am the Word no words can rescind,
> For I am the Word who has never sinned:
> Pristine! Indelible! I made the wind!

Sunday

Jesus and I were riding in a taxicab traveling somewhere beyond the outskirts of a large city. Jesus was sitting in the front, in the passenger's seat, and I was in the backseat directly behind the driver. I began to sniff the air swirling through the taxi's rolled down windows, trying to identify the stink wafting its way into my nostrils. "Where are we going?" I asked. "And that stench ... so thick ... so heavy in the air—what is that foul smell?"

"We're near a landfill," said Jesus, "and not all of the trash and garbage have been buried and covered properly."

"Excuse me, driver," I said, "can you do something about that stench?"

"What do you mean?"

"Are you kidding me? I mean the stink in the air—the stink filling the cab—can't you smell it?!"

"Sure thing, mister, I smell it."

"Well?!"

"Well, what?"

"Well—do something about it! I tried to roll up this window but the handle won't budge!"

"I've tried, mister, but I'm not strong enough to turn the handle, so maybe—"

"So maybe I'm not strong enough?! That's what you really mean, isn't it?! You better watch your mouth, or I'll show you how strong ... that does it! Hey, driver, what's your name? And I want the name of your supervisor! I'm going to report you!"

"Cabby, spelled with a 'y'—that's my name, and I own this taxi, mister. I'm my own supervisor. So, you can report me to me ... know what I mean?"

"Well, Cabby, spelled with a 'y,' here's my report. So far your customer service is like the air in this place—it stinks! You're your own supervisor, you say. How convenient for you! Well, Cabby, there's an organization called the *Better Business Bureau!* I'll bet they've a load of complaints about your service! And I wonder what they'd say about the shabby condition of this joke of a taxi— this jalopy! You still have handles for the windows! Haven't you heard of electric windows? And you've got no air conditioning! Your tires are bald! The paint is chipped and peeling, with corroded metal showing through. There are dents and scrapes all over this hunk of junk. This taxi is just another piece of trash that deserves to find its rightful burial plot in this landfill! Know what I mean?! And you think I'm not strong enough to roll up this window! Watch this!"

I drew both my feet up onto the seat, and with both hands grabbed the handle, arched my back, and with all the strength I could summon in my legs drove my full body weight forward while my straining shoulders, arms, and hands pushed as hard they could on the handle. The rusty and faded silver handle, upright and locked in place, was holding fast against all the force I was exerting. With my back and leg muscles quivering and my arms and shoulders pinched with spasms, I pushed myself backward, sagging against my seat, too weak to make another attempt at turning the handle.

"Not strong enough to turn the handle, mister?" asked Cabby. "I wouldn't worry about it too much. Maybe the windows are meant to be broken ... for a reason we can't figure out. Know what I mean?"

"My name is not 'mister,' Cabby. My name is Travis, spelled just like it sounds! Know what I mean?!"

The smug certainty in Cabby's words caused my fists to tighten, and I refused to acknowledge to him any failure of strength on my part. I sat there, my jaw clenched, my eyes fixed on the back of his head. I grinned as I pictured myself grabbing his greasy, hole-ridden yellow taxicab hat and flinging it out of the window and into the foul-smelling air.

"No, it wasn't that I'm not strong enough, Cabby. You're wrong about that. The issue is your taxi. It's a clunker. Parts of it are so caked with rust—they're frozen in place! Nobody would be strong enough to move one of these handles, and you'd need a blowtorch to cut through the fused pieces of metal. A cab with windows that don't work, a cab without air conditioning, a cab with parts that haven't been properly serviced, lubricated, and where necessary, replaced, well, these undeniable facts make me want to throw up, and never want to ride with you again. You should keep your cab in top shape! You must realize that giving you a tip is out of the question—no! Wait! On second thought: you should pay me to ride with you! Know what I mean?!"

"I wish I could help you, Travis, I really do. Trust me, I know you're real teed off! And sure thing, you're right, something's wrong with the handles, no doubt about that. Maybe the threads are stripped and rusted, it's like they're welded together. I really don't know why the windows don't work. They just quit on me. Things are like that sometimes: they just quit on you, and you can't figure out why ... you've got to accept that ... know what I mean?"

"Yes—I—do," I said, coughing out the words, the stench making me feel sick in my stomach.

"Hey, Travis, you shouldn't blame me for riding with broken windows. The guy sitting next to me is the one who ordered my cab. He called me—asked for me by name. I told him the windows didn't work, that they'd quit on me. But he said he liked broken windows, that broken windows let in air, and he liked the feel of the open air blowing on his face while he was riding. So, I'm not the one you should be teed off at, Travis." Cabby pointed at Jesus. "He's the one who's putting you through this, teeing you off—not me! Check it out: Ask him if what I'm saying is the truth."

Jesus! ... he wanted this stench to fill the cab, I thought. *He wanted to feel the air filled with stench blowing on his face ... he wanted me to feel queasy ... feel a growing sense of disgust ... maybe he's lost it ... gone crazy?!* I stared at the back of Jesus' head, somehow believing that if the force of my stare could pierce his skull I could get inside his mind and see his motives for exposing me to this stench. Suddenly my eyes became hot and watery ... couldn't hold my stare.

"Why are you doing this to me?" I asked Jesus.

"The wind blows where it wishes and you hear the sound of it, but do not know where it comes from or where it is going," Jesus replied.

"Yes," I retorted, "but just because you quote from *John's Gospel,* that doesn't mean that your response is a direct answer to my question."

"There are many times when an indirect answer is a counselor's wisest answer."

"A counselor's wisest answer" echoed inside my skull, the sound loud, thick, and heavy. I felt judged by that bludgeoning echo: I was a fool in the way I unleashed my anger on Cabby, and the weight of Jesus saying "a counselor's wisest answer" was surely his way to show me how stupid I was, and that I was a long way from becoming called to be a counselor. I wanted to get even, to pay back Jesus by judging him—a judgment for a judgment! Yes!

I struggled to form sentences, but I couldn't collect my words, words jumbled and jangled as they bounced off the boney walls inside my head. I needed time to shape and then rehearse a perfectly logical judging response, and then, after memorizing my response, unload on Jesus—get even! I slowly cleared my throat, and then let out a long, husky yawn. I started smacking my lips, as my way to announce that I'd completed my yawn, and then I noticed that the smacking sound was what I was hearing, that "a counselor's wisest answer" was gone from inside my skull.

Even though Jesus' words were no longer judging me, I still wanted to judge him, to pay him back. So, I announced triumphantly, "The stench you like blowing on you is the same stench that's starting to suffocate me. And the Scripture you quoted about the wind blowing where it wishes, well, there's no mention of the wind carrying stench from wherever it's coming from and to wherever it's going! If I gagged to death on this stench, I wonder if that would even matter to you! Drive on, Cabby! Faster, Cabby, faster! How much farther do we have to go in this heap of junk?!"

The taxi chugged up a steep rise in the road, and when the cab edged over the top of the road, I saw a wide space stretched out before us, and in the middle of that expanse stood the landfill. We drove toward the landfill, and as we drew nearer, the sizes and contours of mounds of garbage and clumps of trash began to take shape.

The taxi stopped—Cabby let the engine idle. Through my windowless door I saw at least thirty rows of tiered seats arranged in a semi-circle, the seats facing a man squatting on a mound of garbage, the first row of seats eight to ten feet from the man. "What are those seats doing there?" I asked Jesus. "They don't look like trash that someone dumped here … they look like bleachers … the kind of setup used to watch a sporting event."

Jesus and Cabby appeared to be observing what I was observing. Neither one of them responded to my words.

Confused, I searched for words to frame another question but the stench from the landfill was like a piece of rancid meat lodged in my throat. I cupped both my hands and used them as cover over my nose and mouth, and as I was breathing in and smelling the familiar odor issuing from my own skin, my own odor seemed to become like teeth that chewed through the stench, chopping it into tiny parts, the parts seeming to slide off my hands and scatter into the drifting air, taking most of the stench with them.

With the stench in my throat noticeable but very much weakened, I caught sight of a second man. He was pacing to-and-fro, clutching under his left arm what appeared to be a large notebook while his right hand flailed about, inches from the squatting man's head. The second man, his teeth bared as his lips moved rapidly, seemed to be shouting at the first man, but I heard only spurts of noises barking from his agitated mouth.

Cabby moved the taxi forward until the faces of the men were clearly visible, and then the taxi stopped, the engine running. The squatting man stood up. The second man turned his head toward the taxi, dropped his arms to his sides, and then became quiet and still.

Jesus opened his door and eased out of the taxi. I looked to him for direction. He beckoned to me, and so I joined him. As we stood there, nearly shoulder-to-shoulder, I surveyed the situation, trying to figure out what purpose Jesus might have in bringing me to a dumping ground.

Both men seemed to be scanning us, as though they were looking for those unique signs that confirm the identity of a person for whom you've been given a vague description but whom you've never met.

Without asking us to pay our fare, Cabby turned the taxi around and sped away. "Good move! At least you've got a shred of honesty! You should've never been hired!" I shouted. "Know what I mean?!"

"I know what you mean, Travis," said Jesus. Then he draped one arm around my shoulder, and with a sweeping gesture of his other arm, asked, "Well, Travis, what do you think of it?"

"Think of ... it!" I replied, my voice halting, "think of ... what—a landfill threatening to blanket me with stench! ... that makes me want to throw up! ... a bunch of bleachers ... in the midst of garbage ... and trash ... that—"

"Yes, Travis, all off that—and more! Think bigger, put together all you see, hear, feel, and smell. Use your imagination! Be like a counselor—a man with a vision!"

I shrugged my shoulders, and shaking my head, admitted in defeat, "I'm completely lost ... " I stood there, unable to think of another word to say, and I was feeling increasingly separated from Jesus by a long and thickening silence.

"This is a specially constructed theater!" said Jesus, his voice excited, filled with daring. "This is the theater that must be here, on this landfill, the theater that must reek of decay, the only kind of theater that will suffice for the performance you're going to witness! And what you're about to witness is a one-man show performed by an actor who also pieced together the script, and this is the dress rehearsal of a play, before the play opens tomorrow. Come on, Travis, let's meet the actor and the director."

We walked over to the two men. One man stepped forward, his index finger in his left ear, seeming to probe at something, his outstretched right arm and open palm an invitation to shake his hand. "Hello," he said, "I'm Janus Tribes, the writer and the actor of the one-man show that you'll be seeing. It's a pleasure to meet you—but wait!" Tribes withdrew his hand. "I need to be upfront with you. Janus Tribes is my stage name. The name on my birth certificate is Ichabod Wanes. Ichabod means 'fading glory,' and the public would never want to see someone perform whose name is 'fading glory'—a 'fading glory' that wanes! Nothing could be worse!"

"I can see why you'd want to change your name," I remarked, "it's—"

"But my performances—they're glorious! The best art critics and the most serious reviewers have lavished me with praise. My acting is the very opposite of 'fading glory' and of 'waning!' So, I changed my name to Janus Tribes. Janus is a deity from Roman mythology, and he is shown with two faces: one looking forward and one looking backward. As an actor I have to look backward into myself, to be in touch with and draw on the real me while at the same time I have to be looking forward into the character I'm playing, to ensure that I am being real in the role I'm playing out. Tribes is a name I chose to let people know that I can relate to any and all people in the human race, can empathize with any and all 'tribes,' so to speak."

Tribes folded his hands and let them rest on his chest, sighed, and said, "Later, when I became an adult, I legally changed my name to Janus Tribes. And then I disowned my parents ... I mean ... what kind of parents name their child 'fading glory' and then have the unmitigated gall to claim that they love that child? For years they refused to explain to me why they chose to name me Ichabod, refused to show any compassion for the years of mockery and bullying I took because of cruel jerks calling me 'Icky.' Don't misunderstand me, I know that I'm not a psychologist, but my guess is that my parents and their parents, and generations of parents far, far back into time, got labeled the 'Wanes' family because people saw that everything the Wanes family attempted to accomplish in their lives waned, faded into failure or sank into meaninglessness. And so the label 'Wanes' stuck because they were too weak to deal with their failures on their own, stuck all the way through the generations until the day I was born. So they believed that their only way out from carrying generations of failure was to dump all their psychological baggage on me, believing they could get free of the stigma of being people who fade out, who wane, who sink into voids where their lives are nothing, lives that don't matter to anyone. I was their ... uh ... there's a term for it—"

"Scapegoat?" asked Jesus.

"Yes!" said Tribes, his voice triumphant. "That's right! Scapegoat! But I escaped from being their scapegoat! One day, I got fed up being their scapegoat, fed up to the point of hating them for what they did to me. I decided to do something about it— something for me! I erased them from my life as fast as I erased the name Ichabod from all my memories. I haven't seen them ... even refused to see them ... for decades. Good riddance to their revolting presence! They made me go through a living hell, and they can both go straight to hell—and burn there! ... oh! ... wow! ... sorry! ... so sorry about the long soliloquy ... the actor in me ... you know ... never rests ... don't know where all that came from ... just ... don't ... know."

His eyebrows raised, his cheeks tinged with red, Tribes rubbed at the tip of his nose, and then gingerly extended his open hand.

Jesus shook Tribes' hand, and asked, "Did you write the play?"

"Yes," replied Tribes, "and there's nothing 'icky' about my creativity! I have a gift for creative writing—my words are glorious! You'll see!"

"So they are your words—no one else's?!" asked Jesus, his tone incisive.

"Well ... strictly speaking ... no," said Tribes, his fingers brushing at his left ear, "they're not my words. I selected direct quotations from the *Book of Job*, and then I arranged them in a way that I believe will reveal deeper meanings from *Job*, meanings that will inform the lives of men and women in our post-modern world. As

I am acting the agonizing life of Job, you will hear to the letter but not in exactly the same order the words Job speaks in the Bible. I believe in God, and I want my acting to reveal the truth of Scripture. Do you understand my point, understand where I'm going?"

"I think so," said Jesus, "but I do have one more question."

"Fire away, I'm all ears, and I have nothing to hide."

"Are you saying that you'll be revealing the true meaning of God's word by rearranging the words of Job as they originally are ordered in Scripture?"

"Yes, I do. The truth of Scripture is not in how the words were originally ordered. The truth for post-modern men and women is in keeping the words as they were originally written, but rearranging the order of the words. That way, Job's story can be reshaped and reordered to match each and every story of each and every man and woman. That way, Job can remain universal regardless of whatever changes occur in time, place, and situations. That's why I have titled my play *Job: A Man For All Reasons*. Now, are you really sure you see where I'm going with all of this?"

"Yes, I know exactly where you are going."

"Great! I sense that you're a man who knows his own truth."

"I am."

"Super! Now I'm convinced that you'll enjoy the play!"

Tribes offered me his hand. As my fingers closed around Tribes' hand I felt something stinging and slimy on my palm. I jerked my hand away from his, and, staring and pointing at the bloody-white paste smeared on my palm, said in a tense voice, "What's this ... this nasty gunk?!"

His left index finger gingerly moving in and out of his ear, Tribes laughed, and said gleefully, "Gotcha! That's actor's make-up! I use it to convince the audience that what they're seeing is real bloody pus oozing from my body—from Job's body! All you had to do is feel it and see it on your hand, and it made you scared, made your stomach churn a bit, and made you a little bit angry. Am I right? ... oh ... you? ... oh ... I forgot to ask: What's your name?"

Tribes removed his index finger from his ear, glanced at it, and turned his head away from me, looking at the other man, as though he was waiting for the man to deliver a cue. There was a moment when the entire left side of Tribes' face was caught in direct sunlight, and I glimpsed the full view of his ear, and from inside his ear a tiny ray of light flashed out. I rubbed my eyes, and thought, *What was that? Is there something in his ear? Is the stench playing tricks on my mind?*

Tribes turned back to me, and said, "I'm sorry ... bad manners ... distracted for a second. Now, what's your name?"

"Travis," I replied. Feeling my hands clench into tight fists, I quickly tried to hide them, burying them inside the front pockets of my blue jeans.

Glancing at my hands bulging in my front pockets, the other man grinned and nodded his head. The man wore around his neck a gold chain, the chain supporting a rectangular-shaped gold object which seemed on prominent display near the center of his chest. The man nodded his head, and announced, "Welcome to *Universal Players Theater*. I am Hector Mapps, the director of this production. By the way, Travis, I like the way you improvised with your hands, the way you used them to put on display one emotion while, at the same time, using them to conceal a different emotion. Very impressive! Have you ever considered becoming an actor?"

"No," I remarked, "at least ... not really ... well ... no. Until this moment, I've never been asked that. Do you really think I have talent?"

Mapps cradled the gold object in the fingers and palm of his right hand. "Yes, I do. Of course, you would need to work at the craft of acting, and you would have to be under the tutelage of a director with my kind of commercial and artistic success. Perhaps we can talk later, after the performance."

Looking at Jesus, I said, "Well ... I suppose ... Okay. Maybe. I guess so."

Jesus appeared to be focused on Mapps.

Fingering the gold chain on each side of the gold object, Mapps turned to Jesus, and said in a commanding voice, "I want to apologize for Janus' bad manners ... for not asking you what your name is. At times Janus can be forgetful. You know how it is with artists ... lost in their own worlds ... aware of nobody but themselves. So, please, may I know your name?"

"You may call me 'Sunday,'" said Jesus.

"Sunday," said Mapps, his tone curious. "Don't you have a first name?"

"Sunday will do."

"Sunday ... strange ... when I hear you say your name, the sound of it, and even the way you pronounce it ... it makes me think of church—but don't get me wrong, I don't believe in any of that church stuff, but I bet you get a lot of that."

"A lot of what?"

"You know ... people you meet ... when they hear your name ... telling you that your name—Sunday—reminds them of church."

"Yes, I do, as you say, get a lot of that."

"Hey, wait a minute! I just remembered something: Around a hundred years ago, in America, there was a famous preacher named Billy Sunday. Any relation?"

"Yes."

"Related in what way?"

"Through blood."

"I knew it! I have a gift for reading people! That's why I'm such a good director! You know, I remember seeing photos of Billy

Sunday, remember being struck by the features so compelling in Billy Sunday's face—a consummate actor's face if ever there was one! If he were alive today, I would easily become a multi-billionaire by directing him to heights of stardom that even he wouldn't be able to imagine! Don't get me wrong: being filthy rich is not my primary goal as a director, but even great artists need—"

"Speaking of the features of a person's face," interrupted Jesus, his words like the stroke of a carving knife, "Travis and I will be sitting in the first row of bleachers. We want to see clearly Janus' face as he is acting the part of Job, as well as be able to see your face as you're directing. We also may be halting the action, at times, to ask questions or to make our own comments on what's happening."

Mapps held out his hands, showing both palms, opened his mouth, took a deep breath, and then deftly pressed both his palms over the gold object, as if he was protecting it from something before he'd risk speaking. "That's not acceptable, Sunday!" snarled Mapps. "That will disturb the integrity of the action and destroy the whole meaning of the play. A real audience is not allowed to criticize the ongoing acting and directing of the play, why should you?"

"Did you receive and read the memo that was sent to you?" asked Jesus. "I have with me a copy of the memo, in case you've forgotten what's in it."

His nostrils flared, Mapps clutched the gold object, drew his lower lip between his teeth, and then let out a choppy sigh. "Yes… I … read it," his voice prickly.

Jesus smiled, looked into Mapps' eyes, and said, "Then you know that the memo comes from the person making this entire project possible. He is providing the funding to build the props, to purchase materials for the tiered seating, to obtain the permits to use the landfill—and much more! The memo from that person makes it clear that Travis and I are to be allowed to participate in the play in any way that we think will make the play what it should be by opening night, or else—"

"I know! I know!" said Mapps, his voice edgy, "or else the person will pull the plug on the entire project. All right, Sunday. You and Travis take any seat you wish, and Janus and I will pick up the play at the place where we were rehearsing when you arrived in the taxi and broke our flow."

Mapps and Tribes walked behind a row of large trash bags stacked one on top of the other, the bags forming a ragged and concavely-shaped wall at least ten feet high, the wall a few feet behind the low mound of garbage where Tribes was to sit while he was performing. Torn rugs, dirty carpets, and maggot-ridden blankets were draped over the wall. Rotting garbage and carcasses of decomposing cats, dogs, and rats, were strewn in haphazard clusters on the dirt, along with bleached skeletons of large and small birds, while dung beetles and cockroaches scurried from shadows cast by all that was dead, wasted, diseased, castoff, littered, damaged, ruined, destroyed, or decaying.

A bull snake slithered across the top of the wall, pausing to raise its large head, its flicking tongue tasting the air for prey. Then the snake began to move with what seemed to be calculated and focused speed as it glided away from us, disappearing behind the wall, and for an instant I was struck by how sun and earth appeared to converge in the yellow and brown markings that covered the body of the snake.

Jesus and I took our seats in the front row of the bleachers. In the congesting stench we waited for the play to begin. I moved closer to Jesus, our shoulders touching. I tilted my head toward his shoulder, and took a deep breath. A light-scented bouquet, that renewing smell of the first scent of spring, seemed to emanate from him and flow into my nostrils. The congesting stench began to dissolve.

Mapps made his entrance, his fingers and thumb framing the rectangular-shaped gold object.

"What is that thing hanging around your neck?" I asked, my voice grating. "You keep touching it, almost caressing it! It's distracting!"

Mapps shook his head. "I'm very disappointed in you, Travis! You're not the potential star actor I thought you might be! This is a specially designed smart phone I'm wearing proudly around my neck. It's in a solid gold case. My brother gave it to me as a combination tribute and birthday present. And by the way, my brother, Miles Mapps, has studied all the great plays, actors, and directors in history. So Miles is an expert in recognizing directorial talent. Let me read the engraving on the back of the case. It's in capital letters, so I'm surprised that you can't read it from where you're sitting. The words were written by the immortal Shakespeare, and they say:

IN THY FACE
I SEE
THE MAP
OF HONOR,
TRUTH,
AND LOYALTY

His voice quavering, Mapps said, "Each time I read these words … each … every … time … excuse my emotion … I'm filled with humility and gratitude. Did you notice how brilliant Miles was in his choice of Shakespeare's wording? The word 'MAP' is a play on my last name Mapps! Miles and I come from a history of cartographers—mapmakers!—and that's how centuries ago our family got the surname Mapps. No one could make, or ever has made, maps the way we've made them for countless generations! So, when I or anyone else sees the word 'MAP' on the gold case, it's both a reminder of the truth that the director is the only loyal map—the only direction!—for the actors to follow, and, at the same time, in my face—the face of Hector Mapps!—the actors can see the map of honor, truth, and loyalty—the only living map to follow: that it is my face that will make the actors face the characters they're playing, and in facing their characters through seeing my face, they can bring honor, truth, and loyalty to the play—and embody art in its highest expression!"

Mapps' words set off a loud buzzing in my ears, the buzzing the only sound I could hear. I felt dizzy. *I'm going to faint,* I thought. I grabbed the sides of my seat and put my head between my knees. I sucked at the air, but gusts of stench grabbed at my mouth, trying to force their way into my throat. I stood up, wobbled, and looked at Jesus. He was leaning forward, his elbows on his knees, his face cradled by both his hands, his eyes appearing to focus on the horizon. I turned to face Jesus, dropped to my knees, clutched both his hands, drew them to my face, pressing his open palms over my nose and mouth and breathing the air inside the envelope made by his hands. My ears popped—I could hear!

"Travis, you're all right!" said Jesus, his tone reassuring. "Take another breath—a deep one!"

As I breathed deeply, my nose and mouth soft against his skin, Jesus slowly withdrew his hands, placed them under my elbows, the uplifting push of his hands nudging me to stand up. Jesus took my hand and gently guided me back to my seat.

"Hector," said Jesus, "May I ask you a question?"

"Another one, Sunday! You've got a bunch of them, don't you? Go ahead—ask! But you're delaying seeing the play!"

"Have you ever lost your direction in life?"

"Never, Sunday, never!

"What about Miles?"

"My brother?"

"Yes, your brother. Has Miles ever been in a place where he had no direction in his life, a time where he was lost but couldn't face it?"

"What does that have to do with the play you're about to see?"

"Remember the memo, Hector?"

Mapps folded his arms, turned his back on Jesus, and walked toward the wall, kicking at dirt and trash. Mapps spun around and glared at Jesus. "Oh, you can bet your life on it, Sunday! I remember the memo! When are you going to stop using the memo to blackmail me to talk?!"

"Well, Hector, are you going to—"

"Okay! Okay! Okay! Miles once owned a business with global reach. He was the president and chairman of *Miles of Wine*, a company which took people on guided tours of all the great vineyards and wineries in the world. In his head he carried pictures of every vineyard and winery on the planet. He could've been blindfolded and still he could've guided people through any vineyard and winery of their choosing. With the maps he'd memorized, he was a true example of the Mapps family tradition. He always knew where he was going. And Miles was renowned as the greatest living connoisseur and auctioneer of wine. He was constantly in demand around the world, giving lectures on every aspect of wine."

"Wow! What a success story," I said, "but how did Miles lose his direction?"

"Miles lost his way in stages," replied Mapps, his voice unsteady.

"In stages?"

"Yes, Travis, in stages so small that no one saw what was going to happen until it was too late."

"When you say 'too late,' what do you mean by that?"

"Miles was so consumed by the wine business that he wasn't aware of how much wine he was drinking every day. He became an alcoholic, so drunk every day that over time he couldn't recall the names of any vineyard or winery, and no matter how hard he struggled, he could no longer picture in his head the maps of any of them, so—"

Interrupting, I said, "That is so sad, you must have—"

"So, one day, while Miles was driving, he passed out, veering from his lane and slamming his car into a crowd of pedestrians crossing the street, injuring many people, six of them with serious and permanent damage to their bodies, and killing one of them. The court ordered him into a prison hospital for treatment for alcoholism and to be evaluated for a wide range of mental disorders. And while—"

"I read that chronic alcoholism can cause a variety of severe mental disorders, such as—"

"Travis, please, let me tell the story! As I was saying, while Miles was in extended treatment, he was sued by the people he'd hit, lost all his money, lost his business, and became bankrupt. Physical examinations, blood tests, and scans revealed advanced cirrhosis of his liver. The doctors told him that if he detoxed, quit drinking immediately and followed a strict diet, he might live for years—they wouldn't give us a number."

"Did he follow the doctors' advice?" I asked.

"Yes and no," said Mapps. "And let me make clear: I was a loyal brother, visiting him when I could, always telling him that he could start over, and, in time, make a new map for his life! That's what a true Mapps would do!"

"I still don't understand … is there more to the story?"

"Yes, but to tell the rest of the story … is too complicated a story to tell. Let's just say that it didn't turn out for the best."

"It's not that the story is too complicated to tell! It's that what happened next is actually a director's nightmare. Right, Hector?" said Jesus, his words incisive and pressing.

"You don't know what happened next, Sunday! You weren't there on that fateful day when Miles was to be discharged!"

"That sounds like a declaration of fact," said Jesus, "that you're certain that I wasn't there!"

"You're not talking crazy, are you, Sunday ... you can't be saying that you were there, are you?!"

"I am saying that a reverend was there, someone who knows me, and someone who's spent time with you, and the reverend says he saw and heard—"

"Denton Foils! That miserable excuse for a reverend! After years of being confined to the prison hospital, Miles was finally to be discharged and put on parole, and on that day, Foils asked if he could pray for me and Miles before Miles left the hospital. I'll bet that phony cleric threw out his vow of confidentiality, watched and listened at the sliding door of Miles' room, and then blabbed everything to you, Sunday. I'll bet my smart phone that it was that hypocrite Foils who's been spreading vicious rumors about me! He's the reverend who knows you, Sunday! Right?!"

"Yes, he knows me."

"And I'll bet that you're in his church!"

"I am."

"So I'm right, Sunday, you know everything that went on that day."

"I know."

"If you know, then you can't blame me for what happened! Miles wanted it to happen! He'd just given me my gold-plated and engraved smart phone, the phone that celebrated my birthday and would be a sign of my position as the greatest living director. And I'd brought two small bottles of Miles' favorite *Cabernet Sauvignon*.

He wanted one last drink as his way to mark from that moment forward that he'd be sober for the rest of his life. You see, we're identical twins, and to make the whole celebration especially fun, I reminded him of the time we celebrated our twenty-first birthdays by each one of us guzzling in one go a whole bottle of wine, I—"

"Hold it!—just for a minute!" I interrupted. "A whole bottle of wine—each?! Surely you can't mean—"

"Cut! Travis, that's a director's command for 'Stop and shut up!' Now, I'll continue. I took the two bottles from my briefcase, and told him that it would be great for the Mapps brothers to start a new map together, as we did when we became adults at twenty-one, by each one of us guzzling a bottle of wine, and the first one draining his bottle would win the right to pick the restaurant we eat at when we leave the hospital. I popped the corks, handed Miles a bottle, clicked my bottle against his, toasted him, and celebrated his birthday and the new direction for his life, a direction that he could start mapping out the second he set foot outside the prison hospital. We happily poured the smooth red wine down our gullets, and Miles emptied his bottle first, declaring that he was still first at drinking even though I'd been born first! Then he lurched forward, staggered a few steps, dropped his bottle, grabbed his head, and shrieked 'My head's exploding!' Blood the color of the cabernet gushed from his ears, eyes, and nose. He collapsed to his knees, reached for me, his fingers clawing at the air, and then slumped to the floor."

"When Miles reached for you, did you take hold of his hands ... to ease his fall ... to the floor?"

His brow clenched into a frown, Mapps ignored my question. "Doctors and nurses rushed into the room, trying hard to revive him, but he was pronounced dead at the scene. I caught sight of Foils shrinking from the sliding door and then scurrying away. I never saw that fraud of a minister again. Why didn't he come into the room? Where were his prayers when Miles really needed them?"

"Did you ever think that you needed any prayer?" asked Jesus.

"No, Sunday, why would I have needed prayer? There was nothing wrong with me! Miles was the one in trouble! Besides, I told you: I don't believe in any of that church stuff!"

"But, Hector, you knew Miles was an alcoholic, and yet you talked him into drinking a whole bottle of wine in seconds, enough wine to kill him. Where was your compassion for him in his pain? And what were you thinking when you decided to convince him to do that?"

"Sunday, how do you know that it was the wine that killed him? The autopsy report stated that the alcohol content and the speed of consumption of the wine very likely killed him—but the coroner would not state with absolute certainty that the wine killed Miles! Besides, Miles knew more about wine than any other man on the planet. He must've been convinced that his body could absorb that much wine—and live!"

"I didn't know that a coroner could know anything with 'absolute certainty!'" said Jesus. "But since you claimed that the coroner was not absolutely certain about—"

"Look, Sunday, you didn't read the autopsy report, and yet you talk as though you yourself are a wine connoisseur or a medical doctor who knows a lot about which wine and how much wine can kill a man. Why don't you face it, Sunday, when it comes to wine, you're a lost cause!"

"Am I lost when I say to you that I know that Miles used that bottle of wine to commit suicide, and that you helped him kill himself?!"

Mapps grabbed his smart phone with both hands, angled it so that he could see its face, and began to tap different spots on its face, mumbling all the while. "That's an outrageous lie, Sunday!

No! Worse! That's slander! I can sue you for defaming my character! I have witnesses! You've damaged my reputation! My lawyers
will take you for all you're worth!"

Mapps stared at his smart phone, his brow glazed with sweat,
his eyes expectant, as if his phone was going to inform him how to
combat Jesus' story.

"You have no basis to claim that Miles committed suicide!"
shouted Mapps, "and you couldn't have gotten that bit of malicious
gossip from Foils. There's no way anyone could've heard us!"

"How can you be so sure?"

"Because there was a moment—just before we drank the wine—
that we put on some loud music, hugged one another, our faces
cheek-to-cheek, and we began—very slowly—to turn in circles, a
kind of dance to celebrate Miles' ending his treatment and court-
ordered confinement. Then Miles spoke in a low whisper, his lips
next to my ear, his words barely audible to me, and I whispered
back, speaking in the same low whisper. Even if Foils was listening at the sliding door, he couldn't have heard a word. What was
said was a secret between Miles and me, a secret that he took to
his grave, and I'll take to mine!"

"No, Hector, you've missed something of utmost importance,
something neither you nor Miles ever considered."

"You don't say, and what's that, Sunday?"

"Foils is not only a senior pastor of a church. He also has a ministry to the deaf. The deaf are dear to his heart, because his parents
were deaf, and Denton promised his parents and vowed to God
that he would minister to the deaf as long as he lives. And because
his parents were deaf, Denton at an early age learned to read lips.
He is so adept at it that the F.B.I. has called him in on difficult cases, to look through telescopes and read the lips of suspected criminals, and his expert testimony has led to many convictions over
the years. That day, when you and Miles thought no one could

possibly hear you, Denton was reading your lips. He knows what the two of you really planned to happen that day, and so do I."

"Foils! That money-grubbing so-called man of the cloth! He's pure slime, and I've no doubt that he's told you everything he heard, but I don't believe he knows anything about my secret talk with Miles! You're just trying to bait me! Or Foils is lying through his capped teeth! I demand proof that you know what Miles and I said, or shut up once and for all about this, and let us get on with the play!"

"Which play," asked Jesus, "the play about Job or the play about you and Miles, the one you're trying so hard to stage and direct now?!"

My heart pounding, I blurted, "King Solomon says in *Proverbs:* 'The eyes of the Lord are in every place, watching the evil and the good.'"

"What lord?!" shouted Mapps. "That's hogwash! Besides, who asked you for your opinion about anything?"

"You asked for proof," I said, "and I'm giving you the highest proof: that whatever happened between you and Miles, God was reading your lips and hearing every word. God is everywhere and he knows everything, and King David made that clear when he wrote: 'Even before there is a word on my tongue, behold, O Lord, you know it all. Where can I go from your Spirit? Or where can I flee from your presence?'"

"There!—Is!—No!—God!" boomed Mapps. "Of course, if you're telling me that Foils is God—or that you have direct access to the voice of God!—then you need to be rushed to a psychiatrist, be locked in a nut house, and be put on heavy medication for your delusions!"

"No, Foils is not God," I said, "and neither am I. I was only quoting the Bible, proving to you—"

"Hey, wait a second, Travis! Do you know Foils?" asked Mapps.

"No, I don't."

"Have you ever been in his church?"

"No, I haven't."

"Then your opinion is a fairytale. And your slur on my character is worse than Sunday's! At least Foils knows Sunday, talked to him, and Sunday has been in Foils' church!"

"But Travis is facing in the right direction, Hector," said Jesus. "Your lips and Miles' lips were read."

"I want the proof!" demanded Mapps. "The text! That's my kind of proof, the only proof a director can believe in! Show me the text of this pathetic play you're conjuring up, for some reason trying to attack my character! The text! That's the only proof that's sacred to me! Show me the text, Sunday! Or give up your feeble attempt at being a director of the theater of the absurd!"

"I won't show you the text, Hector," said Jesus. "I'll tell it to you. Miles whispered in your ear that he couldn't picture in his mind a single map of any of the vineyards and wineries he could at one time recall at will. And the best neurologists in the world told him that the damage done to his brain from the daily assaults of alcohol was irreparable. And so, for the first and only time in the history of his family, a Mapp would not be able to make a new map for his life. He didn't want to bring shame on the Mapps family and their centuries-long tradition of each Mapp always being able to make a new map for his life—no matter how despairing his condition. Miles knew that if he left the hospital, then he would live long enough for everyone to see that he could no longer make a map for his life."

"You're impressive, Sunday!" snapped Mapps. "I don't know what you do for a living, but you should quit your job and start reading palms for a living. You'd fit right in with those charlatans!"

"Hector, you agreed with Miles: that he would bring shame on the family that for generations had a perfect record in making maps for their own lives. You suggested that Miles could avoid all shame, not lose face, and continue to project the public image of having a new direction, but in order to accomplish this, he would have to die in the prison hospital—drop dead on the floor!—just before leaving. That way, no one outside the hospital would ever see him fail to make a new map."

"No, I was wrong, Sunday! Predicting a person's future through reading Tarot cards—that's where your talent lies!"

"You told Miles that many characters in plays commit suicide to solve their personal dilemmas, and that you've brilliantly directed these characters so that their suicides were seen as noble and selfless acts. Miles started to shake, squeezed you tighter, and asked if there was another way. You showed no compassion for your brother, but you went on to offer to direct him through the suicide, as if he were a character in one of your plays. His face went blank, his confused eyes fixed on the floor. Then you told him that if he committed suicide by overdosing on his favorite wine, he would be making a kind of new map on his own terms, a map no one could ever know about—except you, Hector." Jesus paused, seeming to wait for Mapps to respond.

Mapps glared at Jesus, and then pinched shut both his nostrils, and retorted, "The stench in this place is getting thicker. I can't catch my breath!" Mapps darted out of sight, somewhere behind the wall of trash, and then came back carrying a small silver canister. "It's an oxygen tank," he announced. He placed the mask over his nose and mouth and took a few breaths. "As the director of the play, I need to be free of the stench in this place, need clean and fresh air to keep a clear head, so I can be the map for all to follow—but no one else is allowed any oxygen, because that would alter the mood created by the stench, and playgoers need the stench to identify with the pain Job is experiencing. If those who are watching the play don't feel compassion for Job, then the play will be a flop!"

Mapps scanned Jesus from head to toe and back again, and said in a challenging tone, "Is that it, Sunday, the climax of your trumped-up excuse for a play?"

"No," said Jesus, "there's more to the story. Miles wavered, unable to decide what to do. But when you reminded him of the time you both celebrated your birthdays by guzzling an entire bottle of wine, and then related that ritual to how it confirmed your becoming adults together—Miles said it was that very special memory that helped move him closer to choosing the final map on his own terms, and—"

"Tea leaves, Sunday!" cried Mapps. "Reading tea leaves! That's the ticket for your future!"

"And then you directed his face to what you were proudly displaying in your hands, the smart phone he'd given you, and you asked him to read the inscription engraved on the gold cover. He read the words of Shakespeare, and then said to you that your face exemplified Shakespeare's words, that your face was Miles' map of honor, truth, and loyalty. It was then that he told you that he was ready to follow his final map—to commit suicide. You handed him a bottle of his favorite wine, he drank it all quickly and urgently, and within seconds what you'd scripted and directed was over—Miles had dropped dead—the Mapps' reputation forever untarnished!"

Mapps sank to the ground. Sitting on the mound of garbage where Tribes was to act the part of Job, Mapps, his face a mask of sweat, pressed the oxygen mask over his nose and mouth and sucked in large gulps of air. Then Mapps removed the mask, and shouted triumphantly, "Ha! I don't believe in God, but I agree with

Job when he said that he is guiltless and that he does not take notice of himself."

Twitches riddled Mapps' eyes, and he gasped for air, then quickly buried his face in the mask, taking rapid breaths. He rolled his body onto his side, his left forearm supporting his weight and securing the oxygen mask while with his right hand he tilted his smart phone toward his face, seeming to search for something on the face of his phone. He mumbled, the sounds from his slack mouth like whimpers aimed at the face of the phone. He turned the phone over and leered at its gold-plated back, and then let it slide from his hand. Mapps' face appeared pale—almost bloodless— as he haltingly managed to lug himself to his feet.

Mapps glanced at his smart phone, sighed, and stumbled his way to the wall of trash. Leaning against the wall, his back toward us, he paused, his head drooping, and then he stepped behind the wall, as though the drooping weight of his head dragged him forward.

"The Lord gave and the Lord has taken away!" cried Tribes as he made his entrance from behind the wall of trash. "Blessed be the name of the Lord!" Tribes surveyed each one of our faces. "You all look disappointed. Now please look at me, and see if I lie to your face! Aren't you just grabbed by Job's words? I'm sorry I took so long to make my appearance as Job, but to create the full artistic and real effect, I had to put on the entire costume and all of the make-up. Quite frankly, I can't tell when the words I'm speaking are mine or are Job's. When I'm on stage—I am Job!" A tiny ray of light glinted from inside Tribes' left ear. With his little finger Tribes tapped lightly inside the opening of his left ear.

"Quiet on the set!" shouted Mapps, appearing composed as he stepped into view. "Janus is obviously ready to act, and our rehearsal is behind schedule because of needless interruptions!"

Jesus gestured to Mapps to continue.

"Janus, take your place on the mound of garbage."

Tribes flopped down, fidgeted with his left ear, and nodded at Mapps.

"Action!" Mapps boomed, his voice commanding.

"Let the day perish on which I was to be born," said Tribes, "and may that day be darkness. Let not God above care for it, nor light shine on it!"

"Stop!" I demanded. "What Job is saying is sin against the Father's plan! Job wants to cancel out that plan and substitute his own plan for the Father's! And you don't sound like a man who knows he's in deep sin! You sound arrogant and angry!"

"No, Travis—you stop!" Tribes fired back. "Read the *Book of Job*! Job doesn't believe that he's sinning! Job believes that he knows what's best for Job! And that's how I'm playing him! Sunday, tell Travis that even you must agree that I've grasped the core of Job's experience in my delivering Job's words!"

"First-rate performance, Janus!" Mapps interjected. "You're a director's treasure!"

"Continue your acting," said Jesus.

Mapps pointed at Tribes, and shouted, "Action!"

As Tribes turned his head to speak, a small circular object squirted from his left ear and landed in the dirt. "Wait," said Tribes, his voice quavering as he scooped up the object. "I can't go on ... need to put this back ... into my ear."

"What is that thing?" I asked.

"It's something ... without it ... I can't ... hear my lines ... can't act, I—"

"Hold it right there!" I insisted. "Hear your lines?! What do you mean by that?"

"You better fess up," said Mapps. "Tell them what it is, and let's get on with the rehearsal."

Tribes pressed the object into his ear. "It's a radio-controlled receiver. And inside my shirt is a concealed transmitter, a filament so thin that it's virtually invisible to the naked eye. About ten yards directly behind the wall of trash I have a trained parrot. His name is 'Playback.' He's memorized the play I made up from the *Book of Job*, and he speaks into a microphone that transmits the lines I need to deliver, and as I hear his words in the receiver in my ear, I speak them out, and when I speak them out, he hears them in the receiver I've strategically placed in the blind I have him hidden in, and then he speaks the next lines, and so forth."

"Are you saying that you haven't memorized the lines of Scripture?" I asked.

"I've never been able to do that, but with Playback feeding me the lines, I don't have to memorize anything. Playback frees me to completely identify with the character I'm playing, and gives me the confidence to be the great actor that I am."

"Let's be honest," remarked Mapps, "without Playback, you'd be worthless as a performer! Don't get me wrong: you are a great actor! But your greatness is totally dependent upon your trusty parrot, who's really more like an idiot savant when it comes to the words in the Bible!"

"As long as we're being honest, Hector," Tribes retorted, "let's get into the open how your greatness as a director is totally dependent upon what's on your smart phone."

"I say let's return to the rehearsal," insisted Hector, "no need to waste time on talking about my phone."

"All right," said Tribes. "Then I'll just say one word, actually say one name—Stanislavski!"

"Who's that?" I asked. "And what does that have to do with Hector's smart phone?"

"If Stanislavski wasn't on Hector's smart phone, Hector would not only be stupid, he'd be incapable of directing anyone to do anything worthy of being called Art. Go on, Hector, tell Travis and Sunday how you work the phone!"

"No, that's a trade secret!"

"Not anymore! You see—"

"Shut—your—mouth!" yelled Mapps. His hands stretched toward Tribes' neck, Mapps went on, "Or I'll shut it for you!"

"Hector!" said Jesus, his tone the force of decree. "Someone wrote that anyone who restrains his lips is wise, but any fool will quarrel. Are you wise or are you a fool?"

Mapps dropped his arms to his sides. "Hey, Sunday, I'm no fool ... you can see that ... because I'm not really quarrelling ... just protecting ... one of my trade secrets ... and so that must mean I'm a wise man, a man of restraint. So, go ahead, Janus, tell them whatever story you want. Who's going to believe someone whose credibility as an actor is based on what an idiot savant parrot tells him what to repeat on stage?"

"Hector, we'll let them decide who's more credible—me or you!" declared Tribes. "Stanislavski was a theater director, an actor, and a teacher of those who wanted to become actors. Hector has the writings of Stanislavski on his smart phone, and Hector is constantly tilting his phone so that he can read what Stanislavski has written about how to direct actors in any given situation."

"Okay, Janus, I think they get the point," said Hector, a tic making his eyes squint rapidly. "Now, let's move on from—"

"Hector is a great director, but he would be a mapless fool with no idea of how to direct anyone to say or to do anything—if you took away his smart phone and made Stanislavski disappear with it!"

I looked at Jesus, and said, "Why did you bring me here, to be in the presence of such blatant hypocrites? One of them can't quote Scripture unless a parrot gives him the words, and the other one is an atheist who despises God, needs words recorded on a smart phone to give him direction, and, to my mind, is an accomplice to his own brother's suicide."

Just then stench wafted across my face and pushed its way into my nostrils. I started to cough, the cough harsh and grating.

Jesus handed me a handkerchief.

I covered my nose with it and breathed through it, the handkerchief like a filter screening out most of the stench.

Jesus turned to me, his lips next to my ear, and whispered, "Are blatant hypocrites and accomplices to suicide worth the compassion of a counselor?"

My head felt ponderous, heavy—it sank forward and downward, its weight driving my chin against my chest, pinning it there—my eyes fixed on the ground at my feet—saw the dirt split open and widen—further—my feet moving to keep pace with the widening chasm—the chasm dark and bottomless—my tongue tightened into a ball—-pushing hard against the roof of my mouth—unable to cry for help—I squeezed shut my eyes, hurled myself backwards, my shoulders banging against the bleacher seat behind me—I sat there, the hard wood of the seat holding me erect.

I felt the ground beneath the soles of my feet. The chasm seemed closed, filled in with solid earth. I slowly opened my eyes, then cautiously scanned the wasteland stretching to the horizon, looking for a place to hide from Jesus' question—my eyes quickly froze into a bitter stare into this vast exposed space where I knew I could never hide, and all the while a thought was ricocheting through my head—*I am a waste—a waste—a waste—a waste—a waste!*

Jesus let his open palm rest on my knee, and whispered to me, "When you believe in your heart that you are a waste, then you are very close to becoming a counselor to the wasted, to those who suffer in their wastelands."

My head felt clear, my body still a bit shaky. Leaning close to Jesus' ear, I whispered, "I think I know what you mean ... you ... "—Words like a turning kaleidoscope moved through my mind, but I failed to make their changing patterns hold still, failed to shape them into coherent words on my tongue and sounds from my lips.

Jesus removed his hand from my knee, gestured to Tribes and Mapps, and said in a commanding voice, "If anyone wastes time and is not aware of it, then he's running out of time, in more ways than one."

Mapps scratched his head, and said in a hollow voice, "Hey, Sunday, there's no need to go philosophical on us. Say it plain and simple: the opening of the play is just around the corner, and we need to get back on track—right?!"

"I'm ready to act, to become Job again!" said Tribes, a word or two sounding like the tinny croak of a parrot.

"Take your place on the garbage mound, Janus," declared Mapps, "and I know that Playback can hear me and is set to feed you lines. I believe in you as Job, Janus!" Mapps tilted his smart phone, and read out loud Stanislovski's words, "'For the theater, knowing means feeling. You cannot create or come to know a living spirit through your brain, you do it, first and foremost, through feeling.'" Then he raised his right hand, pointed at Tribes, and shouted, "Action!"

"My flesh is clothed with worms and a crust of dirt," moaned Tribes, "my skin hardens and runs, my skin turns black on me, and my bones burn with fever. God splits my kidneys open. At night affliction pierces my bones within me, and my gnawing pains take no rest. I am decaying like a rotten thing, like a garment that is moth-eaten. Horror takes hold of my flesh! I am afraid of all my pains. I am sated with disgrace and conscious of my misery."

I felt a rumble in my stomach, then twinges of pain, acid crawling up my throat. I gulped—hard, blocking the acid, forcing it downward.

"Cut!" shouted Mapps. "Bravo! Janus! Bravo!" Mapps tilted his smart phone and read out loud, "'Truth is inseparable from belief, and belief from truth. Everything on stage must be endorsed by belief in the truth of the feelings being experienced and in the truth of the actions taking place.' Janus, you're doing that as the great artist that you are! Keep your focus, and—Action!"

"I loathe my own life," groaned Tribes, his voice sounding like a resigned pleading, "and I will speak in the bitterness of my soul, so that my soul would choose suffocation, death rather than my pains—"

"Cut!" bellowed Mapps. "No! No! No! Your delivery has"— Mapps tilted his smart phone—"has no connection to life but is said in a formalistic, mechanical, limp, soulless, empty way. It is like a corpse in which no pulse beats.'"

"What you know I also know," said Tribes, his voice loud and flexed, "and I am not inferior to you. Your memorable sayings are proverbs of ashes, your defenses are defenses of clay."

Mapps displayed to Tribes the back of his smart phone, pointing to Shakespeare's words as he read them, "'In thy face I see the map of honor, truth, and loyalty.' Remember, I am the director, and my only overriding concerns are the artistry of your performance as Job and the critical success of your play."

Mapps tilted his smart phone, and read out loud, "'Acting is above all intuitive, because it is based on subconscious feelings, on an actor's instincts.' Perhaps you could bring more life to certain parts of Job by tapping into the subconscious feelings you have toward your mother and father."

"How painful are honest words!" cried Tribes. "How long will you torment me and crush me with words? Let's do another take, and then look at me—at me!—and see whether my performance seems like I'm being intuitive, relying on my instincts. I don't need memories of me and my wicked parents to act out the truth of Job!"

Mapps drummed lightly on the back of his smart phone. "All right," he said, "let's try it again, but let's use a different place in the play, the place where Job starts to justify himself before God, the part that begins with 'Though he slay me ...' Ready! Action!"

"Though he slay me, I will hope in him. Nevertheless I will argue my ways before him. Let him weigh me with accurate scales, and let God know my integrity. Till I die I will not put away my integrity. I will hold fast my righteousness and will not let it go. As long as the breath of God is in my nostrils, my lips certainly will not speak unjustly nor will my tongue mutter deceit. My heart does not reproach any of my days, I—"

"Stop!" I cried out. "I will use Elihu's own words against you: 'Job speaks without knowledge, and his words are without wisdom. Job ought to be tried to the limit, because he answers like wicked men. For he adds rebellion to his sin. He claps his hands among us, and multiplies his words against God.'"

Tears streaming down his dirt-caked cheeks, Tribes turned to us one after the other, and pleaded, "Oh that I had one to hear me! Pity me, pity me, O my friends, for the hand of God has struck me. Why do you persecute me as God does, and are not satisfied with my flesh? O that you would become completely silent, and that it would become your wisdom, and that you would listen carefully to my speech, and let it be your way of consolation. I am not silenced by the darkness, nor deep gloom which covers me."

"God reveals mysteries from the darkness and brings the deep darkness into light!" Jesus proclaimed, the sound of his words seemed to create stillness and silence that encircled all of us.

Three pairs of eyes were fixed on Jesus.

Snickering, Mapps shook his head, pointed at Jesus, and said, "Sunday, I've got to hand it to you: You really know how to stop a show! What a profound comment! Where did you get it?"

Jesus leaned back, resting his elbows on the bleacher behind him, and said, "It's from Job, of course, chapter 12 and verse 27. Isn't it part of your play, Janus?"

"It is now!" cried Mapps. "Sunday, you got us back on track. Janus, pick up the play with 'My face is flushed ...' Ready! Action!"

"My face is flushed from weeping, and deep darkness covers my eyelids, although there is no violence in my hands, and my prayer is pure, and it is still my consolation, and I rejoice in unsparing pain, that I have not denied the words of the holy one."

"Cut!" snarled Mapps. "Janus, you've missed Sunday's key point! There's no feel or sense of mystery in your delivery!" Mapps tilted his smart phone and read out loud, "'Mystery is beautiful and is a spur to creation. And perspective is the planned harmonious relationship and arrangement of the parts of the entire play and the role. There can be no acting without the right kind of perspective, and there can be no beauty of creation without mystery.'"

"Sunday didn't write the play—I did!" growled Tribes. "In writing the play, I became Job, and like Job, I can say with integrity, 'I have treasured the words of God more than my necessary food!' Sunday may have injected into our conversation a quote from Job, but that doesn't make Sunday God! And that doesn't give Sunday the right to change my play!"

Mapps tilted his smart phone, and reading out loud, fired back, "'Simplistic thinking is dangerous. It springs from narrowness of mind, lack of talent, obtuseness in understanding the human soul and one of the most complex processes of its inner life—feelings.'"

Tribes stood up, faced Mapps, and said, "Your opinion as director of this play is trumped by God himself, whose words he inspired in the mouth of Job, 'This is also my salvation, for a godless man may not come before God's presence!' And you, Hector, being one of the most godless men I've ever met, cannot come into God's presence."

"Knock it off, Janus!" Mapps demanded, his tone angry and loud, "that God stuff is garbage and it stinks worse than the garbage in this dump!"

"However that may be for you, Hector, I can come into God's presence because I am a man of God—a true believer! And I insist that the way I wrote my play trumps your grabbing up Sunday's quote from Job and trying to force it into the vision and words God gave me to write the play! Sunday's ideas about mystery combined with your foolish notions of perspective simply have no place in my original vision from God!"

"You've lost your stage presence, Janus," said Mapps, his tone mocking. Mapps tilted his smart phone and read out loud, "'Charisma is the inexplicable attraction exercised by the actor's whole being in which even his faults are turned to advantage and are copied by his admirers and imitators.'"

Mapps pressed the smart phone flat on his chest, glared at Tribes, and declared, "You've no sense of charisma left to make Job come alive in the way he should. I'm afraid the entire project is in jeopardy, and the play may have to close even before it opens!"

"Your mind is in jeopardy!" boomed Tribes. You're going bananas, Hector!"

Mapps tilted the smart phone and read aloud, "'The Stanislovski system is a whole culture which must be cultivated and nourished over many long years. The actor cannot learn it parrot-fashion.' For some bizarre reason I don't fully understand, you've chosen to strike out on your own, ignoring seeing in my face the map of honor, truth, and loyalty, and as a result you've turned into an actor who not only acts in a parrot-fashion way, but who's fallen to the woefully pathetic level of having to rely on a parrot to feed lines to you while you're trying to act!"

"I'll show you I can act, you big fake!" Tribes thundered. "Without your smart phone and the dead words of a dead man written on the phone—your darling Stanislavski!—you'd be a scriptless—mapless!—bumbling idiot with no sense of how to direct anyone! Hear the next lines from my play! Listen to Job's words, you cold-blooded creep, and whine over the fact that you won't be a part of a great production. 'If I called and he answered me, I could not believe that he was listening to my voice. For he bruises me with a tempest and multiplies my wounds without cause!'"

Mapps rubbed his eyes and scratched at both his ears. "Oh, yes! Janus, yes! When you're raging, all that energy rushes through your body, creating in you a charisma that's truly infectious! When you're like this, an audience will have no choice—they'll be riveted on you and your performance! Keep going! Come on— keep going! What's next?!"

"Bull," said Tribes, quickly covering his mouth with both hands.

"Bull?!" asked Mapps. "That word is nowhere in your script! Look, you're rolling in your role! Don't stop now! Action!"

"Bull!" Tribes blurted.

Stunned and staggering backwards, Mapps appeared desperate as he tilted the smart phone and read out loud, "'In the creative process there is the father, the author of the play, the mother, the actor pregnant with the part, and the child, the role to be born.'"

Mapps scanned Tribes' dumbfounded face, his lips quivering, bubbles of saliva gathering at the corners of his mouth. "Father, mother, and child—that's the trinity of the consummate theater actor! ... Janus! ... listen! ... I said 'trinity!' and that must resonate with your belief in your God and his Trinity. My insight is genius at its highest level! A new level of artistic height and depth for you!"

"Don't blaspheme my God, you atheistic cretin!" Tribes blasted.

"No, Janus, I'm not! Your God is a Trinity who made the artistic building blocks for theater as a trinity! There can be no other conclusion to be drawn: the trinity of the theater is the unity of author, actor, and role—father, mother, and child—and therefore the closest expression of your God's Trinity! And your belief in the trinity of the theater brings you into the very presence of your God as father, mother, and child! You must keep acting, to serve your art and to glorify your God. The charisma is yours for the taking—it's a gift from your Trinity to the trinity of the theater embodied in your life! Ready! Action!"

Tribes grabbed at his chest. "God will not allow me to get my breath, but—Bull!"

"Cut!" shouted Mapps. "What's wrong with you?! This is the role of a lifetime and you're fully immersed in it! You are Job! Charisma personified! Ready! Action!"

"But God saturates me with—Bull! It's Playback! He keeps repeating the word 'Bull' in my earpiece. His voice ... he seems frightened ... I've never heard him so scared!"

"It must be the bull snake!" I shouted. "I saw it taste the air with its tongue, crawl over the wall of trash, and disappear. It must've sensed the heat of the parrot, and then went after Playback as its next meal!"

We rose as one and rushed to a place behind the wall of trash. "There's the bull snake!" I cried. "I see its yellow and brown body moving toward the blind you built to protect Playback, Janus."

"I hate that stupid parrot!" screamed Mapps. "He's a coward, and his refusal to stay at his post, well, that only shows just how quickly he falls apart at the least sign of trouble. He's ruining the performance of the decade ... maybe of the last 100 years!"

"Playback's been loyal to me since he was hatched," insisted Tribes, "and he's the only real family I've got!"

I cried out, "The snake is closing in on him—it's coiling itself—its tongue flicking the air—preparing to strike!"

"Fly, Playback, fly!" yelled Tribes. "Save your life!—do it for me! Live!"

Wings flapping wildly in thick dirt and thatched weeds that made up the floor and protective screen of his blind, Playback, dragging his feet, struggled to get airborne, as the bull snake struck, its barbed teeth grazing the tips of Playback's tail feathers, slowing his ascent, making it lower and longer, but then he began to move upwards on the air.

Mapps picked up a stained and pocked dish, its serrated edges encircling its circumference, and flung the dish in the direction of Playback's flight path, shouting "Die, you gutless squawker!" as the spinning jagged edges of the dish nicked Playback's underbelly, causing him to drop to the ground, flecks of blood on his pale yellow feathers. The bull snake sensed Playback's presence, and the snake quickened its sinuous pace, its focus locked on Playback. The parrot turned its eyes toward Mapps, hissed at him, and flapped its wings, lifting its body high into the stale air, his green and purple back visible as he climbed higher, curving away from us.

"I hope you bleed to death!" yelled Mapps. "You're nothing more than an idiot savant birdbrain—birdbrain in every sense of the word! You've ruined a great artistic performance—you should die for it!"

Jerking his head around to face Mapps, Tribes' earpiece squirted from its hidden place in his ear, flitting across a stretch of space, and then falling to the ground. A dung beetle scurried from a pile of garbage, snatched the earpiece, and vanished into a tangle of debris and shadows. "Leave my friend alone, Hector!" said Tribes, his words biting. "He has every right to live!"

"It's a moot point now," Mapps replied smugly. "Playback's flown your coop! And you've lost your earpiece!"

His fingers shaking, Tribes probed every contour of his ear. "My earpiece! It's gone! I'm helpless without it!"

"I saw it fly away and fall into the dirt," said Mapps, his voice vindictive. "Don't bother to look for it. Without your friend the parrot, the earpiece is worthless and so are you as an actor. You've failed the Trinity of your God when you and your parrot failed the trinity of the theater! From this day forward, your life will be meaningless, the kind of meaninglessness that can drive a person to sink into despair, sink even to the point of committing suicide!"

"Well you and your twin brother would certainly know about that, wouldn't you, Hector?! Feeling any desire to chug a bottle of wine?!"

"Be careful, Janus! You're nothing but a mediocre actor who'll be unemployed—forever! As long as I have my smart phone and Stanislavski's words to map my way forward, I will always be employable and seen as a great director, as Shakespeare's words say with so much truth: I am a man whose face is a map of honor, truth, and loyalty."

As Mapps was berating Tribes, Playback suddenly appeared high above, hovering directly over Mapps' head. Playback was holding in his beak a filthy but intact half-gallon jug of *Thunderbird* wine, and like a skilled bombardier the parrot appeared to be aiming the jug of cheap wine to detonate on impact with the top of Mapps' head.

Playback released the bottle, the bottle gaining speed, hitting Mapps with a loud "Thud!" knocking Mapps to his knees and causing him to lurch forward, the force of the lurch propelling his smart gold-plated phone and its gold chain to be launched into the air and land on the wall of trash. Playback swooped down, clamped his beak around the gold chain, and hoisted it into the air, the smart phone swinging to-and-fro as he flew away.

Mapps scrambled to his feet, his body swaying, his steps moving in a tight circle of stumbles as he checked his head for injuries. "My phone!" bawled Mapps. "Bring back my phone! I'll hunt you down! I'll capture you!—pluck your feathers!—kill you!—fry your meat!—eat you for lunch!—until—there's nothing—nothing!—left of you!"

"Call me 'Thunderbird!'" squawked Playback as he flew in zig-zag patterns, moving toward the horizon.

Mapps ran after Playback, matching the parrot's every zig and zag, but Playback's winged speed in the air outdistanced Mapps' trudge across the potholed and garbage-strewn dirt.

Screaming at Playback and ever-rushing toward the horizon, Mapps stopped, here and there, to pick up stones, rusted soup cans, and broken parts of chairs and couches, to throw them at Playback, each attempt missing the mark, and each miss met with Playback squawking back, "Call me Thunderbird!"

At one point in his raving pursuit, Mapps came to a halt and doubled over. While Mapps was doubled over, laboring to catch his breath, his hands on his sagging knees, his head facing the ground, Playback circled left until the parrot was directly behind Mapps, and then Playback, his flapping wings almost a blur, flew over Mapps, skimming his back with the dangling smart phone and, as Mapps raised his head, the gold-plated phone clapped the base of Mapps' skull, and the parrot cried out to Mapps— "No one puts old wine into new wineskins—the wine will burst the skins— the wine is lost—the skins as well!"

As Playback was descending toward the horizon, he lowered the pale yellow crown of his head, and let the gold chain slide out of his beak and fall from him, the chain and phone quickly vanishing from sight. Gliding on fully spread wings, the parrot glanced at Mapps, squawked, "Playback! Playback! Playback!" and then he disappeared behind the horizon.

As Mapps witnessed the last moment of the irrecoverable loss of his smart phone and chain, he shuddered, his body appearing to be made of parts that no longer fit together, each part seeming to have a will and direction of its own. Mapps collapsed, his body looked like a completed jigsaw puzzle that someone just pushed off a table, the completed picture now isolated pieces falling through the air and then crashing to the ground, exploding into random, chaotic, and detached bits of cardboard.

Face down and his body flat on the dirt, Mapps appeared dead. After a few seconds, Mapps lifted his head, drew his elbows to his sides, and using the points of his elbows, he began to dig them into the dirt, one in front of the other, slowly dragging himself forward, moving closer to the edge of the horizon—then he stopped—sat up, turned around, looked at us, and exclaimed, "Shakespeare was wrong!—all the world's not a stage—no!—all the world's a map—a map in search of its mapmaker!" Then he slumped back onto his left side, and with his left elbow he dragged himself within reach of the horizon, to that place where earth and sky meet—then he stopped, folded in on himself, his body seemed as lifeless as the piles of boulders on either side of him.

Then—suddenly—words, electric and affirming, sounded from somewhere on the other side of the horizon, power-releasing words sending shockwaves through Mapps' body, making his arms and legs quiver, and jolting him forward. He seemed put back together again, all the parts of his body somehow a living whole. He rolled onto his left side again, his right arm bent at the elbow and lifted into the air, his neck stretched to its limit, his head peering over the edge of the horizon, and then—suddenly— the power-releasing words surged through him again, making his arm shoot straight up, his hand open, his fingers splay, his hand rotate left then right, in a small circle, in what seemed like a kind of acknowledgment of someone he was seeing, someone on the other side of the horizon, someone I couldn't see, the someone who—now a third time—spoke those power-throbbing words to him, the urgent sound of the words like strong magnets, seizing him with animating power, infusing him with strength to cross over the edge of the horizon and to disappear.

As I watched Mapps pass from my sight, the words proclaimed to him were so alive with radiating power that I was feeling their lingering presence rippling across my skin even as I was continuing to hear their resounding appeal—"New wine in fresh wine-skins!"

My hands, open and upturned, I extended them toward Jesus, as though I was offering him a prayer I couldn't put into words, the silence of my hands seeming more like a burning request for an explanation for what I'd seen and heard, for what I was still experiencing.

Jesus gazed softly into my eyes, and said, "What's on your mind, Travis?"

Then words rose in me: "What's this all about?"

"All about?"

"Yes, this ... all of this that happened ... all that I'm still feeling ... what does all this mean?"

"Job points the way to an answer: 'Ask the birds of the heavens, and let them tell you!'"

"Birds of the heavens?! Are parrots birds of the heavens? Is this about—"

"Help me!" whimpered Tribes as his body pitched headlong into the wall of trash, causing the wall to rupture and cave in, burying him under layers of garbage and pieces of junk.

"Travis, help me with him!" Jesus commanded. We cleared away the refuse, lifted Tribes to his feet, walked him to the bleachers, and sat him at a place that supported his back. Jesus and I sat on either side of Tribes, each of us with a comforting hand resting on a grimy and bruised shoulder. Tribes' forehead, cheeks, and chin, were bleeding, caused by slivers of shattered glass, some slivers still wedged inside his torn flesh. Greenish slime was oozing from a swollen corner of his mouth, the thick discharge seeming to come from somewhere deep inside him.

In Tribes' hand he was holding a large piece of broken mirror, rivulets of blood from his sliced open fingers beginning to spread across its reflecting surface. He raised the mirror to his face and stared at the image looking back at him, the image being covered with blood until the image and the mirror were dyed with blood. He drew the mirror close to his face, and yelled, "Worthless! Failure! You're a Wane and you'll always be a Wane!" He grasped the mirror with both hands, screamed "Die!" and smashed the mirror against his face, snapping the glass in two and slicing open a ragged gash in the middle of his face, blood streaming from his hairline to the point of his chin, making his face appear fractured and out of kilter. Sobbing, Tribes went limp, fell sideways, his head drooping toward Jesus. I caught Tribes' wrist and held fast, trying to prevent him from falling out of control onto the dirt.

With his hands Jesus cradled Tribes' head, and in a commanding voice, said, "Lift Janus' feet and legs while I guide his head to rest on the bleachers, and look for something here that can act as a pillow."

A wave of stench crashed against me, knocking me off the bleachers, the stench thick, intrusive, and pervasive. I struggled to my feet, hastily walked backwards, gathered my strength, and shouted defiantly, "No! I won't do it!" The stench drove itself into my nostrils and pried open my mouth. I pushed against the rush of oppressive air, feeling the force of an attacker I couldn't see, the flood of stench breaching and overflowing every barrier my body set against it. My stomach began to heave, bursts of acid like sharp fingernails scratching and clawing their way up my throat, the fingernails now a scalding fist punching wildly inside my belly, my hands, one over the other, pressing down on the spot where the blows were beating my insides into hard bulges, desperate to keep the bulges from ripping through my belly and skin, my pressing hands failing to contain clumps of thick and sour goo erupting from my throat, mouth, and nose.

I fought back the urge to spit on Tribes, to spew my vomit all over his face. I pointed at Tribes, and raged, "The stench! It's coming from you! You're infecting me! Your stench! It's inside me! You're making me puke! You're disgusting!"

I started to gag, my stomach seething and retching, blood trickling from the corners of my mouth, each breath feeling blocked by clots of blood in my throat, clots so dense and swollen that I struggled to suck in enough air to stay focused, to remain in control of my arms and legs, my gasps weaker and shorter—"I ... can't ... breathe," my words stretched thinner than a whisper, "I'm ... a ... waste ... wasting ... away," my words using up the last pocket of air left in the cavity of my mouth.

My legs felt like bags of ice water—I slumped to my knees. The landfill appeared watery and blurry, spinning—faster—faster—I blinked hard, hoping the force of my clenched eyelids would seize the spinning, disable it, and make it stop, stand still.

I flashed open my eyes—stupefied—everything was gray: the wasteland and everything in it, extending to the horizon, to the clouds, to the sky, to the sun, to the bleachers, to Tribes, to Jesus, and to what I could see of my body—all was saturated with the dullest gray—gray was everywhere and was in and on everything.

I wiped away some vomit from my chin, and looked at the tips of my fingers—the vomit and my fingers were gray. I searched my mind, scanning it for an image or a memory that was three-dimensional and vivid with color, and I found the inside of my head crowded only with thick gray fog.

I strained to recollect a single example of a thought that was either black or white, a thought with a clear-cut definition of what is right and what is wrong, some cut and dried category of what is good and what is evil, some way I could gain ultimate clarity in my mind, so that I could order my final moments of my waning life, some precise and certain framework to secure a personal meaning for my life that made sense to me but—no!—I was awash with gray, the gray dissolving everything solid inside me, flooding me with gray even as the gray was enveloping and absorbing me into everything gray outside of me.

I—all—of—me—was fading—into—suddenly—I sensed someone behind me, then felt what seemed like contours of hands on my shoulders, with firm, smooth and gentle motion, the hands turned me over and laid me on my back, on the dirt. My eyes shut, my eyelids like rocks too heavy to lift, I felt fingers close my nostrils and ease apart my lips—felt welcoming lips encircle my mouth—felt blown into me a breath of renewing air so cleansing and permeating that it drove out the gray inside me, pouring into me a presence, radiant, real, and expanding, filling the inside of me with this welcoming presence even as this presence was feeling accepted by me as his welcoming home.

My eyelids sprang open, and I saw a face, distinct, vibrant, smiling—"Jesus!" I cried. "It is really you! I was fading, wasting away, and you came to help me, bring me back to life!"

We rose to our feet. I turned in a circle, surveying the landfill. Everything was in sharp focus and clothed in its own color. "Oh!—My!—God! You are really here—with me!" I threw my arms around Jesus' neck. "Thank you for your compassion," I said, "for not giving up on me, not even when I believed I'm nothing but a waste."

"There's someone else who needs compassion," said Jesus, his voice tender and exhorting.

"I know," I said, waves of sadness moving through me as I looked at Tribes. "It's Janus. And, Lord, I know you feel the same compassion for him that you feel for me, and I know that you'll show him that compassion."

"Help me, Sunday!" begged Tribes. "Help me, please!"

"Travis, I want you to show him my compassion."

"I want to help ... I care about him now ... but the stench—I'm afraid ... the stench will hurt me again! I can smell it right now!"

Jesus moved behind me, put his arms around my waist, his chin on my shoulder, and pressed his cheek against mine. "As I breathe out," he said, his voice comforting and validating, "you breathe in."

Jesus let a breath flow from his mouth, and I breathed it in deeply. His chest against my back, Jesus nudged me forward, Jesus breathing out, and I gulping in his breath. As each step brought us nearer to Tribes, I sniffed the air, the stench issuing from him moving toward us. I tensed, stopped, stepped back.

"No!" insisted Jesus, "keep breathing me in, and my breath will dilute the stench, the expansive fragrance of my relentless presence will free you to show my compassion while my enveloping aroma is shielding you from the encroaching stench."

Feeling Jesus at my back, I moved forward—Jesus breathing out, I breathing in him—each step bolder, each breath of Jesus making me stronger, his presence lighter against my back—Jesus breathing out, I breathing in—his chest and my back feeling like one flesh moving through space, the rhythm of our synchronized breathing carrying us forward to within an arm's length of Tribes, Jesus' breaths moving deeper into me, until I no longer felt the weight of his chest against my back or sensed his breathing coming from outside me—he was inside me and we were breathing as one!

I bent over Tribes, draped his arm around my neck, lifted him to his feet. "I'm a waste," Tribes said, choking back tears, "I'm Ichabod ... my name ... glory fading away ... away from God ... away into a worthless nothing ... "

I felt his crushing pain, the same pain that crushed me, I felt his self-contempt and tasted the poisonous lie that he's a waste, the same self-contempt I felt when I swallowed the belief that I was a noxious waste who has no right to live.

I wept as I squatted, low enough to press my shoulder against his belly, and let his limp body slump over my shoulder. "Let's leave this wasteland together," I said, my voice triumphant, "brothers in suffering, brothers in helplessness, brothers in hope, a living hope that will never be cut off!"

"That sounds like something Sunday would say," said Tribes, his voice laced with longing. "Where is Sunday?"

The staccato blaring of a car's horn distracted me from giving an answer. I turned toward the direction of the blaring and spied a yellow taxicab—with Cabby behind the wheel! All the taxi's windows were up. Jesus waved at me from inside the cab, beckoning me to come to the cab and to bring Tribes with me.

"Did I hear a car alarm go off?" asked Tribes.

"No. It's a taxicab, and the driver is honking at us."

"But where's Sunday?"

"He's in the taxi, and he wants me to bring you to the cab."

"Okay ... sure ... but I still don't think I can walk. Will you carry me ... to Sunday?"

"Yes, I will."

As I was carrying Tribes to the taxi, Jesus opened the back door facing me. Jesus slid over, to the center of the seat, and I lowered

Tribes onto the back seat. Jesus motioned to me to go around the cab and enter through the other back door.

I took a place next to Jesus. Surprised as I felt my lungs being filled with a long breath of cool air, I shouted, "Cabby, you installed an air conditioner!"

"Sure thing, Travis," said Cabby, "I know how much the stench around this dump bothered you, so I got air for my cab ... know what I mean?"

"Yes, I do, and I know it must have cost you a bundle to put in the air conditioning. Thank you."

"Hey, I almost forgot: I got some air fresheners in the glove compartment ... shaped like little pine trees ... and I can break one out for you ... if the smell of pine will help you."

"No, thanks, Cabby, but that's very nice of you to think of that."

"Hey, oh wait, wait a second, wait ... almost forgot again ... my head must be on crooked! I also got some CDs with me, in case you want music during the ride ... you want to hear one?"

"Maybe ... I—"

"Wait!" cried Cabby, "I forgot the CDs! I left them back at the office! I'm sorry ... really sorry ... know what I mean?"

"No problem, Cabby," I said trying to console him, "it's the heart that counts, and your heart's in the right place."

Still smiling, Jesus leaned forward, put his hand on Cabby's shoulder, and said, "It's time to go!"

The taxi moved ahead, slowly accelerating, and then maintaining a steady speed and smooth ride.

Smiling, I glanced at Jesus, then turned to Cabby, and said, "Lower the windows!—lower them all the way!"

"Sure thing—hey!—what?! ... you're putting me on—right?!" yelped Cabby! "The stench!—remember the stench!—you were ready to toss your cookies! ... know what I mean?!"

"Lower the windows," I said, my tone firm, "I like the feel of the wind blowing on my face!"

A soft whir signaled the locks on the windows being released, and I watched the windowpane next to me disappear from view, then felt the rush of air pouring over me.

Smiling, I took a deep breath and declared to the stench, "The love of Jesus is riding on the wind, and his love is radiating a fragrant aroma, and as long as I'm breathing in his love, his fragrant aroma is bigger and stronger than any of your stench!"

Cabby adjusted his cap, pulling it down, stretching it, straining to force it over the length of his ears. "Hey, I don't know what you mean. Air is air ... it can smell good or it can stink ... either way, you've got to breathe ... know what I mean?"

"The breath of God is not just air, Cabby. When God is breathing, his breath is carrying his voice, and his voice is releasing his power. If God withdrew his fragrant life-giving breath, to keep it for himself—in that moment—all the life on the planet would suffocate and turn into piles of dirt, dirt surrounded by stench, like the stench polluting this wasteland you're driving on!"

The engine made a grinding metallic sound as Cabby stepped on the gas pedal. The taxi speeding up, Cabby gasped, "Better to get away from here real fast ... know what I mean?"

Stirring, Tribes turned his face toward his open window, gulped in breaths of rushing wind, and asked, "Is this Sunday?"

"No," said Cabby, his breathing shallow and choppy, "it—is—Thurs—day."

"Ease off the gas, Cabby," said Jesus as he leaned forward, his lips inches from Cabby's ear. "Take a deep breath with me and then let it out slowly." Jesus and Cabby breathed together, Cabby letting out an audible and relaxing sigh.

"That's better," said Cabby. "Thanks a lot ... I can still smell the stench ... but I'm a little better ... know what I mean?"

Leaning back against his seat, Jesus replied, "Yes, I think I know: a little better can feel like a lot better!"

"Sure thing, you do know what I mean." Cabby cleared his throat of rattling phlegm, tugged at his collar, and asked, "The other guy in the back, what's his name?"

"Janus is his name," I said.

"No," said Tribes, his voice confident, "my name is Ichabod ... Ichabod Wanes."

"Ichabod!" said Cabby, the sound of the name seemed to daze him, his hands slipping off the wheel, causing the taxi to swerve, then Cabby quickly regaining control of the taxi. "Never met an Ichabod ... that's a weird name—no offense! ... know what I mean?"

"No offense taken," said Wanes. "But am I an offense, Sunday? There's something about being around you, something that makes me breathe easier, feel precious and free, shining and fully alive. But, Sunday, I'm afraid that my life will always be an offense to other people, always be mocked as a fading glory, always despised as a zero of a man."

"No, you're time of fading glory is over!" proclaimed Jesus, his voice jubilant. "The ministry of the Spirit is abounding in glory, and the Spirit of glory breathes out the glory of God wherever he wills, and he is breathing out that glory and—right now!— breathing into you the truth that you are a son of glory!"

"Thank you, Sunday!" Wanes shouted joyfully as he set his glowing face against the foul-smelling air. "Thank you for the Spirit of glory! ... I can feel the Spirit's rest ... I can rest ... a son of glory ... Sunday ... Sunday ... Sunday ... I love your name," his voice seeming to glide into a peace-embracing silence.

Jesus began laughing, the sound like the soft flutter of wings, the wings rising, their flutter now a voice singing a name— "Sunny!" Jesus laid his hands on Sunny's head. "You'll never again be called Ichabod! Sunny is your new name, a name like a sunny day shining with the glory of God, a name the constant reminder of Sunday!"

Everything inside me was resonating to the melodies still vibrating in the singing of Jesus—then a memory-picture appeared inside my head—"Sunday!" I shouted, the resounding force of "Sunday!" a knockout punch landing on the mouth of the stench, and then I drew back and sat flush against my seat.

"Yes! Now I remember a Sunday, a very special Sunday." I turned to Jesus, my eyes secured on his gaze. "Years ago, it was my first time at church. It was Easter Sunday, and the pastor was preaching, 'For we are a fragrance of Christ to God among those who are being saved and among those who are perishing; to the one an aroma from death to death, to the other an aroma from life to life. And who is adequate to these things?'"

"Were the pastor's words sweet to your soul?" asked Jesus.

"Lord," I replied, "the new covenant in your blood makes me adequate as your servant, and the Holy Spirit breathes in me your resurrecting power so I can live as your servant, so my breath can be the sweet aroma of the knowledge of you in every place. Lord, if the Father ever calls me to be a counselor, I know the name I would give to the counseling I'd do, a name that would serve those who are suffering and would glorify you."

"And what name would that be, Travis?" asked Jesus, his tone serious and fervent.

"Eastering!" erupted from my mouth, the geysering thrust of the word shooting outward and upward, catching me by surprise.

"Eastering?" asked Jesus. "Is that the name you truly meant to choose?"

"Eastering!—Yes!—That is the name! Before you say 'No,' please hear me out, Lord. There is one God and Father of all who is over all and through all and in all, and everything is from him and through him and back to him, and the Father has made you head over all things for the good of the church, and the church is your body, and you are making it full and complete, you who are filling all people everywhere with the aroma of your life-giving presence. Do you see it, Lord?! You are breathing everywhere and breathing all the time—your never-ending breathing is never-ending access to your resurrecting power! That, Lord, is Eastering! Counseling your people who are suffering is more than helping them at church on Sunday, more than helping them on Easter Sunday, for the Father of glory, and for you, the Lord of glory, and for the Spirit of glory—every moment is a glorious Eastering moment, because your resurrected and resurrecting life is arising in every moment of every single day and in every single place, making every person new in you. Eastering is the name I chose because I believe the Holy Spirit gave me this name. Lord, what do you think of Eastering?"

"Travis, I like Eastering more than any other name I've ever heard for what is called Christian counseling."

"Why is that, Lord?"

"It got a rise out of me!"

Transfusing Rest

Night. Exhausting day. Working. For the Lord. Working. Ended. At last. Edge of bed. Sitting. Weary. Longing for sleep. Restless. Head. Images swirling. Dim. Monstrous. Noises. Loud. Grinding. Recognition. Fleeting. Real. Phony. Smiles. Crooked. Dissolving. Half-sentences. Garbled words. Broken faces. Chaos. Broken hearts. Pain. Broken spirits. Godless. Broken souls. Anonymous. Broken bodies. Afflicted. Broken promises. Betrayed. Broken purposes. Hopeless. Broken mouths. Propaganda. Broken hands. Useless. Broken me.

Doubts riddled me, my thoughts interrogating words: *People who crossed my path ... today ... did they see my faith in Jesus?*

Or did the homeless woman I felt tender toward feel the blunt ache of my doubt clubbing my heart when I showed her kindness?

Or did the crippled man I was laboring to feed see the thick drops of sweat stinging my faithless eyes as I longed to be anywhere but with his mutilated body?

Or did the demented man with terminal lung cancer sense my fear of death tightening its grip on my lungs as I turned my head away from the foul odor issuing from his rotting chest?

Or did the woman holding her sick infant, searing wet pain awash in her wounded stare, feel abandoned by me, as she waited in agitated silence for comforting words to bridge the lonely gulf between my distantly-polite eyes and her wounded stare? But no comforting words sounded from me to connect my life with hers, no compassion filled my eyes to soothe her wounded stare. I was mute, imprisoned inside the dumb skin covering my body, skin contracting, tightening along the surface of my entire body, skin stretched so tight around me that it threatened to suffocate me.

You're a hypocrite—not a real Christian! ... but ... wait ... slow ... down ... you do have faith in Jesus ... you can prove it ... to people ... to yourself ... just redouble your efforts ... rely on your willpower ... try harder to believe!—believe!—believe! ... even if you're so tired you can't see straight, you should always—

A lump with grainy teeth forced its way into the base of my tongue, blocking my words, an image of a tapeworm flashed inside my eyes, the tapeworm sinking its grainy teeth deeper into my tongue, the tapeworm gathering into one place its unyielding heft, the drag of its heaviness making me wearier, its feeding on my waning stamina adding more weight to my weariness. The heft of the tapeworm's heaviness was beyond my strength to move, depleting me to the point of utter exhaustion.

"I can't breathe!" spurted from me as a guttural cry for help. I strained to rid myself of the lump, swallowing in hard gulps, muscles in my neck moving in cramping undulations. The tapeworm thickened, lengthened—the heft of my fatigue grew heavier. I grabbed at my throat, heels of my hands pushing at the lump, desperate to break up the dense impasse separating my lungs from the life-giving air I needed to breathe, my grabbing producing a rasping sound that slid from behind my clenched teeth.

I struggled to breathe.

The tapeworm thickened, lengthened—the heft of my fatigue grew heavier, the veins in my face and neck near to bursting, my lungs filled with lashing fire. The tapeworm thickened, lengthened, spreading throughout my body, its jagged entrails dotted with blunted teeth, the dull relentlessly scalding teeth chewing through me, creating a gaping hole in bone, muscle, internal organs, rupturing the sheath of skin containing my insides, leaving me exposed, with no barrier to protect what was inside me from what was outside me, my insides now falling through that hole, the gravity of that hole emptying me of everything alive in me, everything holding me together, everything in me of substance, thickness, height, depth, structure, and weight.

As my life was being sucked out of me through that hole, my eyes were growing dim, the sound of my breathing growing fainter. With all my fading strength I strained to keep my eyes focused on the spine of a Bible in my bookcase, and then—quickly and surprisingly—my breath was sucked out through that hole in me, the spine of the Bible seeming to snap in two as my eyelids fell shut, my eyes falling through that hole, and then my heart imploded, its blood and shredded tissue falling through that hole. From somewhere inside or outside of me—I couldn't say where—I heard "Dead-tired!"

With an anguished breath I lamented, "I'm weary, helpless without Jesus," the sound of my words clenched into a nail, sharp and hard, the nail's force aimed at the head of the tapeworm, the nail piercing the lump, the heft of the lump's heaviness shrinking, its thickness, length, and width shriveling, releasing sobs from my throat and tears from my eyes. I gulped in air as I wept, the thin lines of my tears jagged and halting as they moved down my cheeks and onto my lips.

A large smear of blood arose as an image behind my eyes, on the inner surface of my skull, the crimson blotch so bright with radiant light that my eyes and head were ablaze with pain. "I hurt," I moaned as I stared at the blood, unable to erase the searing pain bursting from the radiant light shooting throughout my brain and skull. "I'm dead-tired … deadweight," I whimpered, the sound of my words encircling me as I spoke, forming coils around me, squeezing my temples and brow, adding constricting pain to the burning light that was erupting in scarlet flashes against the inner space sealed by my skull.

Suddenly the large smear of blood exploded in my head, hurtling sunbursts of crimson agony onto muted bone and dumb flesh, crashing, stabbing against the back of my eyeballs, releasing in me a long, tortured and torturing scream—"My eyes are bleeding!"

Unsteady and weak, I struggled to move my arms and legs, but controlled only my fingertips, feeling them claw feebly at my bed sheets. I sagged onto my side, and then rolled over, onto my back. "I'm drowning in blood!" My head flopped from side to side, saliva trickling from corners of my mouth, my fingers clutching at my pillow. "Blood that's not my own!" I drew in a deep breath, and spoke, my words coming in short wheezes, "I'm dying! ... dead-tired! ... deadweight! ... I need ... the blood ... of Jesus!"

I felt a quickening inside me, a gladdening and welcoming presence, this presence embracing me, an enlivening hope inside my weariness, an accepting touch inside the incessant urge to reject Jesus as my Savior.

"Travis, the blood in you is my blood!"

"Is that you, Lord?"

"Yes."

"And it's your blood in me?"

"Yes, Travis, I call it my Shaping Blood."

"Shaping Blood?"

"Yes, because it transfuses your weariness and shapes it into rest, resting in me."

"I'm dead-tired, Lord. I need your Shaping Blood. May I have it?"

"Yes."

That "Yes" felt like a cradle embracing my body, the firm, resonating press of that "Yes" like palms on that cradle, rocking me with quieting tenderness and affirming safety.

I dabbed at the hot ooze trickling from my eyes, and smiled when I saw red streaks on my fingertips. "The Shaping Blood! Yes! Now, Lord?!"

"Yes!"

Christ's "Yes!" released a torrent of Shaping Blood—healing balm streaming to the gaping hole in me, its thick lotion sealing the hole—blazing red juice shaped into teeth of fire consuming the tapeworm—crimson streams shaped into a crown of thorns around my skull, each blood-dripping thorn feeling like an unerring missile firing through my veins, arteries, organs, muscles, bones, and skin, each blood-dripping thorn seeking a target of clotted weariness, to explode the weariness, to reshape it—Shaping Blood—exploding pride clotted with flawless self-estimation—Shaping Blood—exploding anxiety clotted with unerring setting of goals—Shaping Blood—exploding depression clotted with faultless performing of routines—Shaping Blood—exploding anger clotted with entitled control—Shaping Blood—dissolving, bathing, soaking, washing, cleansing—Shaping Blood—reshaping pride into saturating preciousness—Shaping Blood—reshaping anxiety into transforming union—Shaping Blood—reshaping depression into expanding freedom—Shaping Blood—reshaping anger into peace-filling safety—all weariness exploded, dissolved, reshaped into transfusing rest—the beats of my heart, easy, steady, serene— Shaping Blood—transfusing rest—bathing, soaking, washing, cleansing me in unwinding repose, releasing in me warm liquid quiet, loosening, deepening, lubricating, luminous red juice, my heart resting in brimless, rimless silence.

As the Shaping Blood drew me deeper into its liquid quiet and transfusing rest, I began to see the shapes of everything in my bedroom in a new way: tables, chairs, pictures hanging on walls, the carpeted floor, the ceiling, the door, the mirror, the bed sheet, the blanket, my pillow and the case covering it—they were somehow clean and clear, clean and clear like a cloudless sky in summer: warm, weightless, limpid.

Nothing in my room moved and yet everything in it seemed to be dancing inside me. Nothing in my room gave off a sound and yet everything in it seemed to be singing inside me. And as the Shaping Blood became warmer, the cleaner and clearer the sizes, shapes, angles, and lines of all the things in the room showed themselves as things wedded to other things and wedded to me. I felt whole, alive, resting in a nameless mystery, a presence real, true, and actual but beyond the defining brand of a name.

As the Shaping Blood became warmer, its rest more transfusing, everything in my room, including me, seemed nameless. It was as though the names of things themselves somehow were clotted with weariness, and the Shaping Blood was cleansing each thing of its name, each thing being reshaped to reveal its truth and how its truth was connected to the truth of every other thing in the room, and how my truth was connected to the enlivening truth of the Shaping Blood, its delicious calm playing lyrically across my skin, its cadences of lambent quiet filling me, its lilting melody gracing me, uplifting me, bathing, soaking, washing, cleansing me, until, being transfused and overflowing with blood-shot light, light so brilliant with Shaping Blood that my bed felt reshaped into a cradle of frictionless air, a cradle I was suspended in, held aloft only by hallowed air, resting—gliding—resting—gliding—resting—gliding on truth-filling music of a white song of silence.

Love Is Patient:
Fifth and Sixth Deliveries

A mother and a child approached me. I was sitting alone, balanced in the middle of a seesaw. The mother asked, "Is it all right with you if my daughter plays seesaw with you?"

Not sure where I was, I scanned the place. It was an enormous grassy park filled with people enjoying places and objects of relaxation and fun: swings, picnic tables, sets of monkey bars, a merry-go-round, a basketball court with a basket at each end, two volleyball courts, a quarter-mile running track, three tennis courts, a narrow river running along the park's outer edge, and a large, circular wading pool made of concrete, at its center a fountain shooting into the sunny air plumes of burbling water.

Put at ease by the mother's warm smile, I said, "That's fine with me."

"My name is Frieda, and this is my daughter Annie."

"Hi, I'm Travis." Fishing for the name of the park, I asked, "Frieda, do you come to this park often?"

"For sure," replied Frieda. "Every Saturday afternoon unless it's raining. We love to play here, don't we Annie?"

"Uh, huh," said Annie, her grin showing braces fitted to all her teeth. "And then we leave, and go meet Daddy."

"My husband works Saturdays, and so we meet him at Annie's favorite restaurant—"

"But we play first!"

295

"That's right, Annie," Frieda chuckled, "we always play first."

"Do you ever wonder about the name of this park?"

"Wonder about the name?" asked Frieda, her tone probing. "What do you mean?"

"You know ... the name ... don't you think it's odd to call a park—"

"Neversink?! What's so odd about that name?"

"Well, Frieda, when I hear you say 'Neversink,' it makes the park sound safe."

"Safe?" she asked, her look puzzled.

"Yes," I said, "people who play or walk in this park feel safe ... because ... well ... they'll never sink ... you know ... never sink into any bad place ... always have solid ground under them ... sure footing ... so to speak"—words babbling from my mouth, the sound of the voice speaking the words seemed like someone else's voice, a voice I couldn't control—"and that's probably why I like etymologies of words ... you know ... roots of words ... their origins ... where they came from ... if you can see where I'm going ... with this line of reasoning ... how all of these words ... if we can make sense of them ... can make us better communicators"—words kept erupting in my mouth—I struggled to hold them on my tongue—desperate to piece together a way to wriggle out of the web of words I'd weaved and caught myself in—"I ... uh—"

"You're a thinker, aren't you, Travis? A guy who gets excited about words and what they mean—true?!"

Using the palm of my hand to wipe away beads of sweat leaking onto my forehead, I said, "You've got my number, Frieda," relieved that her interruption halted the surges of words.

"Do thinkers ever play?" Annie asked me.

"Yes, they do," I said.

"Then let's play seesaw!"

"Okay, Annie! Hop on board!"

Her hands on one end of the seesaw, Annie paused, turned, looked at Frieda and started walking toward her. "Momma," she said, "your ears are bleeding again."

Frieda gently fingered her earlobes, then studied her fingertips, and said in a comforting tone, "It's nothing serious, Annie."

"I do see a few dots of blood," I said, my tone serious. "If you have a compact in your purse, maybe you should look in the mirror, just to make sure you're all right."

"No, Travis, I'm fine—for sure! I got my ears pierced this morning and put earrings on right after the piercings."

"Can't that be risky ... cause infection ... putting earrings in too soon ... don't the inside of the holes need to stay open, so that—"

"I couldn't wait! You see, my husband and I have this friend—Oscar—and his ministry is to take actual nails, melt them down and then recast them as earrings—earrings in the shape of the Cross of Jesus! Can you believe it! The Cross! Come over here, Travis, check out Oscar's jewelry for Jesus—the man's an artist!"

I drew closer. Frieda's earrings were crosses, each one pressed firmly against an earlobe. "They're exquisite!" I exclaimed. "The way Oscar shaped the metal to combine the loving attraction of salvation with the jagged ugliness of sin—Wow! His work is glorious! But ... Frieda, your earlobes—they do look a bit inflamed ... a bit swollen."

"It's no big deal! Besides, what's a little pain when your faith is involved? The second I saw the earrings, I knew I had to wear them immediately!"

"Why?" I asked. "What difference would waiting a day or two make?"

"All the difference in the world, Travis. I wanted to honor the Lord by wearing the earrings right away, so that from that moment on, everything I'd hear would be filtered through the Cross—the Cross of Christ!"

Annie tugged at my pocket. "She told you she's okay, Travis. C'mon! Let's play!"

Frieda said with verve, "For sure! I feel great! Go on, Annie! Show Travis how kids have fun!"

Annie slid onto the seesaw, flung her loosely-braided pigtails over her freckled shoulders, grabbed the T-shaped metal handle bolted to the seesaw, and like a cowgirl riding a bucking bronco, cried out "Yippee!" as she pushed her feet hard against the worn-down grass, causing her to spring upward. I matched the vigor of her push, and we soon created a smooth, continuous up-and-down rhythm.

Noticing that Annie was pushing herself higher and faster, I asked Frieda, "Are all right with how we're playing?"

"For sure," said Frieda. "Go for it! I'll chime in if I have to!"

"Higher, I want to go higher!" bawled Annie. "Yippee!"

"Okay, Annie," I said, "but slower ... build up slowly."

"No, Travis. Faster! Faster! You're not a scaredy-cat, are you?!"

"No, I'm not a scaredy-cat, but—"

"Annie, slow down!" shouted Frieda, her voice insistent. "And be nice to Travis. He's being nice to you."

"Okay, Momma," said Annie, her tone compliant. "But I still think Travis is a scaredy-cat! Momma, I feel sad for him"—Annie turned her head, her eyes fixed on mine—"sad for you, Travis."

"How old are you, Annie?" I asked, trusting that I wouldn't hear 'scaredy-cat' somewhere in her answer.

"Almost eight!" she replied, her voice bold. She tossed back her head, flared her nostrils, and stated bluntly, "And that's old enough not to be a scaredy-cat! How old are you, Travis?"

"Old enough to know when it's okay to be a scaredy-cat!"

"Then you are a scaredy-cat!"

"No—right now, I'm not—but sometimes it's okay to be one."

"Uh, huh—you are one! But you shouldn't be!"

"Stop it, Annie!" said Frieda, her voice pressing. "Travis told you he isn't a scaredy-cat! Go ahead—play!"

"But, Momma, he is one, and Jesus doesn't want Travis to be a scaredy-cat," said Annie, her tone frisky. She swiveled off the see-saw, and said, "Jesus said adults should be like kids, and Travis is afraid to be like a kid, and that makes him a scaredy-cat!"

"I'm sorry, Travis," said Frieda, her voice soft and inviting. "I know that Annie comes off as rude, and I know you'll find this hard to believe, but Annie only talks this way with people she really likes!"

"Really likes?!" I responded, surprised at the volume of my disbelief. "I can't imagine how she behaves toward adults she really doesn't like! But I'll say one thing: Annie is relentless when she's decided that she's right. One day, when she grows up, I could see her as an attorney whose force of will alone could win her cases in any court of law!"

"Momma, is Travis being a thinker again? This is boring! I want to play!—play with Travis!"

"Settle down for a second, Annie—just cool it! I need to tell something to Travis."

"Okay, Momma, okay … for a second … for a second." She bent down and untied and then retied her shoelaces, mumbling "for a second … for a second" as though she'd determined a set number of times she'd repeat "for a second" before she pressed Frieda to release her into playing.

"What I want to tell you, Travis, is that Annie won't go near people she really doesn't like, won't talk to them, and won't play with them, even if they ask politely to play with her. She has a sixth sense, a kind of feel for people she knows she can trust … people who're safe." Frieda studied my face, smiled, and said, "You do understand what I'm talking about, don't you, thinker?"

"Yes, I do, but—"

"I've waited for more than a second," interrupted Annie, her voice eager and soft. "Do you want to be like a kid, Travis?"

"What adult doesn't? But it's not always easy, Annie."

"The seesaw was fun, wasn't it?"

"A lot of fun!"

"Wasn't that easy?"

"Yes ... you are right about that, Annie. It was easy."

"And you wanted to shout out 'Yippee!' when I shouted it, didn't you?"

"I wanted to ... wanted to real bad!"

"Why didn't you?"

My head feeling heavy and hot, I buried my face in my hands, my eyes stinging with tears, then my arms dropped to my sides, and looking into Annie's accepting eyes, I blurted, "Because I was a scaredy-cat!"

Annie took my hand in hers—palm-to-palm—and said, "Let's play ... be kids together—Jesus likes that!" She began to skip, leading me toward monkey bars, and I skipped along with her, struck by how quickly my body remembered how to move with a child's fluidity and freedom, as though the memory of once being a child was enough to release throughout my legs the rollicking movements of a child.

Annie let go of my hand, shouted gleefully, "Follow me, Travis!"—her words a dancing fire, fueling my every action to match hers—as the force of her arms swinging from below her waist upward catapulted her forward, her hands deftly grabbing the lowest rung of the monkey bars, her legs like a speeding pendulum driven by the momentum of her forward-moving body carried her feet to the next rung, her feet supporting her weight as her hands gripped the sides of the rung and lifted her body to the highest rung, and, once at the top, we both hung there by one arm while with the other arm pounded our chests, scratched at our armpits, and grunted "Nuh—Nuh!—Nuh!—Ew!—Ew!—Ew!—Eeee-yah!—Eeee-yah!" the nasal and guttural sounds laced with "Tee—Hee—Hees!" as both of us bellowed in unison, "I want a banana!"

Frieda applauded us, and shouted, "You'd better watch out! You two are so convincing that I'm worried that the zoo is going to come, capture you, and make you the stars of their monkey house—for sure!"

Annie and I laughed, and then rung-by-rung we swung our way back to the ground.

"C'mon, Travis!"

"Where to?"

"To the merry-go-round! You come too, Momma!"

Music began to swell from the merry-go-round, announcing that a new ride was starting up, and so we raced to the merry-go-round and jumped on. A cluster of only three lifelike creatures bobbed in their places as the rotating floor moved in its fixed circular orbit.

Frieda spied the white horse with a thick mane flying in the wind, and she leaped onto the saddle. "A horse will die serving you, sacrifice its life for you—and all with such beauty ... such loyalty! What an animal! This one's mine!"

Annie's eyes caught sight of a dolphin carved to appear as if it had just broken the surface of the sea, and she exclaimed, "She's mine! Dolphins know how to play!" The dolphin's back was hollowed out, creating a seat inside, and Annie grabbed the dolphin's dorsal fin and pulled herself into the seat.

Only an ostrich remained as a choice. I managed to crawl onto its wide back, struck by the length and power of its legs. I leaned forward, both my arms hugging its long and curving neck, and I pondered how such a homely three-hundred pound bird could survive among so many predators.

"Let's give them names!" cried Annie. "My dolphin's name is 'Smiley.'"

"And my steed is 'ShowDown,'" declared Frieda as she patted the horse's neck.

"What's your ostrich's name, Travis?" asked Annie.

At a loss to come up with a personalized name, I said, "'Ostrich' ... I guess that's his name."

"You can't name an ostrich 'Ostrich,'" Annie retorted. "That's not part of our game!"

"Why not?" I asked. "It is an ostrich, so I can call it what it is!"

"Making up a new name!—that's what's fun!"

"You're overthinking this, Travis," Frieda observed. "Be spontaneous—play along! What's the first name that comes to your mind—don't think!—just say it!"

"Ostrich!"

"Ostrich?!" blurted Frieda, her tone moralizing. "Again!? That's the best you can come up with?! Travis, I saw you on the monkey bars! You were having a ball, like a kid you—"

"'Ozzie'—that's the name!" I declared, cutting her off. "Is that acceptable ... to play the game?"

"'Ossie'—that's a cop-out name!"

"No, 'Ozzie,' with a double 'z'—not a double 's'!"

Frieda looked at Annie, and asked, "What do you think: can Travis still be in the game?"

Annie's eyes traced the lines of the long curving neck of the ostrich, then leaned over, her small eyes peering into the ostrich's large eye, and exclaimed knowingly, "Your eye is bigger than my head, Ozzie! I'll bet you can see farther than Smiley and Show-Down—but Smiley can beat ShowDown and Ozzie to the finish line! Let's race! The winner gets a treat!"

"Ready!" I said, leaning my chest against Ozzie's shoulders and neck.

"Set!" said Frieda, tightening her grip on ShowDown's reins.

"Go!" shouted Annie, her chin pressed on Smiley's back, her hands clamped on his dorsal fin.

As the "Do—dee-dee—do—dee-dee—do" of the tinny organ music piped from a metal enclosure inside the merry-go-round and each animal moved up and down in its fixed place on the floor, the dolphin's snout, the horse's nose, and the ostrich's beak were dead even as they moved in unison in their circular orbit.

"I'm going to win!" whooped Annie, "because Smiley's hearing is much better than both of your animals, and she'll hear when you're tired out and then she'll make her move!"

Frieda shouted, "No, the treat is going to be my reward for victory! My horse is the white horse from *Revelation*, and I'm riding out to conquer both of you!"

"Momma that's not fair! Jesus wouldn't let you use His best horse on a merry-go-round!"

Frieda muffled her laughter, and boomed, "Giddy-up, Show-Down! These two are headed for a showdown with us, and they have no chance to win!"

"Wait a minute—just hold it right there! You both don't stand a chance against Ozzie and me! He can run over forty miles an hour, faster than your horse and faster than your dolphin! You won't be able to keep our pace! You'll tucker out!"

Frieda reached into her purse and whipped out a thick pad of rouge and rapidly smeared red blotches on ShowDown's body. "Now I'm riding on the red horse from *Revelation*," and brandishing a bent fingernail file, she pointed to it and declared, "I have this great sword to make certain that no one beats me!"

"Frieda, that pathetic file isn't scary enough to threaten the dead tissue at the base of my fingernails! But Annie's right! Ozzie does have the largest eyes of any earthly animal who's a vertebrate, so he'll see far in advance any tricks coming from either one of you! If you get too close, he'll kick you with his lethal toes—a kick that can kill a lion!"

"Smiley's full of joy, the joy of a kid—free of worries and problems that weigh adults down. And I'm a kid! So, I don't weigh as much as an adult. So, Smiley carries less weight to slow her down. We'll flash by both of you at the finish line!"

Rummaging in her purse, Freida cried, "There it is! I feel it!" She drew out an eyebrow pencil and quickly drew large black circles all over ShowDown. "Behold! I'm astride the black horse from *Revelation*, and I hold a pair of scales in my hand, scales to weigh your worth against mine—and the scales are in my favor … for sure! I mean, the uglinesss of an ostrich and the goofy smile made by the mouth and teeth of a dolphin—they pale in the face of the beauty and elegance of my horse!"

"Courage will be a key factor in determining the winner to be crowned!" I bellowed. "Ozzie warms and guards newly-laid ostrich eggs all night long, and he'll fight to the death any animal who tries to hurt the eggs and his little hatchlings—now that's courage!"

"I don't need to ride the ashen horse from *Revelation*," proclaimed Frieda, "because I don't need Death to defeat both of you. Those faulty creatures you're riding will cause their own demise before we reach the finish line!"

"It doesn't matter what you do to Smiley and me. Dolphins can be bitten by sharks, be torn open, have deep wounds—and they heal so fast that no scientists can explain it. So, while you're trying to stop Smiley and me, we'll be having fun surfing, catching a big wave, the one that jets us across the finish line!—Look!" shouted Annie, "the man who controls the merry-go-round is waving to us that the ride's almost over!" She shot her right arm straight out from her shoulder, her index finger pointing to an object only she could see as we were bearing down on it—"There! I see it! It's the finish line! Who's going to be the winner!?" Annie shouted.

"Where?!—where is it?" Frieda and I shouted as one voice.

Annie sprang from her seat, scrambled over Smiley's dorsal fin and clamped against the fin the insides of both her knees while lengthening her body across Smiley, her full weight supported by Smiley's back, head, and snout, her head slightly arched, her right arm around Smiley's head, she then stretched out her left arm and fingers, extending her reach just beyond Smiley's snout, Showdown's nose, and Ozzie's beak, and exclaimed in a voice both official and exuberant, "Across the finish line first! I'm the winner—by a hand!" She slid from Smiley as the merry-go-round slowed, and then stopped. "I want my treat!"

Struck by her playful creativity and dramatic flair, I said, "Well, Annie, I'll give you a hand!" I clapped my hands, my applause wholehearted and good-humored. Then, my curiosity piqued, I asked, "Is that a fair way to win, Annie?"

She laughed, and declared with certainty, "It is—for kids!"

"And it is for adults who want to be kids," Frieda added.

"That was loads of fun!" I said, the sound of my voice almost a giggle.

"For sure," agreed Frieda. "Now your treat, Annie, what would you like?"

"A snow cone!"

"Okay, but a small one. Remember, we're meeting your dad soon for dinner. Care to join us, Travis?"

My mouth watering at the invitation, I quickly accepted, "I'd like that very much!"

"Can we eat them at the wading pool, Momma?"

"No," said Frieda, "we wouldn't want to let them drip into the water. There's a bench on the grass. It's close to the pool. We can eat them there."

"Aww, Momma, I won ... it's my treat ... I—"

"Excuse me," interrupted a voice behind us.

We all turned to put a face to that voice.

It was Jesus ... dressed as a vendor and holding three snow cones in his hand!

"I had so much fun watching your race! It would give me pleasure if you'd accept these snow cones as a gift."

Three of us looked at one another, surprise filling the faces of Frieda and Annie. My eyes blinked rapidly—then shut tight—then blinked rapidly—then shut tight—my head swiveling from looking at Jesus to looking at Annie and Frieda. Annie and Frieda were smiling. I felt a smile slowly form on my lips.

"Please don't hesitate," said Jesus. "I can assure you, the snow cones are free. And trust me, if there had been another creature to ride on the merry-go-round, I would've enjoyed jumping on him and playing with you."

Annie plucked a snow cone. Then Frieda took one. My hands felt too leaden to lift as *Jesus as a snow cone vendor* weighed heavy on my mind.

Moving the last snow cone closer to my hands, Jesus asked, "Don't you want one?"

"Go ahead, Travis," said Annie, her voice firm. "You and Ozzie were second, but ... it's okay ... you can have a snow cone."

"Hey, wait a minute, Annie!" Frieda said in mock disbelief. "I placed second—not Travis! But he put up a good race and deserves a snow cone."

With both hands I cupped the snow cone, said thinly, "Thanks," and brought the mound of cherry-colored ice toward my mouth.

"Wait!" shouted Annie. "The snow cones—they're all the same flavor! That's not fair! Mister ... I mean what's your name?"

"People call me Snowman, and—"

"Is it fair, Snowman, that we all have the same flavor?"

"Annie," said Frieda, "Snowman is giving you a snow cone for free. You should be grateful."

"Why? I didn't ask for a free one. I don't want a cherry cone! You'll pay Snowman for the flavor I want, won't you, Momma?"

"The cherry-colored cones are the only ones I have," said Jesus. "Each cherry-colored snow cone may look the same as every other cherry-colored one, but they never have the same flavor! Go, ahead, Annie, taste and see!"

Annie licked at her snow cone. Then she looked at Frieda. Frieda held out her snow cone. Annie licked the side where icy syrup had gathered near the rim of the cone. Then I offered Annie a lick of my cone. She quickly took it, her tongue skidding across the top of my cone. She smacked her lips, scanned Jesus' face, and shouted, "Snowman, you're right! Each one tastes different, but they all look the same!"

"That's why many people call me 'Snowman,' Annie. My snow cones are like snowflakes: On the surface all snowflakes look the same, but when you take a closer, deeper look, each snowflake is unique, beautiful, and precious. And so each snow cone I make is created for one person and only for one person: for her to taste and see how unique, beautiful, and precious she is."

"You're really someone very special, Snowman," I said ephatically. "I think you know that!"

"For very sure," said Frieda, "he is!"

"Will you teach me how to make snow cones, Snowman?" asked Annie.

"I'm sorry, Snowman," said Frieda. "She's so full of questions ... C'mon, Annie, it's time to go meet your father for dinner. We're going to be late! You can finish your snow cone in the car! Thanks, Travis, you're a good sport! It was a fun day! And thank you, Snowman! The snow cone you made for me was the sweetest tasting treat I've ever had!"

Frieda and Annie turned and started to walk away, then Annie stopped, wheeled around, looked straight at me, and shouted in booming certainty, "Travis, you are not a scaredy-cat! You're brave and strong—like Ozzie! I'm going to call you Ozzie—the big ostrich who plays like a little kid! You're fun, Ozzie, you're fun!" As Frieda grabbed Annie's hand and led her away, I turned in their direction and shouted, "Good-bye, Smiley! Good-bye, Show-Down!"

I spun around, eager to see Jesus—he was gone!

Confused and stunned by Jesus' sudden disappearance, I sat on a bench, my thoughts of Jesus a jumble laced with clear and invigorating images of Annie, Frieda, and me racing on the merry-go-round. In the distance, waving hands caught my eye. The hands belonged to a familiar person sitting on the coping of the wading pool—it was L.C.!

I waved back.

She beckoned me to join her.

Excited to see L.C., I walked toward her. She stood up, opened her arms, took my hands in hers, drew me close, and hugged me. "What a joy to see you here on my day off!" she said. "This is one of my favorite places!"

"I've been having a great time here ... and now—to see you! I'm delighted beyond words!"

"Take off your shoes and socks, sit next to me and let your feet and legs dangle in the water. Don't worry about your khaki shorts, the water isn't high enough to get them wet, and yet the water is deep enough so that while you're sitting here, your feet can dangle in the water but not touch bottom."

I removed my shoes and socks and set them next to hers.

We sat on the coping, and then eased our feet and legs into the water.

"Have you ever seen a snow cone vendor in this park?" I asked.

"Yes," she said, "there's always one here ... well, almost always. He pushes one of those carts with long handles and large round wheels."

"Did you ever buy a snow cone from him?"

"Of course, especially on a hot day. Then a snow cone is quite refreshing."

"Do you know his name?"

"Yes, his name is Wally. He's been bringing his cart here for years. Everybody knows him as 'Rainbow Wally' because of the many colors and flavors of his snow cones."

"Not just one color—cherry?"

"Never! Rainbow Wally wouldn't set foot in this park with only one flavor. He'd lose his right to be called Rainbow Wally!"

"Did you ever hear anyone call him 'Snowman'?"

"No ... Travis, I haven't. Why all the interest in Rainbow Wally?"

"A vendor gave me a free snow cone today. Did you see the vendor who gave it to me?"

"No, Travis. When I first spotted you, you were sitting on the bench. I didn't see any snow cone vendor. Besides, I heard some folks talking about how disappointed they were that Rainbow Wally wasn't here today—that nobody was here to fill in for him!"

I paddled the water with my feet.

"And one more thing about Rainbow Wally," said L.C. "He'd never, never give anyone a free snow cone! Whenever I've seen someone try to get a free one from Wally, he'd say in a stern tone, 'If you can't pay, try another day, and, in case you're supposing, I don't make loans to buy my snow cones!'"

"Wow! As stingy as he is, I'm surprised that anyone would want to make 'Rainbow' part of his name."

"'Rainbow' labels the product he sells, Travis, it doesn't name the character of the man."

"Very insightful, L.C.! Really ... very insightful!"

L.C. paddled her feet, her pace matching mine. Then she leaned back, quickening the pace of her paddling—then stopped! "Travis, in your pocket, isn't that one of those envelopes I've been delivering to you?"

I fingered the edge of my back pocket. "Oh ... yeah, it's one of those verdant green envelopes. I must have stuffed it into my pocket when I picked up my mail—and then forgot it was there!"

"Aren't you going to open it ... see what's inside?"

"There's no rush. I know what's inside—it's always the same!"

"Always?"

"Yes ... so far."

"May I ask—"

"Yes, you may. Inside is a verdant green note card and written on it is *Love is patient.* There's no return address on the envelope— well, you know that, since you've been delivering them to me!— and there's no signature or any other way to identify who sends them."

"Still ... unless you open it, you can't be sure that—"

"I'll show you how certain I am of what the note card says. Look at that father and son wading directly across from us. You can tell by the father's knitted brow and the son's staring at the water, that the father is scolding the son for some reason, frightening and shaming the boy."

I scanned the area around us, and noticed a discarded newspaper lying a few yards from me. I grabbed it and folded it into the shape of a rowboat. I slid into the water, and with only my shoulders, arms, and head above water, I placed into the paper boat the verdant green envelope, aimed the prow of the boat at the father, then I pushed—the boat moved smoothly and swiftly across the water, the prow tapping the father on his thigh.

The father looked around, and he caught sight of me gesturing to him to pick up the boat. His eyes seemed to be searching for answers to a kaleidoscope of 'Why?' questions. He ran his thumb across his lower lip, and then he picked up the boat. Seeing the verdant green envelope, he grabbed it and held it in his left hand while he squinted at me, pointed to the envelope, and shrugged his shoulders.

I gestured to the father to tear open the envelope and read what's inside. Nervously gaining access to inside the envelope, the father removed the note card, read what was on it, and, with his palm covering his gaping mouth, slumped back against the coping of the wading pool. Then the father wept as he scooped up his son, enfolding the boy in a gentle embrace, slowly rocking his son from side-to-side, and then he let the boy glide into the water.

His hands on the coping, the father paused, then reached into a bag on the grass, soon drawing an object from the bag. A pen in his hand, the father appeared to be writing something on the note card. He placed the note card on the boat and pushed it back to me.

I took the note card and read what the father had block lettered on it:

AND YOUR LOVE IS KIND
YOU MUST KNOW JESUS!
THANK YOU!

Joy surged through me, and I jumped up and down as I waved to the father. He waved back, then raised his arms straight up, his palms wide, his head tilted back, his eyes looking skyward, his lips appeared to be praising the Lord. Then he looked at me, and smiled—nodded his head—smiled—nodded his head, and then the father began to play with his son, both of them laughing, splashing, and flopping in the water.

L.C. sprang into the water. "What is it, Travis?" she asked, "You and that boy's father seem wildly excited about something that just happened between the two of you! Are you all right?"

I handed her the note card. She read the words:

LOVE IS PATIENT

Then turned over the note card and read:

AND YOUR LOVE IS KIND
YOU MUST KNOW JESUS!
THANK YOU!

Her arms and hands flung wide open, her body whirling in the water, L.C. shouted, "Glory be to God!—Your Word is alive!—Glory be to God!—Your Word is alive!" I joined her, our right hands clasped as one, our eyes an unwavering embrace, whirling together in the water, shouting as one voice "Glory be to God!—Your Word is alive!—Glory be to God!—Your Word is alive!" Then we stopped, took deep renewing breaths, and for a moment stood motionless, holding hands, and then in one fluid motion, my palms moved to her shoulders as hers moved to mine.

As I gazed into L.C.'s face—suddenly—I felt the magnetic pull of her presence—the same captivating loveliness I felt the first time I gazed into her face—the same exquisite strength of her head—the same gracious simplicity and beaming elegance of her face—the same majestic forehead, the expanse of its curving space an alluring call to joy-filling revelations—"Joy-filling revelations!" I cried out. "That's what happened, L.C.!"

"I think I know what you mean, Travis, because—"

"I know you do, L.C., but—forgive me for cutting you off—there's much more. As I was tracking the course of my paper boat carrying its cargo of *Love is patient*, glints from droplets from the fountain's spray caught my eye, the fountain seemed to hold and protect the column of water as it erupted into sparkling droplets dancing in sunlight. As I continued to track the boat, the word 'fountain' stayed with me, and then when the scolding father was convicted of his impatience and was moved to being loving and patient, Solomon's words rose in my mind, 'The fountain of wisdom is a bubbling brook,' the words 'bubbling brook' sent tickles through me, making me laugh, and then Isaiah's words—'You will joyously draw water from the springs of salvation'—geysered in me, flowed through me, swelling my laughter, and my laughter coming in torrents, torrents becoming joy expanding in me, overflowing me, making me think of that father's salvation, my salvation, and your salvation, and when I thought of you and of how beautiful you are, then words from *Song of Songs* gushed through me, heartfelt words that say how I feel about you, 'You are a garden spring, a well of fresh water,' and I believe Jesus is a fountain of life … a fountain of love … and love never fails … and I love … "

Her smile a dazzle across her face, L.C. drew me into her arms, my head on her shoulder, her head on mine, our hearts pulsing as one, then we drew apart slightly, the embrace of our eyes a covenant to keep one another precious inside the encircling peace of our lives awash in Christ's living water, and we surrendered our lives to one another, letting them dissolve into streams of sheltering warmth, a living circle of promise and promising, then our lips, open and rounded, moved toward one another, my lips brushing the smooth heat of her lips, an invitation to be bathed in the love flowing from Christ's life-giving water offered without cost, then our lips met in a kiss, our kiss a holy seal unfading on our hearts, our kiss the pulp and juice of love, electric and dancing along nerves of a new beginning with radiating tingles for words, our kiss a quiet dwelling place for the hush of love to rest within the enclosing peace of our trusting silence, our kiss a joy-inspiring vow to the infusing love being impressed on the soft contours of our fluent lips, breathless and eternal in the melting—merging— melting—merging—mouthwatering moment!

Love Is Patient: Seventh Delivery

From somewhere a faint "tap—tap—tap" sounded through my front door, wafted into my bedroom, and brushed my ears. I rolled onto my side, doubled the corner of my pillow, pulled it closer to my face, and snuggled deeper under my blankets.

The "tap—tap—tap" grew into a "knock—knock—knock" followed by a voice, calling, "Awake, sleeper, arise from the dead, and Christ will shine on you!" The words were familiar but I couldn't place them, the voice familiar I but couldn't place it. I sighed, buried my head under the blankets, and thought, *I want to sleep!—stop that noise!—go away!*

The "knock—knock—knock" swelled into a "bang—bang—bang" followed by the same voice, shouting the same words, "Awake, sleeper, arise from the dead, and Christ will shine on you!"

I bolted upright, my legs dangling over the edge of the bed, the blankets in a heap on the floor. Groggy, I rubbed my eyes. The chilly air in my bedroom nipped at my head and hands, and I snarled, "It's winter ... you know ... whoever you are ... pounding on my door ... it's cold in here ... I haven't turned up my heater yet!"

"Travis, I hear your voice. Will you come to the door?"

That's L.C.'s voice, I thought. "I'm coming!' I shouted. "I need a minute!"

"Take your time," she said, "I can wait—but I think what I've got with me is very important."

I turned up my thermostat, smiled, blew into my cupped palms, and then rubbed them together as I heard the heater begin to chug warm air through wide open vents. I slipped on a long-sleeved flannel shirt, a pair of blue jeans, thick socks, and leather hiking boots, making sure that the boots were laced tight, secure and firm along the length of my calves and shins.

I walked to the door, opened it, stepped onto the welcome mat outside my door, then quickly closed the door, to keep out the be-low-freezing air, and looked for L.C.—but saw staring in my face petals of a large flower, the petals covering L.C.'s face! She flipped the petals away from her face, squealed, "Peek-a-boo!" threw her arms around my neck, and said in delightful tones, "I'm so glad to see you!"

I slid my arms around her waist, drew her close, kissed her cheek, and said, "You're still the most beautiful woman I've ever seen—even though you're dressed in layers of winter clothes!" I stepped back, stroked my chin, and remarked, "Now I remember the words you were shouting through the door! They're the apos-tle Paul's words from *Ephesians* ... 'Awake, sleeper, and arise from the dead, and Christ will shine on you.' That was so cute, and so celebrating of Jesus—to pick from his Word that particular verse to wake me up!"

"How sweet of you to think I would do that! But it wasn't me!"

"It sounded like your voice! C'mon, own up! It's not prideful to admit that you're creative, really smart, and know God's Word inside and out!"

"I'm serious! I didn't shout Scripture through your door. And I didn't hear any voice quoting Scripture. The only sound I heard was the one I was making as I was banging on your door, trying to wake you up. Maybe what you heard was the Bible on CD and you forgot to turn off your CD player."

"I heard an audible voice—from somewhere—calling to me, in Paul's words from *Ephesians*."

"Travis, you're so immersed in Scripture ... you could've heard Paul's words in your spirit, heard them at such a high volume that they seemed to be coming through the door—"

"No, my beautiful L.C., the words came through the door ... why the door? ... why those words? ... I don't know ... only God knows. What I do know is that Jesus loves us, you're beautiful, it's Saturday, and it's a day of play for us—and you're hearing my real words face-to-face and not through a closed door!"

"Oh, Travis, I hear you loud and clear, and I want you to hear this: You're my guy—my love! And you always will be! Isn't Jesus gracious, bringing us together?"

"Yes! And oh, what mercy, and—" The flower flopped onto my head, cutting off my flow of words, a large petal angled across my forehead and draped over the bridge of my nose. We burst into laughter! "I feel like I'm back in time—in the sixties—and I'm one of the flower children!"

"I'm sure glad it's Saturday!" said L.C., her voice jubilant.

"Me, too!" I exclaimed through muffled laughter.

"A day off—with no deliveries for me to make today ... well, that's not quite true."

"You mean you do have to work part of today? I thought you said—"

"No, Travis, it is my day off, and I have no official deliveries to make for the Post Office, and oh, do I ever want to have fun with my guy today—all day! But this flower ... this flower is a different matter, I guess I'd have to call it a kind of delivery."

"Did you buy it for me? You know it's January—too early for a Valentine's Day gift!"

L.C. chuckled, then said, "No, someone wanted me to give it to you."

"That sounds mysterious! Please, tell me more."

"I was on my way to your place, to meet you, and I spotted a man standing on a street corner. He was holding this flower in his hand. He called to me. Believing he was homeless and probably had sold all his flowers but this one ... but, you know, Travis, now when I think about it, it wasn't that he looked homeless that drew me to him. There was something about him, something—"

"Yes!" I said knowingly. "I see what you mean. There was something familiar about him. It was like you met him before ... somehow ... somewhere, but you couldn't quite remember the place or the time?"

"Well ... yes—but no, not exactly. It was more than that—much more. I can't put it into words ... yet ... maybe later ... it will come to me ... the way to describe it. Okay?"

"Of course. No problem. You were saying ..."

"Saying? Right—back to my story. I was saying that I walked toward the peddler, opened my purse and took out a twenty-dollar bill. The man glanced at me! Travis, his eyes were like wells of the deepest and clearest water, and for a moment I seemed to be float-ing, feeling so light and so free. Then I became self-conscious, suddenly aware of my outstretched arm and my hand with money wadded in it. I heard myself telling the man that the flower was gorgeous, and that there was no doubt that when it was picked it must have been in full bloom, and how very rare it was to see a flower like that at this time of year. I offered to buy the flower, and I asked him whether twenty-dollars was enough."

"You sound like you were rambling, that maybe you were in that place where you seem to be outside yourself, see yourself talk-ing, and you want to stop yourself—but you can't! You knew you'd been moved by the man's eyes, and you wanted to stay inside his eyes, floating there, but you felt awkward about it, so you kept talking."

"You're right about that, Travis. I'd stepped—no, was drawn by the man's eyes!—outside myself, and I couldn't get back. To be honest, a big part of me didn't want to go back to myself, and yet part of me did. So there I stood: My body felt frozen, but my mouth kept gushing words."

"That can be a very scary place to be stuck. And then what happened?"

"Well, the peddler smiled at me, told me that twenty-dollars was a kind offer, and that he knew I'd be blessed for my kindness! And then he said the most surprising thing."

"What was it, L.C.?"

"I want to remember it all—exactly!" She paused, looked at the flower, drew it to her face, and then let it glide across the length of her cheek. She seemed to have drifted away, her mind focused somewhere else.

"L.C., are you all right? Please, continue the story, the suspense … I'm breathless …"

Still holding the flower, she lowered her hands. "Yes … sorry … lost my train of thought … the flower … its bouquet … so fragrant … like a lovely caress on my face. The man said that he'd been waiting for me to come his way! Me?! That took me off guard! Shocked and confused, I felt my mouth open but no words came out. I pointed at myself, shrugged my shoulders, and then stood there with my palms open. The man gently took my hands in his, and he asked me whether I knew you!"

"Whether you knew me—he asked that?!"

"Yes, he did! I told him that I knew you—but then I asked him how he knew you. The man told me that there are stories that are too long to tell in a short time. His response took me aback. I paused, and then reflected on why he wouldn't give me an answer to my question. I couldn't think of a reason to explain his response, and yet I thought I needed to protect you. I felt uneasy about challenging him, but I demanded that the man tell me whether you knew him. He said emphatically that you knew him well, and that you and he had become very close!"

"Very close to a flower peddler! Me?! I've never met one!"

"I asked the peddler whether he'd be willing to tell me his name. The man smiled the widest smile I'd ever seen, and then told me to tell you that I'd talked with 'Sunday,' and that you'd know who he is!"

"Sunday! L.C., did the man say his name was Sunday?"

"Yes, Travis, but—"

"Really?! Are you certain that he said the name Sunday?"

"Yes, Travis, yes! I know that you may think that the man was a crazy flower peddler, but let me continue—please! I told him that I meant no offense, but that Sunday was an odd name for a person. He assured me that he wasn't offended. He offered me the flower, and then handed me one of those verdant green envelopes you keep receiving in the mail. Now it comes to me—"

"What does?"

"What there was about that man that drew me to him."

"You said it was his eyes—remember?"

"Yes, oh, yes, but it was much more than his eyes! He radiated a magnetic kind of warmth and safety combined with confidence and strength. It was like he was the center of a circle of trust, and anyone who was drawn inside that circle could trust him with her life. I realized that I was inside that circle, and I trusted that he was telling the truth. I accepted the flower and the envelope, and asked whether he wanted me to give you any message. The man told me to give you the flower, say that Sunday wishes Travis a Happy Eastering, and then hand you the envelope!"

"Eastering! Sunday spoke the word Eastering—not Easter?"

"Yes, he did. But, you know, Travis, just hearing Eastering springing from Sunday's lips felt so strange and yet the very sound of that word was deeply moving! I felt like I was starting to float again! I mean, Sunday even emphasized the 'ing' when he spoke that word. Do you think Sunday might have a speech defect, or—"

"Are you certain—really certain!—that Sunday said Eastering?"

"Definitely—without a shred of doubt—Sunday said—no, it was more like he proclaimed the word—'Eastering!' Then I told Sunday that God would bless him, and that I hoped that people would always buy all the flowers he'd bring to this corner. I started to walk away, and then I heard Sunday declare in words so honeyed and so hallowed, 'Go in peace.' I spun around, to thank Sunday for his blessing, but he was gone. Travis, if you'd have been there and told me that Sunday was Jesus—I would've believed you!"

"L.C., Sunday is Jesus!"

"Sunday!—Is!—Jesus!?"

"Yes, he is Jesus."

"But ... how? ... when? ... Happy Easter-ing!—not Happy Easter?"

"Yes, Eastering!" I shouted joyfully.

"Thank you for your blood, Jesus!—praise you for the Cross, Jesus!—thank you for your resurrection, Jesus! ... but, Travis, why ... how ... did you—"

"Slow down ... L.C. ... slow ... down ... I'll tell you the whole story later. I believe that you have a flower for me."

"Yes, and you'll notice that it's an Easter Lily. Isn't it gorgeous?!"

"It is! The petals are so long, full, and the slight curve at their tips makes them look like fingers of soft purity, reaching out to embrace anyone who's willing to be touched."

"Travis, the way the petals are clustered makes them seem to me like a trumpet about to blast out the truth of Easter, a blast so loud that 'Christ is risen!' are the only words that can be heard above all other words!"

L.C. handed me the Easter Lily, and said, "I want to follow what Jesus—I mean Sunday—asked me to do. So, Travis, Sunday wishes you a Happy Eastering, and he wants to give you this envelope." She handed me the verdant green envelope.

"Hmm ... I wonder what's in here?" I said, my tone feigning ignorance.

"Travis, look! ... on the front of the envelope—there's something written there!"

I looked at the envelope—stunned!—at what was written there:
LOVE IS PATIENT

"That's a new wrinkle—*Love is patient* is written on the outside of the envelope. I wonder what—if anything—is written on the note card inside?"

"Can you hurry up ... just a bit, Travis? It's cold out here ... and it is mid-January!"

"Just a few more minutes ... I've got to see what's on the note card—I've got to!"

"I know how important this is to you, my love, but I'm afraid for you, afraid that—"

"Afraid for me?! Why?"

"It's below freezing, and the temperature is dropping ... it's getting colder ... supposed to go below zero ... and you're standing there—in your bare feet! You could catch a bad cold, and the flu is going around—people die from that, you know!"

"What are you talking about? Bare feet?! I put on my thickest socks and my warmest hiking boots before I came out to meet you." Suddenly my feet felt very cold. I looked down—my feet were bare!

I tore open the envelope, grabbed the note card, peals of rollicking joy surging heavenward from deep within me when I saw the shining words:

MY FATHER MAKES COUNSELORS WALK BAREFOOT!

About The Author

Jim Foreman is a Christ-centered licensed marriage and family therapist (L.M.F.T.), in private practice and on staff as counselor at Faith Community Foursquare Church. As an organization consultant (Ph.D., Sociology) he specializes in conflict resolution, forgiveness, and reconciliation. He speaks to groups as varied as church leaders, nurses, physician's assistants, attorneys, military officials, therapists, and students, on topics that include Anger, Anxiety, Depression, Domestic Violence, the Cross and Transformation, the Holy Spirit, and the Presence of Christ. Jim leads Christian retreats which explore areas such as Peace, Grace, Love, Mercy, Worth, Being Single, Being Married—all designed to experience the living Christ. He also teaches classes on topics as wide-ranging as Walking in the Resurrecting Power of Christ; Friendship; Jesus, Paul, and You; The Glory of God; and Communicating God's Way. He is married and lives in San Diego.

www.ingramcontent.com/pod-product-compliance
Lightning Source LLC
Chambersburg PA
CBHW051335250626
47155CB00007B/2614